THE
MAN
– FROM –
WACO

T0015009

**LOOK FOR THESE EXCITING WESTERN SERIES
FROM BESTSELLING AUTHORS
WILLIAM W. JOHNSTONE AND J.A. JOHNSTONE**

The Mountain Man

Luke Jensen: Bounty Hunter

Brannigan's Land

The Jensen Brand

Smoke Jensen: The Early Years

Preacher and MacCallister

Fort Misery

The Fighting O'Neils

Perley Gates

MacCoole and Boone

Guns of the Vigilantes

Shotgun Johnny

The Chuckwagon Trail

The Jackals

The Slash and Pecos Westerns

The Texas Moonshiners

Stoneface Finnegan Westerns

Ben Savage: Saloon Ranger

The Buck Trammel Westerns

The Death and Texas Westerns

The Hunter Buchanon Westerns

Will Tanner, Deputy US Marshal

Old Cowboys Never Die

Go West, Young Man

Published by Kensington Publishing Corp.

THE MAN
– FROM –
WACO

WILLIAM W. JOHNSTONE
AND J.A. JOHNSTONE

PINNACLE BOOKS
Kensington Publishing Corp.
www.kensingtonbooks.com

CHAPTER 1

Kitty Bannack pushed the screen door open far enough to stick her hand out and ring her little silver bell to call the boys to supper. Tommy, six and Billy, four, ran from the barn where they had been playing, but there was no one else in sight. "Tommy, run down to the other end of the corn field and tell your papa and Uncle John that supper's ready." She knew the men were working down there, clearing some more of the land near the creek. They couldn't hear her little bell that far away from the house. Warren complained that he couldn't hear the tiny silver bell even when he was no farther away than the barn. He said she should use a cowbell if she was really serious about calling him. Kitty didn't have many really nice things like that little bell, a wedding gift from her aunt Sophie, so she enjoyed an opportunity to use it. She held the screen door open to let Billy in. "Go to the pump and wash your hands," she told him. He went over to the other side of the back porch where there was a bucket beside the pump. She remained at the door watching Tommy until he disappeared behind the corn. *I declare,* she thought, *I just patched that boy's trousers and he's wearing through the patches already.* She sighed and went back into the kitchen. "Let me see 'em," she said to Billy and grabbed the back of his collar when he walked past her. "Go back to the pump and wash 'em like I taught you to."

"I washed 'em, Mama," Billy protested.

"You watch your papa and Uncle John when they come in for supper," Kitty said. "That's the way you need to wash your hands. Use that soap. I made it to take the dirt off your dirty little paws." Still holding him by the back of his collar, she turned him around and gave him a little push back toward the pump.

After a few minutes, her husband and Tommy joined Billy at the pump. "You still washin' your hands?" Tommy asked his brother.

"I done washed 'em once," Billy complained. "Mama's gonna wear the skin offa our hands."

"Where's John?" Kitty asked, concerned that the biscuits were going to get cold if they didn't sit down and eat.

"He volunteered to put the horses away, so you wouldn't give us a scoldin' for being late for supper," Warren said.

"I'll give him a scoldin', then," she joked, well aware of John's tendency to make sure he didn't eat more than his share of the food they were able to raise. No one worked harder than her husband's younger brother. Only eighteen years old, he was already as big a man as Warren. It was a shame, she thought, that all he knew was hard work with none of the pleasures of life that many men his age pursued.

Her thoughts were brought back to her husband then as she filled his cup with coffee. She was saddened when her eyes rested upon the recent appearance of gray streaks in his sideburns, far too soon for a man as young as he was. She knew the cause for his rapid aging was because of the poor performance of the crops he had planted. The farm was not providing a sufficient living for two families. And while John had no prospects for starting a family of his own in the immediate future, that had been the grand plan from the beginning. As the situation stood now, however, they needed more land to support another family. And there was no money for them to buy more land. That was the cause of Warren's sleepless nights and the ever-increasing silent moods noticed by Kitty and John.

It was a pleasant spring morning in Waco when the unthinkable happened. Warren went into town alone, having been pushed to the desperate position of asking the bank to make him a loan with his farm as collateral. He stood outside the bank for a while trying to summon the willpower to go inside and ask for the loan, so reluctant was he to put a lien on his property. He only needed a few hundred dollars to get him by this slack period. And he hesitated to tie his land up for that small amount of money. Looking through the window, he could see both tellers taking their cash drawers to the back of the bank to fill them with money from the safe. It would be so easy to walk in right then with his gun drawn and demand that they dump their trays into a bag and he could be gone before they knew what hit them. No one in the town knew him, other than a couple of store clerks. He looked around him, the thought taking root in his desperation. The *OPEN* sign was on the door, but there were no customers as yet. All the signs were right. *Just do it!* He thought and in that insane moment, a normally honest man changed the pattern of his and his brother's life forever.

"No customers yet," James Feldon, the bank manager, said, "both of you fill your drawers."

Robert Tice and Wilbur Davis followed him through the door to the back and the safe room, which Feldon had already unlocked. Both tellers were confused when Feldon turned to face them and appeared to be stunned. They were both startled then when they heard the voice behind them. "Just do like I tell you and nobody will get hurt," Warren Bannack advised them. They turned to discover the bank robber, his hat pulled down low on his forehead, a bandanna tied around his face, and a Smith & Wesson revolver in his hand. Seeing a couple of canvas sacks lying on a table in the corner of the room, he said, "Take one of them sacks and fill it with money and be quick about it. The rest of my gang will be in here if I ain't out pretty quick."

Feldon sensed the desperation in the robber's tone, so he made one attempt. "You're making a big mistake, mister. You don't wanna do this. If you'll just turn around and walk out of the bank, we won't press any charges."

"If this is a mistake, it's already been made," Warren said. "And if you don't hurry up and fill that sack with money, I ain't got no choice but to shoot you down." Davis and Tice took him for his word and started filling the sack. "That one sack's enough," Warren said. "I ain't lookin' to clean you out." He would have liked to have more but figured he could only handle one sack and his gun, too. They filled the sack quickly, so he took it and told them to sit down on the floor. Then covering them with his pistol, he backed out of the safe room, closed the door, and locked it. Running back through the door to the lobby, he took the key out of that door, closed the door, and locked it from the lobby side of the door.

When he got to the front door, he was relieved to see there were still no customers. He holstered his pistol and ran to his horse with his bandanna still in place. Holding onto his sack full of money, he stepped up into the saddle and wheeled his horse away from the hitching rail, almost running over a man and his wife heading to the bank. Realizing at once what was happening, the man started yelling, "Hold up! He's robbin' the bank!" Other pedestrians picked up the outcry, loud enough to bring Sheriff Hank Bronson running out of his office in time to see Warren gallop past. With no time to raise a posse, Bronson ran for his horse and was soon in the saddle, racing out the south road after the robber.

In a panic now, Warren pushed his horse for everything the animal had. He had not counted on the sheriff giving chase this soon. He thought about dropping the sack of money and maybe the sheriff would stop to pick it up. But what if he didn't? Or even if he did stop to pick it up, he would still be coming after him. "Oh, my Lord, my Lord," he groaned. "What was I thinking? My wife, my children, I've got to get away from the sheriff!" With no other choice, he laid low on the dun's neck and encouraged the willing horse and it responded. When he reached the narrow trace that led to his farm, he saw that he was out of sight of the man chasing him. So he turned the dun onto the trace that led to the river through a heavy patch of oak trees. He was sure the sheriff didn't have him in sight when he veered onto the trace. It turned out that he was right. He was out of sight when he reached the trace, so the sheriff did not see him turn off the road. The sheriff didn't go very far before realizing that the obvious trail he had been following was gone. So he turned around and backtracked until he found the narrow trace and the tracks of the galloping horse that he had missed before.

Alert now that he might be riding into a dangerous situation, Bronson reined his tired horse back to a walk, allowing for the possibility of riding into an ambush. It occurred to him that he might have been wiser to raise a posse, instead of chasing the thief all by himself. When he cleared the trees, however, he found the narrow trace led him to a clearing with a cabin and a barn in the center. One tired horse stood in front of the barn and standing in the open door of the barn were two men, seeming to be waiting for him. One of them held the sack of money from the bank. Neither man was holding a weapon, but there was a gun belt hanging from the saddle horn on the horse. Hank Bronson was not quite sure if he had ridden into a trap or not. He drew his rifle from his saddle scabbard and stepped down. "I know you," he said, looking at Warren. "Your name's Bannack, right? I reckon you know why you're under arrest."

He paused then when Kitty Bannack came out the back door of the cabin, followed by her two young sons. "Warren, what's going on?" Kitty asked her husband. When he didn't answer right away, she turned to Hank. "What is it, Sheriff Bronson. What's going on?"

"I'm afraid I've got to arrest your husband for bank robbery, Miz Bannack. He just held up the First Bank of Waco." He held his rifle on Warren, not sure himself what was going on, for Warren just stood there as if frozen, while his wife registered genuine shock upon hearing what he had done.

The one person who remained calm spoke then. "This ain't what it looks like, Sheriff," he said. "My name's John Bannack. I robbed the bank. I just didn't figure on you gettin' on my tail right away. I did it because we needed the money, but when I gave it to Warren, he said he's fixin' to take it back to the bank. Said he'd rather starve than turn into a common thief. I told him I'd take it back, but I needed to rest my horse first. It was a bad idea. I'm sorry I did it, but I reckon I'm ready to pay the penalty for what I did." Unable to believe the drama playing out before her eyes, Kitty ran to stand beside her husband. John looked at them and said, "I'm sorry. I hope you'll forgive me." Back to the sheriff then, he declared, "I won't cause you no trouble, Sheriff. All the bank's money is in there. It ain't been opened since I left the bank with it."

"John . . ." Warren started to protest, but his brother interrupted him.

"Enough said, Warren," John declared. "I made a mistake. It'll be tough workin' the farm by yourself, but it'll be easier not having to feed a big eater like me." Back to the sheriff again, he said, "I wore my horse out, so I'll take another one back to town. I won't bother to switch my saddle. I'll just ride him bareback. You ready to go?"

Hank snorted a laugh, still amazed by the weird circumstances of the arrest. "Yeah, I reckon I am," he answered, although he was tempted to tell John to come into town whenever he was ready and he'd see him there.

John didn't want to risk another minute. Kitty knew very well which one of the brothers went into town and which one stayed home, and she looked as if she might lose all control at any second. He counted on her knowing she couldn't afford to have her husband away at prison. He was also aware that either one of her two sons could destroy his story if they thought to say something. "Come on, Sheriff, I'll get another horse," he said, picked up the sack of stolen money resting now beside his brother, dropped it beside the sheriff's feet, and turned to go into the barn to get his horse.

"Just hold it right there," Hank told him. "I don't want to interfere with your arrest, since you seem to be doing such a fine job of it. But my horse is just as wore out as yours is, so I think we'll just go back on the same horses we got here on. Most likely you can understand why I think that would be best."

"Oh, right," John replied. "I didn't think about that. You don't mind if I ride bareback do you? I'd like to leave Warren my saddle. It's a lot better saddle than his."

"Don't mind a-tall," Hank said. "Go ahead and take it off and just leave it right there but take that gun belt off the saddle horn and drop it on the ground first. And be real

careful about it. Then we'll get started back right away."
John took the saddle off and placed it at Warren's feet.
When Warren started to speak, John shook his head, turned
around, and jumped up on the horse's back. Already in the
saddle, Hank said, "We'll take a leisurely little ride back to
town now." He nodded to the still dumbstruck couple then.
"Mr. Bannack, Ma'am, sorry to make your acquaintance
under these circumstances." They rode out of the clearing
at a slow walk, and when they were out of sight of the
couple still standing in front of the barn, Hank informed his
prisoner, "Normally, I'd handcuff your hands behind your
back, but since you've been so cooperative about surrender-
ing, I'll leave your hands free to help you hold on to your
horse, since you ain't settin' a saddle. Besides, if you was
to take a wild notion to take off without me, it's easy
enough to just shoot you in the back. And John, make no
mistake, I wouldn't hesitate to do it."

"I understand," John said. "You won't have to." Behind
him, he could only imagine the hysterical conversation
going on between his brother and his sister-in-law. For
surely Kitty was as shocked by the desperate decision
Warren had acted upon as he was. He hoped that she would
be understanding and forgiving for his brother's foolish
mistake. They were all three in a state of despair for their
poverty. But Kitty, like himself, was determined to survive
until their lot improved, thinking that it surely would.
Maybe it would have, but after Warren's unthinkable act,
John knew that he had been left with only one way to save
his brother's family. So he didn't hesitate to confess to the
crime. Now as he and Sheriff Hank Bronson walked the
horses slowly back to town, he tried to think of anything
that might cause a question about the truthfulness of his
confession. The biggest problem would be the eyewitnesses
in the bank. He and Warren were close to the same height

and build. He was sure that Warren must have tied his bandanna around his face, an identical bandanna to the one he was wearing. As for their work clothes, they were not exactly alike, but they were similar. The only major difference in their clothing was that Warren wore a hat and he often did not. And at the moment, he was not wearing one. Thinking that a possible problem, he asked a question. "If I see my hat, is it all right if we stop and pick it up?"

"What are you talking about?" Hank asked, alert to any tricks his prisoner might be thinking up. "What about your hat?"

"My hat," John came back, "when you were chasing me from the bank, my hat flew off. It was somewhere right along here. If I see it, can I stop and pick it up?"

"I reckon," Hank said, not remembering if John had been wearing one or not, "but only if we see it somewhere beside the road. We ain't gonna stop to go lookin' for it."

"'Preciate it," John said.

CHAPTER 2

When they rode back into Waco, Hank paraded his prisoner down the middle of the main street to the cheers and comments of the spectators they passed. John speculated that his arrest had helped secure Hank's job as sheriff, whether he improved Warren's situation or not. When he got out of bed that morning, going to jail would have been the last thing he could have possibly considered he might be doing before dinnertime. Had he been given more time than the brief few minutes between the time when Warren rode into the barnyard with the sack of money and the sheriff galloping in right after him, maybe he could have thought of something else. But the sheriff was already placing his brother under arrest when it occurred to John that there was only one way to save him and his young family. Now that he had done it, he was glad that he had thought to take the blame. He could not imagine Kitty with those two sons and no husband and he was doubly sure he did not want to step in to take Warren's place at home. So now he was resolved to cause as little trouble as possible and see what the law would decide to do with him. He would just bide his time for however long they decided to imprison him and maybe it wouldn't be too long, since

Warren hadn't shot anybody and the bank got all the money back.

They pulled up in front of the sheriff's office and Hank's deputy, Tiny Sowell, stepped outside the office to meet them. "Hot damn, Hank, you got him!" Tiny whooped. "I was down at Springer's gettin' my hair cut when I heard ever'body hollerin' that the bank was robbed. By the time I ran back here to the office, you was long gone. So I started seein' about gettin' a posse together, but everybody said you was on that feller like a rooster on a June bug. Looks like they was right. It didn't take you long. The only way it'da been any shorter woulda been if he hadda just run from the bank, straight to the jailhouse." The sheriff dismounted, so John threw a leg over and started to slide off his brother's horse. "Ain't nobody told you to get down!" Tiny snapped, drawing his six-gun as he spoke. John just managed to hang onto the horse.

"Take it easy, Tiny," Hank told him. "He ain't give me a bit of trouble. I didn't even bother with the handcuffs. He confessed to the robbery and said he was sorry he done it, and he's willin' to take his punishment. You can go ahead and get down, John." Tiny holstered his six-gun, and John dropped down from the horse. "Let's take him inside and get him in a cell, then you can take his horse to the stable and on your way back you can tell Myra we need to feed a new prisoner. I expect while you're doin' that, I'd best take this sack of money back to the bank and set James Feldon's mind at ease."

They walked John into the cell room behind the sheriff's office. He waited while the sheriff's oversized deputy opened a cell door and held it for him to enter. "Welcome to your new home until your court date," Tiny said. "You make it easy for us and we'll make it easy for you. Ain't that right, Sheriff?" Hank said that it was.

"That sounds fair to me," John said and started to enter the cell, but Tiny stopped him.

"I almost forgot," Tiny said. "We better have a look at what you've got in your pockets before I lock you up." Since John had been doing nothing but chores at the farm all morning, he had nothing in his pockets but a pocketknife. "I'd better take that from you and put it in a drawer in the office. If you need it for anything, one of us'll get it for you." John handed him the knife, then went inside the cell. Tiny locked the cell door after him. "Don't know how long you'll be with us," he said. "There ain't nobody else in here right now who's waitin' to go to trial. I expect you'll have some company before long, but they'll most likely be drunks or rowdies that'll just be here overnight. You'll probably be here until we get another one who has to go to trial. It depends on the judge who tries you how long they'll leave you here if they don't get nobody pretty soon. When they think they've waited long enough, they'll finally go ahead and schedule your court date. But don't worry about it, if they leave you here a long time. It'll still count against the days you get sentenced to serve." He and Hank walked out of the cell room.

"We'll bring you something to eat when we come back," Hank called over his shoulder.

"Much obliged," John answered. After they left, he looked around his temporary home to see what he had to live with. This was the first time he'd ever seen the inside of a jail cell. The first thing he checked was the cot. *Not bad,* he thought when he sat down on it. It would have to be pretty uncomfortable to be worse than the straw mattress he slept on at home. Under the cot he found a chamber pot, and there was one small stand with a pitcher and basin on it. *Just like a first-class hotel,* he japed to himself.

* * *

Other than the fact that he was locked up twenty-four hours a day in a small room with iron bars, John Bannack could not complain. He was treated very well by both the sheriff and the sheriff's deputy. They, in turn, appreciated the fact that he caused them a minimum of trouble, serving his time without complaints or conversation of any kind unless in answer to a question. There was only one other prisoner in one of the other cells on his second night in jail. A drunk, he was released the following morning. It was the third morning of his imprisonment when his brother Warren came to visit him, a visit that John had been hoping would not occur.

"Hey, John, you got a visitor," Tiny announced when he led Warren into the cell room. "Sez he's your brother. Is that a fact?"

"Yes," John answered, "he's my brother, Warren. Good mornin', Warren. He's the law-abidin' one of the family," he said to Tiny.

"I shoulda guessed he was your brother," Tiny said. "You two look a lot alike." He took no notice of the slight wince in Warren's face when he made the remark. "Don't get your hopes up 'cause I checked him over for weapons and he ain't carryin' any," Tiny japed. "Ordinarily, with a prisoner waitin' for trial for armed robbery, I'd set down in that chair over in the corner of the room just so I could keep my eye on you while you was visitin'. But I think I can give you two some privacy. Right, John?"

"That's a fact, Tiny," John answered, "nothin' to worry about."

Tiny left them alone to talk then but Warren could not seem to find the words to even begin a conversation. So

John said, "Warren, you look like hell. What's done is done. Your job now, your responsibility, is to carry on for your family. Don't spend any more time worryin' about me. I'll be just fine. You and Kitty can make it now without me to feed and house."

Warren looked as if he was not so sure. Finally, his words came. "I don't know if God will ever forgive me for what I've done to you. I know I never will. I don't know what I was thinking. I was just standing there, seeing them through the window with no one else in the bank. The money was right there, and we needed it so badly. I don't know what came over me. I thought I could get away with it." He couldn't say any more, so he hung his head and shook it back and forth in his misery.

"Like I said, it's over and done now," John told him. "You owe me nothing. Your responsibility is to Kitty and the boys. Is she standing by you?"

"She is," Warren answered. "Lord knows, it musta broke her heart to know that I'd do such a thing. But she forgave me and I swore to her I'd never do nothin' like that again. It's just so bad what I done to your life can't be fixed unless I tell the sheriff the right of it."

"Don't you even think about doin' something like that," John quickly reacted. "It would destroy your whole family if you were to go to prison. I've got nothin' to lose. I'm still young enough to start over again when I get out. Just promise me you'll take care of Kitty and those two boys and you won't ever get any more wild notions like this again."

"I promise," Warren said. "Like I told you, I just worried myself to the point where I wasn't thinkin' straight. I'll spend the rest of my life makin' it up to you when you get out." He went silent again for a few moments, then asked, "Have they told you when you will be goin' to trial?"

"No, they ain't set a court date. I do know the judge's

name, though," John said. "His Honor, Judge Raymond Grant. I don't know anything about him except they say he likes to try two or three prisoners on the same day, so I might be in jail here until he gets some more cases."

"Maybe they'll let you know when they do set a date and we can come in to hear your trial," Warren speculated.

"I wish you wouldn't even consider that, brother," John told him. "Tiny said it's a one-man show. There ain't no jury, and there ain't no defense. The sheriff caught me with the money, I gave it to him and confessed that I stole it. So the judge decides how many years that's worth, and that's all there is to it. So there ain't no use in you trying to be there. Don't worry about it. I'll write you a letter from prison." When it was time for Warren to go, and he was still in a state of despair, John told him to make up his mind to make peace with it because he already had. "Now go home and take care of your family."

A day after Warren's visit, a US deputy marshal brought in an odd little fellow with a bushy white beard and a black patch over one eye. He was arrested for cattle rustling. Tiny put him in the cell next to John's and informed him that he would be getting a plate of supper in about an hour. Then he said, "John, brought you some company. This feller's name is George Capp. He's goin' to court for stealin' cattle. Maybe ol' Judge Grant will go ahead and try the two of you."

"Judge Grant?" Capp grunted. "Raymond Grant? Is that the judge who's gonna sentence me? That ain't hardly fair. He's the crotchety ol' buzzard that sent me to The Unit last time."

"Well, it don't look like it cured you of your habit,"

Tiny responded with a chuckle. "How long did he sentence you to?"

"He gimme five years for stealin' five cows," Capp complained. "Five puny little stray cows, he gimme a year for each cow," he snorted, "but they cut me loose after four years."

"How many did you steal this time?" Tiny asked.

"I didn't steal a one," Capp insisted. "That damn deputy marshal arrested me because a little bunch of about twenty strays wandered across the Brazos where I had a camp. Hell, if he hadn't arrested me, I woulda drove 'em back across the river the next mornin'."

Tiny looked at John and grinned. Then to Capp, he said, "Ain't many of them deputy marshals that know cows gotta mind of their own. Maybe you can explain that to Judge Grant."

"Hell, Judge Grant is worse than the dang marshals," Capp said. He looked at John then and asked, "What'd they arrest you for, young feller?"

"Robbin' a bank," John answered.

"Did you shoot anybody?"

John shook his head and said, "No."

"Well, maybe they'll go easy on you, but don't count on it with Judge Raymond Grant runnin' the show," Capp commented.

The trials for both John Bannack and George Capp were completed in short order, just as Sheriff Bronson predicted. Since the court for the Western District of Texas was located in Waco, the prisoners remained in the Waco jail and were transported to a courthouse holding cell during the trial, then returned to jail in time for supper. Capp's trial was first, so John got a pretty good idea of the compassion he might receive from the judge during his own trial.

After Judge Grant read the charges against Capp, he asked George how he pleaded, and George promptly pled, "Not guilty, Your Honor."

"When you were apprehended by Deputy Marshal Forrest Bacon on the eastern side of the river, which is the western boundary of the Double-D Ranch, you were in possession of nineteen cows bearing the Double-D brand," Judge Grant said. "Do you want to change your plea to guilty?"

"No, sir," Capp replied. "'Cause you see, Your Honor, I didn't steal them cows, like that deputy thought. And I don't hold no grudge against that deputy for thinkin' that. Truth of the matter is I crossed over to the other side of the river to get away from that bunch of cows. And damned if they didn't chase right across it after me. It was too dark to try to do much with 'em that night, so I was plannin' to chase 'em back across the river where they belonged in the mornin'. If that deputy hadda waited till mornin', he'da seen that's what I was gonna do."

"You were going to drive the cows back in the morning?" Judge Grant responded.

"Yes, sir, that was what I was gonna do."

"Did that include the cow that Deputy Bacon found you in the process of skinning and butchering when he made the arrest?" Grant asked.

"Your Honor," Capp insisted, "that was just a piece of bad luck. Like I said, it was plum hard dark by then and I saw that calf in the bushes and I thought it was a deer. I'd already seen a heap of deer sign around the river that day and I ain't got but one eye, and it don't always give me a good look at somethin'. I was plannin' to do the right thing in the mornin' and tell somebody from the Double-D about shootin' that calf by mistake. But since it was dead, it'da been a sin not to eat it. That woulda just been a waste of a good cow."

The judge just looked at the comical-looking older man for a few minutes before he sentenced him. "Looking back in my records, I saw that I sentenced you to five years in the Huntsville Unit for stealing five cows, one year for each cow. The prison staff saw fit to release you after only four years. So you still owe me for one cow and it appears that five years wasn't long enough to cure you of your bad habits. So George Skinner Capp, by the power vested in me by the state of Texas, I hereby sentence you to be incarcerated in the Huntsville Unit of the Texas State Prison System to serve a term of ten years." He banged on the desk with his gavel. "Court's closed until after dinner."

It struck John that it was such quick work to try the little man for stealing cattle. There was no jury, no lawyers, just the simple ruling of one man designated to act as God. They talked about Capp's sentencing. "It was about what I expected," Capp said. "Any other judge mighta just give me another five-year sentence. Not Grant, though. I shoulda known he wouldn't go light on me. But what the hell, I can think of a lot worst places to spend the time."

John considered Capp's attitude. It wasn't a bad attitude to take to prison with you, but he was not sure he could adopt it. He had no idea what an attempted bank holdup would call for as far as the number of years to be served. But he hoped for a sentence of no more than ten years. He would still be twenty-eight when he got out, not too late to start a new life. "What kinda sentence do you think Grant will give me?" he asked Capp.

"Hard to say," Capp answered. "You held that bank up, so it was an armed robbery, but you said you didn't shoot anybody and you gave all the money back." He paused to think. "Have you got any record before this? Or maybe I oughta ask if you've ever been caught committin' a crime before this one?"

"Nope," John answered. "This was my first attempt to commit a crime."

"You ain't a very lucky feller, are you?" Capp asked.

"Reckon not," John said with a chuckle.

Listening to their conversation, Tiny was prompted to comment. "Both of you woulda been luckier if you'da got Judge Justice."

"Who?" John asked.

"Judge Wick Justice," Tiny answered. "He don't hesitate to render a harsh punishment when he's convinced one's called for. Judge Grant is more apt to hand down a tough sentence for everybody who breaks a law. He wants to teach 'em a lesson. Don't matter what the circumstances were."

"I ain't never been up before Wick Justice, so I'll just take your word on that," Capp said. "But I don't doubt he'da been more reasonable than Grant."

"Wick Justice," John repeated. "I know I like the sound of the name a lot better than Raymond Grant, but I don't reckon they'll ask me if I'd like to wait for another judge."

After dinner in the holding cell, Hank Bronson put handcuffs on John's wrists and delivered him to the courtroom. The same deputy marshal who walked John and Capp over to the courthouse accompanied Hank as well. Sharply at one o'clock, the bailiff commanded all to rise, and Judge Grant entered the courtroom through a door behind the bench. After everyone was seated again, John noticed three men seated off to one side of the room. There had been no one sitting in those chairs during Capp's trial. He wondered if they had anything to do with his trial or were just spectators. The judge banged his gavel and ordered John to stand up.

Then he read the charges filed against him and asked his plea. John said that he was guilty. "Since we're not using a prosecutor on this case, I'll serve in his stead," the judge said. He motioned to the three men seated off to the side and one of them stood up and took a few steps forward. The bailiff walked over and led him to a witness stand and swore him in, then went back to stand beside the bench.

Judge Grant directed the witness to state his name and occupation. "Yes, sir," the man said, "my name's James Feldon, I'm the manager of First Bank of Waco." John almost gasped aloud. He hadn't thought about having to meet eyewitnesses to his crime.

"Is this the man who walked into the bank and demanded money?"

Feldon hesitated as he stared at John before he said, "I think so, Your Honor. It certainly looks like the same man. He was wearing a bandanna over his face and wore his hat down low on his forehead, but he was the same size and build."

"Was he threatening you with a weapon?" Grant asked.

"Yes, sir, he sure was," Feldon answered. "He said if we didn't give him the money, he'd shoot us."

"These two men with you witnessed the robbery?" Grant asked. When Feldon said that they did, the judge asked one of them to step forward. The two men acted almost in competition to be the chosen one. "Just one of you will do," the judge said. "Bailiff, swear him in."

Wilbur Davis was the quickest to step forward so the bailiff swore him in. When the judge asked his name, he said, "Wilbur Bertram Davis, Your Honor. I'm a teller in the bank and that's the man right there that robbed us." He pointed to John.

"Thank you, gentlemen," Judge Grant said. "You may

sit down now." He turned his attention toward Hank then. "Sheriff Bronson, you were the arresting officer?"

"Yes, sir."

"Is this the man you pursued from the bank?"

"Yes, sir."

"Was he in possession of the stolen bank money when you arrested him?"

"Yes, sir, he sure was," Hank said. "There ain't no doubt he stole it, and I'd like to say that he made no effort to resist arrest. He said he was guilty, and he came peacefully. And he ain't caused no problems since he's been in my jail." John gave a silent thanks for the sheriff's kind comments.

"All right, Sheriff," Judge Grant said. "Your remarks are duly noted. You may step back now." He nodded to the bailiff and the bailiff led Hank back to his chair. Ready to issue his sentence then, the judge addressed John, who was now standing before the bench. "Well, Mr. Bannack, it would appear that this is your first appearance in a court of law."

"Yes, sir," John answered, "and I intend to make it my last one as well."

"Glad to hear you have good intentions," Grant said. "John Boyd Bannack, by the power vested in me by the state of Texas, I hereby sentence you to be incarcerated in the Huntsville Unit of the Texas State Prison System to serve a term of twenty years."

For an instant, he felt like his knees were going to buckle. They didn't, but he was unable to stop himself from blurting, "Twenty years?" He was anticipating ten years at the most. "For my first occurrence and no one was hurt?" Both the deputy marshal and the bailiff came at once to take an elbow to control him. He made no effort to resist.

"I'll remind you that this is a court of law," Judge Grant informed him, "and not an auction. Maybe when your

sentence is served, you will have more respect for the law."
He banged his gavel a couple of times and ordered, "Get
him out of here."

While the sheriff and the deputy marshal walked George
and John back to the jail, Hank couldn't help commenting.
"Damned if ol' Raymond Grant didn't decide to make an
example outta you, John. I thought you'd get off with a
lighter sentence than that."

"That's typical of Judge Grant," the deputy marshal remarked. "He likes to stop you in your tracks and at the same
time show all the other young fellers out here what's liable
to happen to 'em if they decide to break the law."

"I reckon you just have to take whatever life's got
waitin' for you," John said. At this point it might have been
the natural reaction to hate his brother for making such a
foolish decision. But he still felt that it was better that he
should live with the results caused by Warren's moment of
insanity instead of witnessing the destruction of his brother's
family. "I 'preciate your kind words on my behalf, anyway,"
he said to Hank, although he wondered if Grant might have
added a few years just to spite the sheriff's efforts.

"I gotta hand it to ya," Hank said. "You're takin' it pretty
calmly now. But for a moment back there, when he sentenced you, I thought you was fixin' to explode."

"That woulda been another brilliant decision, wouldn't
it?" John said, already resigned to the fate that was obviously designed for him. "You mighta had to shoot me down
right there in the courtroom."

"There's that possibility," Hank replied with a friendly
grin.

CHAPTER 3

"I swear, John," George Capp said as they were put back in their cells. "Twenty years! That old son of . . ." he started, then interrupted himself. "Did you say something to make him mad? Act cocky or something?"

"No, he didn't do a dang thing but stand there quiet and respectful," Hank answered for him. "It was just Raymond Grant showin' what a horse's behind he can be when he wants to. I declare, John, I wish you'da just dropped that sack of money and kept runnin'. Then I'da had to stop and pick it up, and I coulda just took it on back to the bank and no harm done." John almost believed he meant it.

"You was just unlucky you didn't get Judge Wick Justice," Capp said. "Hell, we both was." He looked at Hank then. "When they gonna haul us down to Huntsville, Sheriff?"

"They said day after tomorrow," Hank answered. "They're gonna be here sometime in the mornin', probably after breakfast, with a jail wagon and a cook."

"I wish they'd just let us ride down there on horseback," Capp said. "It'll take a week to drive down there in a wagon."

"Are you in a hurry to get there?" John asked.

Capp shrugged and grinned. "I reckon I ain't. I just

druther set in a saddle than bounce on a wagon seat, though." He continued to grin at John until John finally had to ask him why. "Oh, I was just thinkin' you'd be the one who ought not be in a hurry to get down to Huntsville."

"Is that so?" John replied. "Why is that?"

"On account of when they send you to Huntsville, they send you to work. They'll most likely send me back to the cotton and woolen mill, where I used to work. Big strong young man like you, they'll send to the hardest labor job they've got. Cuttin' timber and workin' the sawmill if they're buildin' new cellblocks, bustin' up rocks to use as foundations, they'll have plenty of work for you. They take one look at me and it's back to the textile mill, or maybe the laundry."

"I swear, Capp, you really know how to cheer a fellow up," John said.

As scheduled, two deputy marshals arrived at the jail with a jail wagon. Deputies, Bud Jessup and Dan Pointer informed Sheriff Hank Bronson that they intended to eat breakfast at the hotel before leaving for Huntsville. So he was to feed the prisoners breakfast as usual that morning. The cook and driver of the jail wagon, Mickey Tate, planned to eat at the hotel as well, rather than go to the trouble of starting a fire and cooking a breakfast for one. The deputies came inside the office just long enough to sign some paperwork for picking up two prisoners. Then they took a quick look at their passengers. "One bronco and one nag," Bud Jessup declared casually. "We gonna have any trouble outta the young one?"

"It would sure as hell surprise me if you did," Hank told him. "John Bannack ain't caused a lick of trouble the whole time he's been here."

"Glad to hear it," Bud said. "Let's go eat breakfast."

* * *

In no particular hurry, since the deputy marshals were paid by the day for transporting prisoners, they took six and a half days to make the trip to Huntsville. It was a monotonous trip for the two prisoners with a daily routine of an early breakfast each morning before starting out. Then they stopped to rest the horses and eat dinner at noon and back on the trail again until camping for the night. There was a long chain in the back of the wagon that one of the deputies pulled out to give John and Capp some freedom from the wagon during the rest and overnight stops. One end of the chain was locked around one of the wagon wheels, then John and Capp had one of their ankles cuffed to the chain, giving them the freedom to move about comfortably without being constantly guarded by the deputies.

Covering an area of over fifty acres, the Huntsville Unit of the Texas State Prison System was the headquarters for the whole state. John and Capp were delivered to the impressive red brick facility referred to as the Walls Unit. Within its walls, the main headquarters and records of the entire Texas Prison System were kept, as well as the cells for those prisoners sentenced to execution. Bud and Dan turned their prisoners over to the prison authorities and wished them good luck, thinking they would surely need it.

While the two new prisoners were being processed, Capp explained what the different procedures were for until they were separated and Capp was led off toward another building and John was maintained in the Walls Unit for general prison orientation. He didn't see George Capp for quite some time after that day. When the paperwork was completed, two guards escorted John to a cellblock on the far side of an open yard and told him that was his new home. Before taking him to a cell, however, he was taken to a large building where he was issued new clothes and work shoes as well as a towel and a washcloth. These he carried to the back part of the building where he was ordered to strip off his civilian clothes and stand in a wide trough with a pump at the head of it. After he was wet down completely, he was instructed to take a bar of soap and soap up his new washcloth. His guards then watched him soap up his entire body while they discussed his work potential. "He looks like he ain't no stranger to hard work," one of the guards said. "He's big enough and he's muscled up pretty good."

"How old are you, boy?" The other guard asked John.

"Eighteen," John answered.

"Ol' Gator's gonna have a good time breakin' this one in," the first guard chuckled. Then to John, he said, "All right, that's good enough. We'll rinse you off." He picked up a bucket full of water and turned it upside down over John's head while his partner filled another bucket from the pump, which he threw at John to rinse the soap off that the first bucket left. John stood, shivering slightly, a reaction to the cold water. "Dry off and put your new clothes on," he was told. John did so immediately.

They walked him to the cellblock building they had pointed out to him before his bath. "This is building four," one of the guards said. "We'll take you inside and find your cell. Ain't nobody in there now. They're all at work. They'll be back pretty soon 'cause supper's at five o'clock and you can just go to the chow hall with 'em." They walked into building number four and a small area just inside the door that had a table and half a dozen straight-back wooden chairs. Beyond that, the rest of the building was made up of two-man cubicles with a double bunk bed in each one. Sitting in one of the chairs at the table, a prisoner who had been dozing with his head on the table, jumped to his feet.

"You the barracks guard?" The guard who had been doing most of the talking, asked.

"Yes, sir, Mr. Royce," the man answered.

"I got you a new guest," Royce said. He glanced at a paper he was holding in his hand. "He's goin' in number twelve."

"Yes, sir, Mr. Royce," the barracks guard responded and led them halfway down the aisle between the cubicles to stop at one with the number twelve over it. He turned then to give John a good looking over. "Mack Tatum's sleepin' in the bottom bunk," he said. John didn't make any comment. He just walked inside the small cell and placed the few items he had on the top bunk.

When he came back out, Royce said, "All right, Bannack, when the rest of the men get back, you just follow them and you'll soon learn what to do."

"Yes, sir, Mr. Royce," John replied. "I 'preciate it."

The two guards left him with the barracks guard then, who promptly asked him, "He say your name was Bannack?"

"That's right, John Bannack. What's yours?"

"Squint Johnson," he answered. "What you in here for?"

"Robbin' a bank," John said. "How 'bout you?"

"I shot a man in a gunfight," Squint said.

"You mean like in a duel?" John asked and when Squint nodded, John said, "I didn't think that was against the law."

"It is when the other feller ain't got no gun," Squint said.

"Right," John replied. "Who did you say was sleepin' in the bunk under mine?"

"Mack Tatum," Squint answered. "He don't talk much. He's servin' time for holdin' up stagecoaches. Where you from, John?"

"Waco," John answered.

"I mean where'd you rob the bank?"

"Waco," John answered again.

"You robbed the bank where you live?" Squint asked. "That weren't too smart, seems to me like."

"I reckon I can't disagree with you, seein' as where it landed me," John allowed. He wished he had been given the opportunity to give that advice to his brother before Warren made such an ill-advised move. The interrogation was interrupted then with the arrival of the other men back from work. There were no windows in the cellblock, so Squint walked out on the little porch at the end of the building to watch. John followed him and stood on the porch beside him while a couple of guards compared body counts to make sure no one was missing since they left the job site.

"Just so you'll know," Squint said, "see the big feller at the head of the column? He's the boss man of four-block. That's what they call this buildin'."

"He's a guard?" John asked.

"No, he's a prisoner, same as the rest of us, but somebody's got to be the boss of things. And in here, it's the strongest that takes over the job of boss, and in four-block, he's the man. His name's Gator. I'm just tellin' you this, so you don't start off on the wrong foot."

"That's good to know. I 'preciate it. There ought not be any problem. I ain't gonna cause any trouble. I'm just trying to get by."

"Sounds like you're thinkin' straight," Squint said as the formation of prisoners fell out and headed toward four-block and the washroom next to it.

John stood off beside the table while the men filed into the building, all of them eyeing the stranger as they passed on to their cells. When a graying middle-aged man walked in, Squint pulled him aside. "You got you a new cell mate, Mack. This here's John Bannack. John, this is Mack Tatum."

There was an immediate flicker of alarm in Tatum's eyes when he looked at the tall, ruggedly built young man. "I'm sleepin' in that bottom bunk," he blurted. "I slept in that top bunk long enough, waitin' for Sid to get paroled."

"Right, Mack," John responded. "I'll take the top bunk. I've already put my stuff up there."

Tatum relaxed at once. "It's just so damn hard on me. I've got the rhumatiz in my knees and it got to where it was really workin' on me just gittin' up and down outta that bunk. Young feller like you can probably jump up there like gittin' on a horse."

"Well, maybe not that easy, but it ain't no problem." John smiled when he said it, taking no notice of the huge man coming up the steps behind him. He turned when Squint alerted him.

"This here's John Bannack, Gator," Squint said. "He's a new man, came in from Waco today. He's gonna be bunkin' with Mack Tatum."

John turned to see the big man striding toward him, so he acknowledged him, "Gator," he said. The brute didn't answer but kept coming until almost on John's toes. Then without warning, he threw a roundhouse right cross that landed flush on John's jaw, snapping his head sideways and driving him a couple of steps backward before landing him flat on his back.

Gator stepped forward to stand over the stunned man. "That's just to let you know right off who's the boss of four-block, and you'd best not forget it." He continued standing over the dazed victim of his unexpected assault until he was satisfied John had nothing to say about it. Then he gave Squint and Tatum a look of satisfaction. "If he ain't on his feet in time to go to supper, put him in his bunk."

"He's a pretty big feller, Gator," Mack Tatum complained, "and we'd have to put him on the top bunk."

"Well, let him lay where he is," Gator said, took one last

look at his unsuspecting victim, then turned and walked back to the table at the end of the building.

John slowly began to recover his senses, thinking at first he had been kicked by a horse. He could hear Tatum and Squint talking but couldn't understand what they were saying until his head finally cleared. Then realizing what had actually happened, he struggled to get himself up from the floor. Seeing him getting to his feet, Mack reached down to help him, but John's brain had settled back in its proper place by then. He pushed Mack's hand away and got to his feet and started toward the end of the building where Gator was standing, talking to several of the other prisoners, his back toward the man approaching. The men Gator was talking to suddenly went silent when they saw John approaching, but Gator was doing most all the talking, so he didn't notice their silence. Feeling the strength returning to his muscles, aided by the rage he felt burning inside him, John grabbed one of the heavy wooden chairs by the back of it. Lifting it high up over his head, he stepped into the blow, swinging the hard oaken chair with all the force he could muster, into the back of Gator's head. There were two distinct cracks of sound, the first when the heavy chair caught the back of Gator's head, the second when Gator's face was smashed against the tabletop. "That's just to let you know that I don't take that crap from any man, *Boss*." He emphasized the last word.

The men Gator had been talking with stepped back away from the table as a pool of blood began to spread on the tabletop, coming from both Gator's face and the back of his head. They stared in disbelief at the new man from Waco, unsure if his rage was confined to the man who had struck him, or any man that came to his aid. John stared back at them, waiting to combat whatever reaction they might have. He found it hard to believe that there might be any sense of loyalty to such a bully of a man. "Is there a doctor or a hospital in this place?" He finally asked when it appeared that Gator was not going to get up from the table.

"Yes, sir," Squint responded. "We'd best get somebody from the hospital to take a look at him!" He ran out to the yard where several of the guards were still standing around and told them Gator needed help. The guards came back with him.

"What the hell happened to him?" One of the guards asked.

"He tripped and hit his head," Mack Tatum answered at once. A couple of the prisoners standing next to Mack nodded their heads in agreement.

"Yeah," Squint said, "a big feller like that gets a little bit clumsy and he goes down hard."

Gator wasn't moving, so the guards feared he might be dead. "We'd better get over to the hospital and tell 'em to bring a stretcher to pick him up," one of them said.

"Better tell 'em to bring a big one," another said. He looked at Mack and added, "You know, if this stud dies, you might have to come up with a few more details about what happened to him."

"It's time to go to supper now," Squint said. "We can remember all the details while we're eatin'."

"Right," one of the guards said to the others. "I'll march 'em to the dinin' room if one of you will go to the hospital."

"Come on, John," Tatum said quietly. "Can you chew anything with that broke jaw?"

"I ain't sure. I don't think it's really broke but it's sure tender as hell." He felt it with his hand. "As long as I don't have to chew anything that's real tough, it oughta do all right."

"Hell, they don't serve nothin' in the dinin' room that ain't tough," Tatum said.

All the prisoners in four-block came out of the building and lined up in the yard. Then they were marched off to the dining room for supper where the most common topic of conversation was about the time Gator met the man from Waco.

CHAPTER 4

Gator was kept in the small hospital inside the corrections facility for the better part of two weeks. There were two doctors who worked at the hospital full time, neither one especially trained to diagnose and treat brain injuries. Well qualified in the treatment of broken bones, cuts, and blisters, they could only speculate that Gator had experienced a concussion from which he was slow in recovering. A couple of the guards were sent back to investigate the accident that rendered the fearsome beast helpless, in hope of supplying the doctors with more information about his injuries. Unfortunately, they found that there was no one who claimed to have actually witnessed Gator's fall. So they were left to assume that he had somehow managed to stumble backward and hit his head on a chair that caused him to lunge forward to go face down on the table. Since the investigation shed no light on anything other than a freak accident, the doctors were left with no line of treatment to pursue. So it was decided to put Gator in a ward with patients too old and feeble to do anything but await their deaths of old age. If he recovered his senses, he would be returned to the general prison population at that time.

The incident had created a different situation for the prisoners back in four-block. In the units that housed the prisoners who did the manual labor jobs, there was always one individual, a captain so to speak, who passed along the orders from the guards. In a prison, that man usually took the position through a show of strength. With Gator gone, the natural replacement would be the man who had been strong enough to bring him down, and that would be the man from Waco. The problem, however, was John Bannack, a new inmate, was still trying to learn the prison routine. In addition to that, they were surprised to find that he had no desire to be the captain of four-block. They ended up electing a captain via a voice vote, and the winner was Mack Tatum, since he was older than most of the others, therefore supposedly wiser. It was also thought a good choice, since John Bannack was his cell mate. There remained a sense of anxious anticipation hovering over four-block, however, for the day when Gator returned. And it was generally assumed that he would return. It was just a matter of when. And if that certainty rode heavily on Bannack's mind, it was not evident.

"Hey, Doc," the hospital orderly called out, "the Gator ate his dinner." He held up a tray with empty dishes on it for the doctor to see.

"Who?" the doctor asked.

"Gator," the orderly replied, "Grover Brice, the one with the cracked skull."

"Oh," Doc responded, realizing he meant the big man with the concussion. He was immediately interested then. Brice hadn't eaten much of anything since he'd been brought into the hospital. He went at once into the ward to see for himself. He found the huge man sitting up in the bed with his feet hanging off each side as if on a horse.

"Where the hell's my clothes?" Gator demanded when he saw the doctor.

Ignoring Gator's question, the doctor asked, "How long have you been awake?"

"Long enough to know you folks in here don't give a man enough food to feed a squirrel," Gator responded. "What the hell am I doin' in here, anyway? What happened to my head?" He reached up to feel the bandage around his skull.

"Do you know how long you've been here?" the doctor asked.

"No. All night, I reckon. How'd I get here?"

"You'll be here two weeks day after tomorrow," the doctor told him. "And we were fixin' to send you to the old folks ward where they're waitin' to die. Don't you remember anything about hitting your head?"

He paused to think for a second. "No, I don't remember anything about hittin' my head." He reached up to feel the bandage again. "How did I hit my head?"

"I wish I could tell you, but I don't know for sure. What they say back at your cellblock is that you tripped and hit your head on the table."

"When do I get outta here?" Gator asked. "I'll find out how I tripped soon as I get back to four-block."

"Hell, you can go back this afternoon," Doc said. "Ain't nothin' else we can do for you here. Your clothes are in that box under your bed. I'll get a guard to walk you back to four-block."

"I don't need no guard to walk me back," Gator said.

"Yes, you do, you still woke up in prison. Get your clothes on, and I'll get a guard."

Gabe Horn, that day's barracks guard at four-block, stood in the open door at the end of The Unit, looking out across the yard toward the Walls Unit. His attention had been caught by the two men approaching the gate in the fence that separated the units. One of the men was a guard, who unlocked the gate and held it open for the other man, who Gabe identified as no other than Gator Brice. There had been reports that Gator had never awakened after he was attacked by John Bannack, but there he was, heading straight for four-block. The guard didn't follow him in, just locked the gate and returned to the Walls Unit. "And I had to catch barracks guard today," Gabe muttered aloud. "If he just got out of the hospital, he ought not be feelin' too spunky." He remained standing in the doorway, preparing to greet the bully back. "I swear, Gator," he called out as cheerfully as he could contrive, "we been wonderin' when you was comin' back. You been gone for quite a spell. You feelin' all right now?"

"Yeah, I reckon," Gator answered. "Soon as I get this rag off my head. Wish I had a mirror. Take a look at the back of my head. It feels like there ain't no hair back there." He pulled off the bandage, that had some dried blood stains on it, and tossed it on the table.

Gabe walked around behind him and looked at the wound. "You ain't got no hair on a big part of your head back there. You're right about that. I reckon they had to shave it off so they could sew up that cut on the back of your head. I swear, it was a big ol' place they had to sew up." He quickly added, "Looks like they got it sewed up pretty good, though."

"I'll tell you the truth, I'm havin' trouble remembering how I hit the back of my head like that. Did you see how I did it?"

"No, I didn't," Gabe lied. "I weren't there when you did it."

"Looks like I coulda remembered fallin' hard enough to do that to the back of my head and bustin' my nose at the same time." He shook his head slowly. "It feels like everything's like it oughta be. It'll come to me, I reckon." He looked at the clock on the wall. "The boys oughta be gittin' back from work pretty soon now. I'm ready to eat. They like to starved me to death over at the hospital."

"Yeah, I'm ready, too," Gabe said. He wondered if Gator remembered John Bannack, and if he did, what would happen when he saw him again. *Wonder what he'll do when he finds out Mack Tatum is the boss of four-block now?* he thought.

"I think I'll catch a little shuteye while we're waitin' for the boys to get back," Gator decided. He went into his cell and laid down on his bunk. Gabe was thinking how lucky it was that Mack hadn't decided to move into Gator's cell yet. He would not have wanted to be the one to explain it to Gator. "They still got us workin' at the sawmill?" Gator called out from his cell.

"That's right," Gabe called back. "The last couple of days we've been cuttin' down trees and haulin' logs to the sawmill." He had hoped Gator would go to sleep and save all his questions until all the men were back. That was not the case, however, because evidently Gator's memory was coming back.

"What about that new feller?" Gator asked then. "I don't reckon he gave anybody any trouble." Since he was lying on his bunk, Gabe couldn't see the grin on Gator's face when he recalled the welcome he gave Bannack.

"Nah, he ain't give nobody no trouble," Gabe answered him. *Not since he dang-near knocked your head off,* he thought. It was pretty obvious that Gator was telling the truth when he said he had no memory of his *accident.* There was likely to be a killing when he did find out what sent him to the hospital. So far, everybody in four-block had kept a tight lip about what had happened on Bannack's first day in the unit. One thing for sure, he decided, he'd best catch the men before they came back inside to see Gator. So he continued staring out the door, watching for the return of the work detail. A few moments later, he heard the sounds of snoring coming from Gator's cell, for which he was grateful.

Brief minutes later, he spotted the column of men approaching the exercise yard gate, so he quietly slipped out the door and hurried to meet them to give warning. "What's up, Gabe?" Mack Tatum asked, suspecting something must be.

"Gator's back," Gabe said. Mack looked at once toward the door of the cellblock. "He's layin' in his bunk, takin' a nap," Gabe continued. The rest of the column gathered around the two men to hear the reason for Gabe's anxious appearance. Before Mack could ask the question, Gabe said, "He remembers that he knocked hell out of Bannack, but that's all he remembers. He don't know it was Bannack that damn-near tore his head off with that chair. And he don't know nothin' about you bein' the new boss of four-block."

"Damn," Mack uttered. "He don't remember gittin' hit with that chair? What does he think sent him to the hospital?"

"He thinks he tripped or something and he can't figure out how he did it," Gabe said. "He asked me how it happened and I told him I didn't see it, so I didn't know how he did it."

"I'm thinkin' we'd best not tell him what really happened," Squint Johnson spoke up. "He's liable to kill John Bannack and he might come after you for takin' his job as boss."

"If he ever gets enough of his memory back, he might remember he wasn't doin' nothin' but standin' by the table talkin' to some of us right after he punched Bannack on the jaw when his lights went out," Mack said. "There's bound to be some trouble outta Gator before this is done with."

"Mighta been better if Bannack had just took that lick and figured it was the price to get in four-block," Squint said.

"Hell," Mack said, "I wish Bannack hadda hit him a little harder and then we'da been done with Gator for good." He looked around him at the questioning faces. "I 'preciate the fact that you all decided to make me the boss, but I think till we find out if Gator's sick in the head or not, it'd be best to let him think nothin' ain't changed. Now we might as well go on and get ready to eat supper." They dispersed then as they normally would have, most heading for the washhouse to clean up a little bit before eating. One among them, young John Bannack, had made no comments during the discussion just finished. No one said anything to him about the problem, but he was aware that they all knew he was the cause of it.

As they filed into the cellblock, John noticed a much quieter entrance than on days before. When he walked past Gator's cell, he saw the reason. The huge man was sound asleep and no one was eager to awaken him. So he went to cell number twelve to get his washcloth and towel to take to the washhouse. When he came back, Gator was still sleeping, so he asked Mack, "It's time to go eat. Are we gonna wake him up?"

"Oh, hell, yeah," Mack replied. "He'd really raise hell if we let him miss supper."

"There are what, twenty-nine or thirty inmates in this unit? Why do you let one man intimidate the whole lot of you?"

Mack responded with a look of tired patience. "Some of us mighta thought like that a long time ago. But after you've been in here for a while, you'll learn that every man acts for himself and has to look out for himself. So

they're ready to march us to supper. Let's wake Gator up."
He hesitated, then said, "On second thought, you go on
ahead. I'll wake Gator up. It might be a good idea if Gator
don't see you right away."

John shook his head. "Whatever you say, Boss." He
walked on outside where the men were already lining up for
supper. And went over to join them. When it was time, one
of the guards blew his whistle and the men formed into a
ragged formation, then were marched off to the dining hall.
After going through the line, John took his tray to the end
of a table away from the one Gator chose. He couldn't help
noticing that, unlike days before, no one else chose to join
him at his end of the table. It was almost humorous, he
thought. They might just as well have hung a sign on him
with a picture of a chair on it. Whether they intended it or
not, their isolation of him worked to call Gator's attention
to him. It was just as well, as far as he was concerned. He
had no intention of being intimidated by Gator or any other
man, or group of men. In his mind, he had made the last
move. He planned to wait for Gator to make the next move,
if there were to be any more moves. If Gator was done with
it, after his visit to the hospital, then he was done with it as
well. Now that he could see the fear the other men had of
Gator, he might decide to enlighten Gator as to the cause of
his headache, so he would know no one else was to blame.

"That's the new feller, ain't it?" Gator suddenly asked
Squint Johnson, who was sitting across the table from him.

"Right," Squint answered, "that's him, John Bannack."

"How come he don't sit with none of the other boys from
four-block?" Gator asked. "He think he's any better'n the
rest of us?"

"Nah, he's all right, Gator. He's just still new, that's all.
He's gettin' along with the rest of the men. He ain't no
problem. Does his share of the work, too."

"Maybe I'll need to have a little talk with him," Gator said, "make sure he don't think he's too good to sit with the rest of us."

"He most likely thought some of the rest of us would be sittin' down there," Squint said. "Like I said, he's just new and he don't wanna cause no trouble."

The longer Gator stared at the rugged looking young man sitting alone at the end of the next table, the more he remembered about their one encounter. He distinctly remembered the satisfaction he had experienced when he knocked the new man senseless on the floor. The memory brought a smile to his face. He promptly got up from the table, picked up his tray and coffee cup, and moved down to take a seat across from the new man. All conversation at the table he left came to a sudden stop. "Mind if I set down here?" Gator asked, a wide smirk on his face.

"Not at all," John answered.

"I thought maybe you figured you was too good to sit with the rest of us common criminals," Gator said.

"Is that a fact?" John asked. "No, I think I can put up with most of you as long as you act like a human being."

"Maybe you don't understand what I do for four-block. I'm the one who makes sure all the new girls behave themselves and do like they're told. Do you understand that or do I have to get your attention again?"

"Oh, I understand," John said. "I'll certainly try to behave. By the way, how's your headache comin' along? You havin' any more pains from the back of your head where that chair hit you? I know that musta hurt. They say you were pretty much out of your head for a long time before you finally woke up."

Gator was speechless for a couple of moments. When he finally replied, he spoke in a smoldering voice. "You lookin' to get your back broke? What the hell do you know about that wound on the back of my head?"

"I know that I put it there," John stated flatly. "I had to get your attention and I couldn't think of nothin' better than one of those heavy oak chairs to do that. I figured you're the one who set the rules when you walked up and slugged me without so much as a howdy-do, like something a lowdown yellow-belly coward would do. So when I found out what the rules of the game were, I thought I'd best be sure I got your attention. Now that I've finally got it, I'll tell you this. I mind my own business, and I don't make trouble for people who mind theirs. I'll not permit any man to raise his hand against me and go unpunished for it. If a man threatens my life, he'd better be prepared to defend his. So Gator, if you've got a grain of sense in that ugly head of yours, you'll just call this a draw and keep a long way away from me from now on. If you don't, I'll kill you. Do you understand that?"

Gator's brain was spinning inside his skull, fairly stunned by the blunt audacity of the new man's warning. Speechless for several long moments, he could only glare in disbelief. Finally, he responded, threatening in a low menacing tone, "You just dug a grave for yourself, big mouth."

"Is that so?" John taunted. "Well, it ain't gonna be so easy next time you come after me because now I know you like to sneak up on a man when he ain't lookin'. And I'm gonna keep my eye on you, you big tub of guts."

It was more than the raging beast could control. Forgetting where he was and anyone else around him, he rose up to his feet, knocking the whole bench over. Then he lunged across the table at his tormenter, his huge hands seeking John's throat. John fully expected a reaction but not one of violent abandon right there in the dining hall. Being quicker in reflex than Gator, however, he avoided his surprise attack, using the only weapons he had. He threw his hot coffee in Gator's face and when the enraged monster recoiled, John jammed his fork up under Gator's chin with such force that the dull tines sank into his throat. Roaring like a wild beast, Gator reached back to pull the dangling fork from under his chin. When he did, John grabbed his arm and dragged him off the table to crash face down onto the floor. Seeing the beast incapacitated for a second, John took the time to get away from the bench where there was more room to meet the next attack. With no time to concern himself with anything but to ready himself for the crazed monster's next attempt, he was unaware of the chaos that had been created with the rest of the dining hall. He could hear the prison guards yelling for order, but he dared not take his eyes off Gator, who was getting to his feet, his eyes like two live coals focusing on him. John waited, his body in a half crouch, ready to meet Gator's charge, knowing he would be crushed if he took him head on.

Gator charged, his head down like a bull. John waited until the moment before the collision, then stepped quickly aside and tripped the charging bull, sending Gator crashing to the floor again. John stood ready for Gator's next charge while the frustrated beast slowly got to his feet. He could hear the guards ordering them to stop, so he called back to them. "Tell him to stop! I'm just trying to protect myself!" The guards ordered Gator to stop, but he was too deep into his fury to obey. He got set and charged again. John got ready to meet the charge but was startled by two shots, fired almost at the same time. He stepped aside as Gator staggered toward him before dropping to his knees and then to the floor.

In a few minutes, there were several more guards in the dining hall, attracted by the shots fired. They talked with the dining hall guards for a few minutes before two of them came over and ordered John to place his hands behind his back. He did as instructed, although he protested that he didn't do anything but try to protect himself. He was told he was a reason for the trouble and would be held in solitary confinement until a hearing was held. He was promptly removed from the dining hall and taken to another part of the prison where he was put in a holding cell by himself.

The prison warden and his staff were greatly concerned by an outright life or death fight between two inmates in the prison dining hall, in which the death of one of the inmates occurred. The warden called for a complete investigation of the incident, which resulted in John Bannack remaining in solitary confinement for almost a week while the warden's staff interviewed inmates of four-block. Ever since its creation, the Walls Unit at Huntsville had been designed to be a model for state prisons, built and operated as a self-sustaining penal unit. With shops and mills within its walls, it would be sufficient to pay for its own cost while teaching its inmates to learn skills that could point them toward legitimate lives upon release. In short, a bloody brawl that ended in the killing of an inmate in the dining hall of the prison was a black eye to the governor's program.

So the question to be decided was how to punish the surviving participant in the dining hall fight. After the warden's investigation, it was evident that the man the guards shot was the aggressor on the day of the incident. However, the other man, John Bannack, had previously assaulted the man who was shot, sending him to the hospital almost two weeks before. They decided that Bannack should be sentenced to a year of hard labor and so he was sent to another cellblock. The work was hard, but the work was the only time he was permitted to leave his cell. So he found himself looking forward to the work. It usually called for working with a pick and shovel, or an axe or saw. He soon began looking forward to the labor gangs the prison contracted with outside businesses even more. These work details called for a small gang of men to work outside the prison walls each day and return to the prison at night. In addition to the guards, a cook and chuckwagon accompanied them to fix one meal at noontime.

His overall sentence was for twenty years, so he didn't bother his mind with counting his days or wondering about the chances of early parole. Almost before he realized it, his punishment sentence of one year of hard labor was over. Instead of returning him to four-block, however, he was transferred to a smaller cellblock, still assigned to the hard physical jobs. Unknown to him, he had established a reputation for himself as a big, strong man, who never complained. In fact, he seldom spoke, and even when he did, it seemed as if he regretted spending his words.

He realized his nineteenth birthday that first year in solitary. His twentieth was passed while he was working out of the smaller cellblock. And by this time, his reputation as the silent man from Waco was well known, not only in his small cellblock, but in the larger ones as well. It was during this year that word reached the prisoners that war had been declared between the north and the south. The cotton and wool mill inside the Huntsville Unit was immediately switched over to start making uniforms and tents for the Confederate soldiers. When John heard that, it brought to mind someone he had not thought of since he had arrived at the Walls Unit. And he wondered if George Capp had been sent back to the mill as the little man had anticipated.

CHAPTER 5

L ike many small towns in Texas, Boonville, the county seat of Brazos County, was feeling the impact of the war on the daily life of the town. The town was depleted of young men. Before the war was declared, the mayor and the city council were intent upon continuing the growth of Boonville. And one of the most important keys to the town's growth was the coming of the railroad. The Houston and Texas Central had already planned to extend their tracks from Millican, but the coming of the war put a halt to that. The town was already a stagecoach stop for coaches from Houston, but the council decided it to their advantage to make it easier for the coaches to reach Boonville to connect with the train. To accomplish that, a plan was proposed to build a bridge across the Navasota River to give the stagecoach a more direct route to their town. Daniel Orton, who owned the sawmill, was the man who could build the bridge. His only deterrent was the lack of ablebodied men to do the work. Since the young men had volunteered to fight the Yankees, there was no one left to do the manual labor required to fell the trees and snake the logs out to be put in place.

At the council meeting one night, Ronald Mallard, the owner of Boonville General Merchandise, made a suggestion that was met with doubt at first but generated more interest as he explained his reasoning. "I'm sure you are all familiar with the warden's outside work program over there at the Huntsville Unit, where he hires out laborers at a reasonable rate. That might be the very thing we need to lay the base for that bridge."

"That sounds like a good idea, Ronald," Rob Humphrey spoke up, "but Huntsville's fifty miles from here. Ain't you forgettin' that? They ain't likely to send any prisoners that far away to work."

"I don't know why not," Mallard replied. "They send 'em out for a day, two days, with a jail wagon, a cook, and a guard. What's the difference?" He looked around for any more objections. "Hell," he continued, "we could make it a lot easier for them, too. Two-and-a-half days to get here, two-and-a-half to get back, that ain't all that far. We could most likely get all we needed out of five or six convicts in four or five days. And the town folks wouldn't have to worry about a bunch of convicts camping near town. We could keep 'em in the jail at night." He looked over at the sheriff. "That'd be all right, wouldn't it, Rufus?"

"I reckon," Sheriff Barnes replied. "Would we have to feed 'em?"

"I don't know," Mallard answered, "maybe, maybe not. They would have a cook with 'em, so he might just keep fixin' three meals a day for 'em after they get here. Whatever, we'll just work out a deal with the prison. Whaddaya think?" He looked around at the men seated there, waiting for their reaction.

"You know, that might not be as crazy as it sounded at first," Rob Humphrey commented. "I reckon it depends on how much the prison expects us to pay for the labor."

"I don't know about the rest of you," Daniel Orton said, "but I'd like to ride over to Huntsville and see what the warden's office has to say about it. What do you think, Ronald?"

"It's certainly worth looking into," Mallard replied. "Might as well go check it out and see what they'll do." It was decided then that Orton and Mallard would ride over to Huntsville to talk to the warden. Mallard had been there before, so he knew where to go to request a meeting with the warden. He also knew it a good idea to inform the warden's secretary that he was the mayor of Boonville. He had heard that the warden would always try to accommodate a visiting mayor. And he saw no reason to inform the warden that he was actually the acting mayor while the real mayor was confined to his bed while he battled a case of pneumonia. They planned their trip for an arrival at the warden's office a little before noon in hopes of getting an invitation to join him for dinner.

Mallard's planning paid off as he had hoped, for the warden was very receptive to the visiting *mayor*. Warden Sims was always up for impressing the leaders of the towns in the prison's neighborhood, even if it extended quite a few miles. In addition, the warden was always open for the leasing of his inmates and services, so the meeting went as well as Mallard and Orton could have hoped. They dined in the staff's dining hall while Mallard presented their proposal for the leasing of half a dozen hard-bodied men for a period of five days. The warden hesitated slightly when he realized how far Boonville was from The Unit. But he was encouraged to continue when his guests informed him that his prisoners would be housed in the jail for the time they were there.

After the time and the price for the deal was agreed upon, the warden summoned the captain of the guards to escort Mallard and Orton to the cellblock where the major portion of the hard laborers were housed. The captain took a couple

of guards in tow and led the visitors to the cellblock. The
guards called for the inmates to line up so Orton could look
them over and select six of them to go to Boonville. To
Mallard, it was an eerie sight as the prisoners stood in line
and glared at him. He encouraged Orton to make his selec-
tions quickly so they could get out of there. One of the
guards smiled at him, knowing what he was feeling, so he
decided to help. "Take that big fellow down at the end of
the line," he said. "He looks pretty tough, but he won't
cause any trouble and I guarantee you he'll outwork any of
the other ones you pick. They all work hard, but he sets his
mind on the work and goes after it until he whips it."

"Good," Orton said. "Write his name down for sure."
He watched as the guard wrote it down on a tablet he was
carrying. "What is his name?" Orton asked, making sure he
remembered it.

"Bannack," the guard answered. "Although everybody
calls him the man from Waco."

"Why is that?" Orton asked.

The guard shrugged. "I don't know. 'Cause he's from
Waco, I reckon." He nodded toward another big man, this
one near the other end of the line. "You might wanna pick
that one, too. His name's Ben Crowe. He's a hard worker
and some of the other men follow his lead. So it's kinda
like havin' a foreman." They continued on until Orton
had his leased crew picked. He and Mallard returned to
the warden's office to take care of all the details, including the
anticipated day of arrival in Boonville. The deal completed,
along with a payment of earnest money to defray the expense of sending the work party to Boonville, Mallard and
Orton headed back home to report that the bridge would
be completed.

* * *

The prison work party arrived in Boonville a little after three o'clock on a Tuesday afternoon. Flanked by two prison guards, the jail wagon with two packhorses trailing, driven by Loafer Bates, rolled to a stop in front of the Boonville jail. It soon attracted the attention of the people on the streets that formed a square around the courthouse. Anticipating their arrival, Sheriff Barnes came out to meet the guards. "Howdy," Rufus greeted them as they stepped down from their horses, "I'm Sheriff Barnes. Understand you've got some guests for my establishment here."

"That's a fact," one of the guards replied. "My name's Benny Cooper, and this ugly fellow with me is Jacob Cobb." Cobb turned his head, pretending to look for someone behind him, then laughed when the sheriff chuckled. "That's Loafer Bates drivin' the wagon," Cooper said.

The sheriff looked at the wagon and said, "Six prisoners, that's what we were expectin'. I'm gonna put 'em in two of my cells. We've only got one prisoner in jail right now, but we've got three cells, so I'll keep him in one by himself. He's goin' on trial for murder one day this week whenever the judge gets here. I know you boys are disappointed that there ain't no room for you, but you're just gonna have to stay in the hotel." He got serious then. "I've gotta be honest with you, though. Nobody said anything about the fellow drivin' the jail wagon. I reckon he's supposed to stay in the hotel, too."

"All the same to you, Sheriff, I'll just stay with my wagon and my horses," Loafer said. "I always do." This was a totally different trip for Loafer. On his typical trips, he was usually charged with taking care of the prisoners, including cooking them three meals a day. There was usually one or two deputy US marshals with him, instead of prison guards, and the prisoners slept in the wagon or on the ground, locked to a chain. He stood up in the wagon and craned his neck to look. "I expect I can make me a spot to camp right down yonder next to that crick. Looks like grass for my horses and wood for my fire. That'll do just fine and all you'll have to do is holler, if you need me."

"Well, I reckon that takes care of that," Cobb said to Cooper. Then he asked the sheriff, "You ready to put 'em in the jail?"

"We're ready," Barnes said, so Cooper went to the back of the wagon to unlock the gate.

They were joined then by Daniel Orton, who came running from the saloon where he had been passing the time. "I swear, Rufus," he said to the sheriff, "you shoulda give me a holler. I didn't see 'em pull in."

"What for?" the sheriff replied. "They ain't goin' to work till in the mornin', are they?"

"That's right, but I wasn't sure you knew that or not," Orton said as he watched his rented crew of laborers climb down out of the jail wagon.

"Ronald Mallard told me they were supposed to get here today to start workin' tomorrow and the hotel was gonna feed 'em just like they fed my other prisoners, except they'd fix their own dinner."

"Wish somebody hadda told me that," Loafer Bates commented. "I woulda just brought one packhorse." He shrugged then and remarked, "I ain't complainin', though. Less work for me."

Inside the jail, in the first cell, Brady Gamble got up from his cot and walked over to stand at the bars when the cell-room door opened. He watched as the six men in prison work uniforms filed by his cell, three going into cell two and the other three in cell three. "What the hell?" Brady mumbled, but Sheriff Barnes and the two prison guards paid him no mind. He understood now why Barnes had taken the cot out of his cell the day before and put it in the cell next to his. There were only three cells in the jail and there were only two cots in each one. So that explained why Barnes had put extra blankets in the third cell. Somebody was gonna have to sleep on the floor. Gamble chuckled when the argument for the two cots started right away. It ended as soon as it started, however, when John Bannack said he would sleep on the floor.

"You tell 'em, Bannack," Ben Crowe called out from the second stall. "Show 'em who's the boss." John ignored the comment and picked up a couple of the extra blankets in the cell to fashion a bed in the back of it.

Once the six inmates were locked in the cells, Sheriff Barnes gave them a little welcome speech. "I want you six men from The Unit to remember that you're in this jail, so you don't have to sleep in that jail wagon or on the ground after you've worked all day. And you'll get a nice breakfast and supper right from the hotel dinin' room. So I'll expect you to act like guests while you're here. If you don't behave, we'll stop feedin' you the breakfast and supper, and you'll just have to get by on what that cook out there on the wagon can feed you for dinner. If you get too rowdy, I'll just kick you out of my jail and you can go back to the wagon. Like I said, the city of Boonville is tryin' to make you as comfortable as we can, but we expect you to act like civilized men."

"You don't have to worry about us, Sheriff," Ben Crowe responded. "We're gonna be like six little angels in Sunday school. Ain't we, boys?"

"You got that right, Ben," Lem Stokes answered, "just like little angels."

Sheriff Barnes shook his head and smiled at Jacob Cobb, who was standing next to him. "It's funny, ain't it? The troublemakers always seem to identify themselves right away." To his new prisoners, he said, "You'll be gettin' supper around five o'clock." He and the two guards turned to leave.

"Hey, Sheriff, who's this feller in the cell next to us?" Ben Crowe asked. "I sure hope you ain't put us in with no criminal." His japing drew a few chuckles from the inmates.

"If he's too bad an influence on you, I'll move him to the hotel," Barnes said.

When the sheriff and the guards went back outside, they found Ronald Mallard talking to Daniel Orton. They paused and Orton said, "These are the guards from the prison. I'm sorry, I don't remember your names." The guards introduced themselves to Mallard and he told them that there was a room reserved for them in the hotel and they could take their horses to the stable. The town would take care of all of it, including their breakfast and supper in the dining room.

"We need to establish our schedule for the workday," Orton said. "You fellows will have to get your horses in the morning and get your jail wagon to the jail. I reckon we'll have to eat breakfast before we go to work. The hotel dinin' room doesn't open until six o'clock, but I think if we keep everybody movin' along, we can still get to the worksite by seven."

"I understand what you're sayin'," Cooper said. "Jacob and I will be ready to go. Loafer will be up cookin' his breakfast at five o'clock, so he'll be here at the jail while the prisoners in the jail are still eatin'."

"Good," Orton replied. "I reckon I'll see you back here in the mornin' and I'll take you to the place where we're gonna build that bridge."

According to the report Mallard and Orton gave to a gathering of some of the other members of the town council in the Lone Star saloon that evening, the plan to span the Navasota River was proceeding as scheduled. "Those two prison guards brought half a dozen prime studs with 'em that look like they could move those logs without the help of Ernie's mules," Orton told them, referring to Ernie Welch who worked at his sawmill.

"You reckon them two guards are enough to handle them prisoners, if they're as tough as you say they are?" Franklin Norsworthy, the president of the bank asked.

"They look like pretty good men," Sheriff Barnes answered. "I was talkin' to 'em, and they've both been workin' with the toughest inmates in the prison for a lot of years." He let Norsworthy think about that for a few seconds. "And I'll be helpin' 'em out, too." He laughed then and added, "Besides, I think ol' Daniel is plannin' on workin' 'em so hard they ain't gonna have the strength to lift much more'n a knife and fork by quittin' time. Ain't that right, Daniel?"

"Let's just say I plan to get all the value I can for the money the town's spendin' to hire those convicts," Orton answered. "I figure it's my civic duty."

Norsworthy was still somewhat concerned about the potential for disaster with six hardened criminals in town. "I don't know how much help you can offer when those men are out of their cells," he felt the need to point out to the sheriff. "You have a murderer who will still be in the jail, so I hope you aren't planning to spend the day by the river with the inmates from Huntsville. You are also responsible for the duties of sheriff of Boonville, which require you to be present in town."

"Why, of course I ain't plannin' on goin' to the river to watch 'em work, Mr. Norsworthy," Barnes responded immediately. "When Brady Gamble's trial starts, I expect I'll have to go to court, too. That wouldn't be no problem if I had a deputy, but as you know, the town council ain't seen fit to hire one."

"That's a discussion for another time," Norsworthy replied. "So far, we really haven't needed a deputy, mostly because of the fine job you've done as sheriff." He favored the sheriff then with a benevolent smile.

There was another meeting taking place in the jail across the street from the Lone Star saloon, also on the topic of the work to be done in the morning. This meeting was of a much quieter nature and was held at the iron bars between cell two and cell three. Most of the talking was being done by Ben Crowe but in almost whispered tones. So much so, that Brady Gamble, the lone prisoner in cell one complained about it. "What the hell is all the whisperin' about?" Brady asked. "You scared I'm gonna tell the sheriff what you're talkin' about? Hell, they're gonna hang my butt. If you're plannin' to escape, I wanna go with you."

"Who said anything about tryin' to escape?" Ben replied. "Did that sheriff stick you in here to try to see if we was plannin' to break out? You might be his deputy for all we know."

"I ain't his damn deputy," Brady said. "He ain't got no deputy. I ain't got no reason to help him. They're gonna hang me 'cause I shot a man in the back. I'da shot him in the front if he'd turned around. I told him not to walk away from me."

"Ain't nothin' we can do for you," Crowe said. "They're gonna take us outta here to work at the river. They ain't gonna take you with us. You're stuck here." He turned back to the huddle of men at the iron bars and whispered low, "But I ain't plannin' on going back to that prison cell in Huntsville. So we've gotta take our chance when we see it."

John Bannack was not up close to the bars while Crowe was talking about his intention to escape, if the opportunity presented itself. He had not really given thought to the possibility of escape since he had been incarcerated, even though it was for a crime he did not commit. He had made a commitment to stand good for his brother's terrible mistake, whatever the length of time it required. He had set his mind to tolerate the dreary existence of prison life and take advantage of the hard labor to make his body strong, determined to make his prison sentence a positive thing. Now, Ben Crowe and his sidekicks talked of a possible escape for all six of them. If it's possible, would he choose to go along? The more he thought about it, the more he began to think, why not? It would be nice to be free. His mind distracted by his thoughts, he didn't realize that Ben Crowe was watching him closely.

The big silent man, Crowe thought to himself. *What is he thinking? I need to make sure he's with us.* He studied Bannack's face and decided the mysterious man was thinking hard about something. "What about you, Bannack?" Crowe asked. "Are you with us?"

"It depends on your plan," Bannack answered. "Cooper and Cobb are both good men. I have never been mistreated by either one of them, so I would not like to see them come to any harm."

"You're right," Crowe said. "They are good men, so naturally, I would hope we could slip away unnoticed without harming anyone. At least, that's the plan."

"If you mean that, then I'll help you," Bannack said.

"Good, we're glad to have you with us," Crowe told him, but he was thinking he didn't need his help, he just wanted to make sure he didn't interfere.

"When?" Bannack asked.

"It won't be tomorrow," Crowe said. "We'll just see how the work goes tomorrow. Then we'll be better able to decide when and how is best."

"That sounds like a reasonable approach to the problem," Bannack said.

* * *

The first day of bridge construction went pretty much as planned. When the prisoners arrived at the riverbank, they found that Daniel Orton had already taken an axe and marked the trees to be felled. He brought two crosscut saws to do the work, so four of the inmates stepped forward to man them. The other two grabbed axes and stood ready to start trimming the limbs away as soon as the first tree fell. "I notice nobody jumped up to grab the other end of this saw," Alton Walker japed when he grasped the handle on the other end of the saw John Bannack had picked up. "I know you boys was wantin' to see me and Bannack go at it to see which one went to his knees first. But don't you worry, Bannack, I'm plannin' on takin' it real easy on you. I wanna be sure you last out the whole week." Walker's japing brought a chuckle from the others but just a questioning look from Bannack. The solemn man did not realize he had been carrying a reputation for his strength.

When the first tree was felled and trimmed, Ernie Welch hitched his mules to the log and dragged it down to be put in position by Orton's direction. It was obvious to the prison work crew right away that their labor was not going to simply be felling trees and trimming them. They were going to be the labor to sink the logs in place for the base of the bridge. "So we're gonna be doin' a lot of swimmin'," Lem complained.

"Maybe so," Crowe replied. "We're gonna be doin' a lot of things and it's gonna make it a whole lot harder on Cooper and Cobb to keep an eye on all of us all the time." He looked to see the two guards standing together, talking, while they watched the trees being felled. A short distance farther down the river, Loafer had parked his wagon and was just standing watching the activity. He would no doubt start a fire in a little while to prepare the noon meal. "Yeah, boy," Crowe quipped, "there's gonna be a lot goin' on around here for two men to keep an eye on." He also noticed that Orton was wearing a sidearm and that might be a good place to get one when the time came that one was needed.

Knowing Crowe was planning the escape, Lem asked again, "When?"

"Not today," Crowe told him. "Let's give 'em a day or two to get used to everything goin' smooth and no problems, till they get careless. That's when we'll ride outta here free men."

Back in town, Sheriff Barnes received a message that Judge Wick Justice had arrived at the courthouse, so he went immediately to meet with him. Justice told the sheriff that he wanted to have Brady Gamble's trial the next day, so if he needed any witnesses to be subpoenaed, he'd best get that done today. Barnes assured the judge that would be no problem, the shooting was witnessed by many. A room at the hotel had been reserved for the judge and one for his assistant, Elwood Wilson. The judge told Barnes he and Elwood would check into the hotel, then they would eat dinner in the hotel dining room. After that, Elwood would visit the courtroom and set it up the way the judge wanted it. And the trial was set for nine o'clock.

"Well, tomorrow's your big day," Sheriff Barnes told Brady Gamble when he returned to the jail with Brady's dinner tray. "Judge Wick Justice just rode into town and he's lookin' forward to meetin' you at nine o'clock in the mornin'."

"All the same to me if the judge has the trial without

me bein' there," Gamble said. "Hell, you know he's gonna sentence me to hang."

"I expect so," Barnes said, "but the trial will provide a little bit of entertainment for the citizens of Boonville, and I know you wouldn't wanna cheat them outta that."

CHAPTER 6

The second day of construction of the bridge was much like the first with the exception of a few more heavy logs in place. To John Bannack, the first day accomplished very little in the establishment of a solid base for a bridge. By the end of the second day, however, Orton and his employee, Ernie, had directed the prison laborers into the successful planting of log columns that would act as the supports for the crossbeams Ernie brought from the sawmill. Bannack decided that maybe Orton knew how to build a bridge after all, and he found himself looking forward to seeing the final product. He was disappointed when he was told that he wouldn't see the bridge completed. There were two reasons for that. The first reason he learned from Orton, who said the prisoners would be returned after the basic framework was completed. Orton and Ernie would nail the finished surface of the bridge, as well as the railings.

The second reason was because Ben Crowe was finally ready to make his move. It had come later than his close compatriots could understand, they being of a more anxious nature. Bannack saw the reason, for he was aware that Orton, Ernie, Loafer, as well as the guards had become accustomed to the prison inmates casually going about the work asked of them. There were no problems and no complaints for the guards to worry about. Much of the conversation was about Brady Gamble's trial and the fact that he was sentenced to be hung at the end of the week.

"Justice?" Ben Crowe demanded. "Did you say the judge's name was Justice? Judge Wick Justice? He's the one who sentenced me to life in prison. If them guards hadn't held me down, I'da settled his bacon right there in that courthouse. And they coulda hung me, instead of sending me to that damn prison." He could feel the familiar fiery bitterness in his veins when he thought of the judge barely more than a mile away from him.

Judge Wick Justice had delayed the date of execution simply because the gallows behind the courthouse was in need of some repair. Since that was also one of Daniel Orton's responsibilities, he was called away from his bridge construction for a brief period, and he took Ernie with him. Their absence resulted in an unscheduled rest for the laborers and some casual conversation between the prisoners and their guards. Always anxious, Lem Stokes stared directly at Crowe and it was unnecessary for him to ask the question again. "When Orton gets back," Crowe said softly and smiled. He had already told Lem and Walker what they were to do when he gave the signal. The three of them would run the show. The other three would blindly follow once they saw Crowe and his two pals take charge. So all they waited for now was Orton's return.

"I reckon we're gonna have to go back to work now," Walker sang out. "Here comes Mr. Orton."

"Yeah," guard Jacob Cobb remarked, "now me and Benny have to decide whether or not we oughta tell him you fellows ain't done a lick of work while he was gone."

"You tell him we've been loafin' and I'll tell him you and Benny almost went to sleep settin' on that log." Crowe chuckled. "You oughta get in that river with us. That'd keep you awake." He nodded his head in Walker's direction and said, "Alton, why don't you go take care of Mr. Orton's horse for him?"

"Right," Walker said and went to meet Orton. He walked up and took hold of the horse's bridle. "I'll take care of him for you, Mr. Orton."

Orton didn't know what to say. He didn't expect an offer of assistance. "Why, you don't have to do that." When Walker just continued to grin at him, he said, "But thank you." Seeing the two guards just getting to their feet, he started toward them. The prisoner named Ben Crowe was standing between him and the guards and gave him a friendly smile as he passed by him. Crowe wheeled to follow close behind him and with one quick move, pulled the Smith and Wesson revolver from his holster. Not even aware what had actually happened, Orton suddenly went sprawling face first on the ground before the two startled guards, a result of Crowe's firm foot on his backside.

Both guards started to reach for their rifles, still propped against the log. "First one grabs his rifle gets the first shot in the head," Crowe warned.

Startled but now fully aware of what was happening, both guards froze before Cooper stammered, "You're makin' a helluva mistake, Crowe. You don't wanna do this."

"Oh, I'm pretty sure I do," Crowe said. "Walker, pick up those two rifles." When Walker picked up the rifles, Crowe ordered the two guards to sit on the ground with their backs against the log they had been sitting on. Motioning with Orton's revolver, he then ordered Orton to sit down next to the guards.

Meanwhile, Lem Stokes hurried up the riverbank to the jail wagon where Loafer was sitting close by his fire, having a cup of coffee. Loafer said nothing, only halfway curious until Lem went to the wagon and pulled his rifle out from under the seat. "Whoa," was all he said as he put his cup down and got to his feet.

Lem cocked the rifle and said, "Just walk right on down the bank where they're settin' and I might not shoot you."

"Whatever you say," Loafer replied and started down the bank, his hands raised in the air. Lem picked up his coffee cup and finished his coffee for him, then followed him down to the others where Walker was busy tying their captives' hands behind their backs.

"What are you gonna do with us?" Benny Cooper asked Crowe while Walker tied his hands behind him.

"I ain't decided yet, Benny," Crowe answered him with a smirk. "Depends a lot on whether you and Jacob and ol' Orton, here, give us any trouble. I'm gonna put you in the jail wagon for now, while I'm decidin' what I'm gonna do with you. If you don't give me any trouble, I'll just leave you in the wagon. If you get in my way, I'll just put a hole in your head and be done with it."

"For God's sake, Crowe," Jacob Cobb pleaded, "think what you're doin'. You'll have every lawman in the state of Texas lookin' for you. Call it off right now and me and Cooper won't even report that it ever happened. Will we, Benny?" Cooper immediately agreed, which only served to bring a smirk to Crowe's lips.

"Sorry, boys, this is sure as hell gonna bring your careers as prison guards to a slidin' halt, ain't it?" Crowe said. "Matter of fact, you might as well be dead. Ain't that right, Lem?"

"That's what I'm thinkin'," Lem answered.

"You're not including me, are you?" Orton pleaded then. "I didn't have anything to do with you men being in prison. You don't have any reason to kill me."

"I ain't decided," Crowe said, playing with the man's

obvious fear. "You tried to work my ass off." Thinking he was wasting time amusing himself, he ordered, "All right, let's put 'em in the wagon, so we can get ready to leave this place." Lem and Walker pulled the two guards to their feet, while two of the other prisoners pulled Loafer and Orton up. One prisoner had made no effort to help or hinder the capture. John Bannack was not yet committed to the escape plan. He had decided he might as well accept the chance for freedom but only because Crowe had told him it would be at no cost of lives. And whatever occurred here today, he had definitely decided to part company with Crowe and his friends. Because of that he had made only one aggressive move and that was to pick up one of the guards' rifles from the log when Crowe ordered it done. Whatever happened, he felt it was not to his advantage to be disarmed.

They marched their captives back up the bank to the jail wagon and locked them in while Crowe considered what their resources were. "We've got three horses with saddles," he said. "I'll take Orton's dun. Lem and Walker can ride the guards' horses. We've got Loafer's packhorse and we're gonna need a packhorse. That leaves the two horses pulling the wagon, so two of you fellers can ride them bareback and you can decide which one of you will take one of Ernie's mules."

The two other prisoners immediately looked at each other, thinking of a fight for one of the wagon horses because they both figured Bannack would take the other horse. Neither man gave any thought toward challenging the mysterious man from Waco for the horse. With a desire to hurry them on their way, Bannack eased their minds when he volunteered, "I'll take the packhorse. You can use one of the mules to carry the packs."

"Yeah, I reckon we could," Crowe said. "I wonder why nobody thought of that before." He was ready to see how well he and his men were supplied as far as food was concerned. They were going to need a lot of things, guns and ammunition, as well as clothes to exchange for their prison uniforms. Orton might be carrying some cash and maybe a little from the guards, but that would be about it. So they were going to have to knock over a general store pretty soon, but he preferred to get away from Boonville before robbing a store. In spite of what he had told Bannack, he did not intend to leave living witnesses to the takeover of the bridge-building party. He had told Lem and Walker, but none of the others that he intended to leave no witnesses. The simple reason he hadn't shot them all down to begin with was because the bridge project was only a little over a mile and a half from the center of town. And he didn't want the sound of the gunfire to bring a posse to investigate it. Since they had a sturdy jail wagon handy to hold them, their captives were out of the way until they were ready to ride. And they would be confined in that one tight wagon so they could be executed quickly like rats in a cage. Crowe and his gang would be long gone before anyone in town could come to investigate. With that thought in mind, he told Bob Yates to hitch Loafer's horses up to the jail wagon and pull it down the bank close by the water. He thought it would be better to move it down where a chance passerby might not notice it.

On a day that seemed to be aligned perfectly with every plan Ben Crowe had in mind, there was one thing that he had not counted on that he could only explain as a wish come true. "Somebody's comin'," Edgar Rice, one of the convicts Crowe had sent up the bank to act as a lookout, called out. "Three fellers on horseback, leadin' two pack-horses." Crowe, Lem, and Walker all readied their weapons. Then Rice called out, "It's Ernie comin' back, but there's two riders with him."

"It ain't the sheriff, is it?" Crowe called back.

"Nah, two older lookin' men," Rice replied. "I'll see what Ernie says." He waited for the party to approach. "Hey, Ernie, we was wonderin' if you was comin' back today or not. Who's this you brung with you?"

"They're on their way to Houston," Ernie said. "I was just showin' 'em a shortcut to strike the Houston road. What are you doin' up here on the bank?"

"I'm a lookout," Rice replied. "Crowe sent me up here to keep an eye out."

"Crowe sent you?" Ernie exclaimed. "What are you talkin' about? Eye out for what? Where's Mr. Orton?"

"He's down there at the wagon with the rest of 'em," Rice answered.

By this time, Crowe was becoming impatient with the man he had sent up to watch the trail from town, so he yelled out. "Ernie, come on down and bring your friends with you and they can take a look at how the bridge is comin' along."

Ernie talked to one of the riders, then yelled back to Crowe. "They said, thank you just the same, but they need to get started to Houston." He paused, then decided he should explain, "He's a judge and he's got business to take care of in Houston."

Crowe felt the blood in his veins turn to ice, and he gasped as if he had had the wind knocked out of his lungs. A judge! *It had to be Judge Wick Justice!* He had tried Brady Gamble and sentenced him to death. He sucked his breath into his lungs to fill them, then he exhaled, thinking that the devil must answer prayers, too. Wasting no more time, he ran up the bank. Lem and Walker followed, catching fire from his flame without knowing the cause of it. When the judge's clerk, Elwood Wilson, saw the three men in prison uniforms charging up the bank, he yelled, "Judge, run!" But it was too late to escape. Ernie's horse was in the way and Rice realized what was happening in time to grab Judge Justice's bridle. Aware, too, Ernie reached for the forty-four he wore but was stopped by a round from Lem's rifle that knocked him from the saddle.

Crowe charged up to the gray-haired man on the gray gelding, grabbed his coat by the lapels, and pulled him off the horse to land him roughly on the ground, holding him down with one massive fist in his chest. "Judge Wick Justice," he spat. "You remember me? Ben Crowe's my name. You better remember me, 'cause if you say you don't, I'm gonna beat your skull in with the barrel of this pistol. You sentenced me to life in prison, you piece of dung."

Laboring to get his breath, the judge stared up at the ape-like man and said, defiantly, "I spared your life. You deserved the death penalty."

With his rage a little more under control now that he realized he had the man he hated so passionately where he had only been able to dream him to be, Crowe grinned wickedly. "It's your loss for not givin' me the death penalty now, ain't it, judge? 'Cause now I'm gonna have another trial and I'm gonna judge you. And I wouldn't count on a life sentence, if I was you."

Still defiant, Wick Justice glared back up at his vengeful assailant, determined to give him no satisfaction of a showing of fear. His clerk, still on his horse with Walker's rifle aimed at his chest, was closer to tears as he silently prayed for the judge not to antagonize the monster further. But knowing the judge as he did, he had little hope of his prayers being answered. To prove him correct, the judge snarled back at Crowe and said, "It's plain to see that the time you've spent in prison has been wasted. You're no closer to a civilized human being than you were the first time I saw you."

"Why, you snide son of a . . ." Crowe almost choked on his anger. Losing control, he raised the pistol high over his head, prepared to deliver a blow to the judge's forehead. But his arm was stopped so violently when he struck down that he felt a tear in his shoulder muscle, and he yelped in pain. He jerked his head around to see his wrist trapped in the vice-like grip of John Bannack.

"That's far enough, Crowe," Bannack calmly told the infuriated man. "You said there would be no killing and already it's out of hand. An innocent man is dead."

"Hey, he went for his gun!" Lem shouted in protest. "It was self-defense."

"Take the men who want to go with you and leave here now," Bannack said to Crowe, ignoring Lem's claims of justification for the shooting.

"Who the hell do you think you are?" Crowe demanded, his wrist still locked in Bannack's powerful grip. "I'm runnin' this show! Let go of my hand!"

"I'll not give you another chance to escape," Bannack said. "Take those who wanna go with you and leave before there is more killing." Then, using Crowe's extended right arm as leverage, he pulled it upward again, forcing Crowe to back away from the judge, who was still pinned down by Crowe's other fist on his chest. Crowe roared in pain as his injured right shoulder was forced back. He grabbed his right wrist with his left hand in a frantic effort to keep his arm from being pulled back. It was still not enough to overcome the strength of the man literally tearing the muscles of his shoulder apart. "Can you get up, Your Honor?" Bannack calmly asked the judge.

"Yes, sir, I can," Justice answered and scrambled up to take cover behind his clerk's horse.

"Shoot him!" Crowe blurted painfully. "Shoot him!" He screamed again when both Walker and Lem hesitated, not sure if he meant the judge or Bannack. When Walker turned to aim his rifle at Bannack, Bannack forced Crowe's arm back down to point the pistol at Walker.

"Don't do it," Bannack warned and Walker hesitated, uncertain. Then he raised the rifle to fire, but the man from Waco forced his finger on top of Crowe's and squeezed off a shot that caught Walker in the chest. Lem reacted then, aimed his rifle at Bannack and pulled the trigger only to find he had not ejected the empty shell after he shot Ernie. He cranked another round into the chamber while Bannack struggled with Crowe for control of Crowe's pistol. He realized then that Bannack wasn't going to make it in time, so he took dead aim to make sure he didn't miss. His finger was not resting on the trigger yet when the shot slammed into his back between his shoulder blades and he dropped to his knees. Bannack nodded his appreciation to Elwood Wilson and Elwood nodded in response, although shaken to the core for actually having shot a man.

Elwood climbed down from his horse then and hurried to Judge Justice's side to make sure he was all right. He was relieved to see that the judge was none the worse for wear, considering what he had just been subjected to. So he started brushing the dirt from the judge's coat, still shaking from the incident just passed. "Are you all right?" Justice asked his clerk.

"Yes, sir, I think so," Elwood answered, although not very convincingly.

"That was a brave thing you did, Elwood," Judge Justice told him. "You know you saved that man's life, don't you?"

"Yes, sir, I guess I did," Elwood answered. "I wasn't sure I could do it, but it looked like he was going to get shot if somebody didn't do something."

"I'm proud of you," Justice said. "You're right, he was about to get shot. And that man was worth saving. I want to know who that man is." He needed an explanation for the whole incident because the fighting had all been done by men in prison uniforms, including the one who had come to his rescue. The aggressor, Ben Crowe, looked to be totally subdued at present, sitting on the ground, holding his right arm with his left hand. The man who had restrained him now had sole possession of the pistol and was holding it over him as they talked. The other two men wearing prison garb were standing by.

The conversation that Judge Justice and Elwood could not hear was an attempt by Crowe to gain his freedom. "You're right," Bannack said. "I did agree to the escape if the opportunity came when we could do it without killin' anybody. And that opportunity looked like it might happen until you decided you didn't want to leave any witnesses. I told you I wasn't gonna go with you and your little gang after we escaped. But I changed my mind about helping you escape when I figured out you planned to kill the witnesses. That's where you went too far, so that's why I put a stop to you and Lem Stokes and Alton Walker. When you went after that judge, I could see just how crazy you are. So, hell no, I'm not gonna let you ride away from here a free man. You're goin' back to The Unit with me and maybe Rice and Yates, here." He glanced over at the two inmates and said, "The decision I've made is for myself, just like the decision I made to escape, if there was no killin'. So if you two are still of a mind to escape, I'm not gonna make a move to stop you, and I'll wish you good luck. But I reckon your best chance is right now when I take Crowe back down to the jail wagon and we set things right again." Both men decided their odds of survival as free men were not good enough to risk at that time, so they chose to return to prison with him. Not willing to trust Crowe for a moment, he took some rope from Ernie's horse and tied Crowe hand and foot while he went to see if the judge and his clerk were all right.

"Are you all right, sir?" Bannack asked respectfully.

"Yes, I'm fine," Justice replied, "just got a little dirt on the seat of my pants. I think I owe you quite a bit of thanks for preventing that maniac from putting a permanent part in my skull with that pistol. What is your name, young man?"

"John Bannack, sir."

"Well, tell me, John Bannack, I notice you're wearing prison clothes. Are you in fact a prisoner?" When John said that he was, the judge asked, "What crime were you sentenced for?"

"Robbin' a bank," John answered.

"Did you actually rob the bank?"

"That's what the witnesses said," John replied.

"That's not what I asked," Justice said. "I asked if you really did rob the bank?" He could see right away that the young man had difficulty with a direct yes or no on the question.

"Yes, sir, I robbed the bank," John answered positively, for an answer of no would place the crime squarely on his brother.

"Did you shoot anyone?"

"No, sir."

"Did you discharge your firearm?"

"No, sir." He hesitated. "I mean, I don't think so."

"How long have you been at The Unit?" the judge asked. Bannack told him a little over three years, and the judge asked how long his sentence was for.

"Twenty years," he answered.

"Twenty years?" Justice repeated, somewhat surprised. "Who was the judge?"

"Judge Raymond Grant," Bannack answered. Judge Justice didn't comment on his answer. Instead, he just looked at him and shook his head slowly. Finally, he said again that he was in his debt for protecting him from Ben Crowe's revenge, and he extended his hand. Surprised, Bannack nevertheless shook his hand, aware that the judge seemed to be studying his face intently. "I hope you and Mr. Wilson have a safe trip," he said, then looked at Elwood. "And I want to thank you again for steppin' in to help when I had my hands full, Mr. Wilson." He stepped back then while they climbed up on their horses again and rode off to strike the road to Houston.

Bannack picked up the rifle he had dropped when he was engaged in the struggle with Crowe and directed Rice and Yates to pick up the other two, then he untied Crowe's feet so he could walk down to the wagon. He rejected Ben Crowe's snarling offer to carry one of the rifles down the bank for him. "'Preciate the offer," Bannack told him, "but I wouldn't wanna put any strain on your bad shoulder."

Bob Yates remembered seeing Crowe throw the key away after locking the guards, Loafer, and Orton in the jail wagon, so he searched in the bushes and came up with it. Loafer said there was an extra key, but it was in one of the packs his packhorse carried. Bannack herded Crowe into the wagon, but the other two inmates and himself remained free. The afternoon was young, and now there were two graves to dig. The guards were back on duty, so a normal routine could be reestablished.

When Bannack gave Orton his revolver back, he asked if he wanted to carry Ernie's body back to town for burial. Orton said that would be best. He was sure Sheriff Barnes as well as the town council would want to be advised of the recent change in the bridge-building project, as well as the reduction in the number of laborers to finish the work. Feeling he could trust the big man to do a good job, Orton told Bannack how he wanted to place the final supports for the bridge frame. "If you and the other two men could do that, I could get started on the framework of the bridge tomorrow," Orton said. "And maybe all this that happened today won't put us that far behind." He was already worried that the council might change their mind about the bridge and send the jail wagon back. But he felt he had to give Ernie a decent burial. The man had no family that Orton knew of, so it was up to him to take care of the hard-working man.

When it was time to drive the jail wagon back into town for supper, the remaining supports for the bridge were firmly in place as per Orton's instructions. The two guards had to agree with Loafer that the three working inmates seemed to have taken on a measure of pride in showing they could do the work of the original six. And it was all done while ignoring the scornful eye of Ben Crowe, who remained locked in the wagon. The guards would not even allow him to be outside the wagon, locked to the chain.

CHAPTER 7

Sheriff Rufus Barnes was standing out in front of the jail when Loafer pulled the jail wagon to a stop. Behind the wagon, he saw Jacob Cobb and Benny Cooper each leading one of Ernie Welch's mules. "I was sorry to hear about Ernie gettin' shot," Barnes said. "He was a good, hard-workin' man. Daniel Orton told us how it happened. We heard the shots. It weren't long after Judge Justice and his man left town with Ernie. I almost rode out there to see what the shootin' was about, but it stopped right away, so I figure whatever it was, it was over." He waited for the guards to dismount and Loafer to unlock the jail wagon before walking inside ahead of them to unlock the cells.

"I expect you'd best not put Bannack and Crowe in the same cell," Cooper said.

"Right," Barnes replied. "Orton told me I'd have two less prisoners for supper tonight. I already told the dinin' room. He told me about the escape attempt. He said it scared the hell outta him. He thought he was gonna get killed for sure." He watched Ben Crowe, holding onto one arm with his opposite hand, as he walked into the cell. "Something wrong with him? He need to see the doctor?"

"Nah," Cooper replied, "he's just got a sprained shoulder.

Did the town council have a meetin' to decide what they're gonna do about the bridge?"

"Not yet," Sheriff Barnes replied. "They're gonna meet after the close of business to see what they're gonna do. Orton said he was gonna ride back out there before the meetin'."

"Most likely wants to see if they did any work after he left this afternoon," Jacob Cobb remarked. "I expect he'll be surprised when he sees how much got done. Rice and Yates had to really hump it, trying to keep up with Bannack. I believe that man could build the bridge all by himself."

"I wouldn't be surprised," Yates agreed. "Let's go take these horses to the stable and go get some supper. And after that, I wanna go get a drink of likker."

"I reckon in the mornin' we'll find out if we're headin' back to Huntsville tomorrow or stayin' here till the end of the week," Cobb remarked. "You reckon the warden will let us go after we let Ben Crowe get the jump on us?"

"I don't know," Cooper replied. "I reckon, if I was the warden, I'd be inclined to fire us for sure." They both thought about it for a few moments before Cooper spoke again. "I keep thinkin' about the fact that, if it wasn't for that man from Waco, me and you would both be dead."

"I don't reckon we've got much of a chance of convincin' the warden that both of us are dang sure gonna be better guards after this lesson," Cobb declared.

The members of the Boonville Town Council met that night in the Lone Star saloon to discuss the status of the new bridge project over the Navasota River. There was a short eulogy of sorts spoken by Mayor Ronald Mallard for Ernie Welch, a man barely known except by Daniel Orton, who employed him at his sawmill. Then for those in the council who had not heard about it, Orton told them about the attempted escape by some of the prisoners the town was paying the prison to use as laborers. The initial reaction to the news was one of alarm that the town's money had just been thrown into the wind. But Orton maintained that upon his inspection of the project that evening, he was pleasantly surprised to see the work that had been done by the remaining prisoners. "In effect, gentlemen," he proclaimed, "the foundation for the bridge is finished and with the help of the remaining prisoners, we'll finish the basic framework in two more days. Then, hell, I can finish the rest of it by myself if I have to. So let's not kill a project that will help influence the railroad to lay their tracks through Boonville over a little snag in our plans."

"Well, I'm inclined to rely on your opinion," Franklin Norsworthy declared. "Whaddaya say we vote on it?" They voted, and it was unanimous to continue with the project.

"Fine," Orton said. "I'll be back to work on it in the mornin'." He started to sit down but paused to say one more thing. "And when it's finished, I think we should call it the Ernie Welch Memorial Bridge, for the man who gave his life for it." There was no outright hoorah for the suggestion, merely a few low mutterings and questions.

After a night where there was very little conversation between the prisoners in the Boonville jail due to the elephant in the cell room in the form of Ben Crowe, supporting his sprained shoulder with his left hand. The man from Waco seldom spoke under normal conditions and neither Rice nor Yates was inclined to bring up the subject that was on everybody's mind. Yates was especially reluctant to make any comment, since he had the misfortune to end up in the cell with Crowe, a result of Rice's quick move to step into the first cell as soon as Bannack paused when he came to the open door. Even with a sprained shoulder, Crowe was still able to intimidate Yates to the point where he was afraid to close his eyes as he lay on his cot, waiting to hear Crowe's customary noisy snoring. But Crowe was in no mood for sleeping. When Yates stole a quick look in Crowe's direction, he was frightened to find the evil man staring at him. When he finally spoke, it was in a low patient voice. "If you hadn'ta turned belly-up cowards when that double-crossin' snake backed out on us, we woulda been settin' by a campfire somewhere havin' a drink of likker, instead of rottin' here in this jail."

"I swear, Ben, there weren't nothin' me and Rice could do after he sprained your arm and shot Walker. Then that feller with the judge shot Lem. There weren't nothin' we could do then. It was over."

"There was a rifle layin' on the ground," Crowe said. "All you had to do was pick it up and shoot that yellow dog."

"I know, Ben," Yates pleaded, "but he was lookin' right at me, waitin' for me to make a move. If I'da dived for that rifle, he'da killed me before I coulda picked it up, cocked it, and fired it."

"You're as yellow as he is," Crowe said, continuing to stare at the frightened man.

When Bannack finally decided Crowe wasn't going to give Yates any peace, he yelled for the sheriff and banged on the bars until Barnes finally opened the cell room door and came in with his gun drawn. "What the hell are you yellin' about?"

"Sheriff, we've got a problem here," Bannack said. "We've gotta work tomorrow and we can't get any sleep like we are now. There ain't anybody else in this jail but us. So how 'bout puttin' Crowe in a cell by himself and put

Yates' cot in here with us? Or put me in the cell with Crowe, if you have to have two to a cell? Whaddaya say?"

Barnes understood the problem at once, but he knew better than to put Bannack and Crowe in a cell together. He knew one of them would be dead come morning. "All right," he said and pointed to Yates. "Come on outta there, I'm gonna give you a private room." Yates jumped up at once when the sheriff opened the cell. Barnes closed it and locked it as soon as he stepped out, then he locked Yates in the number three cell.

"Thank you, Sheriff," Yates whispered.

Barnes nodded in response and cheerfully sang out, "Goodnight all, I'll see you in the mornin'," as he walked out of the cell room.

They ate breakfast, then rode out to the river crossing in the jail wagon as usual. When they got to the river and climbed out of the wagon, Crowe made a big show of not being able to move his arm without excruciating pain. No one was taken in by his performance but were just as happy to have him out of the way. So the guards locked his foot to the wagon chain and let him sit outside on the ground. Daniel Orton was so complementary of the work the three prisoners accomplished the afternoon before that they were inspired to show him they could do even more. As a result, the day was very productive and the following day was the same, so that the heavy work the inmates were needed for was finished by the end of the week. Consequently, Orton thanked them for their hard work and told them they could start back to Huntsville the following morning. So the next morning they enjoyed one final breakfast from the hotel dining room before climbing aboard Loafer Bates' jail wagon for the three-day trip back to The Unit. Sheriff Barnes wished them an uneventful journey and the guards thanked him for his hospitality.

Traveling all day in the jail wagon must have had some therapeutic effect upon Crowe's strained shoulder because it apparently healed almost overnight. The relationship between Crowe and the other three prisoners did not improve a great deal, however. When Bannack got a chance to talk to Yates or Rice out of Crowe's earshot, he reminded them that the takeover of the guards and the work party was Crowe's idea and not theirs. He emphasized the idea that the two of them were playing along only to keep from being killed along with the guards. He also encouraged them to be proud of the fact that, when the time came, they chose to fight on the side of the right. He was satisfied that the two inmates were thinking the right way, so he now wanted to talk to the guards. But that turned out to be more difficult without Crowe seeing him talking to them. Bannack had an idea that they might be troubled over the escape attempt and their failure to prevent it.

When they got to the point where they were only a half day away from Huntsville, he decided he'd talk to them whether the others saw him or not. So he waited for his chance after he got his plate from Loafer and pulled the full length of the chain out before he sat down to eat the noon meal. He had made it a point to get himself locked to the very end of the chain, so there was no one beyond him. He sat down and waited until one of the guards walked around the end of the chain, then he let his biscuit roll out of his hand, pretending he had dropped it. "Damn," he swore. "I dropped my biscuit." He stretched his arm out to show that it was out of his reach.

"I'll get it," Benny Cooper said as he reached down and picked it up. "Got a little dirt on it. I'll see if Loafer's got another one."

"No need to do that," Bannack said. "A little dirt ain't gonna hurt it. I'll just dust it off."

Cooper handed him the biscuit. "You sure you don't want me to get you another one?" He hesitated a moment, then said, "Me and Cobb owe you a helluva lot more than a fresh biscuit."

"About that business," Bannack stopped him as he was about to walk away, "we were talkin' about that last night, me and Rice and Yates, and how none of it woulda happened if it hadn'ta been for Daniel Orton. He walked right by Crowe with his pistol stickin' up outta the holster like a sign that said, 'help yourself, Ben Crowe.' All Crowe had to do was turn around and take it when Orton walked past him and you and Cobb didn't have a chance. It wasn't a mistake on your part. It was just bad luck. I reckon you can't really blame Orton for being so careless. He wasn't used to workin' around prisoners." Bannack could see a light of hope in the guard's eyes, so he felt sure his message had been received. To be sure Cooper got the whole message, he said, "Anyway, that's the way it happened as far as three of us prisoners saw it. 'Course there ain't no tellin' what kind of story Crowe might make up."

"Thank you, Bannack. You're a damn good man," Cooper said. "If I had the authority, I'd set you free right now."

Bannack laughed. "Then you'd really find yourself in trouble." He blew some more dirt off his biscuit and took a big bite out of it. Cooper hurried off to share his newfound encouragement with Cobb, thinking maybe their careers as prison guards were not yet over after all.

They arrived at the prison in time to eat supper, but at their guards' direction, Ben Crowe was taken to solitary confinement while Bannack, Yates, and Rice were returned to their cellblock. The receiving officer on duty notified the captain of the guards and the warden's office immediately to report the return of the work detail minus two of the inmates sent with the original party and one sent to solitary. Unfortunately, the prison staff had no prior notification, since Boonville did not have telegraph. The next couple of days were filled with interrogation sessions with both guards and prisoners as well as the jail wagon driver. The story was pretty much the same from all parties involved with the exception of Ben Crowe, who maintained that he did not threaten anyone or attempt escape. He maintained that for some reason he was unaware of, the other prisoners and the guards were out to frame him. His testimony was refuted some two weeks later, however, by a visit to Superintendent Wallace C. Conklin by his friend, Judge Wick Justice.

"Come on in, Wick," Conklin said, welcoming the judge into his office. "I got your wire and I've been looking forward to hearing your version of your little mishap over in Boonville." The judge followed Conklin back from the doorway to take a seat in one of the two leather chairs in front of the superintendent's desk while Conklin sat down in the other one.

"I would have been here sooner," Justice said, "but I was committed to some business I had to take care of in Houston."

"When I heard about your involvement with an attempted escape, I thought I might have to have you subpoenaed to get a visit out of you. Did it happen like they said? That one prisoner threatened you?"

"I'll tell you the truth, Wallace, I thought I was going to meet my maker right then and there." He paused then and nodded toward a sideboard. "Is there any coffee in that thing or is it just a showpiece?" he asked, referring to a silver coffeepot sitting on a little stand with a small candle burning under it.

"That's a little doodad my daughter gave me," Conklin said. "My clerk got some coffee from the dining hall and poured it in there. It keeps it pretty hot. You want a cup? I don't have any sugar or cream to put in it."

"I'll take a cup," Justice said and got up to pour it. "It's still got some bite in it," he said after taking a sip, then continued his story. "My clerk and I just happened to ride by this bridge the prisoners were working on. And don't you know, one of them was one of the meanest, lowdown scoundrels I've ever sent to prison, a fellow named Ben Crowe. I sentenced him to life because I thought it was too lenient on him to sentence him to death. Well, evidently he held that against me. He ran up and grabbed me by my coat lapels and jerked me off my horse and slammed me on the ground. You saw him, big powerful fellow. Anyway, when I didn't whimper enough to suit him, he drew back with his pistol, intending to split my skull open. And that's when one of your prisoners took hold of Mr. Crowe's wrist and pulled it back so hard he tore Crowe's shoulder muscles."

"The man from Waco," Conklin said and smiled.

"He said his name was John Bannack," Justice said.

"That's right. He's serving twenty years for bank robbery."

"That seems a little harsh for bank robbery with no violence or killing involved," the judge commented, remembering his questioning John Bannack on the bank of the Navasota River. "Some more of the Honorable Judge Raymond Grant's justice," he said. "How did Bannack wind up in a hard labor cell block?" Conklin told him about Bannack's altercation with Gator Brice. Justice thought about it for a moment, then asked, "So this Gator fellow came after Bannack, and the guards shot him. Bannack didn't kill him?"

"That's right," Conklin replied.

"So tell me, what kind of inmate is this fellow, John Bannack? He cause a lot of trouble?"

"Bannack?" Conklin responded as if surprised he would ask. "He never causes any trouble. From what the guards tell me, he rarely opens his mouth, works hard, and never complains. Model prisoner."

"That would have been my guess," the judge said. "I'm telling you, Wallace, I knew when I talked face to face with him that he was a decent man, right to the core. He doesn't belong in prison no more than you or I. Something is dreadfully wrong about that bank charge. I don't believe he robbed a bank."

"He confessed to the robbery, Wick," Conklin insisted, "and the sheriff caught him with the money. Tracked him right to his house and found him waiting for him with the money in his hand."

"Does he have any family?"

"Just his older brother and his wife and kids. That's all. They live on a poor little farm outside of Waco, so your friend, Judge Grant, figured Bannack stole the money and took it to his brother." Conklin paused then before saying, "I have to admit, I was surprised to think Bannack would be dumb enough to lead the sheriff straight to his home."

"I know for sure he ain't that dumb," Justice said. "And I'll tell you something else. That man's got no business locked up in prison, and I need a man like that to work for me."

"Ha!" Conklin exclaimed. "Doing what?"

"What he did that day on the Navasota River, protecting my life without anybody asking him to," Justice declared.

"You think you need a bodyguard?" Conklin asked.

"Call it that, I suppose. I've had several threats on my life lately from relatives of men I've convicted as well as gang members of outlaw gangs." That caused him to chuckle when he thought again of that day by the river. "You know my clerk, Elwood Wilson, don't you?"

"Sure I do," Conklin said at once. "Did you bring him along with you on this visit?"

"No, he needed to take a little vacation, but let me tell you about Elwood on that day I was attacked by Ben Crowe. Crowe had two prisoners who were in on the escape plan with him. And when he jerked me off my horse and started to strike me, Bannack grabbed his arm and managed to shoot one of the other two with Crowe, then Elwood shot the other one before he could reload to shoot Bannack."

"Elwood did that?" Conklin reacted, having met the mild young man.

"He did and it shook him up so bad that I sent him home to take some time off for a while. I expect him back when I get back to Austin." He smiled when he thought about it but got right back to the subject most important to him now. "I need a man like John Bannack. I seem to be making enemies with damn near every trial I try, and I like the man I see in him. I need him to work for me, and you sure as hell don't need him in this prison. I want to see about having him released into my custody."

Conklin just gazed at his friend in disbelief for a few seconds before responding. "Wick, I can't believe that I have to explain to you, of all people, that the judicial system doesn't work like that. Are you asking me to release a man who's served only a little over three years of a twenty-year sentence for no reason other than you want him out?" He shook his head and looked around him as if searching for an explanation. "You know that ain't the way it works. I don't have the authority to release a prisoner. That's what the courts are for."

"I know you don't, Wallace. I'm not asking you to release him. I'm thinking about your favorite uncle, the

Honorable Andrew J. Hamilton, governor of the great state of Texas."

"You want me to go to my uncle to get him to pardon John Bannack?" Conklin asked in total disbelief.

"Seems like a good idea to me," Justice answered. "Sounds even better coming from you."

"Damn, Wick," Conklin swore. "I know we're friends, but that ain't fair coming to me to ask for something like that."

"I reckon it depends on what you call fair and who deserves fair treatment," Justice responded. "I know without a doubt that John Bannack isn't getting fair treatment. He's no more guilty of a crime than you or me, but he's locked up in this prison for twenty years. That's what ain't fair."

"Wick, you don't know that for a fact. He just might have pulled the wool over your eyes."

"If you get me that pardon and it turns out that he's pulled the wool over my eyes, I'll shoot him, myself," Justice vowed. "I want him released into my custody as my responsibility, and I will take that responsibility to the grave with me."

"How do you know he isn't just playing you and as soon as he gets out he'll disappear?" Conklin asked in one last desperate appeal.

"Because he doesn't have the first inkling of an idea that I'm interested in getting him out of here," Justice said.

"All right, Wick, I'll present your request to my uncle, strictly because I've always trusted your judgement. But I don't know what he'll say."

"I knew I could count on you," the judge said, "and I appreciate it. If you ever get arrested, tell them to send you to my court. And I'll set you free, no matter what you did."

"Yeah, you joke," Conklin said, "but that sounds like what you're talking about doing with John Bannack. You want to visit him today?"

"No, I don't think so. I don't think it'd be a good idea to let him know anything about it until I know for certain you're as good a friend as I always thought you were," he japed. "It's not a kind thing to do, to give false hope to a man in prison. And I don' t have any idea when you will get a chance to talk to the governor."

"Sooner than you think," Conklin said. "In my job here at the prison, I never have occasion to talk to the governor. But next week, Lucille and I will be attending a birthday celebration in Austin for my grandfather, and Uncle Andrew will be there. I'll give it a shot."

"I sincerely appreciate it, Wallace. I want to assure you that I would not ask such a favor of you if I were not one hundred percent certain I was acting in sound judgement."

"I know that, Wick, and that's the only reason I would consider asking the governor for such a personal favor. Now that that's settled, are you going to hang around long enough to have dinner with me in the staff dining room?"

"I was beginning to wonder if I was going to have to remind you that I am your guest," the judge remarked. "And by the way, that coffee is pretty rank. I wasn't man enough to finish it."

"Well, it oughta be. It's been sitting there over that candle since breakfast. I just wanted to see if you were as tough as your reputation."

CHAPTER 8

Of the four returning inmates from the six assigned to the Boonville bridge project, Ben Crowe was sent to solitary confinement for six months for his attempted escape and an additional six months for his attack on a court official. The other three were sent back to their original cellblock, based on the interrogation of the inmates and the two prison guards. Their testimony was further confirmed by a statement from Judge Wick Justice, who was a witness to the happenings on that one particular day when the actual escape was attempted. So life for inmates John Bannack, Edgar Rice, and Bob Yates returned to the dull, daily grind that was prison life. As before, Bannack retreated back into his private shell, approached only by Yates or Rice, who felt they shared a special bond with the man from Waco.

As before, the prisoners in that cellblock were assigned to the manual labor jobs, which Bannack welcomed. With the war in full swing, the cotton and wool mill in the prison was under heavy production demands to supply tents and uniforms for the Confederate soldiers. One day, Bannack was working with a crew hauling lumber from the sawmill to the textile mill for the construction of a large extra room to assemble tents. In the process of unloading the lumber from the log wagon, he heard a sharp voice right behind him. "Hey, you big monkey, who the hell told you you could unload that lumber there?" Startled, he turned to confront a little man with gray whiskers and a black patch over one eye.

"Well, I'll be . . ." Bannack started. "George Capp, I reckon you're the boss of this textile factory now."

"How you doin', John?" Capp asked. "How you likin' prison life?"

"I'm doin' all right. I think I like it better on the outside, though," he answered.

Capp grinned and shook his head. "I ain't the boss yet, but I'm workin' my way up. I see they got you workin' with the grunts. That's what you get for growin' so damn big. I swear, I'm mighty glad to see you. I was worried about you. We heard about you over in our block. Heard you got into it so bad with some feller some time back in the dinin' hall that the guards ended up shootin' him. You know what they're callin' you? The man from Waco, that's what they're callin' you. Hell, I told 'em I'm from Waco, why don't they call me that? They said I was lucky anybody called me at all."

"Well, you're lookin' good, Capp. I think prison life agrees with you better'n rustlin' cattle." He gave the little man another close look before deciding he was right. Then he said, "The last time I saw you, I'm sure you were blind in the left eye. But lookin' at you today, I see you're wearin' that patch on the other eye."

"Oh, you noticed that?" Capp asked. "I never said I was blind in either eye. Fact of the matter is I see 'bout the same outta both eyes. I took this here eye patch offa dead man, six or seven years ago. He got in a gunfight with a feller I was partnerin' with and came in second. Well, I always admired that patch he wore and my partner didn't want it, so I took it. And when I looked in his eye, I expected to see an empty socket, but it wasn't. There was an eyeball in there and that got me to thinkin'. I bet that feller could see outta both eyes and he was wearin' this patch over one of 'em to rest it up while the other'n did the lookin'. Well, that made a lotta sense to me. Keep your eyesight sharp a lot longer by restin' one eye all the time. Just don't forget to switch 'em from time to time."

John didn't say anything for a few moments, waiting to see if Capp was going to suddenly break into a chuckling fit. When he didn't, John asked as casually as he could manage, "Have you been able to tell if it's helped your eyes or not?"

"I believe it has," Capp answered. "And one eye is about as strong as the other'n."

"Then I reckon you've got a good idea going there with your patch," he said. *I just hope you don't run into a man with a pegleg,* he thought. "I expect I'd best get the rest of these boards unloaded before somebody comes lookin' for the wagon. Maybe I'll see you again, Capp. You take care of yourself."

"I always do," Capp replied. "You do the same." He watched John walk back to the wagon and couldn't help noticing the transformation. When he and John were first brought to The Unit, John was a big, strong, strapping young man. The few years in prison had further developed him into a formidable man that would be trouble to reckon with.

Bannack saw Capp a couple of times during the following months and then the word came to the prison that the war was over, Lee had officially surrendered. The everyday work of the prison continued, just as it had all during the war. After breakfast one morning while the prisoners were preparing to march outside the walls for a ditch-digging project, a guard came into their cellblock to escort John Bannack to the Walls Unit. The guard gave him no explanation for his summons but told him to take his personal items with him. Evidently he was being transferred to some other unit, but the guard didn't know which one. Very much to his surprise, the guard escorted him to the administration building and led him to the office of the superintendent, Wallace Conklin. The only reason John could imagine was that perhaps some terrible tragedy had occurred to his brother Warren or Kitty or the boys. But when he walked into Conklin's outer office, the first face he recognized was that of Judge Wick Justice. "Come in, John Bannack," the judge said. John nodded and approached him. "Would you like some coffee?"

The offer fairly startled him. "No, sir. I just had breakfast."

"Well, sit down," the judge said, "and I'll tell you who these gentlemen are." He indicated a chair at the long table, and they all sat down. "First, I guess I should ask if you remember me. It's been a long time since we met, under quite different circumstances I should say."

"Yes, sir, I remember you, Judge Justice. I'm glad to see that you're all right. And this gentleman on your left is Mr. Wilson, if I recall the name correctly. But I don't know the other gentleman."

"Well, let me introduce you," Justice said, "because you owe this man a helluva lot. This is Superintendent Wallace C. Conklin and he's the man who is going to sign the papers that are going to permit you to walk out of this prison a free man."

Bannack did not react, although the three men staring at him were obviously waiting to see his reaction. Instead, he looked back at them, his face devoid of expression. He heard what the judge had said, but he felt certain the words didn't mean what they implied. When he still did not respond after a short pause, Conklin said, "I don't believe your man believes you, Wick." He looked at the confused man and said, "John, it took a long road and a lotta work on the part of Judge Justice and myself to persuade Governor Hamilton to issue a full pardon of the charges that sent you here. But as of eight o'clock this morning, you are a free man."

They got a reaction from him then but not the one they expected. Anticipating a look of joyous excitement, instead they were met with an expression of alarm, for his first thought was that his brother must have confessed to the robbery of the bank. And that would mean the destruction of his family.

Seeing the obvious distress in his expression, Conklin was prompted to ask, "Did you misunderstand what I said? I'm releasing you from prison. There are some conditions that you'll have to agree to, but basically, your prison time has been served." He glanced at Judge Justice, then back at John and smiled. "Most men in here would be tickled to death to hear what I just told you."

"Yes, sir, I understand," John said, "and I ain't any different from any other man in here. But is my brother and his family all right?"

Now it was Conklin's turn to look confused. "Why, I'm afraid I have no idea about that," he confessed. "Have they been ill?"

John realized then that his pardon had nothing to do with the bank robbery. He still had no clue as to his release, but whatever the reason, it had to be good news. He was sorry now that he had mentioned his brother. "I'm sorry, sir. The only reason I could think of to set me free was because something bad might have happened to my family. And the only family I've got is my brother Warren and his wife and two boys."

The three men gaping at him all chuckled in response to his misunderstanding. "No, as far as we know, there isn't any catastrophe with your brother's family."

"In that case, I'm tickled to death to hear you're gonna let me outta here, but I can hardly believe it's true, so I know there must be some reason other than my ability to get along with others."

His statement was cause for a chuckle from Conklin, since the man from Waco had a reputation as a loner. "You're right," Conklin said, "there is a reason for your parole, and some conditions that you must agree to before it's official. The man you need to thank, and who is really the man responsible for your release is Judge Wick Justice. He saw something in you that day on the Navasota River that convinced him you were an honest man." John glanced at the judge, and Justice nodded his head to confirm it. "He was also impressed by the way you restrained the man who attacked him," Conklin continued. "In effect, Judge Justice is vouching for your lawful conduct as long as you are in his employ."

"So you're sayin' that you're lettin' me outta prison to go to work for Judge Justice?"

"I guess you could say that's about the size of it," Conklin answered.

"Doing what?" John asked.

"When he first proposed this pardon, I asked him the same question," Conklin said. "I'll answer it with the same answer he gave me, doing what you did to save his life without anybody asking you to."

"You want me to be a bodyguard?" He looked directly at the judge when he asked the question.

The judge answered his question. "That would fall under

your duties, I would hope. You would just be my assistant, to help with whatever, but I need a man capable of handling trouble and a man I can trust with my life. I should tell you that I have enemies, and I need a man who has dealt with my enemies before, like you did with Ben Crowe. You will go where I go. I'll provide your food and a place to live and put some decent clothes on you."

"That sounds like a better deal than stayin' in here for another fifteen years," Bannack said.

The judge laughed. "I'm sure of that. I guess I should tell you, I would be paying you a regular salary for the job."

"Then I reckon we've got a deal," Bannack said.

"Don't you want to know what I propose to pay you?"

"No, sir. I expect you'll be fair about it, and it'll depend on whether or not I do a decent job," Bannack said. "What is this paper I have to sign?"

The judge explained it to him. "In addition to clothes and such, I will have to buy you a horse and saddle. I'll also have to buy you a rifle and a handgun and the ammunition for them. In other words, I'll have quite an investment in you. The paper you will sign guarantees that you will remain in my employ until all that investment is repaid. Fair enough?"

"Fair enough," Bannack agreed. "I'll sign it." He thought to himself that it was a useless paper to sign. He figured if he gave his word he would stay, then that should be enough, but he would sign it if it gave the judge some sense of guarantee. The judge, on the other hand, felt positive that Bannack would honor the contract no matter how badly he wanted to leave, simply because he had signed his name on it.

After he signed the paper that the judge had referred to, Justice told Elwood to walk outside with John to the horses and give him the plain work shirt to exchange for his prison issue. He thought John might be a little less self-conscious without his striped shirt when they went to the stable and the general store in town. The judge paused a moment to thank Conklin for all his efforts to arrange Bannack's freedom. "I'm sorry it took so long," Conklin apologized, "but, frankly, I'm surprised we got it done. I declare, I'd never seen Bannack up close before. He's a scary-looking fellow. Kinda throws you off guard when he talks so polite and respectfully. I hope he turns out to be the man you think he is."

Justice laughed. "If he doesn't, I'll shoot him, myself."

From the prison, they rode directly to the stable in town where they returned the horse and saddle they had borrowed to fetch Bannack. Then the stable owner, a fellow named Floyd Farmer, showed him the horses he had for sale and the judge told him to pick the one he wanted. He replied that he could get by with the gentle sorrel the judge had borrowed. But Justice told him to pick a better one. "You'll wear that horse out in a week." Taking him at his word, John looked the horses over carefully before choosing a buckskin gelding, about four years old. The stable owner then showed him several different saddles he had for sale. John picked one and saddled the buckskin after he let the stirrups out a little.

"You gonna try him out and see how he feels?" Floyd asked. John said that might be a good idea, so he led the buckskin out to the street and climbed up into the saddle. Standing back in the door of the stable, Floyd grinned at the judge and Elwood. "He might be in for a little surprise. That's a right spirited horse he picked out. He don't generally get along with strangers." They watched then as John gave the buckskin a nudge with his heels and started down the street at a trot. About halfway down, he settled into a comfortable lope and when he got to the other end, he wheeled the horse and came back to the stable at a gallop. Floyd just gaped, his jaw hanging open, as John reined the horse to a stop and dismounted. "That buckskin ain't never let nobody jump on him and ride him like that. I swear, if that ain't somethin'."

"I think he'll do just fine," Bannack said. "It's been a long time since I was on a horse."

The judge looked at Elwood and winked. "Let's go get him some clothes so we can eat dinner at a decent restaurant." As far as he was concerned, John's influence on the spirited horse was another positive sign that all the trouble and expense he had gone to was worth it.

The next stop was at Huntsville General Merchandise where John Bannack said goodbye to his prison trousers and shoes and was outfitted in some ordinary work clothes and a decent pair of boots. Justice also bought him a bedroll, since John didn't even have a blanket. Last, but far from least, was the visit to the gun shop in the back part of the merchandise store. The primary reason for hiring John Bannack was for Wick Justice's protection and with that in mind, the judge wanted his protector to be equipped to handle the worst situations. So he informed John that he had already purchased the weapons of his choice and he expected him to become proficient in the use of each. Maynard Wells, the store owner, reached under the counter and pulled out the 1860 Henry rifle. With fifteen rounds in the magazine and one in the chamber, the lever-action rifle was worth the forty-two dollars the judge paid for it. At ten dollars a thousand for the .44 cartridges it fired, the judge decided a Colt six-shooter modified to use the same .44 cartridges would be the best choice for Bannack's handgun.

By this time, John was quite overwhelmed with the lavish investment the judge was making on his behalf. *Maybe I should have read that paper I signed a little closer,* he thought. *I might not live long enough to pay him all I owe him.* He took the Henry in hand and hefted the nine-pound rifle to his shoulder. "There's gonna have to be a honeymoon before I call her mine," he declared. "It's been a long time since I shot that old single-shot rifle I used to own." His comment caused the judge and Elwood to exchange uncertain glances, but it was too late to reconsider the investment. There was a rifle scabbard that came with the saddle they had purchased for him, so John slipped the Henry in it, then strapped on his new gun belt. Then they rode up to the hotel where Justice and Elwood had rented rooms for the night just passed. The judge wanted to have dinner in the hotel dining room before they left Huntsville.

After a dinner that seemed more a feast to Bannack, the unusual trio of the circuit judge, the court clerk, and the ex-convict set out on the road to the town of Boonville. The judge didn't tell Bannack their first destination was Boonville before they actually left Huntsville. He hadn't planned to tell him until they reached the bridge he worked on as a prisoner, just to see if he recognized it. But Elwood told Bannack the judge was scheduled to hold a trial in Boonville, which was a little over fifty miles away. Elwood and the judge had made the trip from Huntsville to Boonville before, so they remembered a nice little camping spot by a creek about twenty miles away from Huntsville. This was their target today, to make camp there that first night. Bannack was anxious to see if he had been bought to be the judge's general servant and would be expected to do the cooking and wash the dishes. He was to find, however, that Elwood was fairly happy to serve in that capacity. So when they reached the creek, Bannack took care of the horses and built a fire while the judge and Elwood each set up their own sleeping tent. The judge must have thought he would prefer sleeping out under the stars after his years in a prison bunk, Bannack assumed, and he was right about that. He found that he was very comfortable on his blanket roll. The grub that Elwood came up with was inferior to what he would have had in the prison dining hall. But the coffee was good, and he could go a long way on a cup of coffee. Since he was now in possession of a first-class rifle, he decided he would acquire some fresh meat of some kind the first chance he got.

That chance came on their second day of travel. After a breakfast of more of Elwood's sliced bacon and hardtack, they traveled approximately another twenty miles before striking the Navasota River where they stopped to rest the horses. He figured the Lord must have decided to have some compassion on them because when they reached the river, they frightened three deer up from the bushes growing close beside the water. Without hesitation, he drew the Henry rifle from his scabbard and shot one of the does trailing a young buck just before they vanished into the trees. It had to be pure luck to see deer out that time of day, and to fire a kill shot the first time he fired the rifle. Even though he aimed for a high shoulder shot and the deer was struck behind the front leg, it was still a kill shot. When he practiced with the rifle, he would have to remember his shot was a little low. To the judge and Elwood, however, it was a miraculous shot, and confirmed the judge's confidence in freeing the man. It had not occurred to His Honor that he had hired a skilled hunter as well as a protector. He was also pleased to find out that Bannack knew how to skin and butcher a deer as well.

They all enjoyed the fresh venison, eating until they could eat no more, but they knew they were going to waste the majority of the meat. The packhorses were loaded down pretty heavily already. Bannack cut a quantity of the fresh meat for supper that night, but with the weather as mild as it was, it would be chancy to risk keeping it any longer. He cut some strips and smoked them over the fire until the horses were rested, but there was not enough time to get the meat smoked long enough. So he reluctantly dragged the rest of the carcass off away from the river for the scavengers to feed on.

While they sat by the fire, digesting the fresh venison, the judge asked Bannack if he knew where he was. "Yes, sir, I do. I think we're about four or five miles south of that bridge I worked on for the people of Boonville. Did they ever finish it?"

"As a matter of fact, they did," Justice replied. "But it didn't help them get the railroad to come through Boonville. There was a lot of arguing between some of the town people and the state. Then the railroad came and talked to the town council and the Boonville folks all decided they didn't need the railroad bad enough to pay for it. The Houston and Texas Central Railroad decided to extend their tracks from Millican, but instead of laying their tracks through Boonville, they decided to bypass it and run their tracks through Bryan. Boonville is already losing a lot of its people and it isn't the county seat anymore. The people voted to make Bryan the county seat. The last I heard, the US Post Office is planning to route the mail through Bryan instead of Boonville. And if that's true, I expect it'll make a ghost town out of Boonville."

"That's too bad," Bannack said. "I know that mayor, I don't remember his name." He repeated it when the judge supplied it. "Right, Ronald Mallard. He wanted to bring the railroad into his town and Daniel Orton was hopin' that bridge would help the railroad lean their way."

"And that's where Elwood shot his first man," Judge Justice said, grinning at his clerk.

"Ooh," Elwood responded, pretending to shiver all over, "don't remind me, Judge. I've had a terrible time trying to forget that day."

"Well, I appreciate it," Bannack told him. "I wouldn't be here if you hadn't shot that man and you wouldn't have had any fresh deer meat for dinner."

"That's right, Elwood," the judge joked, "if you had realized at the time how important a factor that man's death was going to be on our dinner today, you'd have shot him sooner."

When the horses were rested, they loaded up again and crossed over the river, then followed it to the north. When they had traveled about four miles, they reached the bridge that Bannack had worked on. It looked to be in pretty good shape. He rode the buckskin across it and back, the gelding's hooves tapping a hollow sound on the surface Daniel Orton had nailed in place. *What a waste,* he thought, *two inmates killed and one innocent townsman named Ernie. And the town didn't even get the railroad.*

"We might as well go ahead and make our camp here for the night," Justice said. "The horses are ready for a rest and so am I." Bannack was surprised when he heard that because the town was only a mile or two from the bridge. He figured the judge would ride on into Boonville and stay in the hotel. The judge figured he might be thinking something like that, so he said, "The hotel closed its doors and the last time I checked, there wasn't one opened up yet in Bryan. Otherwise, that's where we would be staying the night."

"Well, sir, we got most everything we need right here," Bannack remarked, "and some fresh deer meat for supper. We might wanna ride on down the river a ways, away from this bridge and the trail." The judge agreed, so they rode upstream to find a spot that satisfied them.

After the rest of the fresh deer meat was eaten, Bannack asked for permission to take his rifle and his pistol away from the camp to get acquainted with them.

"I think that's a good idea," Judge Justice said. "And John, you're an employee, not a slave. Remember?"

"Yes, sir, I'll try to remember that," Bannack replied, but it was hard to forget that he was bought and paid for, just not on the auction block. He might have found it interesting had he known that the judge had experienced some troubling thoughts about how easy it would be for him to simply ride away, now that he had supplied him with a horse and weapons. There was no way that he and Elwood could stop him. So the judge was relieved to see him take his weapons and walk into the woods, instead of riding his horse. Justice knew that Elwood had some fear that Bannack might decide to kill the two of them and take everything. But he knew that John Bannack was not an evil man. He was certain he would never murder anyone. He still believed the man had no business in prison.

Bannack had heard men talk about the Henry rifle and he knew that he already liked the feel of the weapon after firing only one shot. He had always been a good shot, ever since he killed his first squirrel at the age of nine. So he was confident in his ability with any rifle and now he was going to see how a really good rifle performed. After he walked about a quarter of a mile back up the creek, he picked a tree about one hundred yards away to be his target. Setting himself squarely, he levered a cartridge into the chamber, raised the rifle to his shoulder and fired. Then he cranked round after round, firing as fast as he could for six shots. Then he picked out another tree on a rise, maybe fifty yards beyond the first tree. He aimed more carefully and took his time to fire four more shots at the distant tree. When he got to the first target, he found a small circle of splintered bark the size of a serving platter with some bullet holes that could be covered by the span of his two hands. "Not bad," he declared. On then to the distant target where he found four holes ripped in the bark, not so close as the pattern on the closer tree, but all four shots in the tree within the space of a man's shoulder to hip. He held the rifle up to look at it at arm's length and said, "You'll do, Henry."

He propped the rifle up against a tree and drew the Colt .44 from his holster. Then he dropped it back in the holster and drew it a couple more times. He had really never fooled with a handgun before, so he had no notion of trying to become a fast-draw gunfighter. But he wanted to see how easily the six-shooter came out of the holster. He was more interested in how accurate he was, once the gun was in his hand. So he holstered it again, then drew it as fast as he could and fired three quick shots into the tree. He was much faster with the Henry, so he decided he would work on the six-shooter whenever he had the occasion. Satisfied with where he stood with his new weapons, however, he walked back to the camp and got the cleaning rod and gun oil the judge bought with the weapons.

"Whaddaya think?" the judge asked him when he walked back to the campfire.

"I think we're gonna get along just fine," he said, "and I want to thank you again for the chance you're taking on an old ex-convict."

"An old ex-convict," the judge repeated and grinned at him. "How old are you now, John?"

"I'm twenty-three, if I haven't miscounted," he replied. "In prison, sometimes you're busy havin' so much fun, you forget and let a birthday slip by you."

The judge laughed. "I'm sure that must happen a lot.

Twenty-three, all is not lost, you're still a young man. Hell, Elwood's older than you. How old are you Elwood?"

"I'm thirty," Elwood said. "I just turned thirty yesterday."

"What?" Justice exclaimed. "Yesterday was your birthday and you never said a word about it? Why, we'd be remiss if we didn't acknowledge your thirtieth birthday. We're going to right that wrong when we get to a saloon."

"Oh, that's not necessary, sir," Elwood was quick to say, already embarrassed to have mentioned it.

"I beg to disagree," the judge insisted. "I'm sure I didn't celebrate it last year, either."

"No, sir," Elwood replied.

CHAPTER 9

At the judge's suggestion, they packed up their camp and rode into town, hoping to find some place to eat breakfast. They knew that the hotel was closed, but the judge hoped to find some little café or perhaps a saloon that was still open for business. Surely, he thought, the whole town can't have died so fast, since he was scheduled to try a man for robbing the stagecoach. That means they still had a jail and a courthouse. He decided it best to go to the sheriff's office to let him know he was in town. And then the sheriff could send them to the right place to eat.

Sheriff Rufus Barnes saw the three men through the window of his office at the jail, so he walked out to meet them. "Good mornin', Judge Justice, Elwood," he greeted them. He acknowledged the big serious-looking man on the buckskin horse, finding him familiar-looking.

"Good morning, Sheriff Barnes," the judge returned. "With all the rumors I've heard lately, I was wondering if I was going to ride into a ghost town this morning. But it looks like there's still some life here."

"Oh, yes, sir," Barnes replied, "the town's still hummin', it just ain't hummin' a tune that everybody likes to hear, I reckon." He gave Bannack a nod of his head. "Looks like you added another man to your party since you were here to try Brady Gamble."

"That's a fact," the judge responded, "you remember John Bannack. He'll be working with Elwood and me from now on."

Suddenly recalling why the man was familiar to him, the sheriff said, "Well, I'll be! He's definitely a good man to have around." He extended his hand to Bannack.

"Are we gonna hold Curly Price's trial in the courthouse as usual?" Justice asked.

"Yes, sir," the sheriff answered. "The courthouse is still open, but there ain't no county business there no more, since Bryan is the county seat now. But you'll try Curly Price there, same as you did Brady Gamble."

"Any witnesses?" the judge asked.

"Signed statements," Barnes said, "by two of the passengers and the stage driver and shotgun."

"But nobody here in person, right?"

"No, sir, nobody could hang around here waiting for the trial to start."

"So how do you know this fellow you have in jail is the man who held up the stagecoach," the judge asked.

"There was four of 'em that stopped the stage," the sheriff answered. "They was all wearin' bandannas over their faces. But one of 'em's bandanna fell down, and both the driver and the shotgun recognized Curly Price. They told the deputy US marshal where to find Curly, and he went and arrested him."

"I see," Justice said, obviously unhappy with the tools he had to work with in the trial. "Well, let's go ahead and get it done tomorrow. Now, we haven't had any breakfast. When I was here last, I stayed in the hotel and I ate there. I know they've closed up. Is there any place in town where we can buy a decent breakfast?"

Barnes gave him a wide grin. "Yessir, there sure is, the Lone Star Saloon, right across the street." When he was met with a somewhat skeptical look from the judge, he chuckled. "When they closed the hotel, Bert Wheeler, who owns the Lone Star, hired Arlene Durham to come to work for him. Arlene's the same woman who did the cookin' for you when you were stayin' in the hotel." That brought a smile to the judge's face, so he made another suggestion. "I expect you'd like a place to spend the night, too, so I'd recommend the Widow Bowen's boardin' house. I know she's got some empty rooms because she told me she lost a couple of her boarders when they moved to Bryan. Then if you druther, you can eat at Sally Bowen's. But the food's better at the Lone Star in my opinion."

"Well, let's get over there while it's still a reasonable time to expect breakfast," the judge said. "Sheriff, will you join us?"

"I don't mind if I do," Barnes responded. "Let me lock my front door."

"Good," Justice said. "Then we'll see if we can get some rooms in that boarding house before we take the horses to the stable." He paused to ask, "The stable's still there, isn't it?" He got an affirmative nod from Barnes. "Then we'll go to trial at nine o'clock tomorrow morning. We can set up the courtroom this afternoon."

"Well, I'll be . . ." Ned Bradley started, "look who's comin' in the door." The two men sitting at the table with him turned to see. "It's Boonville's fearless sheriff."

"Who's that with him?" Shorty Reese asked. "You reckon that older feller is the judge? I bet he's the judge."

"He looks like he oughta be a judge," Ned declared. "Looks like they're really gonna have a trial for Curly."

"I wonder who that big feller is," Jim Turner remarked. "Reckon he's the judge's bodyguard?"

"He ain't no gunslinger," Ned replied. "I can tell you that. Look at the way he's wearin' that six-shooter. He'd have to make two separate moves just to draw it." They didn't bother to even speculate about Elwood, who obviously looked like a clerk but watched as the sheriff led his three guests through the bar area to the eating area, which was partitioned-off by a half wall.

"Howdy, Rufus," Bert Wheeler, owner of the Lone Star greeted them. "You back already? Didn't Arlene feed you enough this mornin'?"

"She always does," the sheriff replied, "but I brought her some more customers who ain't et breakfast. Is it too late to get them something to eat?"

"I don't think so," Wheeler said. "Let me go make sure she ain't started cleanin' up yet." He hurried into the kitchen and was back right away. "She said she'd be happy to cook you some breakfast. Set yourselves down and she'll be out here with some coffee in a minute." They took seats at one of the tables, and once they were settled, Wheeler asked, "Who's this you brought in with you? Is this the judge for the trial?"

"Yep," the sheriff answered. "This is Judge Wick Justice and his assistants, Elwood Wilson and John Bannack."

"I was in the Lone Star once before," the judge said. "It's been quite a while since then. You didn't have this eating section then." He started to say that he had not met him on that occasion but Arlene appeared at that moment carrying a tray with silverware, napkins, and four cups of coffee.

"I didn't think you would be eating again, Sheriff," she said, "but I thought you might want a cup of coffee."

"Bless your heart, I surely do," Barnes said. "Thank you, ma'am." Arlene went back into the kitchen to fix their breakfast, leaving them to their coffee. "I don't know for sure," Barnes answered when the judge asked if he thought the town was going to continue to lose population. "Things are sure lookin' that way. The town council talked such big talk about gettin' the railroad through here. And then when it got down to the time to help the railroad with some of the expense, they backed away. So the railroad bypassed us and put Bryan on the map. And you know, some of the biggest talkers about building the town were the first to pull their businesses out of Boonville and move to Bryan. I reckon I have to see the writin' on the wall. We're losin' folks every day."

"What about your position," the judge asked. "Are you going to stay on as sheriff?"

"That's a question I've asked myself a dozen times," Barnes said. "The question ain't really whether I want to stay on or not. It's more like who's gonna pay my salary to stay on. I've had an invitation to go over to Bryan and talk to the sheriff about a job as his deputy. By the time I'm forced to leave, that offer might be off the table."

Thinking it better to change the subject, the judge asked, "How old a fellow is this Curly Price?"

"He's a young feller. I reckon Curly's in his early twenties. Unless you're talkin' about his brain. Then I'd say about six."

"He have family around here anywhere?" Justice asked.

"If he does, I ain't ever seen hide nor hair of 'em. He just blew into town with some other drifters a few weeks ago. They'd come in to hit the saloons and bother the women. That was when we had more than this one saloon. They're back in town today. I noticed his other three partners settin' out there in the saloon when we came in."

Bannack and Elwood exchanged a puzzled glance after hearing that, but it was the judge who questioned the sheriff's statement. "You say he typically runs with three other men, the three men sitting in this saloon right now?" The sheriff nodded. "And you say the stagecoach was held up by four men?" Barnes nodded again. "And the man in your jail was positively identified as one of the robbers?"

"That's a fact," Barnes said with a wide smile.

"Has it ever occurred to you that the other three stage-coach robbers are the three men Curly always rides with? And they're sitting here in the saloon right across the street from the jail?"

"Your Honor," Barnes said patiently, "I know damn well those three drifters settin' in this saloon are the other three stage robbers. And I know they know I know it. But they also know I can't prove it. When that deputy marshal arrested Curly and brought him in to leave in my jail, I told him then that the other three were those three Curly was runnin' with. He told me I might be right, but there wasn't any evidence to prove it. The passengers couldn't identify any of them and the stage driver and his guard both recognized Curly, but that was because the bandanna he was wearin' slipped down off his face. But they weren't sure about any of the others." He sat back and took a big gulp of his coffee. "And now I get the privilege of watchin' those three grinnin' hyenas walkin' around free as birds. When I first locked Curly up, I prepared every day for his three pals to try to break him out. But they never did anything but what they're doin' right now, just hangin' around town, showin' me there ain't nothin' I can do about it."

Like the judge, Bannack could see the possibility of some major trouble from those three before this was over. If he had to guess, he would say they hadn't acted before now because they intend to wait for the trial on the slight chance Curly would be found not guilty because of the lack of eyewitnesses. They would have no knowledge of the statements the witnesses signed. That would mean the time for an attempt to free Curly would come when he was found guilty, and they would most likely strike before he was returned to the jail cell. Bannack wasn't sure what his roll was going to be, but he knew the sheriff was going to need some help. He knew his first priority in that event was going to be to protect the judge and Elwood. He wondered what his chances were of getting a little help from Elwood again.

Further discussion on the matter was postponed for the time being because of the reappearance of Arlene, this time with her tray loaded with plates of food. When breakfast was finished, Sheriff Barnes gave the key to the courthouse to Judge Justice. "I'd go over there and unlock it for you, but with those three in town, I try to stick pretty close to the jail."

"I don't blame you for that," the judge said. "I'm sure we can make sure everything is set up the way I want it. You said the stable is still in operation, right?"

"Yes, sir, it's still open," Barnes said. "Ol' Wilford Deal is like me right now. He can't afford to stay here in Boonville, but he can't leave."

"Maybe we'd best check by this boarding house first to make sure we're got a place to sleep tonight, then take the horses," Elwood suggested, and the judge agreed.

Following the directions Sheriff Barnes gave them, they rode down a small side street, past a couple of small houses until they came to a large, two-story house with a picket fence around the front yard. They left their horses tied at the fence and walked to the front porch steps to find Sally Bowen standing in the front doorway watching them. "Can I help you gentlemen?"

"Good morning, ma'am." The judge tipped his hat politely. "I'm Judge Wick Justice and these two gentlemen work with me. We're just in town overnight and Sheriff Barnes suggested that you might have accommodations for us to spend the night with you."

She smiled, amused by his elegant way of asking if she had any vacant rooms. "Good mornin'," she replied. "I'm Sally Bowen. You lookin' for three rooms?"

"That would be my preference, if you have three available," the judge said.

"I've got three empty rooms," she said. "Matter of fact, I've got the whole upstairs vacant except for one room. I don't have a barn big enough to take care of your horses. Just room for my mare, so you'll have to take 'em to the stable, unless you wanna just let 'em run loose in the field behind the house." The judge told her that they had already planned to take their horses to the stable. "It ain't that long a walk back from Wilford Deal's stable, if you follow that path leadin' from the side yard," she said. "Come in and I'll show you the rooms." They followed her into the house and up the stairs to the second floor where she led them down the hallway past four rooms with open doors. "They're all pretty much the same," she said. "I didn't fix 'em up like hotel rooms because I expected my boarders to be with me for a long time. So I wanted to make the rooms more homey, but since the hotel closed, I've had more folks like you that just want a room for the night."

"I suppose that's the reason you're going to give for the high price you're going to charge me for these rooms," the judge said.

"If you were going to stay here for any length of time, I could give you a much better rate. But for one night, we have to give the room a thorough cleaning with new sheets and towels. Blame the town council for losing our town to the railroad and Bryan."

"Understood," the judge said. "How much?"

"I have to ask a dollar, twenty-five for the room, but that

includes dinner and supper. It would have been a dollar, fifty with breakfast."

Justice reached for his wallet and placed three dollars in her hand, then pulled some change out of his pocket and picked out three quarters. "We'll need to get some things off our horses and leave them in our rooms; the things, not the horses. Then we have some business to take care of in town."

"Dinner at twelve and supper at five o'clock," she said, oblivious of his attempt at humor. "I'll get you your door keys. The washroom is straight out the door at the end of the hall downstairs. I hope you enjoy your stay with us."

They stopped by the courthouse, which was a single-story building that had been used for many purposes other than courts or county business. The main purpose in stopping there before the stable was to leave a large wooden box from one of the packhorses that held routine items the judge used when he was conducting a trial. "We can set up the bench and the witness stand after we leave the horses at the stable."

So the stable was their next stop, and as they dismounted, two men walked out of the stable door. Bannack recognized one of them as Daniel Orton and it was obvious that he remembered the judge. He grinned and called out, "Judge Wick Justice, haven't seen you since that day at the bridge. I'm Daniel Orton. I'm the one who built that bridge. I reckon you're in town for the trial of that stagecoach robber."

"That's right," the judge said. "I remember you."

Only then, did Orton take notice of the two men with the judge, so he only glanced in their direction. But there was something familiar about the one big man, and he returned his gaze to take a closer look. Then it struck him and he could only utter the words, "The man from Waco," for he could not remember the prisoner's name. Then he looked back at the judge. Of course, the judge knew who he was. He had saved the judge's life that day. But what the hell was he doing out of prison?

Seeing that the man was having some problems with his appearance with the judge, Bannack stepped forward. "Glad to see you again, Mr. Orton. I'm John Bannack."

"Right," Orton said. "Right," he repeated. "John Bannack, I'd forgotten your name."

"And this is Elwood Wilson," Bannack said. "He was with Judge Justice that day on the Navasota. I was released from prison a short while back and I work for Judge Justice now."

"Well, that's good," Orton declared, finally taking control of his confusion. "I'm glad to hear it. That's a good thing, working on the side of the law. Good to see you again, John." He nodded to the judge and Elwood and took his leave.

"I don't believe he was prepared to see you when you weren't wearing prison stripes," Elwood said to Bannack.

"What can I do for you fellows?" Wilford Deal asked when Orton walked away. "You lookin' to leave those horses here?"

"We want to leave our horses with you till tomorrow afternoon," the judge told him. "Sheriff Barnes told me you took good care of the horses in your stable, so that's what we're looking for. I was here once before, but it was quite a while ago. I had no complaints about your service. I remember that much. I remember your name, however. Mr. Wilford Deal, I believe."

"Yes, sir, that's me all right," Wilford said, impressed that he remembered. "I'll try to take good care of your horses again. How 'bout a portion of grain at no extra charge?"

"That would be a friendly gesture on your part and greatly appreciated by me and my associates," the judge responded.

Bannack smiled to himself. The judge didn't remember the man's name, until the sheriff told him. They unloaded the packhorses and left the packs and their saddles in an empty stall. Then they led the horses to the corral and released them. "Look at them," Elwood remarked to the judge, referring to Bannack, who was still at the corral gate, stroking the buckskin's face and neck. "Those two fell in love the first time they saw each other. I feel sorry for the horse thief who steals that buckskin."

They left the horses and returned to the courthouse to do the little bit of furniture arrangement to set up the main room as a courtroom. They set a chair beside the table that was to be the judge's bench and called it the witness stand, although the sheriff was likely the only witness to be called. There was no need for a jury box, for there was to be no jury. There were a few chairs for spectators, in the event there were spectators. The judge said if there were not enough chairs, spectators could stand. The trial shouldn't take that long. Bannack couldn't help wondering why they didn't just go over to the jail and hold the trial there. There were signed statements identifying Curly Price as one of the robbers. All that was left to be done was for Judge Justice to find him guilty and bang his gavel and notify the US marshal to come take Curly to prison. All the rest of this fuss was to make it look official, he supposed. If the judge would hold the trial in the jailhouse, it would also make it a lot more difficult for whatever plans those three drifters had on their minds. He wondered if he should suggest that possibility to the judge. But at this early stage of his employment, he was reluctant to suggest anything to the judge.

"Well, that's all we need to do here in the courthouse," the judge declared. "We'll open it again in the morning at nine o'clock and there should be plenty of time to eat dinner before we head out of here to Austin." He pulled his watch out and looked at it. "It's just about time for Sally Bowen to serve dinner at the boarding house. I'll leave it up to you two. Do you want to see what kind of cooking she does, or eat at the Lone Star Saloon? We already know the woman at the Lone Star is a good cook. If we eat at the boarding house, it might help us decide where we'll take supper. What do you think?" He waited for an opinion.

"I expect the food will be fit to eat at either place," Elwood said.

"Bannack?" Justice asked.

He shrugged indifferently. "We could go eat at the boarding house, since it's included in the room rent. Then if it ain't good, or it don't fill us up, we could get something else at the Lone Star."

"Now, there's a practical man's approach to solving the problem," the judge said. "I'm in favor of that." So they took the path back to Sally Bowen's boarding house.

CHAPTER 10

"What time is the trial supposed to start?" Ned Bradley asked the bartender at the Lone Star Saloon. When Sam hesitated before answering, Ned asked, "They are havin' a trial for Curly Price this mornin', ain't they?"

"Yeah, nine o'clock," Sam answered. "But they ain't havin' it in here."

"They ain't?" Ned and his partners had assumed the trial would be held there in the saloon. In most small towns that was usually the case. "Well, where in the hell are they gonna have it?"

"At the courthouse where they always have trials," Sam answered.

"Are you smart mouthin' me?" Ned reacted and dropped his hand onto the handle of his six-shooter. "I ain't seen no courthouse around here nowhere."

"I ain't japin' ya," Sam quickly replied. "It's that buildin' settin' in the middle of the square. That's the courthouse."

"Well, it ain't much of a courthouse," Ned declared. "Nine o'clock, is that what you said?"

"Yes, sir, nine o'clock."

"You hear that, boys?" Ned asked Jim Turner and Shorty Reese. "We've got time to have some breakfast before we go watch ol' Curly go to trial."

"Nine o'clock," Shorty echoed. "Hell, we got time to have a drink before we eat breakfast."

"I expect I'd druther get some food in my belly before I start drinkin' likker," Jim said.

"Hell, little drink of likker will clear your belly out and get it ready for breakfast," Shorty claimed. "Pour me a little shooter, Sam. Ain't that what they call you?"

"That's right," Sam said and poured a shot, then held the bottle ready to pour another. But both Ned and Jim waved him off.

Shorty tossed the shot back, slammed the glass back on the bar and said, "Now I'm ready for breakfast." He tossed a quarter on the bar and followed his partners into the dining area. He almost bumped into Ned's back when his two partners both stopped suddenly. Then he saw what had caused them to stop so abruptly. Sheriff Barnes was sitting at a table in the back corner of the room, eating breakfast.

"Well, lookee here," Ned said. "Good mornin', Sheriff. Reckon you're gonna need a good breakfast this mornin'. I hear tell, you're gonna try Curly Price this mornin' on charges of holdin' up a stagecoach. Is that a fact?"

"I think you know that's a fact," Sheriff Barnes answered. "He's gonna be tried by a Texas state official, and any interference will be dealt with in proper fashion."

Ned turned and looked at his two partners. "Hear that, boys? Dealt with in proper fashion." Back to the sheriff then, he said, "Well, I'm glad to hear it 'cause we're here as witnesses. We're ready to tell the judge that Curly was with us at the time you say that stage was robbed, so he couldn'ta been robbin' no stage."

"Well, I have to say I believe you," Barnes replied. "I expect he was with you, all right, and you were all four at the stagecoach robbery. And from the short time I've known your friend Curly, I believe he might be about ready to tell the judge you were with him at the time. The judge is inclined to lighten his sentence for that information."

Ned didn't respond at once, not sure if the sheriff was bluffing or not, but then a wide smile slowly formed on his face. "I don't know, Sheriff, if any of that was true, we sure as hell wouldn'ta come back to speak up for poor ol' Curly." Then he got deadly serious for a moment. "But we came here to get Curly and we don't plan to leave without him."

"That's mighty strong talk, but you need to know this. My actions are gonna follow the rulin' of the judge's decision. And if Curly leaves here, it'll only be when the deputy marshals come to transport him to Huntsville Unit. If you start trouble in my town, you'll have to deal with me." Arlene walked out of the kitchen at that moment, so the sheriff said, "Arlene, these gentlemen want to have breakfast, so show them to a table. And I'll have another shot of coffee, if you don't mind."

"Enjoy your breakfast, Sheriff," Ned responded. "You never know when it will be your last one."

"Thanks, I will," Barnes replied. He was determined to uphold the law, and he refused to cave in before veiled threats. But he knew he was one man against three conscienceless gunslingers, and he didn't know if he could fight all three of them. He knew without doubt Judge Wick Justice would rule Curly guilty and sentence him to prison. He was going to need a helluva lot of luck. That, or take the sensible way and let them take Curly. He really didn't want any more coffee. He only ordered another cup to demonstrate that he was not cowered by the three drifters. So he had to force himself to drink half of it before getting up and taking Curly's breakfast to him.

* * *

The judge and his two companions were enjoying a pancake breakfast at the Widow Bowen's boarding house with the only three guests left in the house since the exodus of so many of the residents. Bannack realized the hard times that must certainly lie ahead for Sally Bowen, and he couldn't imagine how she could survive when those last three left her. Prospects were poor for new people moving into Boonville with no work for the typical store clerk or bank teller who needed a good boarding house. The judge must have had some of the same concerns for the hard working little widow because when they finished and said their goodbyes, he took her hand. Bannack was sure no one noticed but him that when the judge took his hand away, he left some money folded neatly in her palm in addition to the three quarters for breakfast. He wasn't sure of the soundless words she formed, but he guessed it to be, *God bless you, sir*. It told him one more thing he liked about the man who had seen the good in him.

After leaving Sally's house, they unlocked the little courthouse and got the *Court In Session* signs out of the wooden box, as well as a sign saying no firearms allowed, and placed them on either side of the door. Elwood was actually in charge of the physical arrangement of the courtroom. The judge busied himself with his notebooks and pens, placing the striking pad for his gavel and the easy access to his Colt .45 inside the wooden box. The last thing to be taken from the box was his official robe, which he would put on when it was time for Elwood to unlock the front doors. "John," the judge said to Bannack, "I want you to sit over here in this corner of the room where you can look over the whole court and just keep an eye on anything you don't think looks right." He looked at his watch, then said to Elwood, "Open the doors. I'm going into the back room to put on my robe." He left then to go into the small room meant to serve as the judge's chamber. Bannack could see that the judge was determined to make the trial as dignified as possible.

As soon as Elwood opened the doors, a handful of spectators entered the building and sat down in the few chairs arranged for them. Soon after that, the sheriff came in with his prisoner, Curly's hands handcuffed behind his back. Elwood directed him to the defendant's chairs. The sheriff took the handcuffs off so Curly could sit back in the chair. Elwood went back to the door to tell three men walking in that this was a court of law and they would have to leave their weapons outside on the porch. "You must have missed the sign right outside the door," Elwood said.

"Yeah, I reckon we missed it," Ned Bradley responded. "They ain't no problem. We'll just keep 'em inside the holsters."

"I'm sorry, sir, this is a court of law," Elwood repeated, "so you'll have to leave your firearms outside on the porch."

"Somebody might steal 'em, if we was to leave 'em out there on the porch," Shorty told him. "How 'bout if we promise not to shoot nobody that don't deserve gittin' shot?"

"All three of us are witnesses for the prisoner," Ned claimed, "so you have to let us in."

"Not with your firearms," Elwood replied firmly.

"Look out, Ned," Shorty said, "here comes ol' big'un."

"Trouble?" Bannack asked Elwood.

"You ain't seen no trouble like you're gonna see, if you don't get the hell outta my face," Ned told him. And he squared up to glare at him, his hand resting on the handle of the gun in his holster.

"Is that supposed to scare me?" Bannack asked, his face completely devoid of any emotion. Ned grasped the six-gun and drew it, but Bannack caught his hand before the gun cleared his holster and jammed it back in the holster, then held it there with a grip made powerful after years of close association with a pick and shovel. Ned started to protest, but Bannack grabbed his nose with his other hand, twisting Ned's head around until he was forced to turn his body in an effort to save his nose from being torn off his face. Once he was facing the door, Bannack released Ned's nose and grabbed a handful of the seat of his trousers and hustled him out the door. It had all happened so fast, that Shorty and Jim were as stunned as much as Ned. Consequently, they were too slow to react when Elwood quickly lifted the handguns out of each of their holsters while they were gawking at Ned's exit.

Out on the porch, when Bannack released Ned, the mortified outlaw's first thought was to reach for his six-gun again, only to realize Bannack was waiting for him, his Colt .44 already leveled at his stomach. "Well, go ahead, big mouth, go for it."

Ned hesitated, infuriated, but not to the point where he was ready to draw against a man with his gun already aimed at him. "You go to hell," he growled as blood trickled from his swollen nose.

"In due time," Bannack said. "Elwood, bring those other two gentlemen out here, if you please. Still flustered by the unexpected turn of events, Jim and Shorty dutifully walked back out to the front porch without waiting for Elwood to say anything. "Here's how this thing works," Bannack began. "When people ignore the sign against guns, they're not allowed in the courtroom while court's goin' on. I'm tellin' you this because evidently you can't read."

"I can read," Jim Turner said.

"Shut up, Jim!" Ned barked.

"Well, that just makes it worse," Bannack continued.

"That means you willfully ignored the sign, which is the same as breakin' a law. And we could have the sheriff arrest you for that."

"We've got business here at this trial," Ned declared. "We're witnesses for Curly Price."

Bannack glanced at Elwood, hoping he might know what the proper procedure would be. But Elwood only shrugged, having never had something like this happen before. So Bannack continued. "In that case, we will let you come inside and listen to the trial. But we'll have to hold onto your guns during the trial and return them to you afterward."

"But the sign says we just have to leave them out here on the porch," Shorty protested.

"That's right," Bannack agreed, "but that applies only if you obey the sign and leave your guns on the porch before you enter the courtroom. When you ignore the sign, like you did, then we have to hold your guns until the trial is over." He thought of a little something more then and added, "Usually, we leave them at the sheriff's office for you to pick up later." He could see the heat rising in Ned's face again, so he smiled and said, "We won't do that today, if you behave yourself durin' this trial. I'll keep 'em safe with me, right up front behind the judge."

He took the other two guns from Elwood and followed the three drifters back into the courtroom where they found three unoccupied chairs. He went back to his chair in the corner, and Elwood went up to the bench and announced, "All rise. The court for the Western District of Texas is now in session, Judge Wick Justice presiding."

Once again, Bannack was to witness the simplest of trials, with no lawyers, no prosecutor, no defense, and no jury. Elwood read the charges against Curly, and the judge asked

Curly how he pleaded. "Not guilty," Curly fairly shouted, "and I've got witnesses to prove it." When the judge asked where the witnesses were, Curly pointed to his three partners and said, "Right yonder."

The judge fooled everyone, including Bannack and Elwood, when he told Ned to come forward and take the witness stand. "State your name for the court," Judge Justice said.

"Ned Bradley," he said, looking around at the courtroom as if he wanted everyone there to remember who he was.

"In what relation are you with the accused?" Judge Justice asked.

"I ain't no . . ." Ned started, confused. "I mean, Curly ain't no relative of mine."

"Just tell me this, how do you know the accused?"

"He's a friend who always rides with us," Ned answered.

"Who do you mean by us?" the judge asked. "You and those two men with you?"

"Right, the four of us."

"And you're testifying that Curly Price was not one of four men who robbed the west-bound stage. Is that what you're saying?"

"Yes, sir, that's what I'm sayin', and I'll swear to it," Ned replied, looking around him confidently.

"What day was that?" The judge asked then, which confused Ned a little.

"The day the stagecoach was robbed," he said.

"I mean the date of the month, Mr. Bradley," the judge implored. "How about the day of the week?"

"I remember that," Ned said, looking a little more confident again. "It was a Saturday. That stage always runs that route on Saturday." He hesitated while the judge just gazed at him in disbelief. "And we weren't nowhere near that gulch that Saturday. And Curly was with us, so he couldn'ta been robbin' no stagecoach."

The judge stared at him for a long moment, wishing he had some scrap of evidence to base a conviction on the four of them for robbing that stage, but he had nothing. He was tempted to keep this idiot on the stand, thinking he might eventually talk himself into a conviction. Instead, he said, "You may step down now. Sheriff, do you have any witnesses for the prosecution?"

"Yes, Your Honor, I have three," Barnes answered, causing everyone, especially Ned, to look all around for the three witnesses. He walked up to the bench and presented three separate papers to the judge. "I have three signed testimonies, witnessed and notarized that one of the robbers of the stage was Curly Price. The three witnesses were very familiar with the accused and got a plain, close-up look at him when his bandanna fell off his face."

The judge read each witness testimony over carefully for the sole purpose of showing some degree of deliberation. Then he finally ordered the defendant to stand up. "Curly Price, this court finds you guilty of armed robbery and sentences you to ten years at the Texas State Penitentiary at Huntsville. Court adjourned."

"Wait a minute!" Ned bellowed. "What kinda Shanghai verdict is that? Takin' pieces of paper as witnesses, instead of real witnesses that showed up for the trial."

The small crowd of spectators filed out of the courthouse quickly when it appeared there might be trouble from the three obvious drifters. Bannack, conscious of his foremost duty, that of taking care of the judge, was also aware that Sheriff Barnes would probably welcome his assistance in transporting Curly back to jail. Being in possession of their three firearms gave him a temporary advantage but only for the time it took them to get to their horses and rifles. While he was listening to the judge question Ned Bradley, he had casually emptied all three of their guns of their ammunition. If he was lucky, that might give the sheriff a little extra time to get Curly safely locked away. When everyone was out the front door, he told the judge of his concerns for the sheriff. The judge understood, urged him to help, and agreed to remain in the room where he had put on his robe with Elwood there with his gun until he came back.

When he walked out of the courthouse, he found the three drifters still on the porch, waiting for their guns. It occurred to him then that he might stall them until the sheriff was safely back in the jail. He saw Barnes hurrying his prisoner along about halfway back to the jail. So he said, "I reckon that was a good try to keep your partner outta prison. You know, if you'da talked a little bit longer, you mighta talked yourselves right into a confession that it was you three and Curly that robbed that stagecoach. It sure sounded to me like it was the four of you that did it. I'm just tellin' you, the judge thinks you did it, the sheriff thinks you did it, and I know damn well you did it. Hell, you got away with it. Ol' Curly will do the time for it. Better hope he don't break out. He'll be lookin' for you. If you're smart, you'll get on your horses and put some distance between you and this town. Give people a chance to forget about that stage robbery."

"Just shut up and give us our guns," Shorty said.

Bannack looked down the street and saw the sheriff herding Curly up the jailhouse steps, so he laid the three guns on the porch railing and stepped back. "Sorry, I forgot I was holdin' 'em."

They quickly picked up their weapons. Jim and Shorty dropped theirs in their holsters right away. But Ned hesitated before holstering his, feeling the weight. Then he pointed it up at the porch ceiling and pulled the trigger once, then again, listening to the click of the hammer on an empty cylinder. That prompted Jim and Shorty to pull their guns and check their cylinders, too. "You emptied our guns. Why the hell did you empty our guns?" Shorty asked.

"I didn't empty your guns," Bannack said. "I wouldn't have any reason to do that. I wouldn't have any use for your cartridges. I use a .44, myself. No need for .45 cartridges."

"You're lyin'," Ned said. "You emptied our guns to make sure we didn't jump the sheriff."

"No, you're wrong, Ned. You weren't lyin' when you said you didn't hold up that stage. And I wasn't lyin' when I said I didn't empty your guns. So I reckon ain't neither one of us liars, right?"

"I'm callin' you a liar," Ned stated. "You're a dirty, low-down, yellow coward and a liar. Whaddaya say about that?"

"I say you must think you're pretty fast with that six-gun if you're really callin' me out man to man," Bannack said. He looked at Shorty and asked, "Is he fast with that six-gun?"

Shorty grinned, enjoying what he figured was a coward trying to talk his way out of standing up against Ned. "There ain't but one way to find out," he said. "Are you too yellow to go up against Ned?"

"No," Bannack answered. "There ain't nothin' about Ned that scares me. I'm just not dumb enough to compete with him in something he's practiced a lot and I ain't ever practiced. I'm not scared of my horse, either, but I ain't dumb enough to bet my life that I can outrun him in a footrace. Now, Ned's called me out to find out who's the better man. It's usually a rule when a man calls another man out to duel, the man called out gets to choose the weapons. So I choose bare hands. And we'll find out who the better man is, not who can draw a pistol fastest." He glanced over at Ned, standing there, looking a little confused. "That all right with you, Ned? That's what you wanna do, ain't it, find out who's the best man?"

"Hell, no, you damn fool," Ned blurted. "I'm callin' you out to a gunfight. You're wearin' a gun. Are you too yellow to use it?"

"No, I ain't too yellow. If you won't fight me hand to hand, then I'll have a shoot-out with you, but I ain't had this pistol very long." He glanced down the street and saw the sheriff step back outside his office, so he was satisfied that Curly was back in his cell. Looking back at Ned then, he said, "Well, let's get this gunfight over with. It's gettin' close to dinnertime." His remark brought a chuckle from the three men facing him. "When and where?" he asked, triggering another chuckle from the three.

"Right now, right out there on the street," Ned answered, replaced the missing bullets, then hefted his six-gun a couple of times to make sure it was riding free in his holster.

Bannack walked down the steps and a half dozen paces farther to stop in the street. He pulled his .44 out of the holster to make sure the hammer wasn't set to strike an empty cylinder while Ned walked out and took his stance roughly twenty paces from him. "Does anybody count to three or something?" Bannack asked when he let the .44 slip back in his holster.

"No, you dumb ass," Ned replied, "you shoot when you're ready," whereupon Bannack whipped the .44 back out and shot him, putting two bullets in his chest. Ned dropped to his knees, his six-gun still in his holster.

Bannack looked at Jim and Shorty, who were standing frozen in shock. "I told you I was new at this game. He said shoot when I was ready. I was ready, so I shot him. Seems like a dumb game to me. One of you wanna try it now?"

"Hell, no," Shorty blurted, "we're gittin' the hell outta here." Even though the big man had jumped the gun on Ned, he drew his .44 pretty fast and Shorty didn't trust the dumb act he was putting on.

"Well, take him with you," Bannack said. "I expect there might still be some of his share of that stagecoach robbery left for you two to split." Shorty and Jim exchanged a cautious look before hustling down the steps to Ned's body, still on his knees. They lifted him up on his horse, mounted up, and rode out of town, having no further business to take care of in Boonville.

Bannack watched them until they disappeared beyond the end of the street before he turned around and went back inside. He felt no pang of conscience for having taken advantage of Ned Bradley, for he had reservations about his speed in a quick-draw contest. And he could see no justification in making killing a game. As far as he was concerned, Ned was going to try to kill him, so the normal thing to do was to try to kill him first. He was also certain that Ned, along with Curly, Shorty, and Jim, was one of the four who robbed the stage. Maybe a death sentence was too severe for that crime, but no punishment at all was worse.

Inside the courthouse, he found the judge and Elwood almost finished packing up all the judge's paraphernalia. So he said he would go to the stable and get their horses. The judge gave him enough money to pay what they owed. "I reckon you heard the two shots," Bannack said and started to explain.

"We watched the execution from the window," the judge interrupted. "No need to feel you owe an explanation. The man intended to kill you. What you did showed good sense and rid the world of one more rotten apple." Bannack nodded his appreciation. "When you get back with the horses, we'll pack up and that oughta be about time to eat dinner then. So we'll eat at the Lone Star before we pull out. I see Sheriff Barnes coming this way. Maybe he'll eat with us. I'll tell him we'll stop in Bryan on our way and telegraph the marshal service to send a deputy to pick up Curly."

CHAPTER 11

With help from Wilford Deal, Bannack saddled the horses and loaded the packs, then paid Wilford. He returned to the courthouse, leading the horses, to find Sheriff Barnes there talking to the judge and Elwood. "I was tellin' the judge that I was hopin' nothin' bad had happened when I heard those two shots from over this way," Barnes said. "I didn't know if I needed to get ready to protect the jail or come runnin' to see what the shootin' was about."

Bannack returned the money to the judge left after paying the stable bill, then he explained the reason for the two shots he fired. "I was just trying to hold those three up long enough to let you get your prisoner back in his cell. I didn't figure on rilin' that one called Ned up so much that he would decide he wanted to show me how fast he was with a gun."

"You ain't got nothin' to apologize for, no more'en if you was to shoot a mad dog," the sheriff remarked. "I was darn glad to find out there was one less to worry about. It sure made ol' Curly unhappy, though. He went to cussin' my jail and the town. I'll tell ya, I'll be right happy to see the marshals come to get that boy."

"Well, we're all finished here," the judge said. "Let's go

to the Lone Star and see what Arlene cooked for dinner."
They locked the courthouse door and left the key with
Sheriff Barnes, then the four of them headed for the saloon.
They did not linger long at the saloon because they wanted to
stop in Bryan at the telegraph office before getting started
on the trail to Austin, a trip of about eighty-six miles from
Bryan. Arlene didn't disappoint with her special beans and
rice concoction. A couple of drinks with Sheriff Barnes
and they were in the saddle for the short trip to Bryan.

"I don't know 'bout you, but my belly was startin' to think
my throat was cut," Shorty Reese said when he walked out
the door of the Sundown saloon. "That cook in there ain't
nowhere as good as that woman back in Boonville, but she
sure satisfied my . . ." He stopped talking when he realized
that Jim Turner wasn't paying him any attention. "What the
hell's wrong with you?"

"Hush! Lookee yonder!" Jim pointed down the street
near the railroad tracks.

"Where?" Shorty asked. "What are you lookin' at? I
don't see nothin'."

"There!" Jim said, "on the platform right beside the
tracks."

Shorty tried to look where Jim indicated, but he didn't
see anything but a man outside the telegraph office. Then
he looked at the horses standing beside the platform and a
big man standing with them. He recognized him at once.
"Bannack!" he blurted. "He's come after us!"

"What are we gonna do?" Jim exclaimed. "That man's a
devil!"

"I know what I'm gonna do," Shorty said and ran to
his horse to get his rifle. "I'm gonna shoot him before he
finds me!"

"How'd he know we was comin' here? We left Boonville on the north road. How'd he know we cut back to the west and headed here? Maybe he don't know we're here and he just happened to be comin' here, too. Might be best if we just slip on outta town."

"I'm tellin' you, that man's a devil," Shorty insisted. "He found our trail to this place. He'll find our trail outta here if we run. The only way we're gonna stop that devil is to catch him just like he is right now. The judge must be in the telegraph office and he's just standin' with the horses waitin' for him. We might not get another chance like this. I ain't gonna pass it up." He ran to a watering trough about twenty feet beyond the hitching rail in front of the saloon and knelt down behind it. Inserting a cartridge, he laid the rifle across the trough to steady his aim. Estimating his distance at around seventy yards, he aimed the rifle at the devil he feared. Sighting back from the front sight, he found that the watering trough was too low for his shot. If he pulled the trigger with his rifle fully resting on the trough, his shot would possibly hit him close to his feet. He was afraid that would not stop the devil, only slow him down and make him angry. So he raised the muzzle end of the barrel off the other side of the trough, resting the weapon only on the side of the trough nearest him. By this time, he found himself getting shaky, and the muzzle of the rifle had a tendency to bob up and down while he tried to hold it steady on the broad back of the devil. The more he tried to hold his rifle steady, the more the front sight began to waver to the point where he just couldn't hold it steady. So his only alternative was to anticipate the waver and try to time his shot to pull the trigger when the sight was moving up the back of the target.

Bannack wondered how much longer the judge was going to be in the telegraph office. He glanced up at Elwood on the platform, outside the door, and Elwood shrugged. Bannack smiled to himself. *He must be making a speech on that telegram,* he thought. He was startled then by a sharp smacking sound as a large chunk of wood was ripped from the heavy timber of the railroad platform inches away from him. Almost instantly afterward he heard the report of the rifle. He ducked immediately under the platform and heard the painful squeal of one of the packhorses as another shot rang out. He shouted to Elwood to go into the telegraph office with the judge and to stay away from the window. The platform was about four feet high, leaving little room to move about for a man of Bannack's size, but he quickly crawled to a position a couple dozen feet from where he had been standing. Using a supporting post for cover, he tried to see where the shots had come from but was unable to spot anyone. The most likely place was the saloon about seventy-five yards distant, but he didn't see anyone. He wished he had his rifle because his pistol was useless at that distance. All he could do was scan the store fronts on both sides of the saloon. To make matters worse, there were people running in front of the stores, looking for cover after the two shots were fired. Then a movement behind the water trough caught his eye and he focused on it. After a few seconds more, a figure backed away from the trough and retreated to the saloon. He was certain it was the one called Shorty. "Damn," he uttered, for he knew that if he had his rifle, he could have settled with him for good.

Shorty hustled back to the corner of the saloon where Jim had led the horses. "I missed him," Shorty complained. "And he crawled up under the platform where I couldn't see him anymore."

"Well, that ain't too good," Jim said. "I don't know if he followed us here or not. But thanks to you, he damn-sure knows we're here now. And I expect he's gonna be plum tickled that you shot one of their packhorses." His sarcastic tone suddenly changed to one of panic. "Get on your horse!" He exclaimed, "Here comes the damn sheriff!" Wasting no more time, they jumped on their horses and fled between the saloon and harness shop at a gallop.

Bannack scrambled out from under the platform in time to see the two outlaws ride away. He climbed on his horse and galloped toward the saloon to chase down the alley between it and the harness shop. There was a path behind the stores, and it led him to a road leading out of town to the west. He wasn't in time to see the two drifters, but he figured the chances were that they took that road and headed west. He was inclined to continue down the road after them but thought he had better report back to the judge before he did. So he reined the buckskin to a halt, wheeled him around, and returned to the railway station.

When he got there, he found Sheriff Rudoph Harrison on the scene and very much in charge. "Is this your man?" Sheriff Harrison asked the judge when Bannack pulled the buckskin to a stop and dismounted. The judge said that he was. Then the sheriff asked Bannack, "Did you see which way they went?"

"I didn't get there in time to see them, but it looks like they didn't have much choice but to take that road runnin' west," Bannack said. "Where does that road go?"

"That's the road to Austin," Judge Justice answered before the sheriff could. "That's the road we'll be taking out of here." He paused momentarily, then said, "As soon as I buy a packhorse."

"That is a problem, ain't it?" Bannack remarked. "Too bad Shorty didn't aim at the horse. Maybe he woulda hit me. You ain't in too good a bargainin' position to buy a horse right now. If you ain't in too big a hurry to get to

Austin, why don't you wait here a while and let me go on ahead to see if I can catch up with Shorty and Jim?"

"Unfortunately, I think I might have to take you up on that offer," the judge said. "I'm afraid I've spent more money than I had planned to on this trip." The money the judge had pressed in Sally Bowen's hand came to Bannack's mind. It had caused him to wonder just how much money the judge had brought with him. Not enough to buy another horse, evidently. "If you think you can follow them without getting shot, go ahead and Elwood and I will stay here tonight," the judge continued. "I have enough money to cover that. But damn it, Bannack, you be careful."

"Yes, sir, I will." He climbed back up into the saddle and wheeled the buckskin away from the rail and headed back to strike the road to Austin.

"I reckon you might be wonderin' why I don't call for a posse to go after those fellows for takin' a shot at your man, Bannack," the sheriff said. "To tell you the truth, I ain't had much luck with volunteers for a posse. The town's still so new that there ain't a feelin' to help protect somebody just passin' through. I know that's a terrible thing to say, but that's the way it is. The town council told me my job is to take care of things inside the city limits."

"Don't you consider someone in front of the saloon taking a shot at someone standing by the train station as something that happened inside the city limits?" Elwood felt inclined to ask.

"Why, sure, Mr. Wilson, was it? And if they hadn't gotten away so fast, I would have arrested them. But unfortunately . . ."

"No need to explain, Sheriff," the judge interrupted. "I have more faith in the effectiveness of that one man in dealing with the two would-be assassins than I do with a posse of your average everyday citizens. In the meantime, maybe you can help me get someone to move the carcass of this unlucky packhorse and maybe a cart to carry the packs, saddle, and bridle to the stable."

"I can take care of that for you," one of the spectators who had gathered volunteered.

"This is Tom Murphy," the sheriff told Judge Justice. "He owns the stable."

"Good," the judge said, "then we'll just leave the rest of our horses with you because it looks like we'll be staying the night in Bryan."

Bannack figured he was following a trail of five horses. He remembered the three men having only two pack-horses. So he figured Shorty and Jim still had five horses, after dumping Ned's body somewhere. It was not a simple task because there were many tracks on the road but here and there he would see tracks that were definitely fresh. And they were enough to tell him that the two outlaws were still pushing their horses hard in an effort to put some distance behind them. He, on the other hand, alternated the buckskin's pace between a walk and a gentle lope, thinking he would catch up with them sooner or later, whether they would have to stop to spare their horses or they decided to stop in ambush.

When he finally reached the point where the galloping stopped, at about two miles from Bryan, he became more cautious. He started looking ahead, scanning both sides of the road with no desire to provide an easy target for a bush-whacker. When he came to a likely looking site for an ambush, he stopped well before following the road down a gentle slope to a creek with a thick growth of trees on both sides. It looked too good to pass up, so he turned the buck-skin off the road and cut across the slope for about a quarter of a mile before turning west again to come to the creek. He crossed over to the other side and made his way toward the spot where the road crossed the creek. Taking no chance on the buckskin alerting the outlaws' horses, he dismounted well before approaching the road and proceeded on foot. Creeping closer and closer, his Henry rifle ready to fire, he could hear nothing but the sounds of the creek. Almost to the point where the road went into the water, he realized that they might have set up on the other side of the road. He moved cautiously up behind a large bush that blocked the view of the crossing. With his rifle ready to fire, he gently slid the barrel under one of the heavier branches and slowly moved it aside to reveal the creek flowing peacefully across the road and nothing else.

It was a perfect spot for an ambush. Maybe they didn't have that in mind after all. So he went back to his horse and rode out to the road again. He could see the fresh tracks leaving the water, hoofprints of five tired horses. He gave his horse a nudge with his heels, and the buckskin promptly broke into a gentle lope again. He rode only about half a mile farther when he saw another line of trees that signaled water of some sort. Nothing like the lush vegetation that surrounded the first creek, he guessed it was most likely a sometimes stream, depending on the weather. He judged it not likely a potential ambush site, since they passed up the perfect one. Then a thought occurred to him. Maybe they were smarter than he was willing to give them credit for. He was sure now that he was just wasting time. But he told himself there was no sense in being careless, so he turned off the road again and duplicated his approach at the previous crossing.

There was quite a contrast between the two crossings, however, for as lush as the creek was, this trickle of water supported a ragged line of stunted trees. It led him to believe that the water was not only scarce, it was foul as well. He rode back up the stream toward the crossing, no longer concerned about the horses communicating. Just as a precaution, however, he grabbed his rifle again and dismounted. He started to crank a cartridge into the empty chamber but decided not to as a safety precaution against slipping or tripping and accidentally pulling the trigger. There was no grass beside the gully and he could hear his boots crunching the sand beneath his feet as he walked. Suddenly, he heard a horse up ahead of him nicker to question his horse and it struck him. *He was walking right into the ambush!* Then he heard a man's voice. "Shut up, horse, you got water at the creek." He realized then that they didn't know he was there. He walked past the last stunted tree to discover the five horses bunched together in the middle of the crossing. The two men were on the east bank, lying on their bellies, Shorty on the left side of the road, Jim on the other. Both men were watching the road intently their rifles aimed down the road.

Bannack watched them for a few seconds, thinking about what had come to pass. He was not a lawman. He had not come to arrest them. One of them, Shorty, had tried to kill him, so his intention was an eye for an eye. He had come ready to kill, but he would leave it up to them. If they tried to surrender, he would take them as prisoners and turn them over to the sheriff in Bryan. If they resisted, he would kill them. Ready now to announce his presence, he stepped out onto the open bank behind them and cranked a cartridge into the chamber. The metallic sound of the Henry's lever was like a bugle blast in the confines of the gully. Both targets jumped at the sound. Frantic to get a shot off, they both squeezed the trigger as they turned, sending two shots into the trees. Bannack was already aiming at Shorty before he jumped up, so he was dispatched by the first shot from the

Henry. After Jim's first shot went wide of his target, he reached for his six-gun, for his rifle was a single shot and he had no time to reload. He managed to get a shot off with his six-gun but it was after he was struck in the chest by Bannack's second shot.

Just in case, Bannack cranked in another round before he crossed over the tiny stream and walked up to the two bodies lying there. He felt no remorse in killing the two men. It was a war that they had declared. They were lying in wait to kill him. Had they turned over with hands up, he would not have shot them. He prodded Shorty's body, and there was no response, so he looked at Jim and realized he was still alive, although he was dying. He was still holding his pistol but couldn't make his hand lift it to shoot. So Bannack reached down and took his hand and helped him lift it up. When it was up high enough, he turned his hand and squeezed his finger over Jim's sending a bullet into his brain and ending his misery.

He collected the cartridge belts and holsters and hung them on the saddles of two of the horses. Then he searched their pockets and saddlebags for anything of value. He found a good sum of money, what was left of the stagecoach money, he supposed. He went through the packs their two packhorses were carrying, throwing out everything not of a practical purpose to him. He would give the judge a complete report of everything he found. After he used his horse to drag the two bodies away from the road, he took a look at the five horses to see if they were in any shape to make it back to Bryan right away. They were only about three miles or so from the town. He decided they were up to it, so he tied them on a rope train and headed back to town.

* * *

Tom Murphy was up in the hayloft of his barn when he spotted Bannack coming from the Austin road, leading a string of five horses. "Damned if he didn't do it," he muttered, remembering the judge's response to Sheriff Harrison when the sheriff made excuses for not forming a posse. He continued to watch Bannack until he turned toward the stable, then he went back down the ladder and walked out in front of the stable to meet him. "Mr. Bannack, right?" Murphy asked.

"That's right," Bannack answered. "I reckon the judge left the other horses with you already."

"He did," Murphy replied, "and he said you might be back with some more." He paused, then added, "Looks like he knows you pretty well."

Bannack didn't catch the significance of the remark. "These five horses I was leadin' are pretty much wore out, so I wanna get 'em unloaded and feed 'em some grain. And we can put all the saddles and stuff with the rest of the judge's gear. If you'll just show me where that is, I'll take care of it."

"I'll give you a hand," Murphy said, and the two of them pulled the saddles off and stowed them in a stall with the judge's and Elwood's gear.

When they had finished, Bannack said, "When we leave here, I expect we'll put a packsaddle on that dun there to replace the horse that got shot. That's gonna leave us with four extra horses to drive all the way to Austin tomorrow. I don't know how much buyin' and sellin' horses you do, but it might be a good time to talk trade with the judge." He knew the judge would not want to bother with driving extra horses. In the short time in which he had come to know him, he would not be surprised if the judge might simply give the horses away.

"'Preciate it," Murphy said.

"Do you know where they went after they left the horses with you?" Bannack asked then.

"They said they was goin' to the hotel to see if they could get a room for the night," Murphy said. So Bannack headed for the hotel. He didn't have a watch, but he figured it must be getting close to suppertime and he hoped to catch them in time to eat with them, if only because the judge always paid.

When he got to the hotel, the man at the registration desk told him he was already checked in with a room, told him the number, and gave him a key to the door. Then he told him that the judge and Mr. Wilson had gone into the dining room to eat supper. "Much obliged," Bannack said and took his rifle and saddlebags to the room. Then he went to the dining room where he found the judge and Elwood just having their coffee served.

"Any luck?" the judge asked as Bannack pulled a chair back and sat down.

"Yes, sir," he answered. "They didn't go very far before they stopped and waited to ambush me."

"I take it that it's reasonable to assume their ambush was unsuccessful, since you made it back here for supper," the judge said. "Were you able to get a replacement for my packhorse?"

"Yes, sir, I was. Matter of fact, we picked up five horses to choose from. I told the fellow that owns the stable. I didn't get his name."

"Mr. Murphy," Elwood said, "Mr. Tom Murphy."

"Right, Mr. Murphy," Bannack continued. "I told him we'd keep one of the horses that was totin' a saddle and use him as a packhorse. He's a good strong-lookin' dun. So that'll leave you four extra horses. I think Mr. Murphy might like to do some tradin', so you might want to use those extra horses to settle up with him."

"Excellent," Justice remarked. "Did you bring anything else back with you?"

"If you're referring to Mr. Reese and Mr. Turner, I have to report that they didn't make it back with me. Turns out they were better at robbing stagecoaches than they were ambushin' folks." He pulled out a folded-up paper sack and laid it on the table in front of the judge. "I just did a quick count and I came up with three hundred and twenty-two dollars and some change. I reckon that was what's left of whatever amount was in that strongbox on the stage."

"Damn good work, Bannack," the judge said. He shifted his eyes slightly toward Elwood whose gaze was shifted slyly toward him. There had been some discussion between the judge and his clerk regarding the temptation for a sentenced felon who might find himself with an opportunity to keep riding and never look back. With over three hundred dollars and five extra horses, there was enough to influence a casual conscience. Evidently, the judge thought, John Bannack was not an ordinary man and he was justified in his efforts to get him released from prison. "I expect you're hungry after the day you've had. Elwood and I ordered a steak. How's that sound to you?"

"That sounds to my taste," Bannack replied as the judge turned around in his chair, looking for the waiter. They enjoyed their steaks, knowing that after that meal and breakfast in the morning, they would be back on a coffee and bacon diet for the next two or two-and-a-half days. There was no town between Bryan and Austin to break the diet, so they resigned themselves to saving their appetites until reaching Austin.

After supper, Bannack went back to the stable with the judge to show him which horse he had selected to replace the judge's packhorse. The judge agreed with his selection and then he offered to give Murphy two of the remaining horses as payment for his total stable fee. Of course, Murphy thought this was an extremely generous over-payment for what his normal charge would be. Having no desire to bother with extra horses, the judge was then inclined to offer to sell the other three extra horses for twenty-five dollars each, which was less than the cost of one good riding horse. Bannack convinced him to keep the best two of the three in case of accident or injury to any of their horses. He assured him that both he and Elwood could lead two horses and it would be no bother for either of them. Murphy thanked the judge for his business and when he went home that night, he would tell his wife how he had outsmarted a Texas state judge when it came to horse trading.

CHAPTER 12

They set out for Austin the next morning after eating breakfast in the hotel dining room. With both Bannack and Elwood each leading two horses, they retraced Bannack's tracks of the day before. Curious about the ambush, the judge asked Bannack where the two outlaws had staged their ambush after they had ridden about a mile. "It's about another mile and a half from here," Bannack told him.

"Is this the ambush?" Justice asked about a mile later when they came to the creek. "This looks like the perfect spot for one."

"That's what I thought," Bannack said, "but it wasn't here." He started to say it was another half mile or so, but something caught his eye as the buckskin climbed out of the water and back on the road. So he waited until they were all out on the road again. "Now, Judge, if you wanna know where I got ambushed, look up yonder." He pointed up ahead to a flock of buzzards circling in the distance. "It's a little bit south of those buzzards circlin' up there."

"That's where you left the bodies?" Elwood asked. "Just out in the open?"

"I thought about diggin' graves for 'em," Bannack answered. "Then I got to thinkin' that it was the last chance those two fellows had to do something good for the world. And I think they would have wanted to feed the buzzards. That's most likely as close as those two will ever get up to Heaven, unless those buzzards can fly a little higher." The judge chuckled to himself, thinking that was the first indication he had seen that the somber man from Waco ever had a sense of humor.

When they reached the actual site of the ambush, there was little evidence that anything had happened there. There were only some spots of blood on the sandy bank and the trails left when the bodies were dragged away into the bushes. It was a mean-looking place to die, even for an outlaw. They didn't spend any time there but continued on for about another fifteen or sixteen miles when they came to another creek that they first thought might be a small river. When they forded the creek, the water rose to the horses' bellies before they climbed up the road on the other side. Once on the other bank, they dismounted to let the horses rest and graze on the plentiful grass between the trees. Elwood started gathering wood for a fire while Bannack took care of the horses. In a short while, there was a pot of coffee boiling and some bacon frying in the pan.

Judge Wick Justice fondled his cup of coffee and silently considered his "staff" with John Bannack foremost in his mind. He had to wonder how this whole drama might have played out if Bannack had not been here. In all likelihood, Ned Bradley and his two partners would have freed Curly Price on his way back to the jail, probably killing Sheriff Barnes in the process. Without Bannack's presence, they might not have even waited until the trial was over but would have stormed into the middle of it to free Curly. Such an assault might have taken the sheriff's life but also endangered the lives of Elwood and himself. He felt justified for his efforts to free John Bannack from prison. He glanced over at Elwood then, tending the bacon in the pan. He was certain his clerk was happy to have Bannack on staff. The judge didn't doubt that Elwood would also do his best to try to protect him if called upon to do so, but it just wasn't in the man's nature to take violent action.

The judge realized he was at peace in this Texas wilderness, even with the killing of three men after his recent trial. Out here, at least you could usually see the men who would do you harm. He was on the way back to Austin now, where it was not so easy to see those who would harm you. His mind went at once to His Honor, Judge Raymond Grant. The next couple of weeks trials were scheduled that had been backlogged for various reasons with Judge Justice and Judge Grant splitting the responsibility. Some of these trials were of a high profile, with the defendant a well-known figure or in one case, the railroad. Raymond Grant, being of political ambition, was openly competitive in his quest to hold court over the high-profile cases; in short, the cases covered by the newspaper. Wick Justice had no desire to compete with Raymond Grant in a popularity contest for the top Texas state judge. He had no eye on the governor's office as did Grant. However, much to Grant's annoyance, Justice was born with a better name for a judge, while he was burdened with the name of a Yankee general. In addition, Justice had built a reputation for honesty and fairness for the common man.

Judge Justice suddenly realized he was filling his head with those annoying thoughts of Raymond Grant, so he decided to leave them at that tree. He got up and helped himself to another cup of coffee and sat down to lean against a different tree, one that afforded him casual conversation with Elwood. He might have selected a tree closer to Bannack, but then he would have had to make most of the small talk. For casual conversation was not one of Bannack's strengths. The tree might have contributed more conversation than the solemn Bannack.

When the horses were rested, Bannack saddled them and packed up the packhorses again. Elwood killed the fire and packed up the cookware and the coffeepot, and they left the camping spot pretty much the same as they had found it. They rode another twenty miles before finding a spot to spend the night that was as good as the one they used at noon. After a peaceful night, they spent another day in the saddle that was pretty much a duplicate of the day before, meeting no one on a road devoid of travelers. It was not until the third morning that they came to the first farm with fences bordering the road and a house and barn back a hundred yards or so from the road. The judge told Bannack not to worry about watering the horses because at that point, they were close enough to water them at home. They continued on for another six miles, passing many more houses and barns until finally reaching the town of Austin, located on the bank of the Colorado River. The judge and Elwood led Bannack along the bank of the river until coming to a small creek and a road that led back toward the center of town. When they came to a white frame house and a small barn sitting on a fenced acre of land, they stopped and Elwood stepped down from his horse and opened the gate. "Welcome to your new home," the judge said to Bannack.

They rode around to the back of the barn where Bannack saw an outhouse and a small smokehouse on the other side of the barn. There was no hog pen, but there were some chickens running about and a small fenced-in garden. He was frankly surprised. He knew the judge wasn't married, so he had expected to find that the man rented some rooms close to the capital and the courthouse. They dismounted and were in the process of unloading the packhorses when a man stepped out of the back door of the house. "Welcome home, Judge," he called out. "We was thinkin' you might show up any day now." He walked out to the barn, staring openly at the big stranger with them. "Mr. Wilson," he acknowledged Elwood.

"Thank you, Henry," the judge responded. "Say hello to John Bannack. He's going to be part of the circus now. John, this is Henry Grimsley. He and his wife Lottie take care of the place. Lottie does the cooking and there's not a better cook in the state of Texas."

"I ain't gonna tell her you said that," Henry said, "she's hard enough to handle as it is. I'm proud to meet you, Mr. Bannack." He extended his hand.

Bannack took his hand and said, "It's just John or Bannack. Nobody calls me mister."

"Yes, sir, whatever you say," Henry said when he got his hand back. He was wondering where the judge intended to put the lethal-looking stranger. There were only three bedrooms in the judge's house. The judge slept in the master bedroom, Elwood slept in the small one, and he and his wife slept in the third one.

Justice could read the uncertainty in Henry's face. Guessing what was causing it, he said, "I know you're wondering where we're going to find a place for John to sleep. He's a little too big to tuck in a corner, but we'll work something out." Bannack didn't say anything but turned and led his horse to the barn. "That's the first thing he worries about," the judge told Henry. "He's got to make sure that buckskin gelding is going to have what he needs."

"Well, that tells me he's got his priorities right," Henry said. "Lottie'll have some dinner for you pretty quick. Soon as we saw you come in the gate, she threw some more wood in the stove and started to mix up some biscuits."

"I can always count on Lottie," the judge said. He glanced at the barn again when he saw Bannack standing in the doorway of the hayloft for a few seconds before disappearing again. "Elwood and I better help John take care of the horses. Then we'll go in and see Lottie. Tell her we'll be right in after we turn the horses out in the pasture."

Henry went back to the house and the judge and Elwood went to the barn to help Bannack. On the way, Elwood summoned the courage to speak his mind. "I think I know what you're thinking, sir. But my room's the smallest of the three bedrooms, and that little cot I sleep on isn't really big enough for me. I don't know how we're going to have enough space to walk in and out of the room if he throws his bedroll on the floor."

"I know, I know," Justice responded. "We'll find someplace to put him, if I have to take him in my room."

"How's that?" Bannack asked, just coming out of the barn door in time to catch a word and thinking the judge had directed it at him.

"Nothing, John," the judge answered. "Elwood and I were just talking about where you might be most comfortable to sleep."

"I've already decided on that," Bannack said. "Got my spot all picked out. Gonna spread my bedroll on some of that fresh hay in the back of the hayloft. It's a nice dry loft and I'll be handy to the pump and the outhouse. And I'll be able to keep an eye on my horse. I hope you don't mind if I don't wanna stay in the house."

"No, no," the judge quickly responded, "no offense, whatever you prefer." He heard Elwood exhale. "Let's unpack everything and put it away," the judge continued, "fill up the water trough, and turn the horses out to graze. Then we'll take the rest of our things in the house and see what Lottie was able to fix. I know for sure she's baking biscuits. I can smell 'em."

"I'm glad to see you and Mr. Wilson made it back from your trip all right," Lottie greeted the judge and Elwood when they came in the kitchen door. "Did you have a good trip?"

"Howdy, Lottie," the judge replied. "Why, yes we had a good trip. Any trip we take that ends up back here is a good one. Right, Elwood?"

"Yes, sir, that's a fact," Elwood answered.

"I see you brought someone with . . ." she started, seeing the figure behind them when he was still standing on the steps. But she was startled when they moved on into the kitchen, giving John room to step up into the doorway. "Good grief," she uttered, then quickly recovered her wits. "Henry, you didn't tell me the judge brought a giant home to dinner. I hope I cooked enough of that ham." A tiny woman with a husky voice, she hurried forward to welcome Bannack, aware at once that he was not accustomed to the company of women of a playful nature. "Welcome to my home . . ." she started again, then said, "I should say Judge Justice's home. But it's my kitchen, so welcome to my kitchen." She paused again and looked around her. "Isn't anybody gonna tell me his name?"

"John, ma'am," he said. "My name's John."

"Well, I'm pleased to meet you, John. I'm Lottie, and I hope you'll enjoy this little bit of dinner I put together." She looked around at the other men standing in her kitchen with a look of amazement that they had allowed her to embarrass John as well as herself. "Sit down at the table, and I'll pour the coffee. The biscuits are ready to come out any minute now."

Bannack was not sure if Lottie was the best cook in Texas, as the judge had claimed, but he decided she must certainly be in the running for the title. Then he reminded himself that he had enjoyed the cooking almost everywhere, in hotel dining rooms and cafés and even saloons after his years of eating prison food. He wondered if he was a fair judge. He decided he was impressed that she had made an enjoyable dinner out of such plain fare. When he finished eating, he thanked her for the food and went out to the barn to set up his quarters in the hayloft. Henry offered to go with him to help but was glad when Bannack insisted it wasn't going to be that big a job. So Henry remained at the table to finish up the coffee with the judge and Elwood. "He looks like he don't need no help doin' anything he takes a notion to do," Henry remarked after Bannack left.

"He's pretty capable at his job," the judge said.

"When I saw him walk in the door, I thought you must have brought one of the prisoners back from that prison over in Huntsville," Lottie remarked. The judge and Elwood exchanged a quick glance, both thinking it best not to enlighten her just yet.

After dinner, Elwood asked the judge what he was going to do with Bannack while he was back at his duties in Austin. "I'm gonna take him with us when we go into the office this afternoon," the judge said. "I want him to see where we work and where everything is, since he's never been here before."

"I wasn't sure if you wanted to take a chance on Judge Grant seeing him, since he's the one who sentenced him to twenty years."

The judge could see that Elwood had a legitimate concern, but he wanted Grant to know that he had such a man working for him, just in case he got any underhanded ideas. Grant was sometimes visited by Trace Every, a slick pistolero who lived off his reputation as a fast gun. Grant would certainly deny it, but Judge Justice was certain the gunslinger was a tool Grant used for vengeful purposes. Elwood was much of the opinion that Judge Justice hired Bannack in response to Grant's hiring of Trace Every. He was not that confident in Justice's decision, knowing how inexperienced Bannack was in drawing his recently acquired revolver against a man of Every's skill. He likened it to buying a can opener when all your food came in paper sacks. The only equalizer that Elwood could imagine might be that Bannack would be hard to stop and might be like putting down a buffalo.

Elwood was not alone in wondering what Bannack's role was going to be while the judge was in Austin. Bannack, himself, was puzzled when he tried to imagine what his job was to be. He finally concluded that he was there to help in the event of a threat upon the judge's life and all the rest of the time he was to make himself available to run errands or sweep the floors. "Hell, I reckon it's better than bein' in prison," he muttered. Then another thought occurred to him, one that he had not entertained until that moment. He wondered if he should try to contact his brother and Kitty, now that he was legally out of prison. It might possibly bring them some relief to know he was a free man. At least, he supposed he was free. Judge Justice said he was, but it didn't seem like he was free. And no matter what his pardon said, he couldn't help believing that, if he decided to tell the judge he was quitting, they would send him right back to prison. He was a free man as long as he did the judge's bidding. It was better than prison, so he decided to appreciate the fact that the judge was a kind and considerate master. Maybe he could write a letter and send it to Warren and Kitty to let them know he was no longer in prison. But would they feel they were then obligated to tell him to return to their home to put the burden back as it was before. He liked to think that his having gone to prison made it a little easier for them to get by. "It's better to just let the situation lay right where it is," he said. "Why bring it back to their minds?"

"John, you up there?" Elwood called from the barn below.

"Yep," Bannack answered. "I'm up here in my bachelor's quarters."

"Come on down," Elwood said. "We're going into town. The judge wants to let everybody know he's back and ready to go to work. It'll give you a chance to see where we work when we're in town."

Bannack slid down the ladder to the hayloft and went out in the pasture to get his and the judge's horse while Elwood got his. While they were saddling the horses, Bannack asked, "What's the judge gonna do with the two extra horses we brought back with us?"

"He's probably going to sell them," Elwood answered. "We don't usually keep extra horses on this little pasture. Why?"

"No reason. I was just wonderin'."

"He might give you that job," Elwood said, "to take those two horses to the stable and see what you can get for them. Might give you something to do while the judge and I are in the courthouse. Are you any good at selling horses?"

"You don't get much experience sellin' horses where I've spent the last five years. I don't know what good saddle horses are sellin' for now. But I know enough about horses to know how old they are and what kind of shape they're in. And both of those horses are about ready to hitch up to a buggy or pull a plow. So I hope he don't send me to trade 'em 'cause I might come back short of the money he expected for 'em."

Elwood chuckled. "I'll tell him you don't think much of those horses. Maybe you can get something for the saddles."

"You and the judge were a long way from home when you went all the way over to Huntsville, weren't you?"

"We go farther than that," Elwood answered, "all the way to Houston. That's what a circuit court judge does. We go south as far as San Antonio and west as far as Fredericksburg. Judge Raymond Grant rides a circuit north of Austin. That's why he was the judge at your trial in Waco."

"I reckon if I had known then what I know now, I would have come down here to rob a bank, instead of robbin' one in Waco," Bannack said.

"Did you really rob that bank?" Elwood asked, finding it hard to believe after knowing more about the man.

"That's what the witnesses said," he answered, still reluctant to risk any possibility of throwing suspicion on his brother. "And Sheriff Barnes said the same when he caught me holding a sack full of the bank's money."

Elwood slowly shook his head, still finding it hard to believe. "Well, let's go get His Honor," he playfully suggested, "and go into the office."

The three of them rode into the center of the town built beside the Colorado River. They went directly to a stable not far from the courthouse to leave their horses. "Welcome back, Judge," Sam Garland greeted them when he walked out to meet them. "You've been gone for quite a while." He acknowledged Elwood then. "Mr. Wilson," while eyeing Bannack in frank curiosity.

"Afternoon, Sam," the judge responded, "it has been a while. I want you to meet John Bannack. He works for me now, so just put any business he gives you on my bill. John, this is Sam Garland. He's the owner of this stable."

"Pleased to meet you," Sam said, wondering in what capacity the imposing stranger might be employed but afraid to ask.

"Mr. Garland," Bannack returned simply.

"Are you buying any horses now?" Judge Justice asked Sam.

"Yes, sir," Sam answered, "I do a little buyin' when it's worth the price."

"I picked up a couple of extra horses on this trip over toward Bryan, and I don't need to keep any more horses at that little place of mine than what I've already got. I'll have John, here, bring 'em by for you to take a look at tomorrow or the next day. All right?"

"Yes, sir, I'll take a look at 'em. Be glad to," Sam replied. He looked at Bannack and nodded. *You don't look like you're looking forward to it,* Bannack thought.

They left the stable and walked the three blocks to the courthouse and the judge's office at the back of the building. Elwood produced a key to the outer office and unlocked the door. Inside, the judge unlocked the door to his private office. Both the judge and Elwood carried a briefcase with them when they left the house and now they sat down at their desks to fill out more paperwork to close up the trial of Curly Price and order his transport to The Unit at Huntsville. Bannack was left with nothing to do but wait for them to finish. When the judge could think of nothing to put him to work on, he told him there was really nothing he was needed for when he and Elwood were in the office. "So I'm not going to have you sit around waiting for us all day. We'll work out a routine for you after we catch up here. For right now, why don't you take a walk around and familiarize yourself with the town. We shouldn't take longer than about two hours to finish this up, so I'll look for you then. All right?"

"Yes, sir, that'll be fine," Bannack replied, thinking anything would be better than sitting around this office.

CHAPTER 13

Bannack did just what the judge suggested, walking from one end of the street to the other, then back down the other side, looking at the shops and businesses. Then he walked the side streets, stretching his long legs to cover more ground with each step. When he passed by the stable again, he saw Sam Garland out beside the corral, so he touched the tip of his finger to his forehead in salute. Sam stared but returned the greeting.

Bannack chuckled to himself. *I don't know what the hell I'm doing, either,* he thought. When he figured it was getting close to the time when the judge told him to come back, he walked around to the back of the courthouse and entered the hallway that ran the width of the back of the building. Just as he was reaching the door with Judge Justice's name on it, a door a little farther down the corridor opened and a man walked out into the hallway. Bannack recognized the man he would never forget, *Judge Raymond Grant!*

Grant was stopped cold upon seeing the imposing figure in the dimly lit hallway, seeming to fill it like a great panther poised to attack. He could not help staring at the man staring back at him, for he looked somehow familiar and then a name came to his mind. *John Bannack!* The vision looked like a man he had sent to prison four or five years ago but a bigger, deadlier version of the young man. He had sentenced him to twenty years. He had escaped and come to find him! Grant, fearing for his life, backed slowly up to his door and retreated back inside his office.

Bannack wanted no contact with the man who sentenced him to twenty years in prison, so he went in the door to Judge Justice's office where Elwood looked up from his desk and commented, "You look like you just ate a rotten egg." He couldn't recall ever having seen such an expression of disgust on the ordinarily blank face.

"I ain't surprised," Bannack said. "I just saw a rotten egg out in the hallway." When Elwood looked puzzled by the remark, Bannack said, "Judge Raymond Grant."

"Judge Grant?" Elwood responded. "Did he see you? Did he know who you were?"

"I expect that he did. I saw him when he came out in the hall, and when he saw me, he backed up and went back inside."

"Well, we knew he'd find out about you sooner or later," Elwood said. "We better go tell Judge Justice." He went at once to the judge's door and Bannack followed him inside. "Judge Grant's in town, too, and he just bumped into John out in the hallway."

"Well, we knew he would be," the judge said, "since we'll both be trying cases here in the courthouse. He'll just have to get used to it." Like Elwood, the judge was interested to know if Grant recognized Bannack and how he reacted. "That S.O.B.," he said, "he oughta be worried."

Two doors down the hallway, a discussion about the unexpected meeting was also taking place. "I'm telling you I just saw him in the hall, looking at me like a wild panther getting ready to spring on a lamb. I sentenced him to twenty years in prison."

Clark Spencer opened his desk drawer and took out a

Smith & Wesson revolver. He got up from the desk and went to the door to the hallway, opened it, and stepped out into the hallway. He stuck his head back inside the door. "Are you sure you saw somebody out here in this hallway, Boss? There ain't nobody out here now. This light ain't worth a damn in this hall, anyway. Sometimes the shadows from the two windows make images on the wall."

"Don't try to tell me I didn't see what I saw," Grant fumed. "I remember him. Robbed a bank, and the sheriff caught him right away. He thought I'd go easy on him because it was his first offense and the bank got their money back right away. I taught him a lesson and gave him twenty years to regret it. And he's escaped. Why didn't anyone get the word to me that he'd escaped? They're supposed to alert the judge who sentenced him when one of those lunatics escapes. Look out in that hall again!"

Clark stepped out into the hall again. "Ain't a soul out here but me, Boss. Whoever or whatever you saw ain't here no more. Why don't you pour yourself a drink of likker and settle your nerves?"

"He was standing by Wick Justice's door," Grant insisted. "I bet that's where he went. Where the hell is Trace Every when I need him? What do I pay him for, if he isn't where I need him?"

"I expect he's at the Texas Rose Saloon where he usually is this time of day," Spencer said.

"Never mind," Grant said. "Send somebody to the marshal's office and tell them to send a deputy marshal over here to arrest an escaped prisoner."

"Who am I gonna send?" Spencer responded. "There ain't nobody here but you and me."

"You get your butt over there and bring a deputy back here to this office or you'll find yourself looking for a new job tomorrow."

"Right, Boss, I'm goin'," Clark said, knowing when it was useless to argue past this point. He put his hat on and walked out the door and heard the key turn in the lock behind him. It was a short walk to the US marshal's office and when Clark told them the situation, a deputy marshal was immediately sent back to the courthouse with him. When they got back to Grant's office, Clark tapped on the door. "Open up, Boss, it's me and a deputy marshal."

Grant opened the door a crack, just wide enough for him to see, and when he saw Spencer was telling the truth, he opened it wide. "Good work, Deputy. Come on in."

"Understand you've got an escaped convict in one of the other offices," the deputy said.

"That's right, Deputy. I'm Judge Raymond Grant, and I just saw him in the hallway a few minutes ago. He was convicted for bank robbery, and I sentenced him to a twenty-year sentence in The Unit. And that was just five years ago. I would suspect he has come here to take his revenge on me."

"And you think he's in one of these offices?"

"That's right and I'm sure I know which one, because I saw him about to enter one of them. Clark, show him which one. I'll wait here. He might start shooting if he sees me."

"Do you know his name?" the deputy asked.

"Yes, his name's John Bannack," Grant answered. "I looked through my old case files to be sure."

The deputy looked at Spencer. "You ready?" Clark said he was, so the deputy said, "Let's go then." They went out the door, which Grant immediately locked behind them, and went to Wick Justice's office. "I might have to break that door in, but let's try the knob first." He turned the knob and the door opened to find two startled faces on Elwood and Bannack. With his six-gun drawn and aimed at Bannack, since he seemed the obvious suspect, the deputy said, "John Bannack you're under arrest."

"For what?" Bannack asked.

"For escaping from the Texas State Prison the Huntsville Unit, so get on your feet. Ain't no reason to make this hard on yourself."

"Whoa!" The command came quick and strong from the door of the inner office. "Whoa, Deputy! Who the hell made those charges?" Then he saw Judge Grant's clerk standing in the doorway. "Did Judge Raymond Grant make those charges?" When the deputy realized he might have stuck his foot in something that came out of the south end of a northbound cow, he hesitated to reveal the source. So the judge said, "I'm assuming that's who did. Deputy, I'm Judge Wick Justice. The man you've come to arrest has an official pardon from Governor Andrew J. Hamilton. If he doesn't have his copy of the governor's pardon with him, I can show you my copy of that document. If you're interested in knowing why he was pardoned, it was based on two principles. Number one he was given a sentence far too long for the crime he confessed to, by Judge Raymond Grant I might point out. And number two, he was instrumental in saving the lives of a state circuit judge and his clerk during an attempted prison break that was prevented due to his actions."

The deputy turned to look at Spencer then. "Looks like your boss made a helluva mistake, don't it? You need to have him show you the pardon or are you gonna take his word for it. I'm gonna take his word for it. That's too much to make up right outta the blue." He holstered his six-gun.

"I don't need to see the pardon," Spencer said. "Judge Wick has got a pretty good reputation for tellin' the truth. I'll go explain this to Judge Grant, and I'm sorry to have put you to all this trouble."

"Sorry for the bother, Judge," the deputy said, "Sorry, Mr. Bannack."

"No harm done," Bannack told him.

"And Clark," Judge Justice said as they went out the door, "tell Judge Grant that John Bannack is on my staff now."

"Yes, sir, I'll tell him," Spencer said as he closed the door behind him.

"It's me, Boss," Spencer answered after knocking on Judge Grant's door again.

"Where's the deputy?" Grant asked. "Did he take him off to jail?"

"Well, Boss, the good news is you weren't havin' hallucinations. That really was John Bannack you saw in the hallway. Now the news you ain't gonna like so much is that John Bannack was pardoned by the governor. He's a free man and the really bad news is he's workin' for Wick Justice." Grant was shocked speechless as his mind still held the ominous image of the man in the dim hallway. When he did not respond for several long seconds, Spencer asked, "Did you hear me? He's on Wick Justice's payroll."

"I heard you, damn it!" Grant snapped. His mind was racing, trying to decide if he was in danger or not, for that had been his first thought, that Bannack had come for him. But when he saw him in the hallway, Bannack had not attacked him. "What do you mean, he was pardoned by the governor? Why was he pardoned?"

"Wick Justice claimed Bannack did some kind of heroic crap and saved his life and stopped an attempted escape and that was one of the reasons."

"One of the reasons?" Grant responded. "What other reasons were there?"

Spencer immediately regretted his choice of words. He had not planned to tell the judge it was because of the unnecessarily long sentence he gave Bannack for the bank holdup. He knew Grant was not going to like it if anyone criticized his handling of a trial. "The governor thought Bannack got too long a sentence for the crime," he said, thinking Grant was going to find out from some source, so he might as well tell him.

"Wick Justice!" Grant exclaimed. "He'd do anything to get in my path to the Supreme Court. And now he's brought that animal out of prison to protect him, and who knows what else he's got in mind? Where the hell is Trace Every?" Grant fumed again.

"You want me to go over to the Texas Rose to see if he's there?"

"Yes, damn it," Grant barked. "Tell him I want to talk to him right away. It's time he earned what I pay him."

"Howdy, Clark," the bartender in the Texas Rose greeted Spencer when he walked into the busy saloon. "Pour you a drink?"

"No, thanks, Roscoe, I'm lookin' for Trace Every."

"He's settin' in the back at a table with Paula," Roscoe said.

"I see him," Spencer said. "I didn't see him at first with Paula sittin' in his lap." He walked on back to the table.

"Uh, oh, here comes trouble," Trace Every said to the woman in his lap when he saw Clark Spencer making his way through the crowded barroom, heading straight to his table.

"Ah, you ain't gotta get up and go somewhere, have you?" Paula asked fretfully. "I thought we was goin' up-stairs. Want me to get off your lap?"

"No, you're all right," Trace said. "Let's see what he wants. Howdy, Clark, did you come here to have a drink of likker with me?"

"I hate to disturb you when you're right in the middle of

something so important," Spencer said, "but the judge wants to see you."

"What about?" Trace asked.

"I'll let him tell you. For now, just know that he wants to see you about something important." Spencer waited for his response.

"Hop up, Paula," Trace reluctantly ordered. "I've gotta go see what the judge wants." He gave her an affectionate pat on her behind.

"Can't he wait a little while?" She pouted. "Do you have to go right now? I guarantee you the meeting we was gonna have upstairs will be more to your liking."

Trace laughed. "I expect so, but you don't keep the judge waitin'. He's the one pays the bills, so I can afford to waste money on you."

"Well, I like that," she said, pretending to be insulted. "You think the little bit of money you spend with me is wasted money?"

"I'm beginnin' to think so," he replied, starting to get a little aggravated now. He pushed her up on her feet and got up from the table. "I've got to go now, damn it." Seeing the pout return to her face, he softened his tone. "This is just business, Darlin'." He grinned and said, "The judge has me on a container. Ain't that right, Clark?"

"Retainer," Spencer corrected him. "He has you on a retainer, and he might cancel it if you don't get going." He did an about face then and walked out of the saloon, his patience with the simple-minded gunslinger exhausted. Trace pointed his finger at him and pretended to shoot him in the back. He looked back at Paula and winked, then he followed Spencer out the door.

Paula walked over to the end of the bar to talk to Roscoe. He put a shot glass on the bar and poured a drink of whiskey, which he slid over toward her. "Here," he said, "you need a little shooter to settle your nerves."

"He drives me crazy sometimes," she confessed, tossed the whiskey down, and said, "thanks, Roscoe." She left the bar and sauntered over to a table where six men were playing cards. Roscoe felt sorry for her. Of the saloon girls who worked the Texas Rose, Paula was by far the fairest. Unfortunately for her, she was Trace Every's favorite. Consequently, none of the other men had much to do with her, unwilling to risk a jealous reaction from Trace and an unwanted challenge to a face off. For everyone in Austin knew that Trace Every was the fastest gun in Texas. Only the occasional stranger in town added to his reputation. Roscoe slowly shook his head as he watched her approach the table. A polite nod from a couple of the players but none of the raucous exchanges that usually happened with the other women.

"You wanna see me, Judge?" Trace Every asked when he walked into the office of Judge Raymond Grant.

"Yes, Trace, I've got a job for you and that special talent you have with a six-gun. I have reason to believe there's a plot to take my life by some members of the justice system of this state. They have been out to get me for years, because of my high standards in the punishment of lawbreakers. I've just learned there's a new man in town, who's come to work for Judge Wick Justice. His name is John Bannack, and he knows nothing about the legal system of the state. They brought him from the prison in Huntsville where he was serving a twenty-year sentence for bank robbery."

"You think they got him outta prison to shoot you?"

Trace asked, surprised that anyone in the justice department would be guilty of such a thing.

"I know they did," Grant replied, "because I'm the judge who sent him to prison. So they knew he would be glad to have the opportunity."

"Why, then, hell, we need to get him first," Trace responded. "Just let me get a look at him, and I'll blow him away and that'll be the end of that."

"No," Grant responded, "we can't do that because that would bring a murder charge against you. I might not be able to save you if that happened. The only safe way is for you to call him out face to face in a duel. Then there is no danger of a charge of murder against you."

"Yeah," Trace said. "I like that even better. Is this feller . . . what'd you say his name was?"

"Bannack," Grant said, "John Bannack."

"Right, Bannack," Trace repeated, then paused to try to remember if he had ever heard of anyone by that name. "I ain't ever heard of anybody by that name. Is he supposed to be fast?"

The judge chuckled, "No, you don't have to worry about that. He didn't have a reputation for being fast before he went to prison. And he just got out a couple of weeks ago after never having touched a revolver for five years. Your job will be to get him to face you man to man and then it will be the same as legalized murder."

"That sounds like the way to do it, all right. It oughta be easy enough if he ever comes in the Texas Rose. He might go to one of the other saloons or somewhere I can run into him. Hell, I don't even know who I'm lookin' for. Where can I get a look at him, so I know I shoot the right man?"

"As I said, he works for Judge Wick Justice," Grant said. "He's in their office right now with Elwood Wilson and Wick Justice. I expect they'll be coming out of there pretty soon now to go home for supper. Most likely they'll go to the stable to get their horses. You can get a look at him when they come out the back door of the courthouse."

"How will I know it's him?" Trace asked. "I ain't never seen Judge Justice or that other feller you mentioned, either. Least if I have, I didn't know who it was."

"Hell," Spencer interrupted, "go out and stand in the hallway and watch to see who comes out of office number one hundred and three. You'll know which one Bannack is. He'll almost have to duck to keep from hitting his head."

"Big feller, huh?" Trace responded. "I like a big target."

"But Trace," Grant was quick to remind him, "don't shoot him in the hallway or inside the courthouse. I can't be connected to this thing in any way."

"I gotcha, Judge. I'm gonna call him out for insultin' me."

"If you do this thing right, I'll give you a little extra bonus," Grant told him. "It'll make you a little bit richer, and it'll add on to that reputation you're so proud of."

"Sounds like everybody comes out a winner on this but you, Clark," Trace said. He always enjoyed ribbing the judge's clerk a little bit. "What are you gonna get outta this?"

"Oh, I don't know, maybe the satisfaction of knowing you before you were world famous for beating an ex-convict to the draw."

Trace favored him with a wide smile. "Maybe you oughta test your skills sometime, Clark. You might be faster than you think."

Clark smiled back at him. "I'm more of a shot in the back gunfighter. If I decide I want you dead, I don't believe in giving you advance notice."

"I'll have to remember that and be sure I don't ever turn my back on you," Trace said.

"I expect it would be a good idea if you went out in the

hall now," Grant said to Trace. "They oughta be leaving before too much longer. Clark and I will wait and leave after they're gone." He didn't confess that he would wait to leave because he wanted to make sure he didn't come face to face with John Bannack.

"All right, Judge," Trace said. "I'll see you later." He gave Spencer a smirk and added, "You, too, Clark." Spencer didn't respond.

After Trace left, Spencer said, "I can't stand that smug jackass."

"I know," Judge Grant replied. "He is hard to stomach sometimes. You just have to remember he's no more than a tool that we use for the dirty part of this business that we don't like to do ourselves."

CHAPTER 14

"I'm ready to go now," Wick Justice announced. "Are you ready, Elwood?" Elwood replied that he was ready. "I reckon I don't have to ask you, John. I know you're ready to get out of this office."

Bannack broke out one of his seldom used grins and said, "Yes, sir, it is kinda like a prison cell, only a lot bigger."

"Maybe that's the reason I like riding the circuit better than these sessions in the capital," the judge said. "Do you have that feeling, too, Elwood?"

"No, sir," Elwood answered. "If I have to be honest, I have to say I like it better in town."

They walked out into the hallway and stood for a moment while Elwood locked the door to the outer office. There was a man standing a short distance down the hallway who seemed to be taking a casual interest in them. He was taller than average, a rather slender-looking man, dressed in black shirt, trousers, and hat. Bannack noticed all that in a glance and he also noticed the holster riding just right for a quick draw. The man said nothing but continued to watch them until they walked out the door at the end of the hall.

When they had gone, Trace walked back and tapped on

Judge Grant's door. When Spencer opened the door, Trace said, "I saw him. He's a big cat all right. I'll show him what happens to big cats who come around here lookin' for trouble."

"You've got to get him to stand up to you in a duel," Judge Grant immediately reminded him. "I don't want to see you in my court on a murder charge."

"That won't be no problem," Trace assured him. "He'll either fight or run. Either way, he ain't gonna be around to bother you."

"I prefer him dead," Grant confessed.

"You're the boss," Trace replied and turned to leave.

"Evenin', Judge Justice," Sam Garland greeted them when they got to the stable. "I brought your horses up front for you. They've been fed and watered. I gave 'em a portion of grain, like you said. I saddled yours and Mr. Wilson's horses. I tried to saddle that buckskin you rode in on," he said to Bannack. "But he made it pretty plain to me that he don't want no saddle, so I gave up after a couple of times. I figured it weren't no use gettin' him all riled up."

"He can be cantankerous," Bannack said. "He just needs to know he ain't been sold again, I reckon. I'll take care of him." The judge and Elwood were already in the saddle, so he said, "You can go on. I'll saddle him and catch up with ya." When the judge hesitated, Bannack said, "If I don't catch up, I know the way back." It wouldn't have taken him but a minute to saddle the buckskin, but he wanted to take a couple of minutes to give the horse a little attention.

"Well, we aren't going to be riding that fast, anyway. Are we, Elwood?" The judge wheeled his horse. "Don't be late for supper, though. You don't want to get on the wrong side of Lottie."

"I ain't gonna be that long," Bannack said as they rode off down the street at a slow walk. He turned around and went back to the buckskin standing peacefully since he had returned. Sam watched as the horse stood calmly while Bannack threw his saddle on and tightened the cinch. Then he took a minute to stroke the horse's face and neck.

"Ain't that something?" Sam remarked. "Peaceful as the schoolmarm's mare. A couple of minutes ago, he looked like he was fixin' to kick me out the barn door."

"I wouldn't give you a nickel for a buckskin horse." The statement came from the open barn door behind them. They turned to discover Trace Every, standing in the doorway. Bannack recognized him as the man who was standing in the hall outside the judge's office.

Sam knew him and his reputation. "Can I help you with something, Trace?"

"I notice you ain't particular whose horses you keep in this stable," Trace replied. "And I don't like the way you was lookin' at me back there in the courthouse," he said to Bannack.

It was pretty obvious to Bannack at this point that this was no random meeting, and he had read the low hung holster correctly when he saw him in the hall. Instead of answering Trace's remark to him, he asked Sam, "Does he keep his horse in here?" Sam said that he did. Back to Trace then, Bannack said, "Then I reckon I have to agree with you, he ain't particular whose horses he keeps in here."

"You're like most all big men," Trace said. "Make a lot of noise, but when it comes down to put up or shut up, you ain't got the guts to stand up to the real test."

"So now you're callin' me out? Is that right?" Bannack asked. "When you first opened your mouth, you said you wouldn't give a nickel for a buckskin, so I thought you were callin' my horse out. He didn't respond, so I figured he didn't care what you thought. And I feel the same as my horse. I don't give a damn what you think about big men. So go tell Judge Grant that John Bannack wouldn't play with you. Take your little six-shooter to a saloon. You can likely find some poor soul drunk enough to play your little fool's game with you." He started to lead the buckskin toward the door but stopped when Trace planted his feet as if he was going to block him. "How many men have you killed in a face-off?" Bannack asked him then.

Trace grinned, more smirk than smile. "You'll be number eight."

"I'm afraid you're gonna have to find somebody else to be number eight. I ain't got the time to mess with you right now. You're makin' me late for supper." He started again for the door, leading the buckskin.

Again Trace moved to block him, this time up close. "You yellow bellied coward, you're wearin' a six-gun, so now you're gonna have to use it. And don't tell me it's only for snakes and rats, like all you yellow belly cowhands claim."

"That's exactly what I was just gonna tell you," Bannack said. "I only use it on snakes and rats. Which one are you? I'm guessin' rat." That was too much for the frustrated gun-slinger to tolerate. He reached for his Colt .45 but didn't clear his holster with it before Bannack's right fist caught him flush on his nose, crushing the bone and flattening his nose. The force of the right cross drove him several feet to land on his back, squeezing the trigger of his six-gun in an automatic reaction that sent one wild shot into the toe of his boot. The buckskin jumped, startled by the gunshot, as did Sam. Before Trace could regain his senses, Bannack moved quickly to take the gun out of his hand.

"I swear . . ." was all Sam Garland could come up with for a long few seconds. "You reckon you killed him?"

"No," Bannack said. "He just got his bell rung."

"What's goin' on in here, Sam?" They both turned to see the sheriff making a cautious entrance, his gun drawn, his eyes focused fully on Bannack.

Sam, still recovering from the startling scene he had just witnessed, was calm enough to report. "Trace Every tried to pick a gunfight with Bannack, here, and shot himself in the foot. How'd you get here so quick?"

"I was right outside when I heard the gunshot," the sheriff said. "Who's this fellow? Is he the one Trace wanted to fight?"

"Yep," Sam answered. "This is John Bannack. He works for Judge Wick Justice and although it don't look like it, he was the victim before he decided he didn't wanna be."

"What the hell are you talkin' about, Sam?" the sheriff demanded.

So Sam went through the whole incident and told him exactly what happened to Trace Every. He ended up by saying, "I swear, Sheriff, I never saw anything like that before. I druther get kicked by a mule than get hit like that."

"I'm Sheriff Roger Nicholson, Mr. Bannack. I'm sorry this is the introduction you got to our town. After hearing Sam's account of what happened, looks like you were the victim. Are you thinkin' about pressin' any charges against Every? No? Well I appreciate your efforts to avoid a gunfight." He looked at Sam then and said, "I reckon we oughta get Every to the doctor. That nose looks pretty bad, and I don't know about his foot. Maybe he just shot his boot."

"We can put him in my wagon and take him down to see Doc Bane," Sam suggested. Bannack handed Trace's gun to the sheriff, then he helped Sam carry Trace Every to the wagon.

"You need anything else from me, Sheriff?" Bannack

asked. "I'm afraid Judge Justice is gonna wonder where I am. He thought I was coming right behind him."

"No, ain't no reason to hold you up any longer," Nicholson said. "You stayin' out at the judge's house?" Bannack said that he was. "Good, I know where to find you if I need anything from you."

Bannack nodded his thanks, climbed on the buckskin and rode out of the barn while the sheriff and Sam watched. "I swear, Sheriff," Sam repeated, "I ain't never seen nothin' like that before."

They were prompted to move then by the awakening garble of Trace Every. Unable to understand most of the mutterings coming out of his mouth, the sheriff stood by the wagon while Sam hitched a horse up to it. When Trace managed a question they could actually understand, Nicholson answered him. "What hit you?" Nicholson repeated his question. "I think you just got gall smacked by the real world. The world that ain't got no use for gunslingers and fast-draw artists. Ain't that what you think, Sam?"

"I wouldn't be surprised," Sam agreed. He just hoped that it hadn't earned John Bannack a shot in the back somewhere later on.

"My foot," Trace exclaimed then, just gaining consciousness enough to realize he was feeling pain in his foot as well as his face. "Something's wrong with my foot."

"Good news, I reckon," Sheriff Nicholson answered him, "looks like you didn't miss after all." He stepped up into the wagon and sat down beside Sam. Then they drove Trace Every up to the other end of town to Dr. Bane's office. "I'll see what Doc has to do with him, then I think I'll let him spend a couple days in jail on a disturbin' the peace charge."

* * *

"Well, you did find your way home after all," Lottie said when Bannack came into the house after taking care of his horse.

"Yes, ma'am," Bannack said. "I'm sorry I'm late. I got held up a little while, then I got here quick as I could."

"The judge and Elwood think you forgot your way back to the house."

"No, ma'am," he said, "I didn't forget."

"Well, get on into the kitchen and set yourself down and I'll fix you a plate," she said. "And pour yourself some coffee," she called after him.

He walked into the kitchen and did as Lottie instructed. Both the judge and Elwood stopped eating and looked up at him, waiting for his explanation, as he poured his coffee. When he offered no explanation, the judge finally asked, "What took you so long?"

"Trace Every is what they said his name is," Bannack answered and immediately attacked the plate of beef stew Lottie set before him.

"Trace Every?" the judge exclaimed. "That fast gun that Raymond Grant thinks nobody knows is on his payroll? Where did you see him?"

"In the stable," Bannack answered. "He walked in right after you and Elwood left."

"Did he just happen in or did he come in looking for you?"

"I think he came in looking for me," Bannack said, "because he gave me an invitation to face him in a fast-draw competition."

"When?"

"Well, he wanted to do it right then, but I told him I was late for supper." The judge and Elwood exchanged glances of amazement.

"And he let you off the hook so you wouldn't be late for

supper?" Elwood asked. "I find that hard to believe. Are you sure it was Trace Every you ran into?"

"It was him all right. Sam Garland said it was, and Sheriff Nicholson said it was him." He paused to chew up a tough piece of beef.

"The sheriff was there, too?" Judge Justice asked. "What was he doing there?"

"He came in because he heard the shot . . ."

"The shot!" Elwood interrupted. "I told you that was a pistol shot we heard," he said to the judge.

"Who fired the shot?" the judge asked.

"Well, Trace Every fired it, but I'm not sure he meant to," Bannack answered, reluctant to tell the whole story in detail.

"I declare, John, if you were a witness being questioned in a court of law, you'd drive the prosecuting attorney out of his mind," the judge complained. "In your own words, can't you just tell us what the hell happened after we left you in that stable?"

He went back over the incident and told them basically what Every had in mind when he came to call him out in the stable, probably thinking he could kill him and have it witnessed as a fair gunfight by Sam Garland. "And the shot we heard was actually Trace Every shooting himself in the foot?" the judge asked.

"Yes, sir," Bannack answered.

The judge chuckled delightedly. "Sometimes the Lord sees fit to see that folks get what they deserve," he declared. He enjoyed the thought of the incident for a little while, but then he saw fit to warn Bannack. "I reckon I don't have to tell you that you've made a real enemy now, and you've got to be more careful than ever to watch your back."

* * *

The judge informed Bannack that it was not necessary for him to go into the office the next morning with Elwood and him. "Now that you know where the office is, you can find me if you need to. I'm not going to be holding court until Monday, and that's when I want to have you in attendance. It's the criminal cases where we run into trouble sometimes with members of the accused's family or gang and where I've received threats. So I'll leave you to do whatever you think you need to do to become comfortable with your new weapons or just to familiarize yourself with the town. No point in you sitting in that office all day."

That was good news to Bannack, even though he wasn't sure what he was going to do with himself all day. One thing he decided, however, was that he was not going to hang around there all day at the judge's house. He felt sure that would make it uncomfortable for Henry and Lottie, especially Henry. Lottie seemed to have a woman's confidence that she could manage anything of a male gender. Henry, on the other hand, was cordial and helpful if asked for help, but Bannack felt Henry would be more comfortable if the judge kept him on a chain. The fact that he lived in the barn with the rest of the animals encouraged that thought. So when the judge and Elwood left to go to the office, he told Lottie he was leaving, too, and wouldn't be back until supper. "What are you gonna do for dinner?" she asked, and he told her he had a little money and he could buy something to eat. She looked at him as if she didn't believe him. "You'd best take a couple of those biscuits left over from breakfast with you, just in case," she said.

He threw his saddle on the buckskin, slipped his Henry rifle in the saddle scabbard, and put two biscuits wrapped in a cloth in his saddlebag. Then he stepped up into the saddle and headed back across the river. His intention was to get far enough away from town to practice his quick-draw ability. He was also intent upon avoiding all prospects of participation in a fast draw competition. But he thought it best to make some preparation for a time when he might not have a choice. He was much more at peace when he was far away from civilization, anyway, so he wouldn't mind if he had to ride a great distance to find country remote enough to suit him.

CHAPTER 15

Back in the town of Austin, Judge Justice and Elwood Wilson got a much more detailed account of the confrontation between Bannack and Trace Every when they left their horses at the stable. Sam Garland concluded his narrative once again with the statement that he had never before seen anything like that in his life. "I swear, Judge, I thought Bannack had killed him. Me and the sheriff hauled him down to Doc Bane's office in my wagon. I left the horse and wagon there at Doc's in case the sheriff needed it to haul Trace to the jail when Doc was finished with him. It was close to eight o'clock before Sheriff Nicholson brought the wagon back. He said he left Trace in the jail to sleep off the chloroform." Sam paused to let that sink in, then continued. "I asked the sheriff about the hole in Trace's boot. He said Trace shot his big toe off. Doc had to make a stump out of it."

"Is Trace Every still in jail?" the judge asked.

"I reckon so," Sam answered. "I ain't seen the sheriff this mornin', but from the way he said Trace was lookin', I expect he's still there. The sheriff said he was gonna hold him in jail for a day or two for disturbin' the peace, come to think of it. So I reckon that's where he is."

* * *

That's where he was all right. At the same time the judge and Elwood were leaving the stable, Trace Every was sitting on a cot in a jail cell, trying to drink a cup of coffee without burning his upper lip, which was about three times larger than its normal size in keeping with the rest of his swollen face and flattened nose. "Can you eat any of them grits? Or a biscuit?" Sheriff Nicholson asked him, while looking at the untouched plate of food from the hotel. Trace rolled his eyes up to look at the sheriff, trying not to move his head. He tried to answer the sheriff but couldn't form the words without moving his lips, and that was too painful, so he just slowly shook his head.

"Think you can walk back to the Rose with your bad foot?" Nicholson asked. That's where Trace had a room on the second floor. He nodded his head up and down very slowly. He thought he could make the short walk from the jail to the saloon, even though he was not so sure about climbing the stairs to his room. Any place was better than staying in the jail, however, so he was willing to make the effort to walk to the saloon. Paula could take care of him until he recovered. "All right," the sheriff said, "I was gonna let you sit in that cell for a couple days, but I'll let you suck on that cup a little bit longer and then we'll give it a try." He started to leave him to wrestle with the coffee cup a while but saw his right boot on the floor and was prompted to jape him a little. "You want me to shoot a hole in the toe of your left boot, so they'll look like a pair?" Trace's mouth was too swollen to laugh, but he wasn't inclined to, anyway.

* * *

One street away, in the back hallway of the courthouse, Judge Raymond Grant opened the door to his outer office to find his clerk waiting for him. "Good mornin', Judge," Clark Spencer said. "I saw Judge Justice and Elwood when they came in this mornin'. I was coming outta Riley's Café, so I followed 'em to the courthouse. Wick's panther wasn't with 'em. You think maybe Trace might have caught up with him last night?"

Grant's interest perked up at the thought. There could be no better news to start his day, if that was the case. "I don't know. Let's not count our eggs too soon. Was there any talk in Riley's this morning about a shoot-out?"

"Not a word that I heard," Spencer said. "But Every was pretty anxious to get on with taking care of Wick's panther before he could cause any problems. Did you tell him to come into the office this mornin'?"

"No, but if he took care of that problem last night, he'll be here, all right, to collect his bonus," Judge Grant declared.

"I'm surprised he wasn't sitting here with his back against the door, waiting for me to open the office," Spencer said, "if he did do the job last night." They continued to speculate on the possibility that John Bannack was no longer a threat to them in any capacity until the morning dissolved into noontime with still no word from their gunman.

The man who would soon destroy Judge Raymond Grant's day was in the process of enjoying his. He and the buckskin gelding had followed the winding Colorado River northwest of Austin for several miles before they left it to head farther west into the wooded hills. He was not yet certain if he was going to like his role working for Judge Wick

Justice. But it would be decidedly better than being in prison. The judge said he wanted him with Elwood and him when he was holding court on Monday, so he supposed it would be the same as it was in the court at Bryan. In that case, he was there for the protection of the judge foremost and order in the courtroom secondly. And this was the reason he had ridden off into the wilderness to take more practice time with his rifle and especially his handgun. He was already satisfied with his proficiency with the Henry rifle. A rifle had been part of his life since he was a small boy. But it was the Colt .44 six-gun he wanted more practice with because it was his thinking that if a danger suddenly occurred in the courtroom, he would have to be quick and accurate. And he would not likely carry his rifle in the courtroom. So when he came to a small stream flowing from a narrow valley between two heavily forested hills, he rode up it a little way and dismounted.

He looped the reins loosely around the saddle horn, so the buckskin could graze and go to the stream, knowing the horse would not leave that spot if he dropped the reins on the ground. "We ain't gonna be here long, so I ain't takin' your saddle off," he told the horse. He walked down beside the narrow stream and picked out a target tree on the other side of it. "I'm up against skinny men today," he announced. "That's the reason I'm pickin' on you narrow tree trunks today. Anybody can hit a fat target. It'd help if you'd move some." As if in answer to his request, a gentle breeze began to stir the branches of the trees. "That's more like it," he said. "Look alive." He picked out a branch of the small tree and followed it with his eye until it forked. "That's his hand," he declared. All set then, he checked his six-gun to make sure it was loaded and rotated the cylinder so the hammer would strike a live round. He took another look at his "victim," then turned his back on the target and waited for the breeze to kick up again. When he felt the breeze ruffle the bandanna around his neck, he spun around and fired. He missed the hand target. Without hesitating, he threw a second shot at the narrow tree trunk and hit it dead center.

He repeated the exercise two more times before he shot the gun out of the suspect's hand and did it again on the fifth shot. He reloaded all six chambers then and emptied them at the unfortunate tree, clipping the "hand" fork of the branch three times. He decided further practice would not likely improve his skill. It was what it was. Out of eleven shots, he knocked the gun out of his victim's hand five times. After the first attempt, when he missed the fork and quickly put a kill shot into the center of the tree trunk, he didn't waste any more cartridges on the tree trunk. He just tested his skill on the small target of the branch. He knew he could hit the trunk every time, so if the exercise ever became reality, he decided he would choose to aim to stop the man with his first shot. Never mind shooting the gun out of his hand when his odds were about fifty-fifty. He stepped up into the saddle and directed the buckskin back toward the river, letting the horse select his pace. He was in no hurry. While he rode, he thought about the incident at Sam Garland's stable. He figured it just a matter of time before he was going to have to deal with Trace Every again, if not face to face, then a shot in the back in all likelihood. He had to figure that his reputation as a fast gun was the only thing Trace cared about. So when Trace got back on his feet, he was most likely to call him out for the whipping he put on him. He had no idea how fast Trace was, faster than seven other men, according to his boast. But how fast were those seven men? "I guess I'm bound to find out," he said to the buckskin because he realized he was not going to get the opportunity to handle the next confrontation in the same manner he handled the first. Trace would shoot him before he let him get that close to him again. *I could run from here, I reckon, but I don't know of any place I want to go. Besides, I owe the judge for getting me out of prison and spending all that money on me. So I'd hate to run out on him. What the hell? Maybe I'm faster than I think.* He reached into his saddlebag behind him and pulled out the biscuits Lottie had wrapped in a cloth and was surprised to find a little slice of ham in each one. "Too bad I ain't got my packhorse with me," he said. "I'd go back to that stream and build a pot of coffee."

The object of most of Bannack's thoughts and conversation with his horse was far from enjoying the casual mood that Bannack was. Suffering pain literally from head to missing toe, Trace Every was bitterly trying to recover from the savage attack by Wick Justice's panther, as Raymond Grant and Spencer referred to John Bannack. Starting out that morning with an excruciating limp for thirty-five yards from the jail to the Texas Rose Saloon, he startled the early morning patrons of that establishment with the picture he presented. Not sure it was really him at first, due to the swollen face and the flattened nose, bandaged and held together with Doc Bane's stitches, the bartender and the saloon girls simply stared in amazement. Recognizing the shirt and trousers, Paula was the first to speak when he dragged himself through the door, carrying one boot and limping on a bandaged foot. "Trace?" The greeting was more question than greeting. "You didn't come back to the room last night," she said, telling him something he was already painfully aware of. "You didn't come back for breakfast. You look awful! What were you doing? I waited for you to come back."

"Damn you," he managed to make clear, "does it look like I was havin' a good time?"

"What happened to you?"

"Never mind that. Help me up the stairs. I need to lay down," he said, finding it took great effort to form his words.

She looked at him in the same way she would look at something she might see crawling in the muck underneath an old outhouse. "You need to go to the washroom before you lay down on your bed. You've got blood and stuff all over your clothes."

"I need to lay down, damn it!" He forced between his swollen lips.

"Couple of you women get him upstairs," Roscoe finally ordered. "It's plain he's been beat half to death. Get him up to the room and get a wash basin and clean him up. From the look of them bandages, he musta already been to the doctor. What happened to your foot?" Trace didn't answer the question.

"Somebody oughta go get the sheriff," one of the women said.

"Don't go get the sheriff," Trace managed, forcing the words again.

"He needs to know who did that job on your face," Roscoe said.

"He knows," Trace strained. "I spent the night in jail."

"Oh," Roscoe responded, then paused. "Well, get him upstairs and clean him up. He's payin' the rent on that room. Mr. King ain't gonna like this," he said, referring to the owner, Horace King.

A couple of the heftier women got under his shoulders and carried him upstairs and into his room where they laid him down on the bed. "There you go, Paula, honey," Gladys Hutto, the oldest and toughest of Horace King's soiled doves, said rather sarcastically. "He's all yours, just like always." When Paula just stood there, making a face, Gladys said, "Here, I'll help you get started." She pulled his other boot off his foot, unbuckled his belt, and yanked his trousers off. He yelled in the process when she bumped his bandaged foot, which prompted her to examine the bandage more closely. "I swear," she exclaimed, "I don't believe there's a big toe under that bandage."

"The hell you say," Trixie Howard said. She was in the process of getting his shirt off but stopped to look at the foot. "I believe you're right, Gladys. Hey, Trace, what happened to your big toe?"

"None of your damn business, you nosy whore," Trace managed, lying on the bed now in his long underwear, with the three women staring down at him, two of them amused, the third sickened.

"I declare, Paula," Trixie commented. "Somebody sure rearranged that pretty face of his, didn't they? Looks more like a bulldog now."

"Get outta here," he grunted painfully. "Leave us alone."

"He's right, Trixie, we need to get outta here so Paula can take care of her sweetie." Gladys turned away from the bed and headed out the door. Trixie gave Paula a smile and followed Gladys.

Paula went out the door into the hall after them. "Wait!" she pleaded. "Don't leave me alone with him."

"Why, Paula, honey, that's what you've always wanted, Trace Every all to yourself," Gladys said.

"No, it isn't," Paula insisted. "It's what he always wanted. He had the other men so afraid he was gonna pull his gun on 'em that wouldn't nobody else come near me." She looked about to cry as she said, "I don't know what to do for him."

Softening a little upon seeing the poor young girl's distress, Trixie said, "I declare, Paula, go fill that wash basin with water and I'll help you clean him up a little bit. Has he got anything else to change into?"

"He's got another shirt in the bottom drawer of the bureau," Paula answered, "and his summer underwear and another pair of socks." She emptied the pitcher of water into the basin. "Bless your heart, Trixie, I knew you had a heart of gold. I'll run downstairs and get some more water."

"Yeah, we'll need it," Trixie said. "What we shoulda done was take him to the washroom and throw him in a tub before we carried his sorry behind upstairs. But you can get him in a tub after he feels like he can get up and down the steps on his own. For now, we'll clean him up enough so maybe he'll go to sleep for a while. We'll put his clean shirt on him and you can wash this one he always wears. It ain't tore anywhere that I can see, just got a lotta blood on it." Paula went out the door at once with the pitcher. Trixie looked back at her patient, lying helpless-looking on the bed. "Fast Gun Trace Every, you musta had a bunch of 'em jump on you. You ain't talkin', but maybe the sheriff knows who jumped you." She knew Nicholson would stop in the saloon two or three times a day, and he would tell the story if, in fact, he knew the straight of it.

Trixie was right in her prediction that the patient would feel better after he was cleaned up a little. When they had finished, they dumped the dirty water out the window into the alley below and hung the wet shirt and washcloths on the windowsill to dry. The patient relaxed enough to pass out after a sleepless night on the cot in the jailhouse. Paula thanked Trixie over and over for helping her take care of Trace. "I reckon I oughta be ashamed to thank you for helping me, because you did it all and I wasn't much help. But I don't know what I woulda done without you." She glanced over at the now sleeping patient. "I swear, I still can't stand to look at him. He looks like he stuck his face in front of a freight train." She whispered then, "Do you suppose he knows he's missing two teeth in front?"

"I don't know," Trixie said. "He might not. I expect he mighta swallowed 'em." She fixed the younger woman with a firm look then. "You've really got yourself a problem now, ain't you? When he was all slick-lookin' and had that handsome profile, you were satisfied to be his woman. Now, it's different, him with two front teeth missing and his nose smashed flat. And I'm gonna tell you, his nose is gonna stay that way after it's well 'cause the bone was smashed. People don't grow new noses. So you'd best be thinking about any promises you mighta made him before he ran into that train and whether or not it's time to take a trip to some other town, if you can't stand looking at him." She turned to leave, then stopped and turned back to say one more thing. "On the other hand, sometimes really gettin' your brains kicked in can change a person's whole point of view about things and the way he sees himself. Trace might be a whole different person after he heals up from this. You might wanna see if you like him better with a new face." She paused again, then concluded, "But I know I won't. I think he finally got what he had coming." She went downstairs to get a cup of coffee.

She was still sitting at a table with Gladys Hutto, drinking coffee, when Sheriff Nicholson stopped in to have a cup himself. "Good mornin', Sheriff," Roscoe greeted him. "You lookin' for a cup of coffee or a shot of something with more kick?"

"Just the coffee, Roscoe. Good mornin', ladies," he called out to Gladys and Trixie at the table. He watched as Roscoe poured him a cup of coffee, then he picked it up and walked over to the table. "Mind if I join you, ladies?"

"I reckon we can risk it," Gladys said. "It might not hurt our reputation too much. Is it all right with you, Trixie?"

"I've been trying to improve my reputation lately," Trixie replied. "I hope it don't set me back too much, if I'm seen drinking coffee with the sheriff."

Nicholson chuckled as he sat down, accustomed to the horseplay he usually participated in with the ladies at the Texas Rose. Roscoe poured himself a cup and walked over to join them, since there was no one at the bar. "Trixie," the sheriff pronounced, "I can't believe your mama named you Trixie. What is your real name, the name your mama called you when you were born?"

"Gladys," Trixie answered promptly.

"Is that a fact?" Nicholson responded and looked at Gladys then. "Was Gladys your birth name?"

"No, my mama named me something else," she answered.

"What'd she name you?"

"Trixie," she said.

They all chuckled over that, then Roscoe asked a question he and the women wanted to hear an answer for. "Who jumped Trace Every last night? He came draggin' in here this mornin' lookin' like he got run over by a stagecoach."

"Didn't nobody jump him," the sheriff said. "He called out the wrong man last night. It was in the stable. I didn't actually see it happen, but I can tell you like Sam Garland told me. And I expect it's pretty much the way it happened because I was just passin' by the stable when I heard a shot, so I was in there right after it was fired."

"Who was it? Who'd he call out?" Roscoe asked.

"That fellow Judge Wick brought back with him. John Bannack's his name, big fellow."

"What'd Trace call him out for?" Roscoe asked.

"I don't know," Nicholson speculated, "lack of sense, I reckon, but whatever the reason, he came into the stable and called this Bannack fellow out. Only, Bannack told him he didn't believe in that quick-draw nonsense."

"Then there musta been one helluva fight from the look of Trace's face when he came back this mornin'," Roscoe said.

"There weren't no fight," Nicholson said. "Sam said Bannack told Trace he wasn't gonna draw with him, but Trace wouldn't have it any other way and tried to make him draw. Bannack still wouldn't do it. So Trace said he was gonna kill him anyway and went for his gun. And that's when Bannack hit him square on the nose with his fist and laid Trace out cold. He hit him so hard he made Trace squeeze the trigger and put a hole in his boot and shot his big toe off."

"You tellin' me all that damage to Trace's face was from one punch?" Roscoe asked. "That's mighty hard to believe."

"Ask Sam Garland to tell you what happened, if you don't believe me. Sam hitched up his wagon and we hauled Trace up to Doc Bane's office. Doc had to stitch up his face in a couple places where pieces of his nose bone tore the skin. He was in such bad shape by the time Doc got through with him, so I just took him to the jail for the rest of the night."

"You didn't arrest Trace?" Gladys asked.

"No, if I was gonna arrest either one of 'em, it'da had to have been Trace," the sheriff said. "But I figured he'd already paid a pretty good penalty for tryin' to start a gunfight. I just hope it cures him of wantin' to pad his reputation as a fast gun around here."

CHAPTER 16

It was not until they went to the hotel dining room for dinner that Judge Grant and Clark Spencer received any news about the shooting in the stable on the night just passed. Overhearing someone asking Sheriff Nicholson about the shooting when he walked into the dining room, Grant waited until they were finished talking. And when the sheriff started to head for a table, the judge signaled him. "It's been quite some time since I've had a chance to talk to you, Sheriff," Grant said. "Why don't you join us for dinner?"

"Why, thank you, Your Honor," Nicholson replied. "Sure I wouldn't be interrupting some important business?"

Judge Grant chuckled. "Not at all. We don't discuss business at the dinner table. Do we, Clark?"

"That's a fact, Sheriff," Spencer replied.

"Well, in that case, I'd be honored," the sheriff said and pulled a chair back. He had a pretty good idea why he got this unusual invitation to have dinner with Judge Grant. He had just settled into his chair when the dining room manager, Jim Davis paused by his chair to ask if he would need a plate for a prisoner when he left. "Just one today, Jim, I let one of 'em go after breakfast. I've just got Billy Duncan now."

Presented with a ready opener, Judge Grant didn't wait to get into the matter at hand. "Did I hear someone say there was a shooting in the stable last night?" he asked. "I hope nothing has happened to Sam Garland."

"No, Sam's all right," Nicholson said. "He wasn't involved in the shooting. It just happened in his stable. It didn't amount to much and the fellow who caused the trouble spent the night in jail and I've already let him go." That's as far as he went, knowing full well the judge wanted all the details, but he decided to make him beg for them. He, like some officers in the marshal's office pretended not to know of Raymond Grant's association with the gunslinger, Trace Every. It was one of those associations that was hard to prove but made you wonder about the coincidence of bad luck for people who caused trouble for the judge or criticized his rulings. Trace Every was often seen coming or going from Judge Grant's office, but that made it only a crime of association.

When the sheriff stopped with that vague answer to Grant's question, the judge asked impatiently, "Well, what kind of trouble did he cause?"

"Nothing you'd be concerned about, Judge. It was this gunslinger who's been hangin' around town for a while now, trying to make a name for himself. His name's Trace Every. You've probably never heard of him."

"As a matter of fact, I think I did hear of that name," Grant said. "What did he do?" He wanted to hear confirmation that Trace provoked a gunfight and killed John Bannack.

Nicholson chuckled, as if it was amusing. "Well, this was one time when Trace tried to pick a gunfight with a man who didn't believe in that fast-gun nonsense. This fellow he picked to add to his reputation wouldn't draw, and Trace got so frustrated he drew on the fellow and the man slugged him in the face with a haymaker that made a vegetable outta Trace. He hit Trace so hard that he pulled the trigger and shot himself in the foot. Shot his big toe off. Sam and I had to haul him to Doc Bane's in a wagon. His face is a mess, and he's gonna need a pair of crutches to walk till his foot heals up." He paused then and waited for their response, but there was none beyond the expressions of total disbelief on the two wide-eyed faces gaping at him.

"Well, if that ain't something," Spencer finally blurted when the lack of response was blatantly awkward and it appeared that Judge Grant was speechless.

When the judge finally recovered enough to speak, he asked, "So, I expect there'll be charges against Judge Justice's panther then?"

"His panther?" Nicholson responded, pretending ignorance of Grant's term for Bannack. "You mean John Bannack? No, no charges. Trace drew on him and Bannack just defended himself, and he did it with his fist. He never drew a weapon." He looked around him for the waiter then. "I wonder what they're servin' for dinner today."

A long silence followed the sheriff's report of the incident between Bannack and Every with all three concentrating on the plate before them. Judge Grant was smoldering inside his head and spoke not another word until the word, "Convict," slipped out of his mouth.

"How's that, Judge Grant?" Nicholson responded immediately, delighting in the judge's obvious discomfort.

"Nothing," Grant said and then decided to say what he was thinking. "Did you know that John Bannack is supposed to be serving a twenty-year prison sentence at The Unit in Huntsville?"

"Why, no, I didn't," Sheriff Nicholson responded. "What for?"

"That's not important," Judge Grant answered. "What's

important is that he only served five years of that twenty-year sentence and yet he's walking the streets of Austin a free man. A man so violent, so evil, that he almost killed another man with his bare hands. It would behoove a responsible citizen to shoot him down the same as he would shoot any wild animal stalking the streets." He fixed Nicholson with a stern eye. "Maybe you should have arrested the man while you had the chance. You think maybe?"

"Why no, Judge," the sheriff responded, surprised. "I never thought about arrestin' a man for defendin' himself against another man who came after him with a gun."

"The judge doesn't mean to imply that you should arrest a man for defending himself," Spencer said, afraid that Grant was too angry to think calmly. "I think he means that this Bannack person reacted in such a violent nature that maybe he should still be in prison."

"I know what I am talking about," Judge Grant declared. "I am the judge who sentenced that animal to twenty years and I should have been consulted prior to any talk about releasing him upon society again." He sat there glaring at the sheriff for a few seconds more before continuing. "And maybe Judge Wick Justice should be arrested for getting that animal released from prison. Maybe that's where the real fault lies. What kind of man adopts a panther for a pet?"

"I don't know as I've ever eaten better meat loaf than this they served today," Spencer commented, in an attempt to change the subject before Judge Grant said something he couldn't take back.

"It was good, wasn't it?" Sheriff Nicholson agreed, beginning to get a little uncomfortable, himself. "And I reckon I can't sit here all day. I'd best get back to the jail. I've enjoyed the conversation with you two gentlemen." He got up from the table and fished in his pocket for some money.

"Save your money, Sheriff," Spencer said. "You were our guest today."

"Why, thank you kindly," Nicholson said. "I appreciate it."

"It was our pleasure," Judge Grant was finally able to say.

Nicholson walked out of the hotel dining room wondering if there was any legitimate basis behind the wild accusations Judge Grant made about John Bannack. Grant sounded like he went a little out of his mind for a brief spell back there. But what if everything he accused the solemn-looking man of was fact? He knew beforehand that Grant was highly competitive with Judge Justice, but what if this business about getting Bannack out of prison was just what Grant said it was? I think I need to go have a talk with Wick Justice, he decided.

Nicholson waited a little while before going to Judge Wick Justice's office just to give the judge plenty of time to get back from dinner. He used the time to check by the jail to make sure no one was looking for him. Since Judge Grant's office was only a few doors down from Justice's office, he also wanted to make sure he didn't bump into him and Spencer on their way back from the dining room. He paused at the head of the hallway to make sure all the office doors were closed before he walked down to Judge Justice's. He opened the door and walked into the outer office where he was greeted by Elwood Wilson. "Afternoon, Sheriff, you looking for the judge?"

"If he ain't too busy, I'd like to talk to him for a few minutes," Nicholson replied.

Elwood got up from his desk and started for Judge Justice's door only to be met by the judge coming out.

"Afternoon, Sheriff," Judge Wick greeted him. "What can I do for you?"

"I wanted to talk to you about your man, John Bannack. I thought he might be here, too, but I see he ain't."

"No, I suspect John's out in the hills somewhere," the judge said. "I told him we didn't need him in the office today. Is this about that incident in the stable last night?"

"Yes, sir, partly," Nicholson said. "I talked to Judge Grant a little while ago and he was tellin' me that Bannack was servin' a twenty-year prison sentence for a violent crime."

"Well, that's true in part," the judge said. "John was in prison, but not for a violent crime. When he was eighteen, living with his brother's family on a small farm, he made the mistake of trying to rob a bank in Waco. They were desperately trying to make a living. So he took his brother's pistol and went into the bank and took one sack of money and ran. The sheriff was right after him, and he found him waiting at his brother's farm. His brother wouldn't accept the money and told John he was going to have to take the money back to the bank. I talked to the sheriff. Hank Bronson was his name. Bronson told me Bannack made no effort to resist arrest. As a matter of fact, he said he didn't even handcuff him. Just rode back into town and locked him up." He paused then before asking, "Did Judge Grant tell you he was the presiding judge on John's trial?"

"Yes, sir, he did."

"Did he tell you how long a sentence he put on him for his little mistake, which by the way, was his first and only offense and would ordinarily call for half that sentence at the most?"

"Yes, sir, he did, but he didn't describe John's crime like the one you just described."

"Sheriff Bronson told me that when he heard the sentence

Judge Grant gave him, he wished he had just let him go and had taken the sack of money back to the bank," the judge said.

"Judge Grant says you got Bannack out of prison after he'd served five years. If you don't mind me askin', is that a fact?"

"Yes, it is," the judge said. "It took a lot of work and a lot of time, but we got him out."

"How'd you happen to get interested in John Bannack?"

"I became interested in the prisoner, John Bannack, when he saved my life and the lives of two prison guards and a civilian bridge builder in the little town of Boonville." He went on then to tell Nicholson the story behind the incident on the Navasota River when Ben Crowe was behind an escape event that would have left himself as well as many other men dead beside that river had it not been for John Bannack. "The more I investigated John Bannack, the more convinced I became that he had no business being locked up in that prison. Granted, he had made a stupid mistake when he was eighteen, and that was out of a desperate desire to help his brother and his family. But he served five years in prison, so I figure he did enough time to satisfy that mistake. Then with the help of the superintendent of The Unit at Huntsville, we were able to review John's case with the governor. He agreed with our findings and granted John an official pardon of his crime, changing the sentence to time served."

"So now he works for you as a bodyguard, right?"

"I guess you could call it that," the judge replied. "I placed no obligations on him. He was a free man again, but he had no plans of any kind, no place in particular he wanted to go to. I knew I could use a man like him to work with Elwood and me. So I offered him a job, and he took it. As far as the bodyguard role, I think Elwood will agree that

John has already proven his worth in that capacity this year alone in Boonville and Bryan."

"I wanna thank you for telling me about Bannack," Sheriff Nicholson said. "I had a feelin' he was a good man. I'll get out of here now and let you get back to work."

"No problem, Sheriff, anytime you need to talk," the judge said. "I'm happy you took the time to get both versions of the John Bannack story."

After the sheriff left, the judge turned to Elwood and said, "It's Friday afternoon, Elwood. Whaddaya say we close up and go home early? We're going to be in court Monday morning, so we best try to enjoy the weekend."

"Well, sir, you're the boss," Elwood answered. "I didn't have anything left to do, anyway. I've got everything ready for Monday."

"What's the name of that first trial? I read the charges but I swear I can't remember the names."

"Well, sir, that's one of the reasons you hired me, wasn't it?" Elwood responded.

"Come to think of it, that was one of the main reasons," the judge said. "And that's been a few years back. My memory hasn't improved any, since I've gotten older, either."

"I'd say you do pretty well for a man your age," Elwood said. He didn't want to tell him that he had noticed his loss of memory slipping a little more lately. It seemed to be affecting only his short-term memory because the judge seemed to be able to recall every detail of events that happened long ago. *I've gotta keep the old warhorse going,* he thought.

It was still a little while before Lottie would have supper ready when Bannack returned to town, but he still had a craving for a cup of coffee ever since he ate the two ham biscuits she gave him for his dinner. He had an idea that she would make a pot for him, if she knew he wanted it, but he didn't want to put her to the trouble. Since his bed was in the hayloft over the barn, he could easily get the coffeepot out of the judge's packs, as well as some coffee, and make himself some coffee. However, that struck him as too wasteful and a lot of trouble for one cup of coffee. It would be much simpler to stop in any saloon and buy a cup for a nickel. Most saloons kept a pot going, so that was what he decided to do. He had not had an opportunity to patronize any of the saloons in town, so he just picked the first one he came to. "The Texas Rose," he read the name aloud. "Sounds like they'd have a good cup of coffee." He pulled the buckskin over to the boardwalk and stepped down from the saddle, looped his reins over the hitching rail, and walked through the batwing doors. The saloon seemed moderately busy for a Friday afternoon. As usual, he attracted some looks of curiosity, one especially from the bartender as he walked on over to the bar.

"Howdy, stranger," Roscoe greeted him. "What can I pour you?"

"Howdy," Bannack returned. "Tell you the truth, I'd like to have a cup of coffee, if you happen to have any for sale."

Roscoe couldn't help but chuckle. "As a matter of fact, I do have some fresh coffee. Those women settin' around the table in the corner make sure that coffeepot stays charged up. Two of 'em are livin' on coffee. I'll get you a cup, and I'll have one with you."

He walked over to the coffeepot on the sideboard behind the table where Gladys and Trixie were sitting. "Who is that?" Trixie asked.

"Oh, did you notice him?" Roscoe japed.

"Who is he?" Gladys asked. "It's hard for a man like that to sneak in without gettin' noticed."

"I don't know who he is," Roscoe answered. "Just a stranger walked in wantin' a cup of coffee."

"He just came in for coffee?" Trixie asked. "Hell, when he came through that door, I thought he was one of them angels from hell, comin' in here to clean out all the sinners. And I was afraid we were gonna lose Gladys. Here, let me help you with that. You're liable to spill half of it before you get it back to the bar." She got up and took the cup out of his hand, then filled it.

Gladys got up and took the other cup from Roscoe's hand. "You go ahead," she told him. "We'll bring the coffee." The two women followed him back to the bar, surprising Bannack when they sidled up on either side of him. "Here you are, Sweetie, you wanted some coffee?" Both women set the coffee cup they carried on the counter before him.

"I didn't want but one cup," Bannack said.

"Take your pick," Roscoe said. "I get the other one."

"How much I owe you?" Bannack asked. When Roscoe said a nickel, Bannack said, "That's a pretty good price for that kind of service. I appreciate it. You treat all strangers that way?" He fished in his pocket for a coin and put it on the bar.

"Every one of 'em, Sweetie," Gladys said. "What brings you to town? You gonna be around for a while, or are you just passing through?"

"Right now, it looks like I'll be in town for a while, although I expect I'll be traveling some of the time, too," he replied and took a sip of the hot coffee. "That's not bad coffee. I had a strong cravin' for a cup of coffee, even if it is almost time for supper."

"Where you gonna eat supper?" Trixie asked. "You know we've got a good cook right here. You could eat supper with us."

"That sounds like a good idea," Bannack said, "but I'll be expected at supper at my boss's house, a ways out of town."

"Who's your boss?" Gladys asked.

"Judge Wick Justice," he said and was startled to see all three jaws drop open with no sound coming out for what seemed a long few seconds before Roscoe spoke.

"You're Judge Wick's panther!" he declared, further confusing Bannack.

"I'm his what?" Bannack asked.

Neither Roscoe nor either of the two women answered his question. Instead, they remained shocked, standing there, staring at him as if he truly was a panther. Then, just to be sure, Roscoe asked, "Do you know a man named Trace Every?"

Understanding their strange behavior then, he answered, "I've met him. Why?"

"He has a room upstairs," Roscoe said. "He's layin' up there in bed, trying to get over meetin' you."

"He shouldn't have tried to pull that gun on me," Bannack said, slowly placing his cup on the bar. "I had no quarrel with him."

"Don't get me wrong," Roscoe said at once. "I've got no quarrel with you. Gladys and Trixie ain't, either. I just thought you'd wanna know."

"Why did he want to kill me?" Bannack asked. "Can you tell me that? I had never seen the man before he came in the stable lookin' for me."

"Because you're Wick's panther," Roscoe said.

"Stop calling me that. I'm not anybody's panther. My name is John Bannack. All I did was defend myself. And now I'll apologize for stumblin' into the enemy's camp, and go about my business." He turned to leave but paused momentarily to say, "The coffee was good, worth the price."

Gladys caught his arm to stop him. "Listen, John Bannack, the three of us are not your enemies. I want you to know that, but this business with Trace Every is not over. So you be on the lookout for that little brute to try to kill you for the whippin' you put on him. You be careful, you hear?"

"What is your name?" Bannack asked. She told him and he said, "Thank you, Gladys Hutto, I will be careful." He walked unhurriedly out the door of the saloon under the curious eyes of most of the afternoon patrons of the Texas Rose. But only the three at the bar might have described his walk reminiscent of the deadly walk of a great jungle cat. Judge Raymond Grant had named him well.

When he returned to the judge's house, Bannack found Henry in the barn, pitching some hay down for the cow. "Oh, hey, John," Henry blurted, as if embarrassed to have been caught in the hayloft. "I was just throwin' some hay down for the cow. I'm coming down right now."

"Don't let me hurry you, Henry, ain't nothin' I need from up there. You know, it's your barn. I'm just sleepin' up there. I hope my stuff ain't in your way."

"No, sir, not in my way at all," Henry insisted. "I ain't got no reason in the world to go in the back of that loft where your stuff is. I don't even know what you've got back there."

"Well, next time you go up in the loft, go in the back where my bed is and you'll see there ain't nothing there but a couple of blankets. Then you'll know why I'm not worried about anybody seein' what's back there."

"I don't need to look back there," Henry said. "If you say there ain't nothin' to see back there, I'll just take your word for it." Bannack shook his head, exasperated. He was still convinced Henry would be more comfortable if the judge kept him chained to a tree out in the yard. "I reckon it's gittin' on about time for supper," Henry said. "You ready to go in?"

"Just about," Bannack said and he pulled the saddle and bridle off the buckskin and released him to graze.

When they sat down at the supper table, Lottie brought out the serving dishes and placed them in the middle of the table for everyone to help themselves and pass it along. When she brought the platter with the beef steaks, a regular Friday night main course, she placed it beside Judge Wick. They were all cooked the same, medium-rare, pink in the center. He took his pick, then started the platter around. "Perfect, Lottie, just the way I like my steak," he said while still chewing up the first large bite, "nice and juicy, not burnt black." Everyone agreed with him, even Henry and Lottie, who preferred them well-done. Their steaks were under the rest of the meat and were the last to be served. Lottie kept an eye on the platter. So when John speared one of the two well-done steaks, she deftly speared it with her fork, pulled his fork out and stabbed the remaining medium-rare with it. She smiled sweetly at him while she guided his hand back to his plate with the medium-rare steak. Her actions confused him at first, but then he understood and nodded his thanks to her. He didn't like burnt cow, either.

Once the plates were filled and the eating was underway, the judge asked Bannack a question. "Well, John, how did you spend your day? Lottie tells me you weren't here for dinner."

"I just took my horse out for a little ride to see what the country across the river looked like. While I was at it, I used up a little ammunition gettin' a little more familiar with my firearms."

"Is that so?" the judge replied. "You still satisfied with the weapons?"

"Yes, sir, I am. I spent most of my cartridges on the Colt and I got a pretty good idea of how fast I am with it. So I decided there wasn't any use to keep spendin' cartridges killin' trees."

"Sheriff Nicholson came by the office this afternoon to talk to me about you," the judge said. "He'd been talking to Judge Grant, and you can imagine Grant didn't give him a very good opinion of you."

"No, sir," Bannack replied, "I wouldn't imagine he did."

"I want to let you know that the sheriff didn't buy Grant's story, and he wanted to get the straight of it from me. So I told him how you got your pardon and he's satisfied with that. He knows Grant's mixed up with Trace Every, but Grant won't admit it. The sheriff is also concerned about the possibility of Trace coming after you for that whipping you gave him. So stay clear of him if you can."

"I stopped in the Texas Rose this afternoon for a cup of coffee," Bannack commented. "But I didn't run into Trace Every. They said he was still layin' in bed."

"Damn," the judge swore. "What did you do that for?"

"I didn't have any idea Trace had a room there before I went in. It was just the first place I came to where I thought I could get a cup of coffee." He could see the alarm in the faces of the judge and Elwood. "I met a woman there. Her name was Gladys Hutto. She told me he was the only one there who had any hard feelings against me. She told me to be careful."

"John," Lottie said, "that woman's a prostitute."

"I know that," he replied, "but she was just a friendly woman when she warned me to watch out for my back when Trace got well again."

CHAPTER 17

It was a leisurely weekend with the judge and Elwood spending a good portion of their time in the rocking chairs on the front porch while Bannack helped Henry build a couple of new stalls in the barn. Then John took the buckskin for a long ride across the river again on Sunday afternoon. He was not particularly looking forward to spending Monday morning in the courtroom, but the judge said the trial would be over by dinnertime, so that wasn't a whole day wasted in the courtroom. After a big breakfast, the judge, Elwood, and Bannack rode into town and left their horses at Sam Garland's stable, then took the short walk to the courthouse.

The trial the judge was presiding over this morning was a charge of murder against a young man named Billy Duncan. According to witnesses, Billy and his brothers, Davy and Luke were drinking heavily in the Briar Patch, a small saloon at the south end of town. A couple of cowhands from a ranch three miles from Austin complained that the Duncan brothers were getting too rowdy and making too much noise. One thing led to another and it ended up with one of the cowhands being shot in the back and the accused shooter was Billy Duncan, according to witnesses at the Briar Patch. With a warrant for his arrest, a couple of deputy US marshals were sent to Caleb Duncan's little ranch to take Billy back to Austin to stand trial. Warned beforehand of the likelihood of armed resistance to the arrest by the whole Duncan clan, the two deputies decided it in their best interest to kidnap their suspect if the opportunity could be arranged. With that in mind, they found a place where they could watch the house without being seen. And from that lookout, they watched the Duncan men come out after breakfast to go to work. Studying each Duncan through their field glasses, they identified Billy by his lack of a mustache, in comparison to his two brothers, who grew thick bushy ones. This supplied by the eyewitnesses. All three brothers went into the barn and came out minutes later on horses. They split up then, with one of the brothers riding out in one direction while Billy and his other brother rode in a different direction.

It would have been better had Billy been the one who rode off alone, but at least two against two was better than two against three. They followed Billy and his brother Davy until they had an opportunity to surprise them. Then they made their arrest, taking the guns of both, but putting Davy's gun in his saddlebag. They rode away with Billy as well as Davy's horse, leaving him on foot. They told him they would let the horse go free after a mile but actually let the horse go after about two and a half miles. So Billy Duncan was arrested and taken back for trial, avoiding what certainly would have been a gunbattle with the odds against the deputies. Sunday night, Billy was transported from his jail cell to a holding cell in the courthouse.

Concerned about the chance of disruption of the proceedings by members of the Duncan family, the US marshal assigned the two deputy marshals who had made the arrest to attend the trial. Consequently, the judge, Elwood, and Bannack were stopped when they entered the back door of the courtroom. One look at the menacing figure with the judge and Elwood caused immediate concern for the deputy marshal at that door. "Just hold it right there," the deputy demanded. "There ain't gonna be no guns allowed in the courtroom. What are you doin', comin' in the back door, anyway? Go back and come in the front door and leave your gun with the deputy there." He rested his hand on the handle of his six-gun as he watched Bannack carefully.

"I'm Judge Wick Justice," the judge said. "I'm the presiding judge over this trial this morning. This is John Bannack. He works for me and is authorized to wear a sidearm. His job is to ensure order, since in most cases, we don't have the services of the US Marshal Service. So, in the event of trouble in this trial, he'll be one more to help you and the other deputy." He waited for the deputy to think it over.

"All right then," the deputy finally said, "since you're the judge, I reckon it's all right. I'll tell the other deputy." He stepped aside and nodded to Bannack as they walked into the little room behind the bench.

A little before nine, Elwood went into the courtroom to make sure everything was where it should be to please the judge before he arranged his pads and papers in preparation for recording the trial. Bannack went with him to position himself to watch the proceedings. There were three eyewitnesses on the front row and a few spectators behind them in the courtroom, all of whom were the usual spectators at every trial. Bannack heard what sounded like an argument outside the front door, so he decided to see what the trouble was. Maybe that's what I'm supposed to do, he thought, still not sure exactly what his duties were. He found the two deputy marshals confronted by three men obviously arguing about the weapons the three men were wearing. The older of the three looked up and pointed at

Bannack. "He's wearin' a gun and he just came from inside the courtroom."

One of the two deputies gave Bannack a startled look. The other, who was the deputy at the back door earlier, responded. "He's an official of the court. He's authorized to wear a weapon. You oughta know there's a city ordinance against wearin' a side arm in this part of town. You have to leave those weapons out here, if you wanna go inside and watch the trial."

"Damn it, I done told you," Caleb Duncan complained, "we're family. Billy Duncan is my son and these two boys are his brothers. We got a right to hear his trial."

"Yes, sir, you do, but your guns don't," Bannack said. "So shuck 'em off and give 'em to the deputy marshal. The trial's fixin' to start."

No one made a move for several seconds as Caleb considered his chances against the two lawmen and the formidable figure standing in the doorway. "All right, boys," he finally told his sons, "I reckon we have to respect the law." He unbuckled his gun belt and handed it to one of the deputies. Davy and Luke reluctantly did the same. One of the deputies took all three guns and placed them in a chair by the door. "What's gonna keep somebody from stealin' them guns?" Caleb asked.

"I'll be right here guardin' 'em," the deputy said. "You can have 'em back on your way out."

They walked on inside the courtroom and sat down near the front, just as the prosecutor, Alvin McClain, a lawyer, walked in a side door and sat down at one of the small tables in front of the bench. Right after that, Sheriff Nicholson escorted the prisoner, Billy Duncan, his hands cuffed, into the courtroom and sat him down at the other small table. Elwood stood up and walked over in front of the bench to announce, "All rise. The court is now in session, the Honorable Judge Wick Justice presiding."

The judge walked in and sat down behind the bench and smacked his gavel down hard. "You may be seated." He looked at Elwood and said, "Will the clerk read the charges?" After Elwood read the charges brought against Billy Duncan, including murder and destruction of property, the judge asked Billy to rise. "You've heard the charges made against you. How do you plead?"

"Not guilty, Your Honor," Billy said. "I never murdered nobody."

"Your Honor," Alvin McClain charged, "the evidence will show that Billy Duncan shot the deceased, Wayne Jackson in the back when he was walking out the door of the Briar Patch saloon."

"That's a dad-blame lie!" Billy blurted.

"You just hold your tongue, young man," Judge Wick told him. "You'll get your chance to tell your side of the story." Billy had rejected the offer of a public defender, insisting that he could speak for himself. Judge Wick turned back to the prosecutor then. "You mentioned evidence, what evidence do you have to prove the victim was shot in the back?"

"Mr. Wayne Jackson's body with a bullet hole neatly placed between his shoulder blades in the center of his back," McClain replied. "It was a little too unhandy to bring it into the courtroom, but Your Honor, the body is on display for you to examine at the Austin Funeral Home. Or, if it's more convenient, I have a description of the wound, signed by the mortician, Mr. Theodore Reece." He walked forward and handed Justice the paper.

"Very well, Mr. McClain. I'll accept this as proof that the victim was shot in the back. What evidence do you have to substantiate your claim that the defendant is the person who fired the shot in the victim's back?"

Billy jumped up from his chair at that point. "I never went to shoot him in the back!" he fairly yelled. "It was a face off and he went yeller and turned on me!"

The sheriff grabbed the back of his collar and sat him back down. "The judge will tell you when you can speak," Sheriff Nicholson told him.

"Your Honor," McClain continued, "I have four witnesses picked out of the patrons who were present at the time of the shooting in the Briar Patch. They will all testify that Wayne Jackson turned and started to walk out of the saloon and Billy Duncan took dead aim and shot him in the back."

"Call your first witness," Judge Justice said.

"I call Jason Rivers to the witness stand," McClain said. A bald, middle-aged man came forward, and Elwood got up to meet him, holding a Bible.

"Place your left hand on the Bible and raise your right hand," Elwood said. "Do you swear what you are about to testify is the truth, the whole truth, and nothing but the truth, so help you God?"

"I do," Jason said.

"Now, Mr. Rivers, do you see the man that shot Wayne Jackson in this courtroom?"

"Well, no, I don't see the man who shot Wayne Jackson in this courtroom," Jason answered.

"You don't?" McClain responded, startled.

"No, sir," Jason answered. "I do see the man who shot Wayne Jackson in the Briar Patch, though. He's settin' right over yonder." He pointed to Billy Duncan.

"Right, Mr. Rivers," McClain said, relieved. "Your Honor, please notice that the witness pointed to Billy Duncan." He turned back to Jason then. "I wonder, Mr. Rivers, if you could tell the court how Wayne Jackson got shot in that saloon."

"Yes, sir," Jason said, "it was like this. Billy Duncan and two other fellers that looked like them two settin' right there with the old man, was drinkin' whiskey and makin' a lot of noise. It got to where it was hard to hear the fellers you was trying to talk to at your table. So that feller, Wayne Jackson, finally told 'em they was makin' too much noise. I heard him tell 'em he couldn't hear the fellers he was trying to talk to at his table, so would they kindly hold it down a little bit? Well, Billy told him . . ." He paused to try to remember it word for word and nodded when he thought he had it. "That's when Billy drew his six-gun and fired two shots over Wayne's head that busted the front window out. Then Billy said, 'Did you hear that?' Well, that sure enough stopped all the noise in the place. Wayne told him he didn't much appreciate him firin' his pistol over his head like that. And Billy said he'd aim a little bit lower if Wayne was man enough to stand up and face him in a shoot-out. Well, sir, Wayne got up from his chair and told him he wasn't about to shoot it out with a damn drunk. After he said that, he turned around and started for the door, and that's when Billy shot him."

"In the back, while he was leaving?" McClain clarified.

"Yes, sir," Jason answered.

"He's lyin'!" Billy exclaimed, on his feet again until Nicholson jerked him back down again and threatened to stuff a gag in his mouth. Then Judge Justice told Billy that he was going to have the opportunity to tell his side of the story and to remain silent until then.

Seated on the side of the courtroom where he could watch the bench and the spectators, too, Bannack kept an eye on Billy's father and his brothers, thinking them the main potential for trouble, if there was to be any. So far, the only sign they showed of causing a problem was when Billy jumped to his feet. The rest of the time, his brothers appeared bored and sleepy while his father fidgeted constantly.

McClain called two more witnesses to the shooting and they both agreed with Jason Rivers' version of the shooting. Then Judge Justice gave Billy his chance to refute the testimony of the eyewitnesses and give his own recollection of the encounter. "In the first place, Judge, it weren't like that a-tall in that saloon," he began. "Me and my brothers was havin' a little drink of likker. We mighta been laughin' and talkin' loud, but it weren't no louder'n anybody else in there. And then this feller, Wayne Jackson, says he's gonna throw us outta there. And that's when I made a mistake, and I'm ready to own up to it. I wanted to show him that me and my brothers weren't scared of him, so I pulled my six-gun and put a shot through the window." He paused to point toward the eyewitnesses. "They said it was two shots. I don't remember but one and I'm sorry about that. I thought the window was open. It looked like it was open to let some of the smoke outta the place. I never meant to bust that window out. Well, I reckon he thought I was callin' him out, 'cause he got on his feet and faced me like he was ready to draw down on me. Well, I weren't gonna back down, but I reckon he turned yeller of a sudden. He started to make a move for his gun, but decided to turn and run. But it was too late then 'cause I drew and fired when he started to reach for his gun. If he was gonna turn and run, he shoulda done that in the first place, instead of makin' a move for his gun. So you see, Judge, it was an accidental shootin'."

"Are you going to stick with that story, Mr. Duncan?" Judge Justice asked.

"Yes, sir, that's the way it happened, just a bad accident,"

Billy replied. "I don't know what the man was thinkin', to act like he was gonna draw and then turn and run. Looks like he'da knowed if he made a move for his gun, I'd go for mine."

"I have to say you've got quite an imagination, Mr. Duncan," the judge remarked. He was about to say more but was interrupted when Caleb Duncan got up from his seat.

"Judge, I've got somethin' to say," Caleb called out. "You call this a fair trial and ain't nobody said nothin' but that fancy lawyer for the prosecution. I got two eyewitnesses right here that say what Billy just said is the way it really happened. Is Your Honor gonna take that in consideration with what them other witnesses said?"

The judge looked at him and the two younger men beside him for a few moments before answering. Then he decided. "Yes, I'll take that under consideration. State your name for the court."

"Caleb Duncan," he answered.

"And what are the names of your two eyewitnesses?"

"Davy Duncan and Luke Duncan, they was both there at the time."

"So Mr. Duncan, I assume that you are Billy Duncan's father and you say that his two brothers are willing to testify that his testimony just given is accurate."

"That's what I'm sayin'," Caleb answered.

"Duly noted," the judge said, "we'll enter that in the records. It won't be necessary for your sons to give their testimony individually." He addressed the jury of six men then and directed them to retire to the jury room to make their judgement.

"That won't be necessary, Your Honor," Theodore Reece said. "We took a quick vote and we're all agreed on the verdict."

"Very well," Judge Justice replied. He banged his gavel again and announced, "After seeing the evidence and hearing the testimony of the witnesses, the jury has reached a verdict. What say you, Mr. Foreman?"

"We find the accused guilty of all charges," Reece answered.

Judge Justice expected no less. "In the case of the state of Texas against Billy Duncan, the state finds the accused, Billy Duncan, guilty of the voluntary manslaughter of Wayne Jackson and is sentenced to death by hanging, the sentence to be carried out within thirty days of this date."

Only five people moved at the saying of the verdict, since all others in the courtroom expected it. Billy went rigidly stiff as the deputy marshals each grabbed an arm to hurriedly escort him out of the courtroom. Davy and Luke both jumped to their feet to curse the judge and his decision. One alone, came prepared for such a verdict. Caleb Duncan reached inside his coat pocket to clutch the derringer pocket pistol he had concealed there. Only six-inches long and weighing about eight ounces, it was easily overlooked by the deputy marshal who took his gun belt. He got to his feet, his eyes locked on Judge Wick Justice, only one thought in mind, to kill the man who had just killed his son. He took a step toward the judge and drew the derringer from his pocket, only to feel his hand trapped in a steel-like vise that was Bannack's hand. He struggled helplessly to try to free the weapon from the hand that forced his arm to point to the floor, squeezing so hard until he was forced to pull the trigger and send a bullet into the floor. Only then was everyone else aware of what had happened. The sheriff reacted at once to cover Caleb and his two sons. Bannack pulled the derringer out of Caleb's limp hand and handed it to Sheriff Nicholson. "It's a two shot, so I reckon there's another bullet in it," Bannack said.

"Sneaked it by the deputies, huh?" Sheriff Nicholson said to Caleb. "I reckon you just earned yourself a little more time to visit your son while you're in my jail until Judge Justice decides what to do with you." Then he turned to Davy and Luke. "Now, let's see what you two outstandin' young men have got on your minds."

"Don't cause no trouble, boys," Caleb said. "Somebody's gotta take care of the farm while they do whatever they're gonna do with me. You go on home. Your ma's there by herself, and she can't make it without you boys."

"Listen to your pa, boys," Nicholson said. "He's tellin' you the right thing to do."

Judge Justice and Elwood, both frozen for a few minutes after the gunshot, stood watching the confrontation going on with the Duncan men. "That, right there, is why I got him out of prison and put him to work for me," the judge said to Elwood.

"Amen," Elwood replied. "It looks like Sheriff Nicholson is going to take the old man to jail. Are you going to press any charges against him?"

"I don't know. I was just thinking about that, myself. I know the man is really upset with me after I just sentenced his son to be executed. I don't know if his reactions were just of the moment and he might forget about thoughts of revenge after he realizes his son got what any man would get in a court of law. Maybe I'll just let Nicholson keep him in jail for a while and see if he cools down."

"Even if he does," Elwood said, "what's gonna keep him from going crazy again when we have the hanging?"

"Makes you wonder why any man would want to be a judge, doesn't it?"

Bannack took the three gun belts from the sheriff and walked Davy and Luke back to their horses. "If you're smart, you'll do like your pa told you," he said. "I don't know for sure, but I expect the sheriff will hold him in jail for a few days and then let him go. He could send him to prison for a couple of years just for drawin' a weapon in a court of law. But Judge Justice is a fair man. He knows how hard this is to see a son sentenced to die. But there's one thing you two have to accept. Billy did the crime. He killed a man and it happened just the way those witnesses said it did. You were there, so you know the truth. You shoot a man in the back, you oughta pay for it. Here are your guns. Which one belongs to your pa?" When Davy pointed to it, Bannack hung it on the saddle horn of the horse they pointed out. Then he gave them back their belts. "Sheriff Nicholson unloaded all three of the guns, just for safety sake, but he put the cartridges in the belts." He stepped back and watched them climb up on their horses and continued to watch them until they rode out the south end of the street.

CHAPTER 18

When Bannack walked back to the courthouse, he found the judge and Elwood waiting for him to go to dinner. "Elwood and I were beginning to wonder if you'd gone to eat dinner with Caleb Duncan's two charming sons," the judge japed. "We decided we'd eat at the hotel today. I told Lottie not to plan on us for dinner because I didn't know how long this trial would take. Hotel okay with you?"

Bannack looked surprised to be asked. "You're the boss. Wherever you say suits me just fine."

"I figured I owed you a good dinner, since you saved my behind from getting shot today," the judge said. "It's a damn good thing you happened to be watching him. Who would have thought that old devil would be carrying a pocket pistol?"

Bannack shrugged, thinking he was under the impression that it was his job to watch suspicious characters. "Oh, I just thought I'd watch him for a while and maybe I'd get a good dinner if I saw anything."

"See there, Elwood, I told you the man has a giant sense of humor," the judge said with a chuckle. "Let's get over to the hotel before Jim Davis turns the OPEN sign around." They continued a conversation about Caleb Duncan on the walk to the hotel and whether he had the potential to create a problem as a result of the ruling on his son's trial. "I don't see any way you can predict what a man will do in a situation like this," the judge said. "But also I don't believe it's my right to send the man to prison just because I can. He made a mistake today and I punished him for it. But I only punished him for carrying a gun into my courtroom and an extra day in jail for firing it. And maybe that was not fair, because now I find out that John actually made him fire the gun. Isn't that right, John?"

"Yes, sir, it is, so I reckon I can expect to do some time now, too?"

The judge laughed. "No, you're authorized to fire a gun in my courtroom if it's necessary, and today it was necessary."

Jim Davis welcomed them to the dining room in the hotel and they sat down at the judge's favorite table near the back. They had not been seated long when Sheriff Nicholson and the two deputy marshals came in. Seeing the judge's party sitting at the table in the back, the two deputies kept walking and sat down at the table next to them while Nicholson paused to order dinner for his prisoners in the jail. When he sat down at the table, he commented, "This is the first time I've ever had a father and his son in one of my cells. I'll tell you one thing, I'm gonna have to hire another deputy. I thought I could do just fine after Brady Quinn left to take that job in San Antonio, but I was wrong. Austin's gettin' too big to handle by myself, even with a marshal's office here now. I'd like to hire you away from the judge," he said to Bannack.

Bannack tried to smile as he responded, "The good citizens of Austin might not like it if you hired an ex-convict as your deputy." His remark caused an expression of puzzlement to appear on the faces of both deputy marshals, since they were unaware of Bannack's past. They looked at once toward Judge Justice to see if he was as surprised as they were.

But the judge laughed. "I better not catch you going after my man, after all the trouble I had getting him released from prison."

"And all that trouble paid off today," Elwood saw fit to emphasize. "And that's the reason you have a father-son combination sitting in your jail."

"And I reckon I'm to blame for that old man havin' that derringer in his inside coat pocket," Deputy Marshal Ralph Curry confessed. "I took the sidearm he was wearin', but I didn't notice anything in his coat and sure didn't expect him to be carryin' a pocket pistol."

"Like I said," Judge Justice remarked, "that's the reason I hired Big John—my panther, as Judge Raymond Grant calls him—to take care of things like that." Everyone chuckled at his remark except Bannack. He was not especially fond of the nickname and hoped that they would soon forget it.

"Well, look who's decided to grace us with his appearance downstairs today," Gladys Hutto announced when she saw Trace Every limping down the stairs. Trixie Howard, who was sitting with her back to the stairs, turned to take a look at Trace, who had been holed up in his room upstairs for days.

"I declare, now ain't this special?" Trixie commented sarcastically. The two prostitutes had begun to wonder if he was ever coming downstairs again. With Paula serving as his slave, he had taken all his meals in his room while he continued his healing process of face and foot. "If we'da known, maybe we coulda talked Blanche into bakin' a cake or something."

"Look at that," Gladys said, "he's took all the bandages off his head and he's got his boot on his bad foot." She lowered her voice to a whisper. "Damn, look at his face. He looks like a bulldog. Either end," she added.

"You gonna eat down here with us today?" Trixie asked when Trace approached the table.

"Yeah, he thought he would," Paula, who came down the stairs behind him, answered for him. He sat down at the table next to the one the two women were occupying. "I'll go tell Blanche to fix you up a plate, Sugar," Paula told him and went into the kitchen.

Left with a rather awkward situation, since he had not uttered a word, the two women exchanged uncertain glances. It was Gladys who broke the ice. "Well, Trace, it looks like you're recovering from your accident."

"It weren't no accident," Trace responded. "That yellow dog jumped me when I weren't expectin' it. And me and him are gonna have another little meetin' before I'm done with him."

The two women knew the whole story of the confrontation between Trace and John Bannack, according to the sheriff and Sam Garland. So they knew Trace had tried to draw his six-gun before Bannack smacked him with his fist. But Gladys said, "Well, looks like you're just about back to tip-top shape."

"Hell if I am," Trace shot back, bitterly. "We got a mirror upstairs and I can see I ain't nowhere near bein' back to normal yet."

Staring at his bashed-in cheek bones and flattened nose, Trixie thought, *you're looking for a miracle, but you can't grow a new nose.* To him, she said, "I reckon you've just gotta give it a little time to get back to the way it was."

"I think I kinda like the way you look right now," Gladys lied. "You was handsome before he hit you with his fist.

But now you've got that rugged look that makes women get downright giggly." She glanced at Trixie's grinning face and winked. "Don't you think so, Trixie?"

"Oh, I do," Trixie said. "I was just thinkin' that very thing. I expect Paula already told you that."

"Told him what?" Paula asked, coming in from the kitchen carrying two plates of food. Looking at the two grinning faces looking up at her, she asked again. "Told him what?"

"That his more rugged lookin' face is more attractive to women than his old handsome face was," Gladys answered.

Paula started to scold them but hesitated when the expression on Trace's face told her that he had actually bought their malarky. "I didn't tell him 'cause I was afraid he'd start lookin' around at other women to associate with," she replied instead.

"I swear, you women can come up with some downright loco ideas," he snorted, contemptuously. "Now go get us some coffee."

Paula took a sideways glance at her two grinning conspirators and grinned back at them. It was obvious he had bought it. She was dealing with the relationship with Trace much better since she had talked about it with Gladys. Thinking at first that she could not stand to be with him after his devastating beating and humiliation at the hands of Judge Justice's panther, she decided to stick it out until his money ran out. She figured that when that happened, he would simply leave, drift away, just like he had drifted onto the scene in Austin. And when that happened, she imagined she would wake up one morning to find him gone without a goodbye, and she would be free of him. She wondered now just when his money was going to run out. She was sure it had come from Judge Raymond Grant, but she could not imagine that the judge would still be paying him after he failed to eliminate John Bannack. It had not been difficult for her to become certain that was what the judge had given him money to do. Trace had unknowingly told her a little more than he would have when in a drunken state, boasting about his skill with a six-gun and the reputation he had earned. Now she had to wonder if it had been smart to go along with Gladys and Trixie's little game. If they really have convinced the simple minded gunslinger that he was more attractive to women now, he might not want to leave. And she knew she was definitely in favor of his moving on.

The question of money paid to Trace Every was very much on Judge Raymond Grant's mind, an investment that had so far borne no fruit. The idea of using the young fast-gun as a way to eliminate John Bannack legally seemed a sure bet. While the big man from Waco was as lethal as the cat he and Spencer had named him for, Bannack had no reputation as a gunslinger. Still, Judge Grant assumed he would not back down when Trace Every called him out. Trace had eagerly accepted the proposition. The money was good, and it was an easy way to add to his number of kills. Unfortunately, no one had considered the possibility of Bannack turning the challenge into a single-punch fist fight.

The entire incident had left Judge Grant more obsessed with the desire to kill the man than before. Knowing this, Spencer suggested that he could approach Trace again to see if he had recovered from his unsuccessful first attempt. He further suggested that, this time, he would be paid a large sum of money if he was successful. And if he was successful this time, it would be money well spent. On the other hand, if he was killed, then at least it would not cost the judge any more money. The judge was receptive to the idea, so he gave Spencer the go-ahead to contact Every.

Spencer started dropping in at the Texas Rose for a drink after dinner the next couple of days until he happened to bump into Trace Every. When Trace saw the judge's clerk, his first reaction was to pretend not to notice him. But Spencer walked over to the table where Trace was sitting with the young whore named Paula. "Hello, Trace, I almost didn't recognize you sittin' back here."

"How do, Mr. Spencer?" Trace answered respectfully, but he was already preparing to tell the judge's errand boy where he could go to try to get any of that money back for John Bannack's killing.

"Mind if I sit down?" Spencer asked. "I'd like to buy you a drink. Looks like you had a bad time of it. I figure you might be about ready to do a little payback." Spencer looked at Paula, who was staring wide-eyed at him, wondering why he wanted to buy Trace a drink. He peeled off a couple of dollars and handed it to her. "Here, young lady, why don't you go over there to the bar and get us a bottle." She took the money and got up. When she went to the bar, Spencer asked Trace, "How'd you like to double that money you got to do that little job you were supposed to do?"

"What are you talking about?" Trace asked. "It ain't my fault that crazy man wouldn't draw." He paused then when Paula returned with the bottle and glasses and placed them on the table. "Run along now, Paula, I've gotta talk a little business." Trace motioned with his hand and she left to join Trixie and a man at another table.

"Don't you know why he wouldn't draw?" Spencer asked. "He knew if he did, he was a dead man. He knew you would cut him down before he could clear leather. You played his game and let him get his hands on you. In your business, you don't ever want to let a man get his hands on you, especially one like that panther."

"He wouldn't draw," Trace complained again.

"You have to make him draw," Spencer said. "Keep insulting him and if that don't bother him, tell him you'll go after the people he works for, anything to shame him for not facin' you. And if you do shame him to that point . . ." He paused. "Listen to me, Trace. If you do get him to draw that weapon and you cut him down, then I'll be coming back to see you with the same amount of money you were paid to do the first job." He paused then and poured a drink of whiskey into each of the two glasses. "Whaddaya think? Have we got a deal?"

"The man's a crazy man," Trace insisted. "He might not draw his six-gun but still come after me again, and if he does, I ain't waitin' for him to get his hands on me. I'll shoot him down like the mad dog he is."

Spencer hesitated a moment to picture that, then he said, "If it happens that way, I'll still pay you the two thousand. You'll go to court, but we'll see that you're acquitted, since you'll just be defending yourself. So, have we got a deal?"

"Yes, sir, we've got a deal," Trace said.

"Good," Spencer said. They tossed the whiskey down, then Spencer got up from the table and walked out the door leaving Trace to think about the unexpected opportunity to collect another two thousand dollars just as the first two thousand was running out.

Suddenly, he felt like a big man again, and when he thought about Trixie's and Gladys' remarks about his new "rugged" look, he thought he felt his old swagger return, in spite of his crippled right foot. He got up from the table and picked up the bottle. Then he walked over to the table where Paula was sitting with Trixie and a young cowhand he'd never seen before. "Here," he said and handed the bottle to Paula, "take this up to the room for later tonight."

"Hell, sport," Trixie's cowhand asked, "why don't you just leave it right here on the table with us?"

Trace gave him a cold gaze of indifference before answering, "Because I didn't take you to raise." Back to Paula again, he said, "Take it up to the room. I'm goin' outside to get a little fresh air."

"Good idea," the cowhand remarked, "might improve the air in here, too. Ain't that right, Trixie?" Trixie started to laugh, then caught herself when she saw the look in Trace's eyes. Seeing her reaction, the cowhand asked, "What's the matter? Did I say something to hurt his feelin's? I sure didn't mean to hurt your feelin's, partner. Tell him what a nice fellow I am, Trixie."

"He don't mean no harm, Trace," Trixie said. "He was just funnin'."

Trace seemed to relax his tenseness a little, but the cowhand commented again. "Shoot, no, I don't mean no harm. Besides, it looks like you already had your share of bad luck. It looks like somebody did the Texas Two-Step on your face and didn't even have the good manners to take their boots off." Then he rewarded his clever remark with a hearty guffaw.

"You got a big mouth, cowboy, and I'm sick of hearin' it," Trace told him. "If you wanna see another day of nursin' cows, I advise you to get your sorry ass outta here."

"Whoa!" the cowhand responded loudly. "Look who's talkin' like a stud horse. You need me to work on that face of yours for you. I'd be glad to finish the job somebody already started." He pushed his chair back from the table and stood up. A long, lanky man, he took a fighter's stance and balled his fists, ready to get it on.

Looking at him with contempt, Trace said, "I don't play schoolhouse games. You back your words with your life, or you crawl out of here like a yellow dog. You're wearin' a gun, so get ready to use it."

"Whoa!" the cowhand responded again, this time in

shocked surprise. "Wait a minute. There ain't no cause for this. Like she said, I was just funnin'. You know havin' a few drinks and cuttin' the fool." Noticing for the first time how Trace wore his gun holster, he threw a quick glance at Trixie and asked, "Why didn't you tell me?" Trace stepped backward until he had enough distance. "No, no, sir," the cowhand said, "I ain't pullin' irons against you. If I offended you, I was just funnin', and I apologize. All right?"

"It's too late for that now," Trace said. "If a man can't back up what he says, he oughta keep his mouth shut. Now, you get ready to draw that gun or I'm gonna shoot you down for the coward you are. What's it gonna be?"

"I can't draw against you," the cowhand pleaded. "My gun ain't even loaded. I don't ever ride with my gun loaded."

"Then what the hell do you carry it for?" Trace demanded.

"I so seldom have anything to shoot at that I don't bother loadin' it."

"I'll wait while you load it," Trace said. "So you might as well load it right now."

"All right, all right," the cowhand responded. "I'll load the blamed gun, but it still don't make no sense to me to want to shoot a man for just havin' some innocent fun. The man I ride for is short of cowhands already. It ain't gonna help if you turn out to be faster'n I am."

"You can still crawl out of here after you admit you're yellow," Trace said. "Otherwise, pull your gun out and load it, then drop it back in the holster."

"I ain't yellow. I just ain't a gunfighter. I'll admit to that, but I ain't gonna admit to being yellow. I'll load my gun." He very deliberately pulled his six-gun, being careful not to make any sudden moves. Trace watched him carefully as he broke the cylinder out and loaded each chamber with a cartridge. Then, when he started to return the gun to his holster, he suddenly made his move. Anticipating just such a trick,

Trace whipped out his Colt .45 and fired a shot in the cowhand's chest, causing him to fire a wild shot into the far wall before he dropped.

Trace looked at Trixie and smiled. "One of the oldest tricks a man can try, the old, unloaded gun trick. I'd heard about it, but this was the first time I've ever seen it." His confidence was sky high. He had not only recognized the trick in time to be ready for it, he had been fast enough to draw and fire before the cowhand could turn a gun, already in his hand, toward him and fire. He knew then that there was no one faster than he. He also knew that he would force Wick Justice's panther to stand and face him in a fair duel. Bannack had won the first fight due to his size and physical strength. Now Trace would win the second and most important round due to his speed with a six-shooter. Clark Spencer had offered the motivation to kill Bannack with the promise of another payday. But a stronger motivation was the need to seek revenge for the brutal beating and humiliation he had suffered at the big man's hand. All he needed now was the opportunity.

CHAPTER 19

The days that followed the Billy Duncan trial brought John Bannack back to the courtroom for three more trials, but there was not the drama that was provided at Billy's trial. Billy's father, Caleb, was released after three days in Sheriff Roger Nicholson's jail. And with Billy's hanging not scheduled for two weeks, there was a constant alertness for attempts to free him by his father and brothers.

For Bannack, there was always a personal obligation to remain alert for any threat on Judge Wick Justice's life with Caleb Duncan especially in mind. He, like everyone else in town, had heard about the gunfight in the Texas Rose saloon between Trace Every and an unknown cowhand. Evidently Every had regained his pride and his ability with a six-gun. Bannack hoped that Trace would just steer clear of him. He had no need to visit the Texas Rose because he seldom needed anything sold there. When he did have an urge for a drink, he found the Capitol City Saloon more to his quiet taste and bartender Jug Smith a pleasant conversationalist. The Capitol City was Judge Wick's favorite saloon and the owner, Milton Bailey, a personal friend. Consequently, more often than not, a visit to the Capitol City Saloon for Bannack was solely because the judge felt the need for a drink of whiskey. It was on one of these infrequent occasions when Trace Every finally managed to corner Bannack.

Riding down near the southern end of the town, Trace pulled his horse to a stop when he saw Judge Wick Justice pulling his buggy up to a stop in front of the Capitol City Saloon. It was the large man riding the buckskin horse behind the buggy that captured Trace's attention, however. *This might be the perfect way to spend an afternoon,* he thought. *I knew you couldn't avoid me forever.* He watched as Bannack dismounted and tied the horses at the rail. Then he waited until they went inside the saloon before he rode over and tied his horse beside the buckskin. He walked up to the batwing doors and looked inside. The judge was walking to a table to join Milton Bailey. The judge's bodyguard was down at the end of the bar, talking to Jug Smith. *Good,* Trace thought, *the bright sunlight will be shining through the door behind my back.*

Trace pushed on through the doors. "Well, well, if it ain't Judge Justice's panther," he said. "You're a hard man to find."

"Not hard enough, evidently," Bannack responded.

"You and I have some business we need to take care of," Trace said. "And now's as good a time as any to finish up what we started. You played a trick on me last time that only a coward like you could pull. Well, you ain't gonna get that chance today. You're gonna stand to face me man to man, like you were supposed to do in the stable."

Judge Justice rose up from the table to interfere. "John Bannack has no notion to stand and shoot it out with you. So turn around and leave before I call the sheriff down here."

"You just set down and shut up, Judge," Trace told him. "This ain't no damn courtroom. This is a saloon, and it ain't against the law for me to call a man out to settle an argument. He assaulted me, and I've got a right to call him on it. If you don't believe me, take a look at my face. So you ain't got no say-so in this business between me and this coward. You might as well just set down and watch your man in a fair fight."

"He's right, Judge," Bannack said. "I'll take care of it. Maybe we can take it outside, so we don't have to bother you and Mr. Bailey while you're havin' a drink."

"Oh, no, we ain't," Trace said at once. "We're gonna settle it right here in front of this bar, you at that end and me at this end, fair and square. And if you try to get any closer, I'll shoot you down before you take another step."

The judge was reluctant to give in to the brash gunman and still threatened to send for the sheriff. But Bannack assured him that he would take care of the situation, which amused Trace. "I'm gonna tell you again, you don't stand and draw that gun you're wearin' and I'll shoot you down like the yellow dog you are." *And I'll get two thousand dollars for doing it,* he thought to himself, which brought a smile to his face.

"Let's get this over with," Bannack said. "I know you must be anxious to see what it's like in hell."

Trace smiled in response to what he knew was an attempt to mess with his mind. It was wasted effort and desperate as well, for he knew no man was faster than he was. Bannack stepped away from the bar and took a ready stance. Trace, still smiling, did the same at the other end. "Go for your gun anytime you're ready," Trace said. "But if you don't go for it pretty quick, I'll count to three and when I say 'three,' I'll shoot you down."

"Fair enough," Bannack said and they both got set to draw. He knew Trace had to be fast, but he wasn't sure how fast he was in comparison. The practicing he had done with his Colt .44 tended to make him think he was pretty fast.

But fast enough? He was about to find out. He decided he would let Trace start counting and he would go for his gun on "two," hoping to surprise him enough to disrupt his timing. But he was determined to brace himself regardless.

They stood staring into each other's eyes for what seemed a long time, long enough for Trace to wonder if the big man actually thought he had a chance against him. *There's no way,* he thought, *and I couldn't ask for a bigger target.* Then, thinking Bannack was never going to reach for his gun, he started the count, "One, two . . ." Before he said three, Bannack reached, and Trace reacted in lightning-like reflex to whip his .45 out and fire before Bannack's .44 was fully level. The bullet struck Bannack high in the chest, causing him to take two steps backward, having been braced for the impact. "Ha!" Trace shouted in celebration of his victory, only to discover that Bannack was now taking dead aim with his pistol. Bannack's bullet struck the center of Trace's forehead, killing him instantly before he had time to cock his .45 again. He collapsed to his knees, then over on his side. Bannack dropped his .44 back in his holster and walked over to the table next to the judge's and dropped down on the chair.

The judge, Bailey, and Jug, were all struck motionless by the scene just witnessed. Of the three, Jug recovered first and exclaimed, "Damn! We gotta get him to Doc Bane's. He's been hit in the chest!"

"Put him in my buggy!" Judge Justice urged. "I'll drive him to Doc's. We'd best be quick about it!" They ran to his side and started to try to lift him from the chair.

"Take it easy," Bannack said. "I can walk to the buggy, if you just kinda give me a shoulder to lean on."

They hurried around him to assist him out the door and into the buggy. "Tie his horse to the back of the buggy," the judge said. "I can take care of him, and while I'm up that way, I'll see if I can find the undertaker to collect that gunslinger." Then he drove back uptown at a trot. "You hang in there, John, we'll be there in a minute."

"I'm all right," Bannack assured him.

"I thought you'd lost your mind, standing up to that gunslinger," the judge said. "Did you really think you would beat him?"

"No, I figured I wasn't as fast as he was. I figured I'd have to take a shot to get a chance to kill him. But I think I beat him. He's dead and I ain't." The judge looked at the blood soaking the front of his shirt and wasn't sure he agreed.

By the time they got to Doc Bane's office, Bannack was feeling a lot more pain, although the bleeding had slowed somewhat. When Doc's wife, Lucy, saw who it was, she went at once to get her husband and told him Judge Justice was there with a huge man who had been shot. Doc came at once and helped Bannack lie down on his operating table. "Looks like you took a bullet right in the chest," Doc said unnecessarily. "How'd that happen?" He looked at the judge for an answer.

"That little gunslinger that's been hanging around the Texas Rose called him out to a duel," the judge answered.

"And your boy, here, lost, huh?"

"No, John won. I've got to go tell the undertaker to pick up the loser," the judge answered.

"You mean he just stood there and took a shot in the chest, then shot the man who shot him?" Doc was amazed.

"Right between the eyes," the judge answered.

"Damn," Doc exclaimed. "You mighta been lucky. You don't act like it hit your lung and it's too high and too far to the side to hit your heart. I won't know for sure till I go in and find where that bullet ended up. I'm gonna put you to sleep for a while. You ever had any chloroform?" Bannack shook his head. "Well, if you can stand up and take a bullet in the chest, a little dose of chloroform ain't gonna bother you. Let's get your shirt and your undershirt off." Lucy came in with a cloth folded into a pad, which she poured the chloroform on, then held it under Bannack's nose for him to breathe. He was soon unconscious. Doc told the judge that he was going to take a little while, so if he had some place to go, he could leave and come back in about an hour. The judge decided to go see if he could find Theodore Reece, the undertaker, and send him to the Capitol City Saloon to pick up Trace Every's body. "Just from what I see so far," Doc sought to reassure the judge, "your man here looks strong as an ox. I don't expect any problems. I'll just go in and find that bullet, then we'll patch him up."

The judge found Mr. Reece at his place of business and he informed him of the body awaiting him at the Capitol City Saloon. Reece found it quite interesting that Trace Every had been killed in a duel that he had insisted upon. "I just put a nameless cowhand in a box after this Every fellow called him out. Sooner or later, all these fast-draw gunfighters find another one that's faster than they are and they end up in one of my pine boxes."

"Just so you know," Judge Justice told him, "this wasn't another gunfighter who stopped Trace Every. You know John Bannack who works for me. He's no gunslinger, and he's the one who put Every in one of your boxes."

"Is that a fact?" Reece asked. "Yes, I know who John Bannack is. How'd he happen to shoot Trace Every?"

"Like you said," the judge answered. "Every called him out and John answered the call. He knew he wasn't faster than Every, so he stood there and took a bullet, then took dead aim to finish Every."

"Well, I'll be . . ." Reece started, surprised. "Have I got another body to pick up?"

"No, John's over at Doc's now, getting that bullet taken out of his chest."

"I declare," Reece exclaimed, "that's really something. I've seen your man, Bannack. Somebody shoulda told Trace that going after Bannack was like going after a buffalo. Most of the time, you don't bring one of 'em down with one shot."

"I don't want folks to start thinking John is another one of those fast-gun gunslingers. He's a fine, hard-working young man who doesn't believe in that quick-draw nonsense. He's a peaceful man who happens to be able to handle trouble."

Reece looked at the judge and grinned. "I expect you know that ain't how Judge Grant describes him. He calls him your panther. But I'll take my wagon down to the Capitol City Saloon and pick up some of that trouble your peaceful man handled."

When the judge went back to Doc Bane's office, he found that Bannack was just coming out from under the chloroform. Lucy Bane was fanning his face with a fan in an effort to flush out the anesthesia with fresh air. "It was like I suspected," Doc said. "He took the bullet high enough and to the right far enough to avoid any major organs. It was more toward his shoulder and he's got a lot of muscle in there. That's where I found the bullet, lodged in that muscle. I took it out and patched him up. He lost quite a bit of blood. He needs to build that back. Tell Lottie to make sure he eats plenty of beef, and he needs to take it easy for a few days and keep that wound clean. It shouldn't be too long before he can put himself to the test again."

The judge paid Doc Bane and when Bannack felt like he was over the effect of the chloroform they left the doctor's office and headed home. The buckskin was still tied onto the back of the buggy, but they both agreed it best if John rode home in the buggy. When they arrived at the judge's house, Judge Wick wanted to drop Bannack off at the house first, but Bannack insisted on going with him to the barn to make sure the buckskin was taken care of. Lottie saw them pass by the window and was puzzled to see Bannack riding in the buggy with the judge. Stranger still was the fact that he was wrapped around his shoulders with what appeared to be a sheet or half of one. She sent Henry down to the barn to put the horse and buggy away and to help John if he needed it. They had already been gone longer than she expected them to be, so she knew something was wrong.

"Are you going to be all right sleeping in that hayloft tonight?" Lottie asked after the men returned to the house and she learned why they had been late coming home. John assured her that he would. "Are you sure you can even climb up the ladder?" She insisted.

"Yes, ma'am," he said, "it ain't that much of a climb to go up that ladder."

"I reckon I could trade with you for a couple of nights," Henry volunteered. "I could sleep in the hayloft and you could sleep in the house."

Nobody said anything for a long moment, waiting for him to think about it before Lottie finally told him. "Henry, you sleep with me in the bed."

"Oh," Henry said, "that's right. I forgot about that."

It was not until the next morning that news began to circulate explaining the two gunshots heard the afternoon before. Clark Spencer overheard some diners talking about it when he was eating breakfast at Riley's Café. It seemed that someone had called the final bluff on that cocky gunslinger who had been hanging around the Texas Rose for months. He knew, even before he heard, who the party was that shot him down. It had to be Bannack. He confirmed it when he asked Riley on his way out of the café. *Damn,* he thought, *it was not a good way to start the day.* Judge Grant was presiding over a case of armed robbery today. There was no telling how many years in prison the poor wretch would get after the judge heard the news about Trace Every.

Spencer was reluctant to go to work. So much so, that he went by the hotel dining room to see if Sheriff Nicholson was eating breakfast there as usual. He was in luck. When he stepped inside the dining room, he saw the sheriff sitting at a table, eating. When Jim Davis greeted him, he said he just stopped by to give the sheriff a message. Then he walked back to the table. "Good mornin', Sheriff," he said.

"Clark," Nicholson acknowledged. "Were you lookin' for me?"

"No, I just stopped in to see if the judge might have had breakfast here this mornin'," Spencer lied. "I see he didn't, but I saw you, so I thought I'd check with you to see if what I heard about Trace Every was true."

"Yep," Nicholson replied, "Trace Every finally met up with the wrong man."

"John Bannack?" Spencer asked. The sheriff nodded. "I didn't think Bannack was fast enough with a gun to take Trace Every," Spencer said.

"He wasn't," Nicholson replied. "He was tough enough to stand up to Every and take the shot, then he took his shot and put one right in Trace's forehead."

That could actually be good news, Spencer thought. They shot each other. Bannack's gone and they wouldn't have to pay the two thousand to Trace. "So they ended up killin' each other?"

"No, Trace didn't kill Bannack," Nicholson said. "He stood there and took Trace's best shot. Milton Bailey said

Bannack didn't even grunt when that bullet struck him in the chest. Said he already had his gun out, pointed at Trace, so he took careful aim and put a bullet in the center of Trace's forehead. Then Judge Wick told him to get in his buggy and the judge drove him to see Doc Bane."

"I declare," Spencer remarked, "that sure is something, ain't it?" Trying not to show any strong reaction to the sheriff's detailed description, while very much aware that the sheriff was watching him closely, well aware of Judge Grant's annoyance with John Bannack. "Well, I'd best not disturb your breakfast anymore. I guess Judge Grant must have ate breakfast earlier than I expected. Have a good day." He turned and walked out of the dining room, passing Jim Davis without saying a word.

Jim walked on back to the sheriff's table. "What was that all about?" he asked the sheriff. "Him nor Judge Grant, either, don't ever eat in the dinin' room."

Nicholson chuckled. "He was just wantin' to find out about that shoot-out yesterday. I expect he was hopin' to hear that John Bannack got killed."

"Why in the world would he wanna hear that?" Jim asked.

Nicholson looked at him in surprise. "You don't know?"

"I reckon I don't," Jim answered dumbfounded.

"Well, you must be the last person in town who doesn't," the sheriff said. "Judge Grant hates John Bannack with a passion, but he don't hate him as much as he hates Judge Justice. And that's because Judge Wick got a pardon for Bannack to get him out of prison."

"John Bannack was in prison?" Jim asked, truly surprised.

The sheriff looked at him as if he couldn't believe he had to ask. "I swear, Jim, don't you ever talk to any of your customers that come in here to eat?"

"Not that much, I reckon," Jim said and scratched his head in wonder. "Judge Justice and Elwood Wilson usually eat at home. But once in a while, they'll stop in here at dinnertime. Sometimes John Bannack is with 'em." He paused to picture it. "That big ol' fellow, so quiet and polite, I can't believe he was in prison. What did he do to get sent to prison?"

"He robbed a bank when he was eighteen," Nicholson said. He went on to tell Jim about the robbery and the severity of the sentence given him by the judge. He told him about the extent Judge Wick went to have it reduced and eventually pardoned altogether. Judge Grant considered that a direct insult he told him, and they've been enemies ever since. "That's why Grant calls Bannack Judge Wick's panther. You knew that, didn'tcha?" Jim shook his head. "I swear, Jim, you need to get outta this dinin' room once in a while."

"I ain't ever told anybody this," Jim said, "but I'm a little bit hard of hearing."

When Clark Spencer arrived at the office, he found the door unlocked, which was unusual because he always opened the office in the morning. Judge Grant was not an early riser as a rule. He enjoyed a leisurely breakfast with his live-in cook and housekeeper in the small house he owned close to the capitol. Spencer sometimes wondered who the live-in cook entertained when he and the judge were riding the circuit. But he never brought up the subject for speculation. On this morning, however, the judge was there before Spencer arrived. "You're running a little late this morning, aren't you?" Judge Grant greeted him.

Spencer knew why the judge was early. "Yes, sir, I'm a

little later than usual because I stopped in at the hotel dinin' room after breakfast to see if I could catch Sheriff Nicholson there. I figured you'd want details about the shooting in the Capitol City Saloon yesterday afternoon."

"Was he there?" Grant asked, immediately interested. "Was it a face-off between two men, like we heard?"

"Yes, sir, he was there and he said that's what it was," Spencer replied, reluctant to continue because he knew the judge was eager to hear that John Bannack was dead. "And it was between Trace Every and John Bannack." He paused then, reluctant to get the judge's hopes up, thinking there was a double killing to solve his problem, as he had assumed when the sheriff led him through the story. So he spat it out. "Trace Every's dead. John Bannack's got a wound in his chest, but he's alive and breathing."

Judge Grant's face blanched and then it became red as he clenched his teeth and the veins stood out on his neck. The oath came from his mouth like an explosion. "Damn!" he repeated four times, the last time loud enough that Spencer was sure it was heard three doors down the hallway at Wick Justice's office. Grant was forced to pause to inhale some air before he continued in a soft, almost calm tone. "I want that man dead, that damn panther has no right walking around a free man."

"Killing might be too merciful for the man," Spencer suggested, knowing the judge would charge him with the responsibility for finding another assassin, a job that he had rather not be involved in. "It might be more fitting to persuade Governor Throckmorton to reverse the pardon Governor Hamilton gave Bannack and let him sit in a prison cell for the rest of his life."

Judge Grant paused to consider the suggestion. "You could be right. It would certainly be worthwhile to present my case to the governor. It would be highly proper to put that big cat of Wick's in a cage. Why don't you contact the governor's office and make an appointment for me to talk to him?" The more he thought about it, the better he liked the idea. "You may have hit on the solution for our problems with Judge Wick and his panther," he said.

CHAPTER 20

Bannack tried to turn his body a little more onto his left side, hoping that would relax his right side and let him get back to sleep. It had been only a couple of days since he had taken the bullet in his shoulder, and he had found it most comfortable for him if he laid on his back. He felt pain from his wound, but it was not enough to awaken him from a sound sleep before this disturbance. Maybe he needed some new hay under his blanket, he thought, but he had just freshened up his bed in the hayloft that afternoon. Something else must have awakened him, so he lay still and listened. There was nothing for a minute, and then he heard the buckskin nicker softly in the barn below him. Maybe that was what had awakened him. He rolled out of his blanket and winced when he felt a little shot of pain in his shoulder. Ignoring it, he pulled his boots on, got to his feet, and slid down the ladder to the barn. He went to one of the new stalls he had helped Henry build to see if the buckskin was having any problems.

He took a few seconds to pet the gelding before he walked to the end of the stalls where he was surprised to look out the back door to discover three horses tied at the back corner of the barn. Immediately alert now, he ran to the tack room and pulled his rifle from his saddle. Back out in the barn, he crouched in the darkness and levered a live round into the chamber of the Henry and waited for any reaction. There was none, so he figured he was alone in the barn and he hurried to the front door. There was only a sliver of moon the shape of a fingernail in the dark night. But it was enough to see the three figures creeping along the back of the house, going from window to window. Not likely robbers, he decided, more likely assassins and they were looking for the judge's bedroom, which was at the corner of the back wall. They were at the middle bedroom now and two of the men made a platform with their arms, so the third man could step up on it and be raised high enough to look inside the window. That window would be Elwood's room, Bannack thought as he slipped out the barn door and advanced upon the assassins. Not suspecting anyone to be behind them, the killers hurried to the corner window and created their platform, and the trigger man climbed upon it, one hand steadying himself on the side of the house, the other holding a double-barrel shotgun.

There was no doubt what the trio's intentions were, so there was no reason for Bannack to hesitate. As soon as the assassin lifted the shotgun up to the windowsill, Bannack put a .44 slug into the middle of his back, cranked a second round into the Henry's chamber and knocked the leg of one of his accomplices out from under him, causing the shooting platform to collapse. The uninjured one managed to pull his sidearm, but Bannack's third shot struck him in the shoulder, causing him to drop it. Injured and confused, Luke and Davy Duncan sat on the ground, their father's body lying between them. "Don't make a move, if you want to live," Bannack warned them. He could hear the sounds of frantic activity inside the house, and a lamp came on in the middle bedroom. "Henry! Elwood! Judge!" he called out. "Everything's under control."

In a few seconds, everyone in the house came out the kitchen door. "Who is it, John?" Judge Wick asked.

"Duncans," Bannack said simply. "The old man was fixin' to let you have both barrels of that shotgun layin' on the ground under the window." Lottie turned the wick up on a lamp she brought out with her, so they could see the wounded and the dead. "One in the leg, the other'n in the shoulder," he said and explained how the two sons had constructed a platform. "I didn't have a choice with the old man. He had that shotgun up on the windowsill, fixin' to shoot. I had to stop him cold."

"Under the circumstances, that's understandable," Judge Wick said. "Even Judge Grant would agree with that. Did you get hit?" he asked then, pointing to a line of blood on Bannack's undershirt.

"No, sir," Bannack answered. "That's just some blood from Trace Every's shot that started bleedin' again. It oughta stop pretty soon. I reckon I better see if I can do anything for the Duncan boys. Doc Bane ain't gonna want to see 'em in the middle of the night. I don't know if we can even take 'em to the jail till mornin'."

"We'll just wrap their wounds up enough to stop the bleeding," the judge said. "Then let Sheriff Nicholson take care of them in the morning. We can lock them in the smokehouse for the rest of the night."

Lottie went back inside to get some rags to use as bandages while the men stood guard over the two prisoners. Bannack moved close to Elwood, so Henry and the judge wouldn't hear as he gave the clerk some advice. "Something you might wanna remember if this ever happens again, if you hear something going on outside in the middle of the night, don't light a lamp. Ain't no use in making it easy for them to see you and it's harder for you to see them in the dark."

After Luke and Davy were bandaged up, Bannack helped them into the smokehouse. Although their father was dead, neither son was inclined to put up any resistance against the fearsome man who had killed him. "There ain't many hours left in this night," he told them. "So you won't be locked up in here long. I'm gonna put your daddy on his horse and we'll take him into town with you in the mornin'. I expect the sheriff will take you to see the doctor right away, so I'll ask Lottie if she can fix you something to eat when we let you out in the mornin'." Still partially in shock, neither son was in any shape to protest, so they made no efforts to resist or protest.

At sunup the following morning, Lottie was up cooking breakfast, preparing enough to feed the two surviving would-be assassins as well as her own crew. No one in the house had been able to go back to sleep after the interruption by Caleb Duncan and his sons. "I think it would be a smart idea to never tell anyone that John sleeps in the barn," Lottie commented.

"I think you're right," the judge said. "And I know I'm getting a sore arm from trying to pat myself on the back for being intelligent enough to get that man out of prison." He paused to look toward the kitchen door. "Where is he, anyway?"

"I just came from the barn," Henry said. "He's still up in the hayloft, probably sound asleep."

"Did anybody else go back to sleep?" Lottie asked, looking around the gathering at everyone shaking their heads. "Better go wake him up, Henry. Breakfast is just about ready. I want him to let those two out of the smokehouse.

They mighta decided to get even for their papa while they
were locked up in there."

"I expect they're about ready to come outta that smokehouse, all right," Bannack remarked, having heard Lottie's
comment as he walked in the door. "If you're ready to feed
'em, I'll let 'em out and watch 'em while they eat. Then I
reckon I'll just lock 'em up again while I eat. Then I'll take
'em to the jail and let Sheriff Nicholson take care of 'em,
and I'll take their pa to the undertaker."

"I've got a better idea," Lottie said. "Set your big self
down at the table, and I'll give you your breakfast. Then
you can go out to the smokehouse and feed those two pole-
cats who tried to shoot all of us last night."

"Amen," Judge Wick said. "She's right. Sit down and
eat your breakfast and thank you for saving my life
again."

"Amen to that," Elwood said.

Bannack was touched, unaccustomed to praise as he
was. "Just trying to do what you hired me for," he managed.

Grinning at his embarrassment, Lottie told him to sit
down again and when he dutifully obeyed, she brought him
a big plate of breakfast and a mug of coffee. When he finished, he and Henry took breakfast out to the prisoners.
Bannack let them sit on the kitchen steps while they ate.
They still showed no indication of possibly causing trouble,
although Davy did take the opportunity to tell Bannack he
didn't have to kill their father, that it wasn't right for him to
shoot him in the back. "I reckon that's one way of lookin'
at it," Bannack answered him. "But tell me this, what did
you think your father was gonna do with that shotgun he
laid on the windowsill?" Davy didn't answer.

* * *

Sheriff Roger Nicholson stepped out of the hotel dining room and stopped at once when he saw John Bannack riding up the street, leading a string of horses behind him. The sheriff recognized the two Duncan brothers on the first and second horses behind him, their hands tied behind their backs. And bringing up the rear was another horse with a body draped belly down across the saddle. "Well, it looks like my mornin' is gonna be pretty busy," he said to himself as he walked out in the street to meet Bannack. "Good mornin', John. I reckon I don't have to ask you what you've been up to."

"Mornin', Sheriff," Bannack said. "We had a little visit out at the judge's house last night, so I brought you a couple of prisoners. Judge Justice said he'll be in to see you to verify everything I have to tell you about an attempt on his life. You might recognize the two Duncan boys, Billy's brothers. I reckon this'll make the whole family you've had in your jail."

"They don't even give you time to heal up between shoot-outs, do they?" Nicholson remarked when he noticed the blood spot leaking through from his shoulder wound. "I'm gonna guess that the fellow layin' across the saddle is Caleb, their papa."

"That's a fact," Bannack replied. "His two sons were holdin' him up to the window and he was fixin' to shoot Judge Justice with a shotgun. I was lucky to come along at the right time and I shot him before he could pull the trigger on the shotgun. You want to look him over before I take him to see the undertaker? You'll notice that I shot him in the back and that's because I was behind them, comin' from the barn. So with him raised up by those two boys, he was facin' the window and had his back to me. I didn't have time to ask him to turn around. I just wanted to get that straight in case it ever comes up."

"They might ask you what you were doin' in the barn in the middle of the night," the sheriff suggested.

"That's where I sleep, in the hayloft," Bannack said. "They tied their horses up right under me almost and I reckon that's what woke me up."

"How come you were sleepin' in the barn?" Nicholson asked. "Did you have some kinda idea that they were gonna try something?"

"Nope," Bannack replied. "I always sleep in the barn, in the hayloft."

"Right," the sheriff said. *You wouldn't keep a panther in the house,* he thought. "If you want to take that body to the undertaker, I'd appreciate it. But tell me first about the arm wound and the leg wound."

Bannack went over the incident again, describing the shot to the leg to collapse the human platform, in case Caleb was able to take the shot at the judge after he was shot in the back. "The shot in the shoulder was because he drew his gun and was gonna shoot at me."

Nicholson thought he had a clear picture of the attack, so he said, "First, give me a hand puttin' these two in a cell. Then I'll see if Doc Bane has to have me bring 'em to his office, or if he can just come to the jail to treat 'em." He took a look at the two mournful-looking brothers and commented, "It's too late to feed 'em. Billy's already had his breakfast. They'll have to wait till dinnertime."

"They've already had breakfast," Bannack said. "Lottie cooked 'em some bacon and eggs."

"I hope they won't be too disappointed by the service they get in my jail," Nicholson japed.

Bannack walked with the sheriff back to the jail, leading the horses with the two sullen brothers and their deceased father in tow, causing the people on the street to stop and gawk. When they got to the jail, they helped the two wounded men off their horses and Bannack helped Luke, who had the wound in his thigh, get up the steps. Inside, they untied their hands, emptied their pockets, and put them in a cell next to the one their brother was in. Billy was so amazed, he could only stand and gape at his two brothers for several minutes before he finally mumbled to himself, "What the hell. . . ?"

"You boys just set there and have a little family reunion," Sheriff Nicholson told them. "I'm gonna go see the doctor about treatin' those wounds. Billy can tell you how I run things in the jail. I'll have all the information about the charges against you later today." He and Bannack walked out of the cell room then with still not a word having been spoken between the brothers.

Once the cell room door was closed, however, the three brothers all spoke at once with Billy dominating when he demanded, "What in the hell are you doin' in here? What have you and Pa been doin'? I've been waitin' for you to try to break me outta here. Whatta you been waitin' for? That sheriff ain't but one man! They've got a hangman comin' to stretch my neck in about a week! Where's Pa?"

"Pa's dead," Luke said. "And maybe you ain't noticed, but me and Davy has both been shot and all because you had to shoot that cowhand in the back."

"Pa's dead?" Billy asked, unable to believe his ears. "How'd he die?"

"Gunshot," Luke answered. "Shot in the back, just like that cowhand you shot."

"Who done it?" Billy demanded, at once angry.

"That big gorilla that works for Judge Justice," Luke said.

"Why?" Billy asked. "What was he after you for?"

"He wasn't after us," Davy tried to explain. "Pa wanted to kill Judge Justice for throwing him in jail and sentencin' you to a hangin'. So we found out where the judge's house is and we sneaked up to his bedroom window last night and Pa was gonna shoot him. But that big gorilla showed up behind us from somewhere out there in the dark. Pa saw the judge layin' in the bed and was just fixin' to shoot him when he got hit. Then Luke caught one in the leg and we all landed on the ground. I got my gun out just in time to catch the next shot in my shoulder. So he had us pretty much right where he wanted us."

"You was supposed to be figurin' out how you was gonna break me outta this jail," Billy complained. "How the hell was killing the judge gonna help me break outta this jail? I'm tellin' you, they're gittin' ready to hang me!" He started pacing back and forth from one side of his cell to the other, mumbling to himself. Then he stopped and demanded, "If you was gonna sneak up on somebody and shoot 'em, why didn't you sneak up on the sheriff and shoot him? And get me outta here?" He paced back and forth some more. "We're gonna have to figure a way to jump the sheriff and break outta here. I druther die tryin' to escape than to die at the end of a rope."

Davy whispered aside to Luke, "But me and you ain't sentenced to hang."

Overhearing his remark, Billy exclaimed, "Oh, you ain't, are you? Wait till the sheriff comes back with your charges. You and Pa was trying to kill the judge. You think you ain't gonna get a death sentence?"

"I swear, he might be right," Luke said. "We might be in a bad fix here."

"He's right about one thing," Davy said. "I druther die from a bullet wound than choke to death swingin' on a rope. If I see just a hair of a chance to escape, I'm goin' for it."

"Me, too," Luke said. "Maybe we'll get a chance if he takes us to the doctor."

"I swear," Billy commented sarcastically, "what a nice couple of brothers I've got. I sure hope you get a chance to get away when he takes you to the doctor. Don't worry about your brother. I'll most likely get a chance to get away if the sheriff forgets to lock my cell door."

"You might as well quit your bellyachin', Billy," Luke told him. "If there's a chance for all three of us to escape, we'll take that chance, whatever it is. But if that doctor gets careless when the sheriff takes us to get treated, and we see a chance to make a run for it, me and Davy are sure gonna take it. We'd be pretty big fools not to, just because you ain't with us. If you was in our shoes, you'd do the same thing and you know it."

"Yeah, I reckon I most likely would," Billy confessed. "Matter of fact, after hearin' you two talk about your plans to cut out from the doctor's office, I know damn well I wouldn't worry about either one of you two."

The bickering between the three brothers went on for about forty-five minutes before they heard the sheriff return. A minute later, he unlocked the cell room door and walked in to announce, "Good news, boys, you don't have to walk up to his office. Doc Bane's comin' here to take care of you." He looked at Billy, who started chuckling. "What's so funny?"

"Nothin', Sheriff," Billy answered. "I was just thinkin' about something else."

Just as Billy predicted and Davy and Luke feared, charges were filed against them for the attempted murder of Judge Wick Justice with a trial set for two days after the arrest. It was pushed ahead on the court's schedule of trials because of the possibility of a death penalty if they were found guilty and the fact that the hangman was already scheduled

to be in town for Billy's hanging. Since Judge Justice was
the party charging the attempted murder, the trial was to be
presided over by Judge Raymond Grant. This was not good
news to Judge Justice because of the bad blood between the
two judges. But he made no protest to the court because
the case was hardly questionable. The facts spoke for themselves. The accused, with their father, went to Judge Wick's
house and tried to shoot the judge in his sleep. They were
caught at the scene of the crime and confined until morning
when they were taken to jail. Because of the nature of the
crime, there would be a six-man jury. So Judge Grant would
not decide the case, as he would have in non-criminal cases
of a minor nature, and the accused would be assigned a
public defender.

Unlike their brother Billy, Luke and Davy readily accepted the services of the public defender, a conscientious
young lawyer named Franklin Pierce. Pierce promptly visited the two brothers in jail the day before the trial to hear
their side of the story. Knowing beforehand that he had
little chance of winning, he hoped at best to save the two
brothers from the hangman. As he expected, their primary
defense was that they simply did what their father told them
to do and that he was the guilty party. Young Pierce's inter-
view with his clients was not made easy by the heckling of
their brother Billy from the cell next to theirs.

"If you was any good as a lawyer," Billy teased, "you'd
talk that jury into sendin' Judge Justice to prison for settin'
a trap for my pa and my brothers."

After supper that evening, Davy and Luke were transported
to a holding cell in the courthouse where they awaited their
trial, scheduled to begin at nine o'clock the next morning.
Since Judge Wick and Bannack were both principals in the

trial, they were there early. And since Judge Grant was presiding over the trial, Bannack was not allowed to wear a firearm. The jury, having already been selected, were seated before Davy and Luke were brought into the courtroom by two deputy marshals. Shortly after that, Clark Spencer walked to the side of the bench and announced, "All rise," and introduced Judge Raymond Grant. Grant walked in much like Julius Caesar might have at the height of the Roman Empire. His chin held high, he stood for a moment and scanned the courtroom from one side to the other before telling all to be seated.

The trial moved rather swiftly, as both sides expected. With Alvin McClain again acting as prosecutor for the state and Franklin Pierce representing the defense. Judge Grant read off the charges of attempted murder against the two sons as well as the deceased father. In order to expedite the proceedings, the judge elected to rule on the two together, instead of trying them one at a time. When he asked them how they pled, Franklin Pierce answered, "Not guilty, Your Honor." The judge called on the prosecutor to present the case and McClain went to work. He called Judge Justice to the stand and questioned him regarding what happened on the night in question. And Judge Justice told him he was awakened by a gunshot in the middle of the night, outside his window, and it was a shot from the rifle of John Bannack that saved his life.

"Why do you say it saved your life?" McClain asked.

"Because he shot Caleb Duncan just before Duncan could pull the trigger on a double-barrel shotgun he was aiming through my window at me in my bed," Judge Wick answered. McClain had no further questions for him and turned him over to the defense for cross-examination.

"Judge Justice," Pierce began, "you stated that you were asleep until that shot that killed Caleb Duncan woke you.

Is that right?" Judge Wick said that he was. "Then how could you know who fired the shot that woke you? And how could you know if Caleb Duncan was aiming a shotgun at you, if you were asleep?"

Judge Wick smiled and answered, "Common sense. There was only one man out there who is paid to protect my house and the people who live there, John Bannack. The only other people there, besides Caleb Duncan, were his two sons." He pointed to Davy and Luke. "They were in the process of holding their father up high enough to fire his shotgun through my window. So one of them would have been the only other suspect who could have shot their father. In that case, maybe this trial should be to determine which one of them shot Caleb Duncan. However, John Bannack has already confessed to the killing of Caleb Duncan. So common sense should tell us the two men on trial here are guilty of aiding and abetting their father in a planned assassination of myself in revenge for my sentencing of a third son to death by hanging."

Franklin Pierce could think of no argument to combat Judge Wick's statement, so when he hesitated, Judge Grant said to him, "Are you concerned that the accused may not have intended to kill? Maybe you want to question Bannack." Hearing the judge's coaching, Judge Wick almost called to object, but was able to hold his temper.

"Your Honor," Pierce stated then, "the defense has no more questions for this witness. We call to the stand John Bannack."

Bannack took the stand and was sworn in, then Pierce, in keeping with the hint from Judge Grant, began his questioning. "Mr. Bannack, the court would first like to establish your qualification to testify. Do you happen to possess any supernatural powers that can tell you what people think?"

Puzzled by the question, Bannack answered honestly, "Not that I'm aware of."

"That being the case," Pierce said, "it's quite possible you couldn't know what Caleb Duncan and his two sons had in mind that night at Judge Justice's home. Wouldn't you agree?"

"No, I wouldn't," Bannack replied. "With those two, in the middle of the night, standing under the judge's window, holding their arms together so their pa could stand on them and stick his shotgun through the window—I was pretty sure what they had in mind."

Pierce gave Judge Grant a quick look before continuing. "It didn't cross your mind that possibly they just meant to scare Judge Justice or they were just playing a prank?" He glanced at Judge Grant again, realizing how weak that was. Grant rolled his eyeballs toward the ceiling.

"No, sir," Bannack answered. "That never crossed my mind. What crossed my mind was if I waited to see if they were playin' a prank, most likely I'd be out of a job 'cause my boss woulda been dead."

"The undertaker said Caleb Duncan was shot in the back," Judge Grant mentioned rather casually.

"That's right, sir," Pierce quickly replied. "That was my next question." He turned back to address Bannack again. "How is it possible, if you were in the house, protecting Judge Justice, that you shot Caleb Duncan in the back?"

"I wasn't in the house," Bannack said.

"You were outside the house?" Bannack nodded. "What were you doing outside the house in the middle of the night?" Pierce asked.

"I wasn't outside until those three assassins woke me up when they tied their horses under me where I sleep." He went on to describe his bed in the hayloft and how the three intruders left their horses at the back of the barn while they sneaked up to the house. "When I saw what they were up to, I knew I'd have to shoot the slimy rat in the back. I'da had to run around the house and come in the front door, so I could shoot him in the chest. And that would have taken more time than I had." There were a couple of chuckles and a few snickers from the small group of people watching, causing Judge Grant to call for order.

Pierce had nowhere else to go, so he declared, "The defense rests, Your Honor."

"Prosecution rests, Your Honor," McClain said, confident that every soul in the courtroom knew the straight of the story.

Judge Grant was about to send the jury out to discuss the case, but the foreman said, "I don't think we need to go out, Your Honor. We'll take a quick vote to see if we need to talk it over." They pulled their chairs around to huddle up and the foreman handed each juror a slip of paper and a pencil. They voted and handed them all back to the foreman, who counted each one. Then he nodded his thanks and said, "We don't need to go out, Your Honor."

"Have you reached a verdict?" Judge Grant asked, an obvious smirk of irritation on his face.

"We have, Your Honor."

"In the case of the State of Texas versus Davy Duncan and Luke Duncan, how do you find the defendants?"

"We find the defendants guilty, Your Honor."

Judge Grant stood up and addressed the jury. "Thank you, gentlemen, for your service to your state and county. You are dismissed." Franklin Pierce and his two defendants stood up, as did Alvin McClain. "Davy Duncan and Luke Duncan, this court finds you guilty of attempted murder by a jury of your peers. There will be a thirty minute recess while I review all the testimony, then the court will reconvene for sentencing."

CHAPTER 21

"That imbecile the court assigned to defend those two morons needed to be led by a mule," Judge Raymond Grant complained to Clark Spencer. He vigorously stirred the two heaping spoonfuls of sugar in his coffee, irritated by young Franklin Pierce's lack of imagination in his defense of the Duncan brothers. Contrary to his statement to the court that he had taken a thirty-minute recess to study the facts, he was having a cup of coffee. He knew what his sentence was going to be before the case was tried.

Feeling a sliver of compassion for the task the young lawyer had been handed, Spencer saw fit to remark. "He's still a little green," he said, "but he didn't really have much to work with. It was pretty plain ol' Caleb Duncan and his two boys came to shoot Judge Wick for givin' Billy the death sentence."

"That's what they go to law school for," Grant insisted. "To make up some facts, if they ain't got any real ones." He looked at his pocket watch and said, "I expect I've had time to review the testimony." He gulped down the rest of his coffee and got up from his desk. "Let's go back in and give 'em the sentence. I'm looking forward to seeing how Wick Justice likes it."

They went back into the courtroom and found most of

the spectators still there. Judge Grant called the court to order, and Franklin Pierce stood up with Davy and Luke to receive the sentencing. "After reviewing the testimony given by the witnesses to this crime, it's rather obvious that the only actual defendant to the charge of attempted murder in this case is the deceased, Caleb Duncan. And it seems he has already received the maximum punishment for his crime, death by rifle shot. As for the defendants, Davy Duncan and Luke Duncan, a jury has found them guilty, but guilty only of obeying their father's orders, which were to make a platform for him to stand on. I find it hard to punish a son for obeying his father's orders, as long as he does not participate in the actual shooting. Davy Duncan and Luke Duncan are not without guilt, however. But their crime is trespassing on private property for which they shall be held accountable. So Davy and Luke Duncan, I hereby sentence you to ninety days incarceration in the county jail."

Everyone in the courtroom was surprised, but the two Duncan brothers were confused. Their public defender, however, was stunned, as was Judge Wick Justice, Alvin McClain, and John Bannack. The deputy marshals escorted the two defendants out of the courtroom and Judge Grant and Clark Spencer went out the door behind the judge's bench immediately. Judge Wick Justice and both attorneys were left standing in shock and disbelief after hearing a judge famous for his brutally harsh sentences, administer what amounted to a slap on the wrist to two men obviously guilty of attempted murder. It was unbelievable to Bannack as well, and like Judge Wick, he was immediately aware that in three months' time, the two would be out of jail and free to resume their search for vengeance. There was no doubt in Bannack's mind that it was the motive behind Grant's sentence. What he found hard to believe was that

Grant had the gall to do it, to use his public office to carry out his petty jealousies.

They went home for dinner to enjoy a chicken that Lottie had baked that morning. Elwood, who had remained in the office instead of going to the trial had come to the house to meet them for dinner. He, like the judge, was appalled to hear the story of the sentencing. His first response was to have Judge Wick write a letter of protest to the Texas Supreme Court. The judge told him that he was seriously considering it already but was reluctant to wage an all-out war with Grant. Elwood protested, reminding him that an attempt to murder him was as serious as it could get. Then the judge reminded Elwood that it was the Duncan brothers who attempted to murder him and they were severely punished for it. "That's not funny, Judge," Lottie told him. The discussion went on through dinner with Lottie charging Bannack to keep a sharp watch over every move the judge made. The judge was typically already becoming irritated by everyone's concern for his health.

The atmosphere wasn't helped any with the coming of Billy Duncan's date with the hangman a couple of days later. Everyone at Judge Wick Justice's house was sick of talking about the Duncans, who seemed more a plague than a family, and they hoped that with the execution of Billy that would end the talk, at least for three months. Public hangings always drew a crowd, and it was no different on the day of Billy's appointment with the devil. It was scheduled for eleven o'clock in the morning, late enough to give the spectators time to gather and early enough to allow them to go to dinner and discuss it afterward. Judge Wick Justice planned to attend the hanging, since he felt it his duty to attend when he was the judge who sentenced the man to death.

Not the typical spectator at a public hanging, a frail looking little woman with graying hair and a slight bend in her spine, drove her wagon down to the river's edge to water her horse. Having left her humble farm three hours earlier that morning to make it on time to attend the hanging, she made her camp right there and walked the rest of the way to the public gallows. When Davy and Luke had returned home to tell her and her husband about Billy's arrest, Caleb went to his trial with their two sons. Her two sons came home without their father, who had been put in jail. When he got out, he and the boys went back to Austin to settle with the judge who sentenced Billy to die. And that was the last she had seen of any of her men folk. So she hitched the horse up to the wagon and came to see Billy one last time. In her black dress and black shawl over her head, she made her way through the people already gathered there. "'Scuse me, sir," she asked a man standing near the steps that led up to the gallows, "where will they come from when they bring Billy out to hang?"

The man turned and pointed toward a door in the back of the courthouse. "They'll bring him outta that door right yonder." He smiled down at the meek little woman. "Do you know the man they're hangin'?"

"Yes, sir," she replied, "I'm his mother."

"Oh," the man responded. "I'm right sorry, ma'am. Are you sure you wanna watch this?"

"I wanna say goodbye," she said.

"Yes, ma'am. Well, you stay right here by these steps and they'll walk him right by here. You oughta get a chance to tell him goodbye. I'd better go see where my family is." He walked over to the other side of the gallows having suddenly felt uncomfortable where he was and glad his family was at home.

At the stroke of eleven, the door in the back of the courthouse opened, and two deputy marshals walked out with Billy Duncan between them. They forced him to walk briskly toward the gallows, his arms handcuffed behind his back and a short length of chain between his ankles. When they reached the steps to the gallows, she suddenly stepped in front of them. "Ma!" Billy cried out. "What are you doin' here?"

"I come to tell you goodbye," she said as the deputies stopped to keep from knocking her down.

"You have to step back, lady," one of the deputies ordered.

She paid no attention to him. "You be brave, Billy. You show 'em. I don't know where your pa is or your brothers, either, but you show these folks what you're made of."

"Pa's dead, Ma!" Billy blurted.

"All right, lady, step back outta the way or you're gonna be arrested," one of the deputies told her and pushed Billy along to the steps. She backed away but remained in front of the gallows.

"You just keep your eyes on me, Billy, we'll show 'em. Just look at me and you'll be all right." She stood there through the whole procedure, looking her son in the eye until they finished the talking and sprang the trapdoor. Only then did she gasp and turn away. She saw an older man standing off to the side then. With a full gray beard and a long black coat, he looked like an official of some sort. When the man she had spoken to before walked past her she stopped him and asked, "Who is the distinguished looking man over there?"

"That's Judge Wick Justice, ma'am. He's the judge who sentenced Billy to the gallows." He hurried along then, uncomfortable talking to her.

Bannack stood looking over the crowd, now dispersing. He started to ask the judge if he was ready to go home. But he saw a fragile little lady dressed all in black walk up to the judge to ask him something, so he waited a moment.

The judge started to turn toward Bannack when the little lady spoke to him. "Are you the judge who sent that man to be hanged?"

"Yes, ma'am, I'm Judge Wick Justice."

"I'm Ida Duncan," she said. "Billy was my son." Before he could reply, she reached into her purse and pulled out a derringer and fired, putting a shot into Bannack's side as he stepped between the gun and the judge. Bannack snatched the pocket pistol out of her hand as she gazed up at him in horror, expecting him to strike her with his other hand. Instead, he held her by her wrist and she sank to the ground.

"You all right, Judge?" Bannack asked.

"Yes, yes," the judge answered, obviously shaken. "She said she's his mother!"

"What do you want me to do with her?" Bannack asked.

"Just get her away from me," the judge answered. "She's grieving and I'm sorry for her. But I'm not going to press charges on a grieving mother. No harm done. Just get her away from me, and take that damn pistol away from her."

Bannack picked her up from the ground. "Who else is with you?" he demanded.

"Nobody," she cried fearfully as he held her trapped with a big hand holding each of her arms. "I came by myself."

"Oh, yeah?" he replied. "You got a horse or a buggy?"

"A wagon," she said. "I drove my wagon."

"Where is it?" He demanded and she turned her head back toward the river. "All right, take me to it." He released one of her arms and let her lead him away from the courthouse. While they walked, he told her that her son shot a man in the back. "And the regular punishment for that in a court of law is death. Judge Justice just went according to what the law says. You're blaming the wrong person for your son's death. It's your son's fault. Now you go on home and be glad the judge understands you're grievin' and didn't send you to jail." He put her up on the wagon and untied her horse and gave the horse a sound smack on the rump with his open hand. He stood and watched until the wagon drove out of sight. Then he went back to make sure the judge was all right.

"I guess it's not such a good idea for me to attend these damn hangings," the judge said when Bannack came back. "After today, I might stop coming to them. Did you send her on her way?"

"Yes, sir, I watched until her wagon was out of sight," Bannack answered.

"Good, we can go to dinner now. I'll tell you, though, that gave me quite a start when she pulled that gun out of her purse. But you were right there on the spot. I heard the gun go off when you stepped in front of me. I feel damn lucky she missed."

"She didn't miss," Bannack said, "and I expect I need to go see Doc Bane, if you don't mind goin' on to the hotel by yourself."

Only then was the judge aware of the dark red stain spreading on the side of Bannack's shirt. "You stepped between that gun and me and took the bullet!" He exclaimed in shocked surprise. "I heard the gun go off, but I thought you had grabbed her hand or something."

"I didn't have time," Bannack explained, "but I turned my body to take the shot in the side, hopin' it wouldn't do too much damage. I was lucky, I reckon, because it didn't seem to slow me down too much. But it's startin' to smart a little now, so I think I'd best go see the doctor, if you don't mind goin' to the dinin' room without me."

"We're going straight to the doctor," the judge said. "I feel like a damn fool. You took that bullet intended for me, and I didn't even know it!"

"Don't forget," Bannack reminded him, "Elwood is

supposed to meet us at the dinin' room for dinner." Elwood remained in the office during the hanging, since he didn't like to watch a man being hung. "I can go to the doctor by myself."

"Good Lord, man," the judge replied, "you just took a bullet meant for me. The least I can do is go with you to make sure the doctor takes care of you. Can you walk all right?" Bannack said he could. "Let's go, then. Maybe we can catch him before he goes to dinner."

Ten minutes later, they walked into Doc Bane's office and rang the little bell sitting on his desk to announce their arrival. In a few seconds, Lucy Bane came from the hallway to greet them. Seeing Bannack holding a bloody shirt tightly against his side, she at first assumed he had somehow aggravated his chest wound. "What did you do to that wound?" she scolded.

"Nothin'," he answered. "That one's comin' along just fine. This is a new one. I've got another one. This one's in my side."

"My goodness, Judge, you've got to keep this man from associating with men who carry guns," Lucy said.

"This one came from a little old woman, carrying a pocket pistol," the judge said, "and it was meant for me."

"I'll go get Doc," she said. "You know where Doc's surgery is. Just go on in and sit down on the table. You might as well get that shirt off and your undershirt, if you're wearing one." She went back down the hall.

"No need to hold you up, Judge," Bannack said. "I might be here for a while and Elwood might start worryin' if you don't show up at the hotel pretty soon."

"I'll wait until Doc Bane comes in," the judge said.

A few moments later, the doctor came in. "Good afternoon, gentlemen," he said. "Lucy says you took another bullet and we ain't even had time for the first one to heal properly. I see you're not wearing a bandage on it anymore, so it's looking pretty good. Let's have a look at what you've got now. How'd you get this one?" While the judge told him how it happened, Doc examined the entry wound in Bannack's side. "Well, it looks like you were lucky again. You walked in here, so we know the bullet didn't hit the spine or your pelvis, so it's lodged in there in the muscle. It's in there pretty deep, but I don't think it'll hurt anything, if we just leave it in there. If we do, I'll have some repair work where it went in. It was at extra close range from the look of it. So I expect I'll need to put you to sleep for a little while, either way. So what do you think, you wanna carry it around with you or do you want me to go in there and dig it out?" Bannack hesitated, so Doc said, "If you have trouble with it in there, we can always go in there and cut it out later."

"If it was in your side, what would you do?" Bannack asked.

Doc shrugged. "I'd probably leave it in there." So Bannack told him he'd do the same. Lucy got the chloroform ready while the judge paid Doc for his services in advance. Then the judge left to meet Elwood in the hotel dining room.

It was only about an hour before the judge would normally close his office for the day when Bannack recovered from the effects of the chloroform. So instead of going to the office, Bannack decided to go on back to the house. He needed to put on his extra shirt and see if he could get the bloodstains out of the one he took off. Maybe he would have time to do that before supper was ready. When he was ready to go, Doc Bane said, "You're one helluva man, Bannack, and you've been lucky. But you can't keep taking shots like that. The law of averages is gonna catch up with you."

"Believe me, it's a habit I'm tryin' my best to break." He

left the doctor's office and walked to the stable to get his horse.

"I swear, Bannack," Sam Garland greeted him, "you look like you been rode hard and put away wet."

"Kinda feels that way," Bannack said.

Eyeing the bloody shirt, Sam asked, "Where you been?"

"Just came from the doctor's office," Bannack said. "Tell Judge Wick and Elwood that I've already gone home, will ya?"

"Sure will," Sam replied, "but what in the world happened to you?"

"Ask the judge when he comes for his horse," Bannack told him, "he tells it better than I do."

"Right, I'll do that," Sam said, thinking that maybe the big man had spent some time in a saloon and that was the source of the bloody shirt as well as the whimsical remarks.

Henry was inside the house, talking to Lottie when he looked out the window and saw Bannack ride past the house on his way to the barn. "Yonder's John," he said, "but I don't see the judge and Elwood with him." He walked over to the window to get a better look. "Is that blood all over his shirt?"

Lottie walked over to the window to see for herself. "That's what it looks like. Better go down to the barn and see what's happened." Henry went out the kitchen door.

"John, are you all right?" Henry called out as he approached the barn. "Where's the judge and Mr. Wilson?" Feeling satisfied that he had yelled plenty loud enough to be heard, he walked on into the barn. He was always careful not to surprise the big man because of Bannack's automatic reactions.

Bannack casually turned his head toward Henry as he

pulled the buckskin's saddle off and parked it on the side rail of a stall. "I expect they'll be back for supper at the usual time," he said. "I had to go by the doctor's office, so I just came on home, instead of goin' back to the office."

"Where'd all the blood come from?" Henry asked.

"A sweet lookin' little old lady put a bullet in my side with one of those little pocket pistols," Bannack said.

"Where was that?" Henry asked.

"At the hanging. Turns out she was Billy Duncan's mother. So now, I gotta put on my other shirt and I'm gonna see if I can scrub the blood outta this one."

"Forever more . . ." Henry started. "Billy's mother, well ain't that somethin'? Did they put her in jail?"

"Nah, we took her pistol away from her and sent her home." He went over and picked up a big bucket near the pump and filled it with water. He came out of his bloody shirt and put it in the bucket, then he got a bar of lye soap from a shelf in the tack room and went to work scrubbing his shirt.

"Lottie woulda done that for you," Henry thought to say.

"I know she would," Bannack said, "but I don't want her to have to fool with a mess like this." He worked on the shirt for quite a while, refilling his bucket three times until he got most of the stain out of the shirt. He called it good enough when he reached the point where he feared he was going to wear a larger hole in the shirt than the one the .44 bullet had created. It still had a faint red tint on that side of the shirt, but it was clean. He was hanging the shirt on the clothesline when the judge and Elwood arrived.

"How ya doin', John?" The judge sang out when they rode up to the barn. "Did Doc get that bullet out of your side?"

"No, sir, he left it in," Bannack replied. "He said it wouldn't do any harm where it was, so he just patched up the hole. He said he'd just make a bigger hole tryin' to dig it outta there."

They dismounted, and Henry took their horses for them. "You should have let Lottie wash that shirt for you," Elwood said. "You've probably lost a lot of blood and you didn't even get any dinner."

"I wasn't all that hungry, anyway," Bannack said. "I intend to make up for it at supper."

"Well, if you're through with your laundry duties, let's go see if supper's ready," Judge Wick said.

Lottie was putting it on the table when they walked in the kitchen door with Henry hustling along behind them. She stopped and stood waiting for someone to tell her the news. When no one offered, she said, "For goodness sakes! Is anybody gonna tell me why John rode in here with a bloody shirt?"

"We figured you already knew," Judge Wick said.

"I sent Henry down to the barn to find out and he never came back," Lottie complained. "Then the next thing I see is John hanging a shirt up on the clothesline."

"Billy Duncan's mama shot him when they was watchin' the hangin'," Henry declared.

"My Lord!" Lottie cried out. "You've been shot again?" She rushed over and took his arm. "Sit down." She led him to a chair at the table. "Are you all right?"

"I'm fine," he assured her, "been to the doctor and got patched up."

"And here you were, down there washing out your shirt." She gave Henry a scolding look. "Why the hell didn't you come back here and tell me?" Back to Bannack then, she asked, "Why on earth did Billy Duncan's mother want to shoot you for?"

"You don't quite have the real story about that shooting," Judge Wick interrupted. "It's true, she shot John, but the shot was intended for me. John saw her pull the gun out of her purse, and he stepped in front of it and took the shot himself. Then he subdued the poor woman, marched her back to her wagon, and sent her on her way. And all that time he had her bullet in his side, and I didn't even know it. When he jumped between her gun and me, I couldn't see what happened. I heard the shot, but I assumed she had missed because he had everything in hand. And he didn't act like he'd just been shot."

Lottie turned and set a steady gaze upon the big man, amazed by an apparent devotion to the judge that she had not realized. It occurred to her then that she was probably guilty of underestimating the man, John Bannack. An ex-convict who spoke very little, as if words were too expensive to waste on mundane chatter, he was easily dismissed as untamed. *Judge Wick's panther* came to mind, kept in the barn with the other animals. Judge Wick had been convinced that John Bannack should not have been imprisoned. She was inclined to agree. He was supposed to have robbed a bank, but she was certain there must have been a more important motive for it than stealing the money.

CHAPTER 22

The days that followed the hanging of Billy Duncan were troublesome days for the sheriff of Austin as well as the Texas Supreme Court. It had nothing to do with the hanging, but everything to do with Billy's brothers. The trouble was created by the absurd sentencing of ninety days in the county jail for Luke and Davy Duncan for their part in the attempted murder of Judge Wick Justice. Sheriff Roger Nicholson complained to the court that the county jail was not equipped to handle two prisoners for ninety days. The jail could handle a prisoner for a week at most. There were no exercise facilities for long-term prisoners and no guards to escort the inmates to work details. There was not even a deputy sheriff at the present time, and the sheriff was still charged with his duties to the town as sheriff. The only place that was equipped to handle them was the Texas State Prison Huntsville Unit and a couple of deputy marshals and a jail wagon would be required to transport the prisoners to Huntsville, one hundred and sixty miles away. "Why the hell didn't Raymond Grant just set the two of them free?" the Chief Justice asked sarcastically. "It would have been a helluva lot cheaper."

The decision was finally made to go ahead and transport the two prisoners over to Huntsville to be incarcerated in the prison to serve their three-month sentence. On the day before they were scheduled to leave for Huntsville, Luke and Davy had a visitor. Sheriff Nicholson looked up in surprise when Clark Spencer walked into his office. Judge Raymond Grant's clerk was not a frequent visitor to the jail or the sheriff's office. "Mr. Spencer," Nicholson greeted him, "something I can do for you, sir?"

"Yes, Sheriff," Spencer said, "I would like to visit Davy and Luke Duncan."

"You would?" Nicholson replied before he caught himself, expecting anything but that.

"Yes. I think that's permissible, isn't it? The prisoners are allowed to have visitors, aren't they? Or are there certain visitor hours? Maybe I should come back some other time."

"No, I mean yes, sir, you can visit them," Nicholson stammered. "I reckon I was just surprised you wanted to visit them, what with you being the clerk for the judge that sent 'em to jail."

Spencer smiled patiently. "I guess a lot of folks don't know that Judge Grant is a compassionate man. Some even think he gives harsh sentences, but they don't know all the facts of every case. We found that there were so many important facts that were never brought out in this case that might have called for a lighter sentence than three months."

"I didn't think there could be a much lighter sentence than three months," the sheriff said.

"But that's already said and done," Spencer said. "The purpose of my visit today is to see if the men of the Duncan family have made any provision for the welfare of those they leave behind when they are killed or go to prison. We know that these two boys are leaving their mother a widow now and with one son dead. The judge, in his compassion, would like to know if there is anyone left at home to take care of her. If not, then he is prepared to get her some help until her sons are released from prison."

"I swear," Nicholson responded, "I'da never accused the judge of that. No offense," he quickly added.

Spencer chuckled. "Not many people would. The judge wouldn't want it to get out that he has a soft side. Anyway, can I visit the prisoners?"

"Sure you can," the sheriff said. "I expect they'll be surprised to see you." He walked over and unlocked the door to the cell room and walked inside. "You've got a visitor, boys," he announced, which got them up off their cots. He walked back past Spencer and japed, "I don't reckon you've got any weapons on you, have you, Mr. Spencer?"

"Nope," Spencer returned, "I'm clean."

Davy and Luke came at once to the front of the cell to see who had come to see them. They were both surprised to see the man who had acted as bailiff at their trial. Spencer waited until the sheriff went back into his office before he walked up to the bars. "You might remember me at your trial. I'm Clark Spencer, I work for Judge Raymond Grant. I want to know if you two realize how lucky you were to have Judge Grant preside over your case. Three months for trying to help your father kill Judge Justice? Do you know what you would have gotten if he had been your judge? He tried your brother Billy, and you know what he got, right?" They both stared at him, wide-eyed and confused. "I came here to tell you that Judge Grant thinks you got a raw deal and that's why you got such a light sentence. He's concerned about you and the rest of your family, if you've got family. I know you've got a mother. Judge Grant is concerned about her and wants to make sure there's someone to take care of her. Do you know that your mother was at your brother Billy's hanging?"

"Ma was at the hangin'?" Davy blurted.

"Yes, she was," Spencer replied. "She drove all the way from her home in a wagon to say goodbye to Billy."

"I swear," Luke said, "that sounds like Ma."

"What I want to know is, does your ma have anybody to take care of her?" Spencer asked. "Has she got any money to buy food while you boys are away in prison? Because, if she doesn't, we'll get her some help, at least until you get out and can take care of her."

"I don't think she's got any money," Davy said. "But Ma's tough. She can take care of herself. She's spent most of her life alone while the men were out gettin' in trouble."

"There's nobody left at home to help her?"

"Nah, ain't nobody," Luke said, "she ain't never needed nobody."

"Well, in that case, you wouldn't mind if we arranged to give her a little money to tide her over till you boys can take care of her. Is that right?"

They looked at each other and laughed. "I reckon we wouldn't mind that a-tall," Davy answered him.

"How can we find your home?" Spencer asked.

"You know where Gentry's Store is?" Luke asked. Spencer shook his head. "You know where Black Creek is?"

"No," Spencer said. "Can you draw me a map?" He pulled an envelope and a pencil out of his coat pocket. "Here, draw it on the back of this." He handed it to Luke.

Luke handed it to Davy. "Here, you do it. You can draw better'n me."

Davy took the envelope and drew a rough map for him. "It's about twelve miles from Austin. Just follow the river till you get to Black Creek and Gentry's, then follow the creek till you get to the first log house you come to. And make sure you call out loud and clear or Ma's liable to take a shot at you." Both brothers chuckled at that.

Spencer took a look at the map, then put the envelope

back in his pocket. "All right, boys, I'll give you a little bit of advice. Do your time at Huntsville and don't cause trouble and you'll be out in three months. That ain't a long time, even in prison. Then you can take care of whatever business you think needs taking care of." He turned and went back out the cell room door.

The sheriff got up from his desk and locked the door to the cell room. "Did you find out what you wanted to know?" he asked as he followed Spencer to the front door.

"Yes, I did," Spencer answered. "Like I figured, their mother's by herself with nobody to help her. So I wouldn't be surprised if the judge sent a little bit of help her way." He released a little sigh. "And more than likely, I'll be the one he'll send up to see her." He opened the front door and said, "Well, good afternoon to you, Sheriff." He headed back to the judge's office then, satisfied that he had planted the seed in the minds of the two sons that would persuade them that Judge Grant was their friend and Judge Justice was their enemy. Then, when they came out of prison with revenge in mind for their father and brother, they would target Judge Wick and his panther to pay the price. That would benefit Judge Grant's ambitions. He wasn't looking forward to the little trip to visit Ida Duncan, however.

As far as Judge Grant's nemesis was concerned, it was a period of relative peace for a change for Judge Wick Justice and his crew. He, along with Lottie's help, persuaded Bannack to take it easy for a little while to give his latest bullet wound time to heal. Never one to sit idle for any length of time, Bannack gave it one day of sitting in a rocking chair on the judge's front porch with an occasional sip from the bottle of laudanum Doc Bane gave him. The next day, he was ready to do whatever job Judge Wick had for him to do. He complained that the wound bothered him most when he tried to sleep. Sleeping on either side caused him discomfort and the only way he could go to sleep was to sleep on his back, which caused him to snore, which caused him to wake up. At breakfast the second morning after, he reported that he was ready to go back to work, so he attended a hearing on a land dispute the judge was presiding over. There was really nothing required of him, so he was rather relieved when the judge told him to stay home on the second day of the hearing because he was proving to be more a distraction than a help. Unlike with some of the criminal cases, the judge's life was not in danger, anyway.

Similar to Judge Justice's schedule, Judge Grant did not have a busy week either. So he thought it a good time to send Clark Spencer up the river to visit Ida Duncan. Spencer left after breakfast and set out on a narrow trail that followed the river northwest. According to what Davy Duncan had told him, he had about twelve miles to travel in order to reach Black Creek and Gentry's Store. He planned to get there and back by suppertime, so he started out at an easy lope the bay gelding could maintain for a few miles before reining him back to a walk. It was an easy ride. He came upon several creeks that he thought could have been Black Creek and he wondered how accurate Davy's estimate of distance was. But there was no sign of a store and he began to wonder. Was the store located on the river where Black Creek flowed into it? Or was the store actually on Black Creek? If so, could he see it from the trail beside the river? Maybe the store was on the river, just close to Black Creek. "I should have pinned the knucklehead down on the location of the damn store," he complained to the bay gelding.

　　As it turned out, he couldn't have missed Gentry's Store. It was built on the riverbank beside a creek with a small back porch extending out a little over the water. There was a half-sunken boat tied up to one of the poles supporting the porch. "I didn't need the map," he muttered to himself. "He could have just told me to follow the trail till I came to this store." He decided he'd make sure, though, so he pulled his horse up at the front of the store. Then he saw the small crudely printed sign, Gentry's Store. He got off the bay horse and looped the reins over the hitching rail, took the one step up to the porch and walked into the store to see a large, heavy-set man coming from a door in the back of the store.

"Mornin'. I didn't hear you ride up. Can I help you?"

"If you've got any chewin' tobacco, you can sell me some," Spencer answered. He liked to chew tobacco, but Judge Grant wouldn't allow it in his office or the courtroom.

"I sure do, most all the popular brands," Waylan Gentry said. He walked over behind the counter to a row of big jars filled with plugs of tobacco. "See the one you want?" Spencer pointed to one and held up two fingers. Gentry took out two plugs, ripped a piece of wrapping paper off a roll and wrapped the two plugs up. When Spencer gave him a questioning look, Gentry said, "Ten cents." Spencer reached into his pocket for some change and gave him a dime. "Ain't seen you in the store before," Gentry said. "Where you headed for? Austin?"

"Nope, I was headed here," Spencer said. "I just came from Austin. I figure that's Black Creek on the other side of your store."

"Matter of fact," Gentry said. "You know somebody on Black Creek?"

"I'm going to see Ida Duncan," Spencer replied. "I was told she lives in the first log house I'd come to after I left your store."

"Who told you that?" Gentry asked. "Are you a lawman?"

"I work for a circuit judge, but I'm not a lawman. I told Davy and Luke Duncan I'd deliver a message from them to their mother. They're on their way to the Huntsville Unit."

"I ain't surprised," Gentry remarked. "I heard the judge hung their brother Billy."

"That's right," Spencer said, "but not the judge I work for. We're workin' with Luke and Davy. I've got a message from them to their mama. She lives in the first log house up that creek, right?"

"That's right. They send any money with that message? 'Cause she's got a bill ridin' here at the store, she keeps promisin' to catch up."

"Like I said, the message is for her," Spencer said. "How much is she on your books for?"

Gentry reached under the counter and pulled out a ledger. "As of day before yesterday, she's on my book for eight dollars and fifty cents. That ain't a whole lot, but she ain't showed any sign of payin' anything on it. Caleb and the boys was always goin' off and leavin' her by herself for a long time, and he would always come to the store and catch her up on her bill when he got back. I didn't have no problem with that. Only thing is, this time Caleb nor none of the boys have been back. Least, they ain't been back to the store. I heard Caleb and the two boys was back, but I ain't seen hide nor hair of 'em."

"Since you haven't heard, I can tell you this. They're not coming back to Black Creek. Caleb's dead and the two boys are on their way to prison."

"What's that poor woman gonna do?" Gentry responded. "She ain't got nobody to help her. She's a tough little ol' lady, but she ain't gonna be able to work that place by herself."

"Well, like I said, the judge I work for is tryin' to get her some help. He's already got her two boys a short sentence, so they'll be out pretty soon. I wanna help a little, too. So I'm gonna pay you that eight dollars and fifty cents she owes you."

"Why, that's mighty Christian of you, friend," Gentry said. "I appreciate that."

"Yeah, I'm always doin' Christian things for people," Spencer said sarcastically.

"Drop in again, if you're back this way," Gentry called after him. *I must be really slow witted,* he thought. *Took me long enough to remember that rascal.* "Melva!" He yelled down the short hall to the kitchen. "Guess who just came in the store."

"Who?" His wife asked when she walked into the store.

"That feller that worked for Judge Grant at Bobby's trial four years ago. I recognized him but I couldn't call his name, even if I'd wanted to. I hoped somebody had shot him and he was already in hell."

"Clark Spencer," Melva said. "What did he want?"

"Wanted to find Ida Duncan's house."

Spencer left Gentry's Store and started up the left side of Black Creek, since Gentry said that was the side Duncan's log house was on. He would have taken that side anyway, since that was the side the path was on. He cut off a chew of tobacco before he started and began working up a spit before he came to the first of two little cabins Gentry told him he would pass before he reached the log house. Both cabins looked deserted, although he thought he saw a face disappear from a window in the second one as he rode past it. He figured the distance to be about a quarter of a mile from the river when he came to the log house. Unlike the two shacks before it, it didn't look deserted, and there were curtains on the windows and the weeds were chopped around the house. "Whadda you want?" The shrill voice came from behind him, startling him enough to cause him to spit involuntarily, leaving a brown streak across the bay gelding's breast.

He turned to look behind him to discover a skinny little woman aiming a double-barrel shotgun at him. "Damn," he blurted and wiped his mouth with the back of his hand. "You gave me a start. Where'd you come from?"

"The same place ever'one of us comes from. Whadda you want?"

"Are you Ida Duncan?"

"Maybe I am and maybe I ain't, but if you don't start tellin' me what your business is on my property pretty damn quick, I'm gonna make a mess outta that fancy vest you're wearin'." Recovering somewhat from his initial reception, he started to step down from the saddle. "I ain't asked you to step down," she warned and raised the shotgun to aim at his head.

He paused to say, "You've got a mighty odd way of welcoming somebody who just paid your bill at Gentry's Store for you." He proceeded to step down in spite of the warning.

She took a couple of steps back but continued to hold the shotgun on him. "What bill? What the hell are you talkin' about?"

"That total of eight dollars and fifty cents on Gentry's books that you owe," Spencer said. "You don't owe him a dime anymore."

She was at once suspicious. "Why would you pay off my debts? Who the hell are you, anyway?" she demanded.

"I work for the only friend you and Davy and Luke have left and the only friend who can help you get the two men who are responsible for killin' your husband and your son

Billy. Those two men are Judge Wick Justice and John Bannack. You met them both at Billy's hangin', but you missed your chance."

The memory of that day flooded her brain with the frustration of her failure. "I won't miss next time," she stated.

"You ain't likely to get another chance like that one," Spencer said. "They know you now. You'll be shot on sight. You need your sons to help you get your revenge and that's why I rode up here to find you. They told me how to find you. Now, let me spell it out for you. Your two sons are a hundred and seventy-five miles from here. That's four, four and a half days on a horse, if you made forty miles a day. Thanks to Judge Grant takin' charge of Luke and Davy's trial, they ain't gonna serve but three months for helpin' your husband try to kill Judge Justice. When they get out, they'll wanna come after Judge Wick and Bannack. Trouble is, they're gonna be on foot with no weapons, no food, and no money to buy anything with. Now the judge can't be involved in anything like that, and I sure as hell am not. So what I came lookin' for you today is this. Have you got the backbone to ride a horse that hundred and seventy-five miles, if someone was to buy you a good horse and a packhorse and give you enough money to buy your sons horses, weapons, and everything else they'd need to even the score with Judge Wick and Bannack? You think about that. Could you do it? It's a helluva lot for a woman to take on."

"Hell, yes, I can do it," she said at once. "I've been doin' things a woman ain't supposed to do all my life. How will I know what day they'll be released from that prison?"

"Can you read?" he responded.

"Yes, I can read," she claimed.

"I wrote the day they are set to be released down for you as well as some instructions on where to go to meet them.

It's all in this envelope, along with some money to buy you a good horse and to live on till I meet you when it's time to ride over there with the rest of the money." He reached into his saddlebag and pulled out the envelope. "Here, I'll hold that for you," he said and took the shotgun. She immediately opened the envelope, anxiously looking for the money. When she looked up at him again, he had the shotgun aimed at her. "Make no mistake," he told her, "you don't honor this deal, you pay with your life."

She smiled at him when he handed the shotgun back to her. "You ain't gotta worry about me. I'll get my boys back and we'll take care of the rest of it." He climbed back into the saddle. "You never told me your name," she said.

"Santa Claus," he said, wheeled the bay around, and headed back down the trail toward the river.

CHAPTER 23

The next few weeks brought a peaceful period for the town of Austin, an atmosphere much preferred by the town council and the state capitol complex. There were no shootings or gunfights to be dealt with, nothing more serious than the overindulgence of alcohol that resulted in a night sleeping it off in jail. It was a time of healing for the man from Waco. An unusually big and strong man, Bannack tended to heal rapidly. So before a month had passed since Billy Duncan's hanging, both of Bannack's wounds were forgotten. And it was welcome news to him when Elwood informed him that in two weeks it would be the first of June and time for the judge to ride the circuit. They would be riding back the way they had ended the circuit with a trial scheduled in Bryan, which was now the county seat of Brazos County. "I expect you and the judge will be glad to get back in the saddle and sleeping on the ground again," Elwood said. "But you know I always prefer working in town, eating at Lottie's table, and sleeping in my bed." He didn't hesitate to make the comment because they already knew of his preference for the city. He had not shared the fact that he had been offered a position on the chief justice's staff that would have kept him in Austin year-round, however. He knew Judge Wick would have encouraged him to take the job, but Elwood felt that the judge needed him, so he kept the offer to himself.

"Where is the judge, anyway?" Bannack asked. "I thought you said he was comin' in to work in about an hour."

"I was just guessing," Elwood said. "You know when we ate breakfast, Lottie said she checked on him when he hadn't come out of his room yet. She peeked in his room and he was sound asleep, so she decided not to wake him. We stayed up pretty late last night." He looked at the clock on the wall. "It is pretty late for him, though. He must have been more tired than he admitted last night."

Having had his horse shod earlier, there was really nothing else for Bannack to do in town, so he decided to go back to the house to make sure the judge was all right. When he opened the door to leave, he saw Henry Grimsley hurrying down the hall in his direction. "John!" Henry cried out when he saw him.

"What is it, Henry!" Bannack responded, knowing it had to be something terribly important to bring Henry into town. "What's wrong?" He stepped back inside the door to let Henry in.

Elwood got up from his desk when Henry rushed in breathless in his panic. "It's the judge!" he exclaimed. "Somethin's wrong with him. He won't wake up!"

"You mean he's dead?" Elwood asked.

"I don't know, I mean Lottie says he's still breathin'," Henry answered.

"You go get the doctor," Bannack told Elwood. "I'll go get our horses and meet you at the doctor's office!" He didn't wait for Elwood to reply but went out the door at once.

Sam Garland saddled Elwood's horse while Bannack saddled his, and he was soon out of the stable and on his way to the doctor's office, where he found Doc Bane hitching his horse up to his buggy. They were soon underway and when they arrived at the house, Lottie met them at the door and told the doctor that the judge had awakened briefly before going back to sleep again. "Did he talk to you when he woke up?" Doc asked.

"Not really," Lottie answered. "It was more like he tried to talk but couldn't make the words. He tried to move, too, but it looked like one side of his body wouldn't work."

Doc checked his blood pressure and listened to his heart. When he was through, he told them what he thought. "I wish I was a lot more experienced in this field, but what I think has happened is he's had a stroke." When he saw nothing but blank expressions in the room, including that one on the patient's face, he explained. "Either something's interfering with the blood in his brain, or he's getting too much blood flow to the brain."

"What can we do for him?" Lottie asked. "Have you got some medicine for that?"

"Unfortunately, there ain't nothing I can do for him. The only thing you can do is let him rest and he might start to come back in a little while. He might get well again but still be helpless on one side of his body or one side of his head. All we can do is wait and see. He's gonna be helpless till he does come back from it. So somebody will have to take care of his bodily functions and clean him up."

"Judge ain't gonna like that," Elwood remarked.

"Sometimes it was just some little accident of some kind that caused the stroke and the patient gets well again," Doc Bane said. "Judge Justice is a pretty tough ol' bird. Maybe he'll lick it. I wish there was something I could do for him, but unfortunately there isn't."

"How much do we owe you, Doc?" Elwood asked.

"I usually charge two dollars for a house call," Doc

answered. "But since there wasn't anything I could do for him, let's just call it a dollar."

"I'm sure the judge would insist that we pay your usual fee," Elwood said and gave Doc two dollars.

"I don't know about that," Doc japed. "If the judge was awake, he might say, since I didn't really do anything for him, to just give me fifty cents." But he took the two dollars. When Bannack and Elwood walked out to his buggy with him, Doc asked Bannack, "How's that bullet in your side? Do you still feel it?"

"Nope," Bannack replied, "you were right about that. I don't even know it's there."

"It should give you a good feeling to know you'll never run out of ammunition," Doc japed and chuckled. "'Course I hope you don't ever run into the situation where you need it."

They stood there and watched the departing buggy for a few minutes before Bannack asked, "What do we do now?"

"Well," Elwood answered, "I expect I'll have to go back to the office and get all the files on the few cases we've got left to try here in Austin and take them to the chief justice, so he can turn them over to Judge Grant. I'll have to ask what to do about the trial in Bryan. I expect they might give that to Grant, too. I hate like hell to turn all these files over to that crook."

"I'll help you carry the files over," Bannack said. "Then I don't know what to do. Maybe I can clean up the whole office for you, so it'll be nice and clean when the judge gets well." He couldn't imagine that the judge might not recover enough to return to the bench, but he also had to wonder what he was going to do if the judge never recovered enough to return to the circuit. He wouldn't need a bodyguard if he was forced to retire. There was nothing he could do but wait and see.

So for the next couple of weeks, Elwood went to the office every day, but Bannack stayed at the house, helping Henry with any repairs the house and barn needed. Falling back on the skills he had learned as a boy, he plowed up a garden plot for Lottie. And keeping his shooting skills sharp, he spent a few days hunting to provide some fresh meat for Lottie to cook. The routine became dull and lazy as they all watched the daily progress of the judge. And then one morning, Lottie came to the breakfast table to report that the judge asked if he could sit in a chair. "He asked?" Elwood responded. "Are you saying he talked?"

"That's what I'm saying," Lottie answered. "He talked. At first, it was hard to understand what he said because he still can't move one side of his face. But that's what he said, and I told him I was going to get somebody to help. So are you going to just sit there, or are you going to help me bring the judge to the table?" They stampeded out of the kitchen to transport the judge.

He was overwhelmed to be attacked by such an exuberant staff as Elwood and Lottie managed to get a robe over his nightshirt. Then Bannack lifted him up from the bed as easily as if lifting a child. And while he held him, Lottie stuck a bedroom slipper on each foot. Then Bannack carried him into the kitchen and placed him in his chair at the head of the table. Lottie followed behind him with her arms loaded with pillows and blankets, which she used to prop the judge up in his chair. "I was sick of that damn bed," he managed with only one side of his face working. He was not steady enough to hold a cup or manage a fork, so Lottie fed him a bite at a time, followed by a sip of coffee. He was able to stay with them for about twenty minutes before he announced a declaration of defeat. "I feel a little dizzy, and I need to get back to my room now."

"You ready to get back to your bed?" Lottie asked.

"I'm ready to get back to my bedpan," he told her. His statement triggered an exodus twice as fast as the transport that brought him into the kitchen.

"Don't drop him!" Lottie couldn't help but cry out as she ran after Bannack, carrying the packing for his bed. Hustling ahead of them, Elwood spotted the shiny bedpan sitting on a straight-back chair near the door. He scooped it up and slapped it down, right-side-up on the bed. Then he caught the tails of both robe and nightshirt and pulled them back as Bannack landed his cargo, bare skin to cold metal and the judge expressed himself immediately after making contact.

The following days brought encouraging increments of improvement until the judge seemed to reach the extent of his recovery from the stroke. He did not complain, telling his staff that he was a lucky man. He had survived the devil's dart, and while not restored to his original condition, he was able to drag himself around primarily by using the right side of his body and a single crutch. His brain, though not nimble, was functioning well enough to make sensible decisions. It was obvious to those around him that he was not yet considering retirement from the bench.

With so much invested in the welfare of this one man, it was easy for those who worked for him and admired his spirit to forget other seemingly less important things—like how fast three months pass. To Judge Raymond Grant, the three months he sentenced Davy and Luke Duncan to serve were grinding by as slowly for him as they were for the Duncan brothers. He truly believed that they would have only one thought in mind when they were free, to put an end to Judge Wick Justice and Bannack. So the news of Justice's stroke was of particular interest to Raymond Grant for his first thought was that it might mean the special plan he had arranged with Ida Duncan was no longer needed.

Then upon hearing that Judge Justice might be recovering, he was fully as interested in his progress as Judge Wick's staff. He decided his original plan to get rid of Wick and his panther was his best option. So he told Spencer to make the second visit to Ida Duncan when there was but one week left before the Duncan brothers date of release. It was costing him a lot of money, but it was far less than what he would have to pay an assassin to kill two people.

So, with one week to go before her two sons were to be released from prison, Ida Duncan had a second visit from Santa Claus. "I've been lookin' for you to show up," she said as she propped her shotgun against the wall and walked out on the porch. "I thought maybe you mighta changed your mind and you weren't really Santa Claus after all. But I see you're leadin' a packhorse this trip. You headin' somewhere?"

He ignored her question. "Mind if I step down?" He asked in a sarcastic tone, remembering his first visit to her house.

"Why, not at all, step down and I'll even offer you a cup of coffee. This time I've got coffee, thanks to the money you left me on your first visit."

He stepped down and said, "No thanks to the coffee. Did you get yourself a decent horse?" She said she did, so he said, "Let's take a look at it."

She stepped down from the porch and led him around the house to a shed and a corral where he saw an old sorrel and a gray that looked in good shape. He checked the gray over, a gelding, he guessed him to be around five years old. "You did pretty well," he said. "He looks like he oughta make the trip in good time. You still wanna make that ride to get your boys?"

"Hell, yes, I decided I was goin' to get my boys whether you showed up again or not."

"It's gonna take you four, maybe four and a half days, to make that trip to Huntsville," Spencer reminded her. "That's a long trip for a woman by herself. Are you sure you're up to it?"

"Don't you worry your little head about me, Sonny. I've hoed a few hard rows in my time. That little trip over to Huntsville ain't enough to cause me worry. I've got my shotgun and a Colt .45 I'll be wearin', and I know how to use both of 'em. Me and that gray geldin' has already decided we're gonna get along just fine, so there ain't nothin' holdin' me back."

"You still got that envelope tellin' you what day they'll be released and where you'll go to meet them?" She said that she did, so he continued. "I brought you another envelope with enough money to buy two good horses and saddles. And I'm leavin' you this packhorse with two Colt six-guns and gun belts, some blankets, and some food to cook on your trip to Huntsville. If you ain't too foolish when you buy the horses and saddles, there oughta be enough money left over to buy food and such for your trip back to Austin."

Ida just stood staring at him as if trying to figure him out. "I'm tryin' to figure out why you're givin' all this to me and my sons. It don't really make a lot of sense to me, unless it's just a different way of hirin' somebody to do a killin' for you." He started to reply, but she interrupted. "Don't get me wrong. I'm grateful as hell for everything you've done, and I wanna tell you this. I think you'll be mighty pleased with what you bought 'cause it looks like you and me are wantin' the same thing."

"I think we have an understanding," Spencer said. "I hope you enjoy your trip." He handed her the second envelope and turned as if to leave but paused to say one more thing. "By the way, that judge that sentenced your son Billy to hang had a stroke. It left him crippled up to where he just sits around at home. That big man that works for him, the one who stepped in and took that bullet for him lives in the barn behind the house. He's the one who shot your husband in the back." He left her to absorb all that, got on his horse, and rode back to town.

Ida didn't wait long to make her preparations for her trip to Huntsville. She had already asked Waylan Gentry how to get to Huntsville and he drew her a map to follow. She took the packs off the horse that Spencer had brought her, so she could see what she had and what she would need. She was pleased to see Spencer had provided her with flour, sugar, coffee, hardtack, and bacon. She would add her frying pan and coffeepot and a few other things and be ready to travel. At first planning to start out in the morning, she changed her mind, since there was still plenty of daylight left. So she closed all the windows and bolted the back door. Then she padlocked the front door and turned her old sorrel horse out of the corral. "You'll most likely stick around here near the creek, but if you're gone when I come back, I've got this packhorse to take your place." All set then, she climbed on the gray and started out for Huntsville, riding for what she estimated to be about twenty miles before she decided to stop for the night. She was careful when selecting her camp, following a creek a long way from the trail, so as not to advertise her presence with her campfire. She slept in her blanket with her shotgun beside her and she was not afraid because she knew that anybody who bothered her was going to pay dearly for the visit.

The map that Gentry had drawn for her took her through the town of Bryan, but she decided to skirt the town, thinking it unwise to advertise an old woman traveling alone. She met only a couple of other travelers on the trail. They both stared but offered a "Howdy" as they passed. They were on the road between Austin and Bryan, and she went from Bryan almost to Huntsville before meeting anyone else. When she got to Huntsville, she went directly to the Walls Unit and the gate that Spencer said her sons would be walking out of. Their release date was not until the following day, but she wanted to make sure she knew that was the right place. She pulled her horses up before two men standing talking close by. They looked like they might be prison guards. They stopped talking to stare at her. "Pardon me, fellers, but is that where the prisoners come out that have been released?" She pointed to the gate.

"Yes, it is, ma'am," one of them answered. "But there won't be no prisoners bein' released this time of day. They'll be released about nine o'clock in the mornin'. Was there somebody you were supposed to meet?"

"Not till tomorrow, the seventh," Ida said.

"Well, that'll be about nine o'clock in the morning," he repeated.

"Much obliged," she said and started to turn away.

"Are you lookin' for the campground?" The other man asked. When she looked puzzled by his question, he said, "There's a little campground by the creek about sixty yards over yonder." He pointed toward a little grove of trees. "That's where most folks camp who've come to meet somebody. Since you're by yourself, you might like to camp where some other folks are camped."

"Much obliged," she said again. "That sounds like a good idea."

She rode over to the grove pointed out and found a wagon parked there by the creek. There was a woman cooking something in a frying pan and a couple of little boys playing by the creek. Ida and the woman exchanged nods as Ida rode past her to pick a spot beyond the wagon. When she got down from her horse, the woman got up from her fire and walked over to her. "Looks like we're two women campin' by ourselves," she said.

"Looks like," Ida repeated.

"You're welcome to share our fire if you want to," the woman offered. "Save you from havin' to build your own fire. If you're like me, you might like a little company, too, since we're both alone. My name's Rachael Burns. Those two scoundrels are Billy and Peter. We're here to pick up their daddy in the morning. I'm hopin' they'll remember him. Are you here to meet somebody?"

"Yes, I am," Ida answered. "My name's Ida Duncan. I'm here to pick up my two sons. They're a little older than Billy and Peter. I had a boy named Billy, too, but he's dead." It was obvious that Rachael was frightened to be camped there by the prison, so Ida said, "That's a good idea to share your fire. Let me unpack and take care of my horses, then I'll hunt up some more firewood and see about cookin' some supper for myself."

The night passed peacefully enough to satisfy both women, and they were both awakened the next morning by the sounds inside the prison telling the prisoners to get ready for breakfast. The women revived the fire and cooked breakfast, after which there was plenty of time to pack up and be ready to leave when their men were released. When the hour of nine was approaching, they put out their fire and left the campground to park beside the gate. The first man to come through the gate was William Burns, who trotted to the open arms of his wife and the respectful standoff of his sons who had not seen him in five years. After their initial embrace, Rachael introduced her sons to their father again. Then they climbed on the wagon and pulled away from the gate without a nod of farewell between the two women.

Ida Duncan stood waiting for another fifteen minutes before Davy and Luke ambled aimlessly out the gate. She didn't make a move to signal them, preferring to see if they were ever going to discover her, standing off to the side holding the reins of the two horses. Finally, Davy glanced her way, then quickly took another look. "Ma!" He yelled in disbelief, causing Luke to react with a start until he saw her as well and followed Davy, who was already running to meet her. "What in the world are you doin' here?" Davy asked. "Where'd you get the horses?"

"You didn't think your mama was gonna leave you to walk all the way back home, didja?" Ida asked.

"I swear, Ma," Luke japed, "you ain't brought but two horses. You didn't bring one for you to ride." He laughed at his joke, then asked seriously, "Where the hell did you steal these horses?" He was hoping there wasn't anybody on her trail.

"These horses ain't stole," she said, "and I've got the money with me to buy two more for you boys before we leave Huntsville. So you are gonna have to walk into town 'cause my gray don't want nobody on his back but me."

They were both so amazed that they didn't know what questions to ask her. There was no possible way for her to have what she claimed other than a robbery of some sort. Then Davy considered another possibility, so he asked the question, "You ain't made a deal with the devil, have you, Ma?"

She gave him a devilish grin and said, "Well, there's a good chance I have. I reckon I don't know for sure. But the two of us have got the same thing in mind and that's to kill the maggots who killed your father and your brother." She told them of her two visits from the man who would only call himself Santa Claus. "Waylan Gentry remembered him from Bobby's trial. He told me everything we need to know about Judge Wick Justice and a feller by the name of Bannack."

"Yeah, he's the feller that visited us in jail before we left for Huntsville," Luke said. "He works for Judge Grant and said he was gonna give you some money. And we know Bannack. He's the one who shot Pa and put a bullet in my leg and one in Davy's shoulder. He's the one I wanna settle up with for sure."

"And don't forget that judge you and your pa tried to kill for hangin' Billy," Ida reminded him. "I almost took care of him. If it hadn'ta been for that damn man of his, he'd already be dead." That surprised them, so she told them about her trip to Billy's hanging and the face-to-face meeting she had with Judge Wick Justice. "That man's gonna be hard to kill. I had that judge standing right in front of me. I pulled out my little derringer and that damn man stepped in front of me just as I pulled the trigger. He took the shot and never even flinched, grabbed both my arms and lifted me up like I was a little girl. Then he walked me back to my wagon, set me up on the seat, and told me to take my behind home."

They walked the short distance into town, coming to the stables first where they were met by Floyd Farmer, the owner. "Howdy, folks. Can I help you?"

"That depends on if you're in the mood to make some quick money or not," Ida answered him. "You mighta noticed that two of us are on foot and we'd make better time if we was all three on a horse. So are you in the business of sellin' horses, or do you just board other folks' horses?"

"Yes, ma'am," Floyd answered. "I think I can sell you a couple of good horses. You take a look in that corral back of the stable and see if you see one you like and I'll tell you what the price is. Every horse in that corral is for sale."

They spent the rest of the morning at Farmer's stable, picking out the two horses that Davy and Luke settled on. And since Farmer had half a dozen saddles for sale as well, they were able to strike a deal to put both boys on a horse for the total sum of three hundred dollars. Farmer was a touch suspicious of the threesome at first, but since the woman, who he figured out was their mother, was the only one wearing a gun, he decided they didn't have anything underhanded in mind. He and Ida bargained back and forth a little, but they were both satisfied with the final price. So the boys saddled their picks while mama paid the man, then they rode on farther down the main street to Huntsville Merchandise where Ida bought her sons new hats and clothes. "Another gift from the devil, or Santa Claus," Ida quipped. She surprised them then when she untied part of the packs on her packhorse and produced two gun belts with a .45 Colt in each holster.

They made the journey back to Black Creek and Gentry's Store after four and a half days of travel during which there were several shooting matches between the two brothers for the purpose of becoming acquainted with their new weapons. By the time they reached Gentry's, they were both familiar and confident with their six-guns. They stopped in Gentry's to buy coffee, sugar, and flour and to hear any news on the creek that might be of interest to them. "Ain't nothin' new since you left," Gentry told them. "Creeks still runnin' west to east, ain't seen no new faces."

"Good," Ida said. "You ain't seen that ol' sorrel of mine runnin' loose, have ya?"

"No, not around the store, anyway. You think he mighta got loose?"

"I never tied him up," Ida answered. "I was afraid, if I

shut him up in our little corral, he'd starve to death or die of thirst before I got back."

"Well, like I said, I ain't seen him around the store. Glad to see you boys back. That was sorry business about your pa and Billy."

"'Preciate it, Mr. Gentry," Luke said. "Sooner or later, people like the ones who trade in that kinda business, have to pay up for what they've done."

"Amen," Davy said and gave his brother a firm nod of his head.

Ida smiled her approval of their comments and said, "Let's get on back to the house to see if everything's all right."

"'Preciate your business," Gentry called after them as they filed out the door. "Glad to see you back home."

When they got back to the house, they saw Ida's ol' sorrel standing beside the creek and there was no evidence of anyone having been there since Ida left. While the boys took care of the horses, Ida went inside the log house and got a fire started in her kitchen stove. Then she threw something together to cook and made a pot of coffee. When supper was ready, they sat down at the table and started planning the assassination of Judge Wick Justice and John Bannack. "I don't want no half-baked attempt to get this job took care of," Ida told Davy and Luke. "Accordin' to the man that paid us to do this job, Judge Justice has had some kinda stroke or something and he don't go to court no more. He said he mostly just sets around on the porch when the weather's nice like it is now, 'cause one side of his whole body is dead. So being the nice Christian family we are, we wanna help him get the rest of his body dead, so he can get on to hell where he belongs."

"Where's that big bodyguard of his that's always with him, now that he ain't goin' to his office and he don't hold court no more?" Luke asked.

"Wick's enforcer?" Ida responded with a dismissive chuckle. "Oh, he's still with him, accordin' to Santa Claus. So we oughta be able to catch ol' Judge Wick settin' on his front porch and his gunman oughta be right there with him."

"I wish that damn Santa Clause had brought us a couple of rifles with those six-guns," Davy said. "That'd make the job a whole lot easier."

"Yeah, how come they didn't give us our rifles back when they let us outta prison?" Luke asked. "They took everything."

"Well, think about what you got sent to prison for, dummy," his mother told him. "Did you think they would give you your guns back when you got out?" She let him think about that for a few seconds, but the expression on his face told her he still didn't understand. "Besides," she went on, "I'd rather finish this business with a handgun, up close, so both of 'em know who's sendin' 'em to hell and why. I want the satisfaction of seein' 'em die. We owe your pa and Billy that much." They both nodded their understanding then.

"One good thing is we know where the judge's house is, since you went there with your pa," Ida said, "so we don't have to worry about having to find it."

"Yeah, but that was at night," Luke said. "I don't know if I could find it in the daytime."

She paused to let him think about what he had just said, but he just continued to gaze at her, his mouth hanging open. She turned to look at his brother, who seemed to be every bit as lost. "I ain't believin' I got two sons that dumb. If you could find the place in the middle of the night, it would be easier to find in the daylight."

"We was just followin' Pa," Luke said in their defense. "He found the house. We just followed him." He tried to remember that night, but he couldn't recall much about the way they reached the barn behind the house.

"It was on a road that led into town," Davy remembered, "and there was a creek that ran right along beside the road."

Ida thought about that for a minute. "I know where a road like that is on the south side of town," she said. "Tomorrow, we'll ride into town and see if we can find the judge's house. I need to get a look at the place. Once we get there, you'll most likely remember how you sneaked up behind the barn." *Billy must have been my bright son,* she thought, *surely I must have had at least one bright one.*

They waited to ride into town the next day until after noontime, thinking that it would help find the judge's house if he happened to be sitting on the porch at the time. As Ida had hoped, once they struck the south road into town, both Davy and Luke remembered being on that road on the night they attempted to kill the judge. They remembered that they had not ridden in very close to town, but none of the houses looked familiar to them. So when Ida saw a young woman standing on the front porch of a small house close to the road, she pulled her horse over and called out to her. "Good afternoon, Miss, my sons and I had an appointment to see Judge Justice, and they said he lives on this road, but I'm afraid we musta missed the house. And I'm afraid we're gonna be late for our appointment."

"You haven't missed the house," the young woman replied, "you just haven't gone far enough out yet. He doesn't have any name sign or anything."

"I was told that it's a white house," Ida replied.

"That's all you need to know," the woman said. "It's the

only white house from here on outta town. It's on the creek side of the road, about half a mile farther."

"Thank you," Ida said. "I appreciate it. Come on, boys, let's not keep the judge waitin'."

"Another fine dinner, Lottie," Judge Wick told her as he started to lift himself up from his chair. "No, no, I can make it." He stopped her and Bannack when they both started to get up at once to help him. "You finish your dinner," he told Bannack. "I'm gonna walk out to the porch and sit in my rocking chair. When you finish, you can bring my cup of coffee out with you." He started hobbling out toward the front door using his one crutch to keep him upright. Bannack got up from the table and walked to the kitchen door to watch him shuffle down the hall and out the front door. Then he walked to the door to make sure he made it to his rocking chair. Once he was seated, Bannack turned around and returned to finish up his dinner.

"Slow down, John," Lottie said. "If he's in his chair, he's all right. If you choke on your food, you're too big for me to try to pick up."

"Was I that obvious?" Bannack asked. "I reckon you're right. I'll finish up, then I'll take him a cup of coffee."

Out on the front porch, the judge was no longer interested in a cup of coffee or anything else in this world of pain and grief. For as soon as he had settled into his favorite chair, he suffered a massive stroke that left his body without a soul. He stared with lifeless eyes at the two gunmen who stepped up on his porch with guns drawn and threatening. Behind him, Ida Duncan held her Colt .45 to the back of his head and said, "This time your watchdog ain't here to take this one for you." Before she pulled the trigger, however, she heard the sound of heavy boots coming down the hall to the front door. "Shoot him if he moves!" She whispered frantically to her two sons, then backed quickly away to stand flat against the front wall of the house.

Bannack walked out the front door onto the porch, carrying a cup of hot coffee for the judge, startled to find the two men with guns trained on the still figure of the judge. Davy and Luke, startled as well, were not ready to face Wick's guardian. Bannack, however, was not so distracted. He tossed the cup of hot coffee at Davy who jumped backward in reaction to the hot liquid while Bannack drew his .44 and shot Luke in the chest, then turned and shot Davy before he could recover from the coffee. He was unaware of the angry woman stepping up behind him, her .45 cocked and aimed at the back of his head until he heard the hollow sound of a large iron skillet bouncing off her skull. He turned around to see Ida drop to the floor, unconscious and a determined Lottie Grimsley holding her skillet.

They both rushed to check on the judge, who was still staring with lifeless eyes, obviously gone. Bannack picked up the pistol Ida dropped and handed it to Henry, who came out the door at that moment, his napkin still tied around his neck. "Get me something to tie this man up with," Bannack told him, and Henry went back in the house at once. He was back in a hurry with a coil of clothesline rope. Bannack tied Ida, hand and foot, as she was just starting to come to. He went back to Lottie then and she told him she could find no evidence that the judge had been shot or injured. He had simply died and probably from another stroke. "I'll saddle my horse and go get the sheriff and the undertaker. Maybe I oughta swing by and tell Doc Bane, too. Will you and Henry be all right till I get back?"

"Yes, we're all right," she said. "There's nobody else to worry about."

"Thanks for savin' my life," he said. "I hope you didn't ruin your fryin' pan."

Everyone Bannack contacted was quick to respond when they heard of Judge Wick Justice's death. Sheriff Nicholson came straight away and Theodore Reece, the undertaker, came in his wagon to collect the judge's body after Doc Bane examined it and agreed that the judge showed all the signs of Lottie's diagnosis. Reece took the bodies of Davy and Luke Duncan, as well. Sheriff Nicholson took his very angry prisoner back to town and imprisoned her in the small room built onto the back of the jail that was used to hold women prisoners. With a heavy reenforced door and one small window up near the ceiling, it was considered escape-proof. The sheriff stood guard over her while Doc Bane patched up a bruise and a cut on the side of her head. She began petitioning to be tried by Judge Raymond Grant and no other. Nicholson tried to tell her that she would probably get Grant, whether she requested him or not.

Back at the house, Lottie complained at the supper table that night that so much had happened so fast that there had been no time to mourn the passing of Judge Wick. So she said a little prayer for the judge's soul and received an "amen" from everyone at the table. "He musta died right after he sat down in his chair," Bannack said, "because his arms looked like they just relaxed all of a sudden and he let his crutch fall on the floor."

"I've got a copy of his will that he gave me," Lottie said when Elwood asked her if the judge had ever talked to her about the likelihood of his early death. "It was right after his first stroke. He wanted me to know he left the house and the property to Henry and me. He didn't have any family.

He also left us a little bit of money. I hope that sets all right with you and John," she said.

"I think that was the right thing for him to do," Bannack said. "I didn't expect anything. He already gave me more than I could have expected when he got me pardoned from prison." Elwood said he didn't expect anything, either, and that he would now accept a position he had been offered that would keep him permanently in town.

"So what are you going to do, John?" Lottie asked. "Will you want to keep living in the barn?"

He laughed. "No, ma'am, you don't have to worry about that. I reckon I'll be movin' on. No real plans yet 'cause I hadn't figured on the judge passin' away this soon. But you won't have to feed me. I'll be leavin' in the mornin', I reckon."

"You don't have to be in a hurry," Henry said. "Take your time to decide."

"Thank you, Henry. I'll enjoy another night tonight in my hayloft bed. Maybe I'll have a dream that'll tell me which way to head. I'll probably visit my brother."

They sat around the table and talked about everything that had happened since the judge had brought John home with him, so it was late when Bannack finally climbed up into the hayloft. It was later, still, when Ida Duncan was aroused from her sleep on the cot in her special female jail cell. She didn't know what the noise was at first, then she realized it was coming from the small window near the ceiling. When she sat up, she heard it clearly. It was someone whispering her name. "What is it?" she whispered back.

"It's me, Santa Claus," the voice came back.

She grinned and lit the lamp beside her cot and got up. "I was countin' on you showin' up. I know you work for Judge Grant, so I want you to make sure he's the one who tries my case when they take me to court. I know that damn

Bannack got lucky again, but Judge Wick is dead, and that oughta make you happy."

"It does, it does," Clark Spencer assured her. "And don't you worry about a thing. You'll get Judge Grant. I just wanted to make sure you're all right. Anything I can get you to make you more comfortable?"

"No, I reckon I'm all right for now."

"Well, I brought you a little something to help take the edge off. Come over here under the window and I'll drop it in. Be sure you catch it. If it hits that floor it'll break."

"All right, I could use a little something," she said and went to the wall and stared up at the window as the barrel of a pistol pushed through the bars and the gun went off, putting a hole in her forehead. Spencer sat down in the saddle he had been standing on and galloped away.

John walked up to the house in the morning and went in the kitchen door. "Mornin'," he said to Lottie. "You reckon a fellow can still get one more breakfast here before I head out?"

"You'll notice the table's set for four people," she said. "Of course I'm going to make your breakfast."

"Well, I thought about it," Bannack said, "and I think I'll move on today, maybe go back to Waco to see my brother and his family. That's where I'm from. Maybe push on north and see what I run into after that."

She put her hands on her hips and looked at him. "I declare, John, I hate to see you go, but I can understand why you want to. Now that the judge is gone, there's not much reason for you to stay. I'll at least give you a good breakfast to start you out."

He sat down at the table with Henry and Elwood and she poured him a cup of coffee. In a few minutes time, she brought him his breakfast and sat down at the table with them. "You know, you have gotten to know quite a few people in Austin. It might be that somebody needs a man like you."

He laughed and asked, "To do what?" She shrugged in response. "Come to think of it," he recalled, "Sheriff Nicholson kept after the judge to let him hire me as his deputy." He was about to say more when there was a knock on the back door.

Lottie went to answer it. "Why, Sheriff Nicholson, what brings you here so early?"

Hearing her, Bannack laughed and said, "This must be my job offer at the door right now."

"Mornin', Miz Grimsley, is John Bannack by any chance still here?"

"He's right in the kitchen eating breakfast. Come on in. Can I fix you something?" He shook his head. "Cup of coffee?"

"I just need to talk to John, but I wouldn't turn down a cup of coffee."

"Well, come on in," she said and led him into the kitchen. "John, Sheriff Nicholson needs to talk to you."

"Mornin', Sheriff," Bannack greeted him. "Something I can do for ya?"

The sheriff sat down at the table. "Thank you, ma'am," he said when Lottie set a cup of coffee on the table for him. Turning his attention back to Bannack, he said, "I didn't know if you were gonna be stayin' in Austin or not, since Judge Wick is gone. But I decided to try to catch you this mornin' in case you were movin' on right away."

"You figured right," Bannack said, "'cause I'm leavin' right after I finish eatin' breakfast. Is something wrong?"

"Well, nothin' right at the moment." He hesitated then. "Maybe we oughta go out on the porch to talk."

"Oh?" Bannack replied, puzzled. "All right, grab your cup and we'll go out to the porch."

They picked up their cups and went out to the porch, leaving Lottie, Henry, and Elwood to speculate on whether or not John might be getting a job offer. Nicholson started talking as soon as the door closed behind them. "John, last night somebody rode up to that little window in the cell where Ida Duncan is and musta called her up under it. Then they shot her right in the face." He looked Bannack squarely in the eye. "Now, I know I can't say who done the killin' of that woman, because I didn't see 'em do it. I was asleep at the time. But I know Judge Grant is gonna order me to arrest you for it. Even though Judge Wick is gone, Judge Grant still ain't satisfied. John, Judge Grant has already talked to Governor Throckmorton about the possibility of revoking that pardon and sending you back to prison. I don't know if he'll be able to get the governor to go along with that or not. But if I arrest you for that woman's killin', he's sure to do what Grant wants. Grant told me last night to keep my eye on you because I was likely gonna have to arrest you. As soon as I saw Ida Duncan's body this mornin', I knew I'd be gettin' an order to arrest you right away. So my advice to you is to leave town, so I can't find you." He drained the last swallow of coffee and said, "I think the reason they killed that woman was to shut her up before she tells somebody everything she knows about Grant and Spencer. And if they hang her murder on you, that'll tie up their little plan to kill Judge Wick and you with a big red bow."

"Sheriff, you're a good friend," Bannack said. "I appreciate you comin' here to warn me. I reckon that makes up my mind for me. I'll get my things together and leave right away."

"Well, I'll get out of the way now," Nicholson said and

they went back in the kitchen. "Thank you for the coffee, Miz Grimsley," he said, then he and Bannack shook hands. "Good luck, John."

"Thanks, Sheriff," Bannack replied and walked him to the door. Then he turned back to the three faces watching him, all of them with questioning expressions, but it was only Henry who asked what the sheriff wanted to tell him.

"I expect that's their business," Lottie scolded him. "If it wasn't, they'da took you out to the porch with 'em."

"No, that's all right, Lottie," Bannack said. "I think you oughta know Nicholson came here to warn me that he was pretty sure he was going to have to arrest me."

"For what?" Henry and Lottie exclaimed as one.

"For the murder of Ida Duncan last night," Bannack answered. Then he went on to tell them what had happened at the jail in the middle of the night. He said Nicholson suspected it was going to be used to build a case against him to ensure his execution, or at least his return to prison. He told them that Judge Grant had already met with the governor in an effort to revoke his pardon.

"They can't say you done that murder," Henry protested. "You were here last night. All three of us know that."

"But you can't know if I slipped out of here last night or not," Bannack said. "You can't prove that I was here all night."

"I'll tell 'em I went down to the barn in the middle of the night to check on the cow and I saw you in there fast asleep," Henry said.

"I 'preciate it, Henry, but I don't think they would accept that as proof. Nicholson knows that and that's the reason he came to give me some time to get out of town. So I'll be goin' now. I want to thank the three of you for makin' me feel like part of the family. I wish you all well and maybe we'll meet again sometime." He turned and went out the door then, when he saw the tears welling up in Lottie's eyes.

She followed him outside. "Where will you go?"

"Somewhere they don't know my name, I reckon. I'll not go back to prison, though, that much I can guarantee you."

"You be careful, John Bannack," she said.

"I'll do that, Lottie, and you take care of yourself. Thank you again for treatin' me like family." He turned then and headed to the barn.

"Good luck, John, and Lord watch over you," Lottie called after him, then went back to the kitchen to talk about it with Henry and Elwood.

"Yonder he goes!" Henry announced after a little while. Lottie and Elwood went to the kitchen window to see the imposing figure of the man from Waco riding easy in the saddle.

**TURN THE PAGE
FOR A RIP-ROARING PREVIEW!**

**JOHNSTONE COUNTRY.
BACK IN THE SADDLE. AGAIN.**

**In this rip-roaring new series,
the bestselling Johnstones present a character
who's sure to be a favorite with Western fans.
He's a once-famous Texas Ranger who's given up his
badge and gone fishin'. But when trouble strikes, he's
ready to get back in the saddle—with guns blazin' ...**

MEET "CATFISH" CHARLIE

As a former Texas Ranger, Charlie Tuttle
spent the better part of his life catching outlaws.
Happily retired in Wolfwater, Texas, he's content just
catching fish—namely Bubba, the wily old catfish
who lives in the pond near Charlie's shack
and keeps slipping off Charlie's hook. He also likes
hanging out with his trusty tomcat, Hooligan Hank,
and tossing back bottles of mustang berry wine—
maybe a little too much, to be honest.
Sure, his glory days are behind him. And yes, maybe he's
let himself go a little in his "golden years."
There's no reason for Charlie to even think about
coming out of retirement ...

Except maybe a double murder and a kidnapping.

It starts with a jailbreak.
Frank Thorson and his gang ride into Wolfwater
to bust Frank's brother out of the slammer.
First, they slaughter the deputy. Then, the town marshal.
Finally, they run off with the marshal's daughter and no
one's sure if she's dead or alive. The townsfolk are
terrified—and desperate. Desperate enough to ask
"Catfish" Charlie to put down his fishing pole, pick up
his Colt Army .44, and go after the bloodthirsty gang.
Sure, Charlie may be a bit rusty after all these years.
But when it comes to serving up justice,
no one is quicker, faster—or deadlier . . .

Once a lawman, always a lawman.
Especially a lawman like Catfish Charlie.

**National Bestselling Authors
William W. Johnstone
and J.A. Johnstone**

CATFISH CHARLIE

On sale now, wherever Pinnacle Books are sold.

Live Free. Read Hard.

www.williamjohnstone.net

Visit us at www.kensingtonbooks.com

CHAPTER 1

May 2, 1891

"Bushwhack" Wilbur Aimes, Deputy Town Marshal of Wolfwater, in West Texas, looked up from the report he'd been scribbling, sounding out the words semi-aloud as he'd written them and pressing his tongue down hard against his bottom lip in concentration. He knew his letters and numbers well enough, but that didn't mean he had an easy time stringing them together. He almost welcomed the sudden, uneasy feeling climbing his spine, stealthy as a brown recluse spider.

He frowned at the brick wall before him, below the flour sack–curtained window, the drawn curtains still bearing the words PIONEER FLOUR MILLS, SAN ANTONIO, TX though the Texas sun angling through the window every day had badly faded them.

The sound came again—distant hoof thuds, a horse's whicker.

Silence.

A bridle chain rattled.

Bushwhack, a big, broad-shouldered, rawboned man, and former bushwhacker from Missouri's backwoods, rose from his chair. The creaky Windsor was mostly Marshal

Abel Wilkes's chair, but Bushwhack got to sit in it when he was on duty—usually night duty as he was on tonight—and the marshal was off, home in bed sleeping within only a few feet of the marshal's pretty schoolteacher daughter, Miss Bethany.

Bushwhack shook his head as though to rid it of thoughts of the pretty girl. Thinking about her always made his cheeks warm and his throat grow tight. Prettiest girl in Wolfwater, for sure. If only he could work up the courage to ask the marshal if he could . . .

Oh, stop thinking about that, you damn fool! Bushwhack castigated himself. The marshal's holding off on letting any man step out with his daughter until the right one came along. And that sure as holy blazes wasn't going to be the big, awkward, bearded, former defender of the ol' Stars an' Bars, as well as a horse-breaker-until-a-wild-stallion-had-broken *him*—his left hip, at least. No, Miss Bethany Wilkes wasn't for him, Bushwhack thought, half pouting as he grabbed his old Remington and cartridge belt off the wall peg, right of the door, the uneasy feeling staying with him even beneath his forbidden thoughts of the marshal's daughter.

He glanced at his lone prisoner in the second of the four cells lined up along the office's back wall.

"Skinny" Thorson was sound asleep on his cot, legs crossed at the ankles, funnel-brimmed, weatherbeaten hat pulled down over his eyes.

Skinny was the leader of a local outlaw gang, though he didn't look like much. Just a kid on downhill side of twenty, but not by much. Skinny wore his clothes next to rags. His boots were so worn that Bushwhack could see his socks through the soles.

The deputy chuffed his distaste as he encircled his waist with the belt and soft leather holster from which his old, walnut-gripped Remington jutted, its butt scratched from all the times it had been used to pulverize coffee beans around remote Texas campfires during the years—a good dozen. Bushwhack had punched cattle around the Red River country and into the Panhandle—when he hadn't been fighting Injuns or bluebellies and minding his topknot, of course.

You always had to mind your scalp in Comanche country.

Or breaking broncs for Johnny Sturges, until that one particularly nasty blue roan had bucked him off onto the point of his left hip, then rolled on him and gave him a stomp to punctuate the "ride" and to settle finally the argument over who was boss.

That had ended Bushwhack's punching and breaking days.

Fortunately, Abel Wilkes had needed a deputy and hadn't minded overmuch that Bushwhack had lost the giddyup in his step. Bushwhack was still sturdy, albeit with a bit of a paunch these days, and he was right handy with a hide-wrapped bung starter, a sawed-off twelve gauge, and his old Remington. Now he grabbed the battered Stetson off the peg to the right of the one his gun had been hanging from, set it on his head, slid the Remington from its holster and, holding the long-barreled popper straight down against his right leg, opened the door and poked his head out, taking a cautious look around.

As he did, he felt his heart quicken. He wasn't sure why, but he was nervous. He worried the old Remy's hammer with his right thumb, ready to draw it back to full cock if needed.

Not seeing anything amiss out front of the marshal's office and the jailhouse, he glanced over his shoulder at Skinny Thorson once more. The outlaw was still sawing logs beneath his hat. Bushwhack swung his scowling gaze back to the street, then stepped out onto the jailhouse's rickety front stoop to take a better look around.

The night was dark, the sky sprinkled with clear, pointed stars. Around Bushwhack, Wolfwater slouched, quiet and dark in these early-morning hours—one thirty, if the marshal's banjo clock on the wall over the large, framed map of western Texas could be trusted. The clock seemed to lose about three minutes every week, so Bushwhack or Wilkes or Maggie Cruz, who cleaned the place once a week, had to consult their pocket watches and turn it ahead.

Bushwhack trailed his gaze around the broad, pale street to his left; it was abutted on both sides by mud brick, Spanish-style adobe, or wood frame, false-fronted business buildings, all slouching with age and the relentless Texas heat and hot, dry wind. He continued shuttling his scrutinizing gaze along the broad street to his right, another block of which remained before the sotol-stippled, bone-dry, cactus-carpeted desert continued unabated dang near all the way to the Rawhide Buttes and Wichita Falls beyond.

The relatively recently laid railroad tracks of the Brazos, San Antonio & Rio Grande Line ran right through the middle of the main drag, gleaming faintly now in the starlight. Most businessmen and cattlemen in the area had welcomed the railroad for connecting San Antonio, in the southeast, with El Paso, in the northwest, and parts beyond.

Celebrated by some, maligned by others, including Marshal Abel Wilkes.

The San Antonio & Rio Grande Line might have brought so-called progress and a means for local cattlemen to ship their beef-on-the-hoof out from Wolfwater, but it had also brought trouble in the forms of men and even some women—oh, its share of troublesome women, as well, don't kid yourself!—in all shapes, sizes, colors, and creeds. However, it being a weeknight, the town was dark and quiet. On weekends, several saloons, hurdy-gurdies, and gambling parlors remained open, as long as they had customers, or until Marshal Wilkes, backed by Bushwhack himself, tired of breaking up fights and even some shootouts right out on the main drag, Wolfwater Street. Marshal and deputy would shut them down and would send the cowboys, vaqueros, sodbusters, and prospectors back to their ranches, haciendas, soddies, and diggings, respectively.

The road ranches stippling the desert outside of Abel Wilkes's jurisdiction stayed open all night, however. There was nothing Wilkes and Bushwhack could do about them. What perditions they were, too! When he'd heard all the trouble that took place out there, Bushwhack was secretly glad his and the marshal's jurisdiction stopped just outside of Wolfwater. Too many lawmen—deputy U.S. marshals, deputy sheriffs from the county seat over in Heraklion, and even some Texas Rangers and Pinkertons—had ridden into such places, between town and the Rawhide Buttes, to the west, or between town and the Stalwart Mountains, to the south, never to be seen or heard from again.

In fact, only last year, Sheriff Ed Wilcox from Heraklion had sent two deputies out to the road ranch on Jawbone Creek. Only part of them had returned home—their heads in gunnysacks tied to their saddle horns!

As far as Bushwhack knew, no one had ever learned what had become of the rest of their bodies. He didn't care to know, and he had a suspicion that Sheriff Ed Wilcox didn't, either. The road ranch on Jawbone Creek continued to this day, unmolested—at least by the law, ha-ha. (That was the joke going around.)

Bushwhack shoved his hat down on his forehead to scratch the back of his head with his left index finger. All was quiet, save the snores sounding from Skinny Thorson's cell in the office behind him. No sign of anyone out and about. Not even a cat. Not even a coyote, in from the desert, hunting cats.

So, who or what had made the sounds Bushwhack had heard just a minute ago?

He yawned. He was tired. Trouble in town had kept him from getting his nap earlier. His beauty sleep, the marshal liked to joke. Maybe he'd nodded off without realizing it and had only dreamt of the hoof thud and the bridle chain rattle.

Bushwhack yawned again, turned, stepped back inside the office, and closed the door. Just then, he realized that the snores had stopped. He swung his head around to see Skinny Thorson lying as before, only he'd poked his hat brim up on his forehead and was gazing at Bushwhack, grinning, blue eyes twinkling.

"What's the matter, Bushwhack?" the kid said. "A mite nervous, are we?"

Bushwhack sauntered across the office and stood at the door of Skinny's cell, scowling beneath the brim of his own Stetson. He poked the Remington's barrel through the bars and said, "Shut up, you little rat-faced tinhorn, or I'll pulverize your head."

Skinny turned his head to one side and a jeeringly warning light came to his eyes. "My big brother, Frank, wouldn't like that—now, would he?"

"No, the hangman wouldn't like it, neither. He gets twenty dollars for every neck he stretches. He's probably halfway between Heraklion an' here, and he wouldn't like it if he got here an' didn't have a job to do, money to make." Bushwhack grinned. "Of course, he'd likely get one of Miss Claire's girls to soothe his disappointment. And every man around knows how good Miss Claire's girls are at soothing disappointments."

It was true. Miss Julia Claire's sporting parlor was one

of the best around—some said the best hurdy-gurdy house between El Paso and San Antonio, along the San Antonio, and Rio Grande Line. And Miss Julia Claire herself was quite the lady. A fella could listen to her speak English in that beguiling British accent of hers all day long.

All *night* long, for that matter.

Only, Miss Claire herself didn't work the line. That fact—her chasteness and accent and the obscurity of her past, which she'd remained tight-lipped about for all of the five years she'd lived and worked here in Wolfwater—gave her an alluring air of mystery.

Skinny Thorson now pressed his face up close to the bars, squeezing a bar to either side of his face in his hands, until his knuckles turned white, and said, "'The Reaper' ain't gonna have no job to do once he gets here, because by the time he gets here, I won't be here anymore. You got it, Bushwhack?"

The Reaper was what everyone around called the executioner from the county seat, Lorenzo Snow.

The prisoner widened his eyes and slackened his lower jaws and made a hideous face of mockery, sticking his long tongue out at Bushwhack.

Bushwhack was about to grab that tongue with his fingers and pull it through the bars, pull it all the way out of the kid's mouth—by God!—but stopped when he heard something out in the street again.

"What was that?" asked Skinny with mock trepidation, cocking an ear to listen. "Think that was Frank, Bushwhack?" He grinned sidelong through the bars once more. "You know what? I think it was!"

Outside, a horse whinnied shrilly.

Outside, men spoke, but it was too soft for Bushwhack to make out what they were saying.

The hooves of several horses thudded and then the thuds dwindled away to silence.

Bushwhack turned to face the door, scowling angrily. "What in holy blazes is going on out there?"

"It's Frank, Bushwhack. My big brother, Frank, is here, just like I knew he would be! He got the word I sent him!" Skinny tipped his head back and whooped loudly. Squeezing the cell bars, he yelled, "I'm here, Frank. Come an' fetch me out of here, big brother!"

Bushwhack had holstered the Remington, but he had not snapped the keeper thong home over the hammer. He grabbed his sawed-off twelve gauge off a peg in the wall to his left and looped the lanyard over his head and right shoulder. He broke open the gun to make sure it was loaded, then snapped it closed and whipped around to Skinny and said tightly, "One more peep out of you, you little scoundrel, an' I'll blast you all over that wall behind you. If Frank came to fetch you, he'd best've brought a bucket an' a mop!"

Skinny narrowed his eyes in warning and returned in his own tight voice, "Frank won't like it, Bushwhack. You know Frank. Everybody around the whole county knows Frank. You an' they know how Frank can be when he's riled!"

Bushwhack strode quickly up to the cell, clicking the twelve gauge's hammers back to full cock. "You don't hear too good, Skinny. Liable to get you killed. Best dig the dirt out'n your ears."

Skinny looked down at the heavy, cocked hammers of the savage-looking gut shredder. He took two halting steps back away from the cell door, raising his hands, palms out, in supplication. "All . . . all right, now, Bushwhack," he trilled. "Calm down. Just funnin' you's all." He smiled suddenly with mock equanimity. "Prob'ly not Frank out there at all. Nah. Prob'ly just some thirty-a-month-and-found cow nurses lookin' fer some coffin varnish to cut the day's dust with. Yeah, that's prob'ly who it is."

His smile turned wolfish.

Grimacing, anger burning through him, Bushwhack swung around to the door. Holding the twelve gauge straight out from his right side, right index finger curled over both eyelash triggers, he pulled the door open wide.

His big frame filled the doorway as he stared out into the night.

Again, the dark street was empty.

"All right—who's there?" he said, trying to ignore the insistent beating of his heart against his breastbone.

Silence, save for crickets and the distant cry of a wildcat on the hunt out in the desert in the direction of the Stalwarts.

He called again, louder: "Who's there?" A pause. "That you, Frank?"

Bushwhack and Marshal Wilkes had known there was the possibility that Skinny's older brother, Frank, might journey to Wolfwater to bust his brother out. But they'd heard Frank had been last seen up in the Indian Nations, and they didn't think that even if Frank got word that Wilkes and Bushwhack had jailed his younger brother for killing a half-breed whore in one of the lesser parlor houses in Wolfwater, he'd make it here before the hangman would.

There were a total of six houses of ill repute in Wolfwater—not bad for a population of sixty-five hundred, though that didn't include all of the cowboys, vaqueros, miners, and sodbusters who frequented the town nearly every night and on weekends, and the mostly unseemly visitors, including gamblers, confidence men and women, which the railroad brought to town. It was in one of these lesser houses, only identified as GIRLS by the big gaudy sign over its front door, that Skinny had gone loco on bust-head and thrown the girl out a second-story window.

The girl, a half-Comanche known as "Raven," had lived a few days before succumbing to her injuries caused when she'd landed on a hitchrack, which had busted all her ribs and cracked her spine. Infection had been the final cause of death, as reported by the lone local medico, Doc Overholser.

Anger at being toyed with was growing in Bushwhack. Fear, too, he had to admit. He stepped out onto the stoop, swinging his gaze from right to left, and back again, and yelled, "Who's out there? If it's you, Frank—show yourself, now!"

Bushwhack heard the sudden thud of hooves to his right and his left.

Riders were moving up around him now, booting their horses ahead at slow, casual walks, coming out from around the two front corners of the jailhouse flanking him on his right and left. They were ominous silhouettes in the starlight. As Bushwhack turned to his left, where three riders were just then swinging their horses around the right front corner of the jailhouse stoop and into the street in front of it, a gun flashed.

At the same time the gun's loud bark slammed against Bushwhack's ears, the bullet plundered his left leg, just above the knee. The bullet burned like a branding iron laid against his flesh.

Bushwhack yelped and shuffled to his right, clutching the bloody wound in misery. He released the twelve gauge to hang free against his belly and struck the porch floor in a grunting, agonized heap.

He cursed through gritted teeth, feeling warm blood ooze out of his leg from beneath his fingers. As he did, slow hoof clomps sounded ahead of him. He peered up to see a tall, rangy man in a black vest, black hat, and black denim trousers ride out of the street's darkness on a tall gray horse and into the light from the window and the open door behind Bushwhack.

The guttering lamplight shone in cold gray eyes above a long, slender nose and thick blond mustache. The lips beneath the mustache quirked a wry grin as Frank Thorson said, "Hello, there, Bushwhack. Been a while. You miss me?"

The smile grew. But the gray eyes remained flat and hard and filled with malicious portent.

CHAPTER 2

Marshal Abel Wilkes snapped his eyes open, instantly awake.

"Oh, fer Pete's sake!"

Almost as quickly, though not as quickly as it used to be, the Colt hanging from the bedpost to his right was in his hand. Aiming the barrel up at the ceiling, Abel clicked the hammer back and lay his head back against his pillow, listening.

What he'd heard before, he heard again. A man outside breathing hard. Running in a shambling fashion. The sounds were growing louder as Wilkes—fifty-six years old, bald but with a strap of steel-gray hair running in a band around his large head, above his ears, and with a poorly trimmed, soup-strainer gray mustache—lay there listening.

What in blazes . . . ?

Abel tossed his covers back and dropped his pajama-clad legs over the side of the bed. He'd grabbed his ratty, old plaid robe off a wall peg and shrugged into it and was sliding his feet into his wool-lined slippers, as ratty as the robe, when his daughter's voice rose from the lower story. "Dad? Dad? You'd better come down he—"

She stopped abruptly when Abel heard muffled thuds on

the floor of the porch beneath his room, here in the second story of the house he owned and in which he lived with his daughter, Bethany. The muffled thuds were followed by a loud hammering on the house's front door.

"Marshal Wilkes!" a man yelled.

More thundering knocks, then Bushwhack Aimes's plaintive wail: *"Marshal Wilkes!"*

What in tarnation is going on now? Wilkes wondered.

Probably had to do with the railroad. That damned railroad . . . bringin' vermin of every stripe into—

"Dad, do you hear that?" Beth's voice came again from the first story.

"Coming, honey!" Abel said as he opened his bedroom door and strode quickly into the hall, a little breathless and dizzy from rising so fast. He wasn't as young as he used to be, and he had to admit his gut wasn't as flat as it used to be, either. Too many roast beef platters at Grace Hasting's café for noon lunch, followed up by steak and potatoes cooked by Beth for supper.

Holding the Colt down low against his right leg, Abel hurried as quickly as he could, without stumbling down the stairs, just as Beth opened the front door at the bottom of the stairs and slightly right, in the parlor part of the house. The willowy brunette was as pretty as her mother had been, but she was on the borderline of being considered an old maid, since she was not yet married at twenty-four. The young woman gasped and stepped back quickly as a big man tumbled inside the Wilkes parlor, striking the floor with a loud *bang*.

Not normally a screaming girl, Beth stepped back quickly, shrieked, and closed her hands over her mouth as she stared down in horror at her father's deputy, who lay just inside the front door, gasping like a landed fish.

Abel knew it was Bushwhack Aimes because he'd recognized his deputy's voice. The face of the man, however, only vaguely resembled Bushwhack. He'd been beaten bad, mouth smashed, both eyes swelling, various sundry scrapes and bruises further disfiguring the big man's face. He wore only long-handles, and the top hung from his nearly bare shoulders in tattered rags.

"Oh, my God!" Beth exclaimed, turning to her father as Abel brushed past her.

Like Abel, she was clad in a robe and slippers. Lamps burned in the parlor, as well as in the kitchen, indicating she'd been up late grading papers again or preparing lessons for tomorrow.

"Good God," Abel said, dropping to a knee beside his bloody deputy, who lay clutching his left leg with both hands and groaning loudly against the pain that must be hammering all through him. "What the hell happened, Bushwhack? Who did this to you?"

He couldn't imagine the tenacity it had taken for Bushwhack in his condition to have made it here from the jailhouse—a good four-block trek, blood pouring out of him. The man already had a bum hip, to boot!

"Marshal!" Aimes grated out, spitting blood from his lips.

Abel turned to his daughter, who stood crouched forward over Aimes, looking horrified. "Beth, heat some water and fetch some cloths, will you?"

As Beth wheeled and hurried across the parlor and into the kitchen, Abel placed a placating hand on his deputy's right shoulder. "Easy, Bushwhack. Easy. I'll fetch the sawbones in a minute. What happened? Who did this to you?"

Aimes shifted his gaze from his bloody leg to the marshal. "Thor . . . Thorson. Frank Thorson . . . an' his men! Shot me. Beat me. Stripped me. Left me in the street . . .

laughin' at me!" The deputy sucked a sharp breath through gritted teeth and added, "They busted Skinny out of jail!"

"Are they still in town?"

"They broke into one of the saloons—the Wolfwater Inn! Still . . . still there, far as I know . . . Oh . . . oh, *Lordy!*" Bushwhack reached up and wrapped both of his own bloody hands around one of Abel's. "They're killers, Marshal! Don't go after 'em alone." He wagged his head and showed his teeth between stretched-back lips. "Or . . . you'll . . . " He was weakening fast, eyelids growing heavy, barely able to get the words out. ". . . . you'll end up like me—*dead!*"

With that, Bushwhack's hands fell away from Abel's. His head fell back against the floor with a loud *thump*. He rolled onto his back and his head sort of wobbled back and forth, until it and the rest of the man's big body fell still. The eyes slightly crossed and halfway closed as they stared up at Abel Wilkes, glassy with death.

Footsteps sounded behind Abel, and he turned to see Beth striding through the parlor behind him. "I have water heating, Pa! Want I should fetch the doc . . . ?" She stopped suddenly as she gazed down at Bushwhack. Again, she raised her hands to her mouth, her brown eyes widening in shock.

"No need for the doc, honey," Abel said, slowly straightening, gazing down at his deputy. Anger burned in him. "I reckon he's done for, Bushwhack is."

Beth moved slowly forward, dropped to her knees, and gently set her hand on the deputy's head, smoothing his thick, curly, salt-and-pepper hair back from his forehead. "I'm so sorry, Bushwhack," she said in a voice hushed with sorrow.

"Stay with him, take care of him as best you can,

honey," Abel said, reaching down to squeeze his daughter's shoulder comfortingly. "On my way into town, I'll send for the undertaker."

Beth looked up at her father, tears of sorrow and anger in her eyes. "Who did this to Bushwhack, Pa?"

"Frank Thorson."

Beth sort of winced and grimaced at the same time. Most people did that when they heard the name. "Oh, God," she said.

"Don't you worry, honey," Abel said, squeezing her shoulder once more. "Thorson will pay for what he did here tonight."

Abel gave a reassuring dip of his chin, then turned to start back up the stairs to get dressed.

"Pa!" Beth cried.

Abel stopped and turned back to his daughter, on her knees now and leaning back against the slipper-clad heels of her feet. Beth gazed up at him with deep concern. "You're not thinking about confronting Frank Thorson alone—are you?"

Abel didn't like the lack of confidence he saw in his daughter's eyes. "I don't have any choice, honey."

Aimes was his only deputy, and there was little time to deputize more men. He needed to throw a loop around Frank Thorson and the men riding with him before they could leave town. This was his town, Abel Wilkes's town, and he'd be dogged if anyone, including Frank Thorson, would just ride in, shoot and beat his deputy to death, spring a prisoner, then belly up to a bar for drinks in celebration.

Oh, no. Wilkes might not be the lawman he once was, but Wolfwater was still his town, gallblastit! He would not, could not, let the notorious firebrand Frank Thorson, whom he'd had run-ins with before, turn him into a laughingstock.

Trying to ignore his deputy's final warning, which echoed inside his head, Wilkes returned to his room and quickly dressed in his usual work garb—blue wool shirt under a brown vest, black twill pants, and his Colt's six-gun strapped around his bulging waist. He grabbed his flat-brimmed black hat off a wall peg and, holding the hat in one hand, crouched to peer into the mirror over his dresser.

He winced at what he saw there.

An old man . . .

His dear wife's death two years ago had aged him considerably. Abel Wilkes, former soldier in the War Against Northern Aggression, former stockman, former stage driver, former stagecoach messenger, and, more recently, former Pinkerton agent, was not the man he'd been before Ethel Wilkes had contracted bone cancer, which they'd had diagnosed by special doctors up in Abilene. Abel's face was paler than it used to be; heavy blue pouches sagged beneath his eyes, and deep lines spoked out from their corners.

There was something else about that face staring back from the mirror that gave Wilkes an unsettled feeling. He tried not to think about it, but now as he set the low-crowned hat on his head, shucked his Colt from its holster, opened the loading gate, and drew the hammer back to half cock, he realized the cause of his unsettlement. The eyes that had stared back at him a moment ago were no longer as bold and as certain as they once had been.

They'd turned a paler blue in recent months, and there was no longer in them the glint of bravado, the easy confidence that had once curled one corner of his mustached upper lip as he'd made his rounds up and down Wolfwater's dusty main drag. Now, as he stared down at the wheel of his six-gun as he poked a live cartridge into the chamber he usually left empty beneath the hammer, his eyes looked downright uncertain. Maybe even a little afraid.

Maybe more than *a little* afraid.

"Don't do it, Pa. Don't confront those men alone," Beth urged from where she continued to kneel beside Bushwhack as Abel descended the stairs, feeling heavy and fearful and generally out of sorts.

Beth wasn't helping any. Anger rose in him and he shifted his gaze to her now, deep lines corrugating his broad, sun-leathered forehead beneath the brim of his hat. "You sit tight and don't worry," he said, stepping around her and Bushwhack, his Winchester in his right hand now. "I'll send the undertak—"

She grabbed his left hand with both of her own and squeezed. "Pa, don't! Not alone!"

Not turning to her, but keeping his eyes on the night ahead of him, the suddenly awful night, Abel pulled his hand out from between Beth's and headed through the door and onto the porch. "I'll be back soon."

Feeling his daughter's terrified gaze on his back, Abel crossed the porch, descended the three steps to the cinder-paved path that led out through the gate in the white picket fence. He strode through the gate and did not bother closing it behind him. His nerves were too jangled to trifle with such matters as closing gates in picket fences.

As he strode down the willow-lined lane toward the heart of town, which lay ominously dark and silent straight ahead, Abel shook his head as though to rid it of the fear he'd seen in his daughter's eyes . . . in his own eyes. Beth's fear had somehow validated his own.

"Darn that girl, anyway," he muttered as he walked, holding the Winchester down low in his right hand. *She knows me better than I do. She knows my nerves have gone to hell.*

Fear.

Call it what it is, Abel, he remonstrated himself.

You've grown fearful in your later years.

There'd been something unnerving about watching Ethel die so slowly, gradually. That had been the start of his deterioration. And then, after Ethel had passed and they'd buried her in the cemetery at the east end of town, that darn whore had had to go and save his hide in the Do Drop Inn. The gambler had had Wilkes dead to rights. The marshal had called the man out on his cheating after hearing a string of complaints from other men the gambler had been playing cards with between mattress dances upstairs in the inn.

So Abel had gone over to the inn, intending to throw the man out of town. The gambler had dropped his cards, kicked his chair back, rose, and raised his hands above the butts of his twin six-shooters.

Open challenge.

Let the faster man live.

Abel remembered the fear he'd felt. He had a reputation as a fast gun—one of the fastest in West Texas at one time. "Capable Abel" Wilkes, they'd called him. His dirty little secret, however, was that when he'd started creeping into his later forties, he'd lost some of that speed. His reputation for being fast had preceded him, though. So he hadn't had to entertain many challengers. Just drunks who hadn't known any better or, because of the who-hit-John coursing through their veins, had thrown caution to the wind.

And had paid the price.

The gambler had been different. He'd been one cool customer, as most good gamblers were. As Abel himself once had been. Cool and confident in his speed. That night, however, the gambler had sized Wilkes up, sensed that the aging lawman was no longer as fast as he once had been. Abel hadn't been sure how the man had known that.

Maybe he'd seen the doubt in Abel's own eyes.

The fear. That fear.

Abel had let the gambler make the first move, of course. Over the years, the lawman had been so fast that he'd been able to make up for his opponents' lightning-fast starts. That night, however, Abel would have been wolf bait if the drunk doxie hadn't stumbled against him in her haste to leave the table and not risk taking a ricochet.

She had nudged his shooting arm just as the man had swept his pearl-handled Colt from its black leather holster thonged low on his right thigh. Abel's own Colt Lightning had cleared leather after the gambler's gun had drilled a round into the table before him, between him and his opponent. Abel's bullet had plunked through the man's brisket and instantly trimmed his wick.

Abel had left the saloon after the undertaker had hauled the gambler out feet first. He'd tried to maintain an air of grim confidence, of a job well done, but the other gamblers and the saloon's other customers all knew it to be as phony as he did. If that drunk, little doxie hadn't nudged the gambler's arm at just the right time, the undertaker would have planted Abel in the Wolfwater bone orchard, beside his dearly departed Ethel.

Leaving their old-maid daughter alone in the cold, cruel, West Texas world.

Now he swung onto Wolfwater's broad main drag, dark except for up at the Wolfwater Inn, half a block ahead and on the street's right side.

Abel felt his boots turn to lead. He wanted to do anything this night, except confront Frank Thorson and Thorson's men. Abel didn't know whom Frank was running with now, but for them to do what they had done to Bushwhack, they all had to be every bit as bad as Frank.

No, Wilkes wanted nothing to do with them. But he couldn't very well ignore them. He wanted to turn tail and run home and hide. Wait for the Thorson storm to pass. That's why he did what he did now. He quickened his pace.

There was only one thing worse than being dead.

That thing was being a laughingstock in front of your whole dang town.

Visit our website at
KensingtonBooks.com
to sign up for our newsletters, read
more from your favorite authors, see
books by series, view reading group
guides, and more!

BOOK **CLUB**
BETWEEN THE CHAPTERS

Become a Part of Our
Between the Chapters Book Club
Community and Join the Conversation

Betweenthechapters.net